The Woman Who Came Back To Life

BOOKS BY BETH MILLER

The Two Hearts of Eliza Bloom
The Missing Letters of Mrs Bright

Starstruck
When We Were Sisters
The Good Neighbour

The Woman Who Came Back To Life

BETH MILLER

bookouture

Published by Bookouture in 2022

An imprint of Storyfire Ltd.
Carmelite House
50 Victoria Embankment
London EC4Y 0DZ

www.bookouture.com

ISBN: 978-1-80019-663-6
eBook ISBN: 978-1-80019-662-9

To Liz and Jacq, and that old big magic

PROLOGUE

I last saw Dad twenty-eight years ago, in 1990. Actually, that's not strictly true. For the sake of accuracy I should say that 1990 was the last time I *almost* saw him.

I took the day off from working at the salon, got a train to London, another train out to the coast, then another train to Rye. I hadn't seen him for almost eight years. I planned to show him the letter he had written, force him to look at his own words:

Dear Pearl, please don't come, it's not convenient. Francis.

Not 'Dad'. Francis.

Looking back, I can't believe that I actually set out to do this, or that I got as far as I did. For someone who tended to shy away from confrontation, my behaviour was uncharacteristically bold. I'm sure Dr Haywood would have something insightful to say about that, had I ever decided to tell him.

I bought a local map in WH Smith, and followed the road through town. The centre of Rye was quaint, with cobbled streets and half-timbered buildings, and there were tourists everywhere I looked, spilling out of tea rooms. I started off confidently, but as I went past the shops and into the outskirts of town, I could feel the righteous anger that had propelled me here begin to fade. The pretty streets gave way to a more nondescript residential area, and the nearer I got to Dad's street the slower and less certain I became. I finally made it to Pendlebury Avenue, and actually got as far as his house. But all the fight had gone out of me, and I couldn't bring myself to walk up and knock on the front door. My heart pounded in my chest and I was finding it increasingly difficult to breathe. My legs felt so weak that I had to sit on the pavement while I struggled for air.

There were a few passers-by but I was too embarrassed to ask for help. Then a young man about my age, early twenties, with spiky hair and a nose-piercing, crouched down next to me and after a few quick questions, gently told me I was having a panic attack. It was my first one, so I didn't know that it always feels like you're dying, and I said he was wrong; it must be a heart attack. He humoured me by taking me to the local hospital, though of course, by the time we got to A&E I was fine, but the nurse said it would be a good idea to get checked over. The young man, I don't remember his name, waited with me, and told me about the panic attacks he'd experienced at school. After I'd been given a clean bill of health, he dropped me at the station. I thanked him and we said goodbye. The kindness of strangers.

I didn't even think about trying to return to Dad's house that day. I took the panic attack as an unsubtle sign, and made my slow way home back across the country. I stopped writing to Dad then, and eventually, after some rough years of grieving the father I'd loved, I more or less stopped thinking about him, too.

ONE

PEARL

I was walking through the wood, listening out for birds. To my ear, French birds sounded different to British ones. When I heard one that I thought might be a song thrush, I stopped and put my field glasses to my eyes, their familiar weight settling into the grooves on my face.

As I craned my neck up, my phone started ringing in my bag, shattering the peace of the wood. It was an unfamiliar sound: it rarely rang. I never got those endless scam traffic-accident calls that plagued people with smartphones. I never felt the need to have the internet in my pocket.

I opened my ancient mobile, but when I saw the name of the caller, I almost closed it again. My brother and I hadn't spoken in over a year, maybe two. Occasional emails were our only communication. I knew he must have a pressing reason to call, and I guessed it wasn't good news.

'Hi Greg,' I said, and a faint 'Hi Greg' echoed back at me. Mobile phones were hopeless for actual phone calls. I thought of the squat grey landline phone of my childhood, my dad handing me the receiver when a friend rang, the crystal clarity of the conversations you had on that.

'Pearl. Thank goodness. I wasn't sure you'd pick up.' Greg's voice, tinny and reverberating, plunged me back into the younger, less certain version of myself. 'Is this a good time to talk?'

Would there ever be a good time for us to talk? 'Yes, of course... Everything all right?'

'Not really. I'm sorry, Pearl. It's Dad. He's in hospital.'

I felt a shiver run up my back.

'How do you know?'

'A nurse called me.' He hesitated, then, presumably anticipating my next question, said, 'I suppose Dad must have asked her to.'

'Seriously? Why?' Dad hadn't wanted to see or speak to any of us for more than thirty years. I started walking, the phone tight against my ear. 'How on earth did he have your number?' He sure as heck didn't have mine.

'I don't know. Does it matter? She said he was very ill, that it would probably be today, tomorrow at the latest.'

'What's wrong with him, did she say?'

'Something to do with his heart, I think.'

How ironic; I'd long suspected Dad didn't have a heart.

'Anyway,' Greg continued, 'just wanted to let you know.' His voice caught on the last word.

I arrived at the centre of the wood, my favourite place, where the trees were dense enough to form a canopy overhead, but not so thick that the sunlight couldn't get through. I liked to sit there, my back against the trunk of the smooth beech, and try to capture with pastels or paints the movement of light filtering through the leaves. It was very peaceful. It must be what other people felt when they were meditating, but I'd never been able to do any of that mindfulness stuff. My mind was never empty. Sitting in the woods with my drawing pad was as close to calm as I ever got.

'Are you all right, Greg?'

'Not really.'

I slid down against my tree, sat on its bumpy roots, and watched the fractured sunlight shimmer over my jeans.

'Nothing can be properly resolved now, can it? All the things I never said. It's all too late.' Greg's last few words were almost inaudible. I couldn't remember the last time I'd heard him cry.

'But Greg, he cut us off a million years ago. He wasn't interested in us, he made that abundantly clear time and time again.'

'Still, it hits you, doesn't it?' He sniffed. 'Going to call Benjy now, so I'd best get going.'

A hare darted out right in front of me, startling me, then disappeared again almost immediately in the undergrowth.

'Are you going to try and see him?' I don't know what made me say this. Why on earth would he, after all these years of silence? But my instincts were right.

'I... thought I might, yes.'

'Gracious! That's massive.' I felt a wave of something – annoyance, perhaps – that Greg was allowing himself to be pulled into Dad's final drama.

'Last chance, isn't it? I'd hate to look back after it's too late, and well, you know. Regret not being there.'

I got to my feet, too antsy to sit still. 'Well, good luck with that. Say hi to Ben for me.' I closed my phone without saying goodbye and started walking fast back along the path. Damn Greg, barging into my quiet day, dragging me back into all that stuff I'd worked so hard to leave behind. It felt like hours, but rationally I knew it was only a few minutes before I saw the familiar sight of our cottage, set in a little clearing in the wood, surrounded by a low white wooden fence.

Before we moved here, everyone had the same reaction to photos of the cottage. Everyone except my sister-in-law, Eleanor. At the salon, my colleagues were all: *You're so lucky; it's idyllic; wish I could live there* and so on. Even my brothers admired it. Benjy told me when he would be coming to visit. Greg said it looked very peaceful and pretty.

But not Eleanor. She scrolled through my pictures and stopped at one I was particularly proud of, the wood dark and inviting behind the cottage.

'Looks like the house in that fairy story,' she said.

'Aww, thank you!' I said. 'It does, doesn't it? Like "Goldilocks"?'

'No,' she said, her wry smile barely taking the sting out of it. 'The one made of sweets, in "Hansel and Gretel".'

Denny was in his workshop, which was where a dining room would be in a normal house. He was sawing away at something, but stopped when he heard me come in.

'That was quick!' He turned round, a buzz saw in one hand, and took off his safety goggles. With his checked, open-necked shirt, green chinos and dark silver-threaded hair, my husband looked like he was in a 'keeping active in your fifties' advert for a workbench, or haemorrhoid cream, perhaps. 'You only left about twenty minutes ago.'

'Greg called. My father's dying, apparently.'

'Oh! How does Greg even know?' Denny put down the buzz saw.

'That's what I said!' I walked to the window and looked out at the trees.

'Are you OK?' He came over and put his arm round me. 'That must have shaken you up. I don't just mean your dad, but hearing from Greg – it's been a long while.'

'Greg's talking about going to see him, can you believe it?'

'Well, I suppose these things take people in strange ways, don't they? And Greg always seemed less resigned than you to having lost touch with your dad.'

I pulled away, shocked, and turned to look at him. 'I'm not resigned! What do you mean?'

'Resigned is the wrong word, sorry. I just mean, you

accepted it as how it is.'

'That's the same as resigned! I never accepted it! The fact that I pushed it down, out of mind, doesn't mean I was fine about it.'

Denny raised his hands in apology. 'I'm really sorry. I'm saying everything wrong. Can I get you something? Coffee? I just put some on to brew.'

It was difficult to catch my breath. 'Yes, please,' I said, in a slightly higher octave than normal.

While he was out of the room, I fished my phone out of my bag and quickly pressed the number, so I didn't have time to think about what I was going to do. *Resigned.* Honestly!

'I'll come,' I said, my voice echoing back at me squeakily.

There was a short silence.

'*What* did you say?' Greg said.

'I'll get the next flight.'

'You hate him! You always said you hated him!'

'I know.'

'Pearl.' I heard Greg shift into 'patient older brother' mode. It bugged me now as much as when I was ten. 'You're not thinking straight. You can't—'

'I can. I want to.' Why did I want to? What the hell was going on? The last time I'd attempted to see Dad was almost thirty years ago, and it had ended in a panic attack. Well, I would just have to work out the 'why' part later.

'You're in the south of France!'

'I'm aware.' I turned back to the window, and watched as a bird flew off a branch and up into the sky.

'You're just going to get on a plane, and walk into the hospital room of a man you haven't spoken to in decades?'

'Text me the hospital details. See you there.'

'But Pearl—'

I clicked the phone shut just as Denny came back in.

'Den, I know this sounds completely mad, but I want to get

the next flight out.'

'What? Where?' Denny, holding two coffee cups, looked bewildered. Understandably, because other than Sundays, when we went to lunch in Millau, thirty kilometres away, I never went any farther than our local town.

'For some reason I feel the need to go there...'

Denny did a slow blink. 'You want to go to England? Now? To see... your *father*?'

I nodded, going through in my head what I needed. A change of clothes, a book, my laptop. Where was my passport? I hadn't used it for a while. Oh, why pretend? I knew exactly how long ago we were last in the UK. Five years, one month.

'Shall we just sit down?'

'I can't, Denny, I need to get going...'

He gently took my hand and led me to the sawdust-flecked sofa. 'Only for a minute. So I can get it straight.'

'All right, just for a minute though.' Most of my brain knew I was being irrational. The rest was click-clacking through logistics.

He handed me my coffee. 'Did Greg tell you to come?'

'No. In fact, he seemed shocked that I wanted to.'

Denny looked into my eyes. 'Sweetheart, I know how he feels.'

'I'm shocked myself. But I want to go.'

'Why?' His voice was quiet, reassuring. 'Your family... You've worked so hard to get distance. And as for your *father*... I could strangle Greg for bothering you with this.'

Denny was so protective of me. I usually liked it. But sometimes it meant he couldn't hear what I was saying.

'It's not his fault, he was just letting me know.'

'Are you *sad*?' Denny peered at my face, trying to gauge what I was feeling. To him, the thought of me being sad about my awful father's imminent death would be extraordinary. No, it wasn't fair to put it all on Denny. To me, too.

'Not sad exactly,' I said. 'Greg wanting to go and see him has unsettled me, that's all.' I didn't want to confess to the bizarre pre-emptive grief I was feeling. I thought I'd done my grieving for my father a long time ago, but there was a strange, yet also somehow familiar ache in my stomach that had been there from the moment I heard Greg's voice.

Denny put his arms round me. 'You poor thing.'

I let him comfort me for a minute, then pulled away. 'Right. Better get moving. Can you check flights for me while I get my bag together?'

'Sure. And if you, uh, change your mind, well, that's fine too.'

I nodded distractedly, trying to remember where my weekend bag was. I went upstairs and eventually discovered it on top of the wardrobe, covered in dust. With relief, I found that my passport was still in the front pocket. Then I had a horrible moment when I thought it might have expired, but thankfully there were still eighteen months left. I packed some clothes and my sponge bag, and went downstairs.

Denny was still sitting in his workroom, exactly as I'd left him.

'What did you find out about flights?' I said.

'You know you don't have to give in to pressure, don't you?'

'What do you mean?' I dropped my bag on the floor and sat next to him. 'No-one's pressurising me. I want to go.'

'It's Eleanor, isn't it?' Denny said. 'You never could say no to her.'

'I haven't even spoken to her!' I put my hand on his arm. 'Have you just been sitting here getting worked up?'

'She'll be ecstatic you're coming over; she'll find all sorts of reasons for you not to come back again.'

'Denny, that is complete nonsense. Exactly how spineless do you think I am? I'm going to see my father before he pops his clogs, come back, that's it.'

'They'll try to make you stay. They don't listen to you.'

'They're not the only ones!' I threw my hands up in exasperation. 'You know they've invited me to a hundred things since we moved here! They're forever having birthday parties and Christmas dinners and goodness knows what... Easter picnics and Sunday lunches and naming ceremonies, and I've said no to all of them.'

'Well... you've not exactly said no, have you? You've just not replied.'

'What about Eleanor's forty-fifth last year?' I stood up. My voice seemed louder than usual. 'She told me I was the only person she wanted to see, remember? And even so, I didn't go. Not to that, and not to anything else. Ever since...' And since this morning was all topsy-turvy, and I was feeling rather wild, I said it: 'Gracie's christening.'

We stared at each other, and I could see the fear in his eyes. The fear of what opening this particular can full of worms might mean.

After a moment, he looked away. I knew he wouldn't acknowledge what I'd said.

'What about work? Your clients...'

'I can easily rearrange them. Denny, my father is dying!'

'But you've barely even mentioned him for years!'

'You thought that because I hadn't mentioned him, I wouldn't be upset?'

'Well... yes.'

'So did I.' I sat down again. 'But I really want to go.'

There was a short silence.

'Right.' Denny put his 'made a decision' face on. I was fond of that face. 'If you're absolutely committed to this, I'll come with you.'

'You don't have to.'

'I do. I'm all that stands between you and your family.' He took out his phone. 'I'll book the flights.'

8TH JANUARY 2018

Roberta said they had asked for some more details but it was looking promising. I asked how long it would take though I knew it wasn't up to her; all she could do was pass on the information. I'm the only one with a sense of extreme urgency. I told her, please make sure she knows how sorry I am. This isn't in the least what I wanted. I always wished for things to be different. It is staggering to me sometimes, what a mess I made.

Poor Roberta, having to listen to me! She was very patient. Kept telling me: Francis, don't worry, I'll do my best for you. I gave her the church address for postal correspondence, told her it would be necessary to keep this confidential. Her voice was so kind. I wanted to tell her: Roberta, I have hidden so much from my wife. Even thinking it felt disloyal. I know I would be lost without her.

Roberta said she would be in touch soon, and I had to leave it there. I hurried home, all the way thinking about this person I never knew. For all that I wasn't able to, I really hope that she and you can find a way to make up for lost time.

TWO

PEARL

A frantic drive to Rodez in the van. We knew it was tight, and maddeningly, we missed the flight by fifteen minutes. We had to rebook and wait three hours, then in the UK the trains to Hastings were delayed. In the end, it didn't really matter. We didn't get there in time.

Greg was waiting outside the Conquest Hospital as Denny and I jumped out of a cab. The three of us stood in the forecourt, blinking at each other in the harsh sodium light. Greg shook his head, and his face said it all.

'Don't,' he said, as I started towards the door. 'Jeanie and Andrea are in there.'

Of course. As in death, so in life: Dad's second family were the ones who got to be with him.

'When did he...?' I said.

'About an hour ago. I'm really sorry.'

'Were you there? With him?' I wasn't going to cry; it would be silly and undignified, standing outside the hospital entrance with people coming and going, patients in pyjamas smoking their heads off, ambulances backing in and out of parking spaces. But to have tried so hard to get there, not really understanding why I was trying so hard, and to have failed by an hour seemed terribly unfair. Denny put his arm round my shoulder.

'Jeanie was in with him in his last moments. I did get to see him earlier today. He was asleep.' Greg spread his arms wide in a gesture of apology. 'I wish I'd given you more notice, Pearlie.'

'We could have made it,' I said, pulling away from Denny, 'if we hadn't faffed around so much before we left for the airport.' Even as I said it, I knew it wasn't Denny I was angry with, but myself. Why the *hell* had I come here, opened myself up to these feelings, feelings that should have been done with long ago?

'It wouldn't have mattered, really,' Greg said, trying to make things better in his Greg-way. 'You wouldn't have been able to speak to him.'

'I'm sorry,' Denny said.

'I am, too.' I leaned against him and he put his arm back round me. 'So... what now?'

'The hotel I'm staying at has room,' Greg said. 'Stay tonight and we can work out what you want to do before the funeral.'

'The funeral?' Oh my god. My father really was dead.

He hadn't been part of my consciousness for so many years, and now he was, but I still wasn't going to be able to see him. He was as out of reach as he had always been. I thought briefly about asking if I could go and see him now, but that felt just too weird for words.

'You'll be staying for the funeral, of course?' Greg said.

'I hadn't thought,' I said, at the same time as Denny said, 'No.'

Greg and I looked at him, and he said, 'We only have overnight bags. We're going back tomorrow. We can't stay for weeks or however long it's going to be...'

'Well, look, I'll talk to Jeanie, see what her thoughts are.' Greg was steering us towards the car park. 'She might be willing to have the funeral quickly.'

'Oh, not on our account, please,' Denny said.

'Since when are you on friendly terms with Jeanie?' I said.

'Here we are,' Greg said, unlocking his huge car. Of course he *would* have a people carrier: he and Eleanor had produced so many people. 'I wouldn't say *friendly* terms. We've seen each other once or twice since Dad's been ill.'

Denny and I sat together in the back of the car, and he held my hand, which was nice of him, given my little outburst. The manic energy which had propelled me here drained away, and I sat in numb silence. It was left to Denny and Greg to manfully keep the conversation going, with small talk about our journey (stressful but quick, though not quick enough), the weather in France (nicer than here, *quelle surprise*), Denny's most recent commission (a new staircase for a chapel in Rodez, the most challenging construction of his working life), and what Eleanor was up to these days (busy being a working mother, of course). Denny even fielded some questions on my behalf, though some of the answers weren't exactly the ones I might have given.

'You're still hairdressing, Pearl?' Greg asked.

'Mmm.'

'Yes, she is,' Denny confirmed. 'Has a lot of regular clients. They love her. Visits them in their houses, don't you, Pearl?'

'Mmm.'

'You must miss the salon, though, right?'

'No,' Denny said. 'She was ready for a change. And it means she has more time for her art. She's been doing some gorgeous nature paintings.'

I loved how proud Denny was of my daubings. But Greg wasn't so interested in that.

'Ellie still goes to the salon, of course. Says it's not the same without you. Peaches does her hair now. She's very good, apparently.'

Of course she was! *I taught her everything she knew*, I wanted to shout. *Tell him that, Denny!* But we were already pulling up at the hotel. I was surprised by Greg's choice, a sweet old-fashioned-looking inn, because he usually opted for the most modern, business-like places.

'Premier Inn was full. Rubik's Cube competition, if you can believe it,' he said, which answered some questions, though raised other, possibly unanswerable, ones. I felt about a hundred years old as I got out of the car and allowed Greg to book Denny and me into a room. Being back here felt incredibly strange. Despite having lived in England for the first forty-six years of my life, I fitted into life in France, Denny said, like a hand in a glove.

'I'll see you in the dining room in half an hour,' Greg said as we went our separate ways. It wasn't a question.

Denny and I closed the door to our chintzy room, and flopped backwards onto the bed at exactly the same time.

'Oh. My. God,' I said.

'I'm really sorry.'

'What are you sorry for?' I rolled onto my side so I could see his face. 'You've done nothing. It's me; I've gone crazy. I don't know what on earth we're doing here.'

'I'm sorry your dad's dead, I'm sorry Greg's being so Greg, and most of all I'm sorry we didn't get here in time.'

'None of that is your fault,' I said, and meant it. I sat up against the headboard. 'Why was it so important all of a sudden to come here, when I have scarcely thought about Dad for years?'

'You tell me, sweetheart.'

'I don't know!' I couldn't recapture the feelings of this morning. 'I was so certain I needed to be here, that there would be some last words of forgiveness, or a look of understanding or something. I'm such an idiot.'

I got up, and went into the en suite bathroom, every layer of the long, fruitless journey clagging at my skin. I threw off my clothes, and turned on the shower. It was one of those rainfall

ones that look a better idea than they are. But I was in the mood
to be drenched. I turned up the heat of the water to almost
unbearable levels, hoping to scald sense into myself.

Denny came in as I was washing my hair, and yelled over
the noise of the water, 'There's a return flight at two a.m. We
could make it, if we leave in the next hour.'

I leaned out, shampoo dripping down my face. 'It doesn't
feel right to rush off straight away.'

'But what is there to do here? You don't want to stay for the
funeral, do you?'

I could barely think straight. 'I suppose not. But what about
Greg? He's expecting us for dinner.'

'He'll understand,' Denny said. 'Or, if he doesn't, I don't
much care.'

I put my head back under the spray. 'I can't hear you properly. Wait till I'm out.'

I took my time in the bathroom. As I went back into the
room, my hair wrapped in a large white towel, my phone rang.
It was becoming more familiar a sound than I would like. Greg,
of course.

'I'm already in the restaurant downstairs,' he said. 'I was
starving. See you here in a minute? They have bouillabaisse.'

'Well, I'm – oh!' I looked at Denny. 'He hung up.'

'Oh god.' Denny put his head in his hands. 'The escape
hatch is closing.'

'He thinks we'll be pleased that they're doing Sussex
versions of French dishes,' I told Denny. 'You don't have to
come, you can get room service, I'll go...'

'You think I'm going to let you be alone with Greg? God
only knows what you'll end up agreeing to! He'll have you being
a pallbearer or something.'

. . .

Greg was already eating when we got to the dining room. I ordered a small salad niçoise and a large glass of white wine.

'Terrible day, right?' Greg said, wiping his mouth. 'For all of us.'

This was the first chance I'd had to look at him properly. He was five years older than when I last saw him, and he looked it. He was tall and statesmanlike, with broad shoulders – broad everything, really. His hair was in serious need of a cut. If he was in my chair I'd get those sides tidied, for starters – they were turning in like kiss curls – and I'd thin out the grey.

I wondered what I looked like to him. The last time we saw each other I was in my mid-forties, but I'd tipped over into my fifties now, and discovered how telling those few years were on a woman's face. It wasn't only new lines and wrinkles, though there were certainly more of those. But my blue eyes, always my best feature, had somehow dimmed. They needed a lot of make-up to stand out like they used to; make-up I wasn't currently wearing.

As if Greg was reading my mind, he said, 'Despite the circumstances, it's so lovely to see you. You look exactly the same.'

'You charmer. I'm old.'

'In that case, I'm Methuselah. I'm always going to be older than you.'

'You liked being older when we were kids.' I touched his arm. 'I'm sorry you didn't get to speak to Dad, after all your efforts.'

'Oh. Didn't I say? I was here last week when he was a bit more compos mentis, and we spoke a little.'

'*Really*? How weird, talking to him after all this time.' I'd thought Greg only knew about Dad being in hospital this morning, when a nurse called him. I felt too tired and confused to unpick it right now.

'He was pretty vague. I don't think he knew who I was.' Greg took a sip of his wine. 'So, the funeral.'

'We're going back home tomorrow,' Denny said, quickly. 'We can come back for it, if Pearl wants to...'

'No way.' Greg put down his glass. 'She'll never come back over a second time. Couldn't bloody believe it when you came today, no way am I letting you go back.'

'Now hang on a minute,' Denny said.

'Denny, I know you are both homebodies,' Greg said, 'and that it's not your ideal situation, being over here. But is it asking too much for you to stay a few days? You haven't been here once since...'

The waiter put a plate of food in front of Denny, mercifully cutting Greg off. We all waited until he'd gone. Then Denny said, 'The funeral might not be for two weeks, maybe more. We can't just stay here, hanging about.'

'But we ought to be there, Pearl.' Greg turned to me. 'You, me, Ben. Dad's first family. I'll talk to Jeanie, convince her we should have the funeral quickly.'

I laughed. 'You're always so sure that people will do what you want, Greg.'

'I'm merely optimistic.' He smiled and clinked glasses with me.

'You're the optimist...' I cited our mother's ancient adage. 'I'm the pessimist, and...'

Greg finished it: '...Benjy's the realist. Actually, he's more of a cynic, wouldn't you say?'

'Both of us have work,' Denny said, wearing his 'I'm a patient man but I'm being pushed to my limit' face. 'We don't even have clothes for the funeral.'

'I do,' I said.

There was a small, charged silence. It seemed like a good opportunity for me to drink the rest of my wine, fast.

'You brought something?' Denny said, staring at me. 'I only have the clothes I'm wearing now.'

'Put in my black dress. In case.'

Greg made a strange noise, and we both looked at him. He was crying.

'Sorry. Sorry. Think it's just hit me. Jesus. Can't believe he's gone.' He ran his hand over his face, trying to reset it back to normal. 'And I can't believe you're here, Pearl. I've missed you so much. Ellie and I have both really missed you.'

'Oh, Greg.' I put my arm round his shoulder and he leaned against me.

The Denny I loved, the kind version who had temporarily been missing in action, reappeared. 'Greg, I'm sorry. You're trying to make arrangements, and we're sitting here bickering.' He called the waiter over and ordered three brandies.

'Pearl,' Greg said – or slurred, in fact. I wondered how much he'd drunk before we'd got here. 'I had a call from Dad's lawyer.'

'Oh yes?'

'Dad left something for you, apparently.'

'I'm sorry, what?'

The waiter brought the brandies and I held onto mine as though it was a lifebelt.

Greg nodded. 'Pretty weird, right?'

'What exactly did this lawyer say?' Denny asked.

'He said there's a legacy for Pearl, and she has to get it at the funeral.'

'For *me*? Someone's clearly made a mistake.'

'No, he's really left you something.'

'And to you and Benjy as well, then?'

'Just you, Pearl.' Greg picked up his brandy glass and swirled it round.

'And if I don't come to the funeral?'

'You don't get it. It'll be destroyed, apparently.'

'What the *hell*?' Denny said, shaking his head. 'I have never heard of that before.'

'That does sound quite mad,' I said. 'Are you sure you've got it right? Dad couldn't even be bothered to pick up the phone, no way did he go to the effort of creating a legacy for me.'

'Are we drinking these, then?' Greg raised his brandy glass, and we toasted each other, because none of us could face toasting absent friends. Though weirdly, my father was beginning to feel less absent now, despite the whole being deceased thing, than he had done for over thirty years.

THREE

CARRIE

As I slid the paper back into the thick cream envelope, the word *vellum* came into my mind. Vellum. A heavy, legal sort of word. A perfect description of the heavy feeling that had washed over me as I read the letter.

I peeked into the bedroom, but Emmie was still fast asleep. She would likely be good for another half hour. Enough time to phone Mum.

'Hello darling.' She sounded tired, but alert. I pictured her, sitting up in bed. All my crossness melted away on hearing her voice.

'Is this an OK time, Mum?'

'Always an OK time to talk to my darling.'

'But do they need to do anything?'

'They can do it while I'm talking to you.' I heard her say something to someone, then she laughed. 'Yes, this lovely one, Ling, says she's going to do my pulse and blood pressure and I won't even notice she's there.'

'I'm coming to see you later,' I reminded her.

'I know! Can't wait.'

'But I just received the most extraordinary letter, and I thought you might be able to shed some light on it.'

'Oh, did you?'

'A letter from a lawyer... your name is mentioned...'

She took a sharp breath. 'Blast, I meant to tell you, but I kept putting it off, and what with one thing and another...'

'So you do know what it's about.' I shifted around in my chair, trying to get comfortable. 'It's not a weird mistake, or a scam.'

'Darling, please don't be miffed. I know I should have asked you first, but I was worried you'd say no.'

'You got that right.'

'I'm sorry. But I felt that circumstances being what they are... ow!'

'What's ow? Are you OK?'

'I'm fine, I didn't know she was taking blood. Naughty Ling!' Mum laughed. 'She's already done it, they are so efficient here.'

'I don't want to bug you, Mum, when they're doing things. I'll bring the letter with me, and you can apologise for meddling in person.'

'Don't be too cross, darling. You know my intentions are pure. Why don't you read it out? I'm fine, it will distract me. And maybe I can answer some questions before you get here.'

'All right, though you are firmly in the doghouse, Mother, don't think you're not.' I said this in my lightest voice, so we both knew I was joking. Only I wasn't, exactly. I took out the letter. 'What does "vellum" mean?'

'It says "vellum" in the letter?'

'No, I just thought of the word when I opened the envelope.'

'How funny you are! I don't know. Is it a kind of parchment?'

I smoothed out the letter and read it aloud, my heart fluttering again as it had when I first set eyes on it.

Dear Ms Haskett,

I'm the solicitor acting on behalf of the late Mr Francis Nichols, who passed away on 17th April. He instructed me, further to his recent phone conversations with your mother, Linda, to request your presence at his funeral. He asked me to stress that it is his last wish and as such, he hoped very much that you will attend.

The funeral will take place on Tuesday 24th April at three p.m. at St Augustin's Church, Rye.

With best wishes, and condolences at this time,

Martin M. Claymore

There was silence at the other end. 'Mum? You there?'

A long sigh. 'Yes. So he's gone. Goodness, that's next week. They've arranged the funeral in a hurry. Do you know who he is?'

'I worked it out. Mum, what's going on? I'm certainly not attending the funeral of a complete stranger.'

'OK, we can talk about it later.'

'You can guess my feelings.'

'I can, my sweet. But you know, given everything, I just want you to have the option, in case of—'

'No!' I shouted, because this was exactly what I didn't want to hear. I immediately heard crying from the other room. 'Damn, I've woken Emmie.'

'Go get her, darling. We'll talk later.'

'Fine.' I tried to leave it on a more pleasant note. 'My gruntle is very dissed.'

Mum picked up my cue. 'I'm sorry to hear that, let me see if I can perform a gruntle-ectomy.' She made some weird noises which I believed, though I'd never drilled down too deeply into this childhood routine of ours, was meant to represent her doing some kind of operation. 'There. Your gruntle is back in place.'

'Thanks, Mum. See you this afternoon.'

'Can't wait.'

We hung up, and I hurried along to Emmie's room and pressed my cold face against her warm, damp one. She stopped crying immediately, and I carried her to the kitchen and popped her in her high chair. She was such a good-natured little thing, had already moved on from her rude awakening. She banged on her tray with her spoon until the microwave pinged, then laughed.

'You like that gourmet pinging sound, don't you?' I handed her the Tommee Tippee cup and watched admiringly as she chugged from it, an expert drinker already. 'Your grandmother's being very annoying, do you know that, Emmie?'

She took her cup out of her mouth and said, 'Babble babble.'

'Well, exactly. You are spot on there. I *will* tell her so.'

I picked up the kettle to fill it, and examined my distorted face in its silvery surface. To my reflection, I said, 'I'm absolutely not going to this stupid funeral.' Mum's reason for me going was terrible, and I would tell her so.

I'd been dreading the long slog up the stairs at Iain's flat, so it was a pleasant surprise to see him waiting for us on the pavement outside. He came over to the car, and Emmie started babbling excitedly.

'Oh my god, she's saying "Dada"!' he said.

'It's a coincidence,' I said. 'I read that it's easier for them to say d-sounds than any other letter.'

'Yeah, yeah.' He leaned into the back seat and started

unbuckling her. 'You know who I am, don't you? Don't you? Yes, you do! I'm your daddy! Yes I am!'

I found Iain's baby voice rather grating, but successfully hid my feelings by gritting my teeth hard enough to make them squeak.

'Here's her bag. Nappies, milk, everything.'

Iain scooped Emmie into his arms. She, of course, loved it, being so high up, laughing and fiddling with his baseball cap. 'I've bought some nappies, actually.'

'Really?' This was new. Iain's only concessions to having a baby until now had been a small monthly cheque, and a small monthly visit.

'No need to say it like that. I know I've not been very hands-on.'

I laughed. 'You've been exactly as hands-on as I was expecting.'

'But it's going to be different from now on.'

'It is? Why?'

'She's gorgeous, isn't she? Our daughter. I want to be in her life more.'

'Oh. Well, that's great.' I knew there must be a reason – probably an unedifying one – for this newfound, unexpected interest in Emmie, but not only did I have neither the time nor headspace to probe it, I didn't care. Iain was a fact of life, like cockroaches or drains, and he would always be a fact of life because I'd been foolish enough to choose him as my baby-daddy. Not that that's what I thought he was, of course, when I got pregnant. I was in love and dreamy-eyed, then. What an idiot.

'I've got to go, Iain. Visiting hours are pretty tight.'

'Send your mum my love. We're going to have a great time, aren't we, Em?'

I opened the boot to take out the buggy, but he said, 'No need. I've bought one. Maclaren.'

'You're kidding.'

'If I'm going to have her more, I'll need all the kit here, won't I?'

'So you really are serious?' I kissed Emmie's warm cheek, but she barely registered me, so engrossed was she in taking Iain's cap off his head and putting it back on skewwhiff.

'I'd like to. If it's OK with you. I'm sure it will be OK with Emmie-wemmie, won't it, yes it will!'

'Definitely,' I said, gritting again until my jaw ached.

I thought Mum was asleep when I walked into her ward, but her eyes opened as I sat down beside her bed.

'Oh, darling!' She reached out her hand to me, and I kissed it.

'How you doing, Mum?' She looked pale and had dark rings under her eyes.

'Oh, you know.' She gestured to the tubes that went in and out of her, the machinery surrounding her bed, the technology that was keeping her alive. 'I'm ready to dance at the Palais tonight.'

'I'll come with you. What will you wear?'

'What's wrong with my nightgown?' She preened herself. 'It's so glamourous.' She did a Hollywood-style pout, then ruined the effect by coughing so hard I had to help her sit up. I gave her some water from an infantilising sippy cup not unlike the one Emmie had drunk her milk from earlier. Our eyes met over the top of it in silent acknowledgement about how much we both hated this.

When she'd recovered, she leaned forward. 'No Emmie?'

'I'll bring her next time. Talk to me.'

'Did you put her in the crèche at work?' Mum had never got over the thrill of me having a university job with low-cost child-care on campus. The dream, she called it.

'She's with Iain.'

'Really?' Mum sat up straight. 'That's promising.'

'Yes,' I said heavily. 'It is promising that he wants to be more involved with her.'

'And maybe promising for more than that?' Mum smiled. 'Wanting to be more of a proper family?'

'Mum, stop trying to make me and Iain happen. That ship has sailed. Anyway,' I leaned back in my chair, 'I suspect you're trying to distract me from the main topic of conversation, because you know you've done something you shouldn't have.'

'I'm very ill,' Mum said, still smiling, 'so you have to be nice to me.'

'Playing the cancer card, huh?'

'It's all I've got.' Her face turned serious. 'Sorry darling, I know I may have overstepped, but on this particular matter, I see things very differently from you.'

'How did it even come about?'

'It's a bit of a story.' Mum thought for a moment, wondering where to start. 'You remember years ago, we left our details with them?'

'Vaguely. How long ago was it?'

'About twenty years. You were fifteen. Your rebellious stage.'

We grinned at each other. My rebellious stage had been short-lived, and quite the cliché: a leather jacket, some door-slamming, a few drags of a friend's cigarette and, to my shame, a rather pointed (but very brief) rejection of my kind, loving parents.

'Well, I don't expect you remember this part, but we gave them my details, not yours, because you were under eighteen. And then, a few months ago, Francis contacted me, via an intermediary.'

'You never told me that!'

'I knew how you felt about it, remember? Aside from that

sweet teenage phase, you've always been really clear that you weren't interested, you didn't want to know. I thought I'd just respond, see what the lie of the land was.'

'And?'

Mum took a sip of water. 'I spoke to him on the phone a few times. He was getting on, almost eighty and in poor health. He seemed rather a troubled person. He hinted at a massive rift between him and his children – indeed, between him and pretty much everyone.'

'It'll be a quiet funeral, then.'

'Now, Miss Carrie. That's not very respectful, is it?'

'Sorry. Go on.'

'He certainly had his reasons for getting in touch, at this late stage. A sense of wanting to try to make things right before it was too late. And I have to say...'

'No, please don't...'

'I have to say,' Mum said, with heavy emphasis, 'that I know how he felt.'

'It's *not* the same. You're going to get better.'

Mum smiled. 'I've always appreciated your positive thinking.' She took my hand and pressed it to her lips. 'If I told you – and I hesitate to do so, because it sounds horribly like emotional blackmail – that you going to the funeral would be a real comfort to me, what would you say?'

'That it sounds horribly like emotional blackmail?'

'I'm a shocker, I know. Look, Carrie love, I don't even mean for you to speak to anyone. See some faces, that's all. It's only about being open to the idea.'

'They'll wonder who the hell I am.'

'They won't. Hang back, give a false name, say how sorry you are. There's always at least one person at every funeral who no-one knows, and it's only much later that everyone says, I thought they were *your* friend? Remember your dad's?'

We smiled at each other, remembering Dad's funeral a few

years ago, at which a decrepit old bloke sat at the back of the church, and sang the hymns so loudly and tunelessly that every head turned. 'PRAISE MY SOUL THE KING OF HE-EAV-EV-EN'. It was the one funny thing on an awful day. I assumed he was some random uncle, Mum assumed he was one of Dad's colleagues, but at the wake we realised that no-one knew him.

'I'll have to think about it.'

'Absolutely. It's your call. I've said my bit.' She paused. 'If you do go, imagine the great gossip we can have about everyone.'

A tall, smiley nurse came over. 'Time to do some checks, Linda.'

'I'll leave you to it,' I said, kissing Mum's dry cheek. 'See you soon.'

Mum whispered, 'Think about it, won't you?'

'Promise.'

I kept my promise on the drive back from the hospital; I didn't think about anything else. Mum must be losing her marbles, to think I would be interested in this man, Francis; in attending his funeral. A person I'd never met, and now I never would. All his family there, and honestly, I knew I couldn't face it.

Iain's flat was unusually clean and tidy, and I wondered if the reason for this was also the reason he was suddenly more interested in Emmie: that there was a new woman to impress.

'We had a great time,' he said, gathering Emmie's things together. 'We danced to music, and played with Duplo, and went to the shops, and had a picnic in the park.'

'Gosh, that's a lot for a couple of hours, well done. Did your new girlfriend like hanging out with Emmie?'

'What are you on about?'

'You're relying on Emmie's silence,' I said, 'but you know that pretty soon, she'll be able to tell me who she's seen, right?'

'You're crazy, you know that? I don't have a new girlfriend.'

I picked Emmie up. 'Say goodbye to this man, Emmie, I honestly couldn't tell you who he is but he seems to know you.'

'Ha ha, funny. You're just jel because she says my name and not yours.'

'Bye, Iain.'

Emmie ought to have been ready for a nap, but clearly, being with Iain had been over-stimulating. She didn't sleep on the way home, so instead of going inside, I put her in the buggy and took her for her second park outing of the day. I wasn't the only one there trying to tire out an energetic child; Henry, my next-door neighbour, was watching his daughter Numa go endlessly up and down the slide in the playground. I tried to interest Emmie in the baby swing so I could stand still and push her, but she toddled away, remarkably quickly, in the opposite direction. She knew that the ducks were mere metres away.

'I say it every time,' Henry said, as I wearily trotted after her, 'but we really need to work out where their off-switches are.'

'Or at least put them in a hamster wheel, so they can generate electricity or something useful,' I said over my shoulder. I managed to catch Emmie at the playground gate, and took her hand firmly in mine.

We walked to the pond, and the funeral roiled round my head. I didn't blame Mum, but I wished she hadn't asked me. Even at the best of times I could never say no to her. She knew I'd managed perfectly well for thirty-five years without these people. They didn't know me; they'd clearly never been bothered about me. It would be a lot of raking up, at a time in my life when I didn't have the headspace for it. Emmie, Mum and work were my priorities, in that order, and with a large gap between the second and third.

Emmie tugged my hand excitedly as the pond came into

view. She always liked to get up close and personal with the ducks. She had no sense of danger. 'Your child, for sure,' Mum said, of this trait. Apparently I'd been the same. Intrepid. She actually went into the pond a little way before I noticed that her new blue Start-Rite shoes were getting splashed. I wondered if she couldn't see the edge between water and land. Maybe not seeing it was what made her brave.

Emmie: Babble babble babble!

Me: Oh, totally agree, Emmie. That green duck *is* particularly charming.

Emmie [laughing]: Babble babble babble!

Me: You have a point. I don't know anything about ducks. You're the expert. On a different topic, what do you think about this silly funeral business?

Emmie: Babble babble.

Me: Totally on point as usual, my love. They *are* a bunch of nothings, aren't they? They're nothing to me. But Nana wants me to go to the funeral. Do you think we should go?

Emmie: Yaargh.

Me: I beg your pardon?

Emmie: Yaargh.

Me: That sounded like yes, Emmie.

Emmie: Babble babble.

This was a hell of an interesting time to say 'yes' for the first time. Unless I was looking for a sign and she'd said 'yaargh' before without me noticing. Still, as Mum would no doubt say, if I was looking for a sign, I was probably looking for a reason to go.

FOUR

PEARL

We sat in the back seat of the taxi, the meter ticking away. We'd already had him drive round two extra times while I worked up my nerve.

Denny was right. This was a big mistake.

'Still not ready?' the driver said.

'Not quite,' I said. 'Can you go round the block again, please?'

He sighed, which irritated me. We were paying for him to drive, after all. Denny squeezed my hand, too kind to remind me that he'd spent all week trying to talk me into returning home, not get pulled into this foolish legacy nonsense.

We pulled back up outside the church, in time to see some people I didn't know walking through the gates.

'Funeral, is it?' the taxi driver said.

'Yes,' I said.

'Someone close?'

The nosey so-and-so. 'Both parents,' I replied. 'Horrific factory explosion. Took my sisters and brothers, too. Their funerals are next week.' It was the plot of a saga I'd been reading.

Denny stared at me, his eyes wide. Something – Dad's death, or being back in the UK – had brought out my long-dormant naughty side. I scrambled for the door, my inertia finally broken.

'Jesus, love, I am so sorry.' The driver took the money Denny offered without counting, waved away his attempts to add a tip, and drove off. I felt bad, but not as bad as I ought to.

We stood in the street by the entrance to the churchyard. 'Shall I add that one to the ever-lengthening "my wife's temporarily lost her mind" list?' Denny said.

'How do we know it's temporary?'

He put on sunglasses, and ran his finger round the collar of his new, stiff white shirt, bought along with a cheap suit during yesterday's shopping trip to Eastbourne. Poor Denny, forced to accompany his snarky wife on a week-long trip to England after five years of swearing never again to step foot on this benighted isle. Today was probably even more excruciating for him than for me. The last time Denny and I were with my family, and in a church, no less, he was the one who caused a scene. I took his hand, and we set off into the churchyard, looking appropriately sombre, though not necessarily for the right reasons.

There were a few people I didn't recognise standing around outside. If I'd ever thought about it, I suppose I'd assumed that once Dad disappeared from our lives he stopped meeting people, stopped making friends. But of course, he had decades to build up other relationships, and doubtless stayed active in the church – this very church, probably. These people must be his friends, or his wife Jeanie's friends and family.

I tightened my grip on Denny's hand, in case one of us tried to make a break for it, and panic-scanned the faces. I realised I did know two of them: my oldest niece, Gina, Benjy's only child, looking so grown-up, I hadn't immediately recognised her; and Barbara, her grandmother – Benjy's ex-mother-in-law. Barbara had one hand on Gina's shoulder, the other holding a

cigarette. She was dressed like a black widow, an actual veil
dangling from her hat. She turned her head to blow smoke away
from Gina, caught sight of me, and waved enthusiastically.

Benjy unofficially inherited Barbara as part of his divorce
settlement with Alice. I wasn't the only one to wonder if Benjy
and Alice split up because there were three of them in that
marriage, to quote Princess Di.

'Darling Pearl!' Barb exclaimed, stepping forward so
abruptly that she wobbled on her heels and had to right herself
by clutching Gina's arm.

Benjy and Alice married very young, and moved in with
Barbara after the wedding. When Alice finally had enough of
being Benjy's wife, it was she who left, and Benjy who stayed.
Benjy-and-Barbara had long been a source of amusement to me,
Denny, Eleanor and Greg. When we were in the right mood, so
perhaps not today, we'd drink an imaginary shot every time
Benjy mentioned Barb's name. I don't think it was so much a
Harold and Maude situation, as much as Benjy seeking out as
many parental figures in his life as he could get.

'What a trooper you are,' Barb said, teetering over to us.
'Your father was an *utter* swine.' She never knew Dad, so this
comment was based on what Benjy had told her. Gina smiled
warily at me. Fair enough; my nieces and nephews had good
reason to be wary around me. But I'd once had a good relationship with Gina. There was a time when she would have run
into my arms. Still, why should she? I hadn't exactly been in her
life recently.

'Gina, it's lovely to see you,' I said, biting my lip on any
clichéd aunty nonsense about how grown up she was. I kissed
her unresponsive cheek and got a whiff of expensive perfume.
She was twenty-five now, and a social worker. The last time I
saw her, she was nineteen. I'd missed the end of her youth; it
was already gone. A wave of sadness washed over me. How
could I have let her slip away?

'Hello, Aunt Pearl,' she said, all formal and buttoned.

'Benjy will be thrilled to see you. See you *both!*' Barbara gushed, touching Denny's arm. 'Not thrilled,' she corrected herself immediately, 'not the day for *thrilled*, is it? But he will be so *grateful* to you for coming.'

I kissed Barbara's proffered cheek, getting a mouthful of stiff black nylon lace. The *grateful* lingered. I guessed that this was less about me gracing the family with my presence, and more to do with turning up to unlock the mysterious legacy. I could see in Barbara's over-eager smile the expectation that a) it was surely going to be a small fortune and b) that I would be guilt-tripped into sharing it with my un-bestowed brothers. I wondered if Barbara had already arranged the terms of her cut with Benjy.

I'd spent a reasonable amount of the last week speculating about this legacy, both aloud to Denny, and silently to myself, but I was no closer to working out why Dad would have left anything to me. Why me, rather than my brothers? Sometimes I felt positive about it, that it might be something symbolic he wanted me to have so I would occasionally look at it and think well of him. Other times I just felt angry that he might have thought some lousy token could make up for being a hopeless father, too cowardly to apologise for his shortcomings in life, leaving all the emotional work to me. When I told Denny I was concerned it might be money, which would feel like a heavy burden with a large side-order of guilt-trip, he pointed out that we could donate it to charity. Perhaps one that provided for children of absent fathers would be suitably fitting.

Denny told Barbara she was looking well, and she told him he was too, and with that fascinating exchange done, Barbara ground the cigarette under her heel and the four of us went into the church. I wanted to walk next to Gina but Denny took my arm as firmly as if I was a doddery old lady. I was grateful for his grip when we stepped into the cold church, because there was a

'who's who', right in front of me, of pretty much everyone I'd
been avoiding for the past five years. The people who were
standing up at the back turned to look at us and the people who
were already sitting down twisted round in their seats, and it
honestly felt as if there was a spotlight over my head. It was so
surreal that I was seized with the impulse to rip off my coat,
grab a mic that someone threw in from the side, and burst into,
'If My Friends Could See Me Now'.

I looked at Denny, hoping for a reassuring glance, but he
was still wearing his sunglasses, naff celebrity-style. I turned a
large, vague smile on everyone, deliberately staring straight
ahead at the altar, at a covered coffin, so I didn't have to look
anyone in the face. But out of the corner of my eye I saw Greg
and Eleanor, his wife. She looked chic in an olive dress and not
a day older than when I'd last seen her. She wore her auburn
hair up in a neat chignon, just like I'd taught her. She stood
when she saw me, smiled and waved, gestured to me to join her.
She gave no hint of being upset that I hadn't replied to the texts
and emails she'd sent last week. I took a deep breath and looked
at the seats next to her, but the children weren't there.

The music struck up from a not very proficient organist, and
with an apologetic grimace at Eleanor, I allowed Barb to sweep
me and Denny along to her row. I didn't resist too hard, that's
the honest truth. It wasn't often that I'd consider that sitting
next to Benjy meant I'd dodged a bullet, but I wasn't yet ready
for Eleanor. I knew she had long ago forgiven and forgotten, but
I couldn't easily think of her without remembering how hard
things had been for me back then, and how – though it wasn't
her fault – she had been part of that.

I sat on the hard wooden seat and turned to smile at Benjy.
He was wearing a black T-shirt and jeans, rather than a suit.
Good to see him socking it to the man as always.

'Make an entrance, why don't you, Dame Pill?' he muttered,
tapping his watch.

'Hello to you, too.'

The vicar stepped up to the lectern, and everyone went silent. 'We are here today to commemorate the death of Francis Nichols, a much valued and missed member of this community.'

Barb handed me an order of service. It had a photo of Dad on the front, and his dates: 1939 to 2018. I scarcely recognised him, an old man in his seventies. It looked to have been taken on holiday because he was sitting on a balcony, the sea behind him. He was wearing a Panama hat, his face serious, his eyes squinting into the sun. There was a vase of yellow fluffy flowers on the table next to him that would be lovely to paint. Mimosa, I thought.

'We will sing one of his favourite hymns, "Abide with Me", number 309.'

Denny fumbled through the pages of a prayer book, then held it open so I could see the words. There was no need, though; I knew them by heart. Dad went to church every week when I was a child, and I usually went with him. I enjoyed it, our quiet time together, the way we'd talk about all sorts of things on the walk there and back. I didn't have any interest in Christianity now, nor any religion, not for decades, but these hymns were part of my DNA. I sang automatically, eyes fixed piously on the covered coffin until I realised – surprisingly late in the day – that it was Dad in there. The tune caught in my throat, and I looked away, focusing on a stained-glass window in which the young Jesus was piously teaching elders in the temple. Speculating about how the elders had felt about that, I managed to distract myself from the coffin long enough to get through the hymn.

The singing came to a ragged end, and the vicar announced that we would now hear a reading from the *Book of Job*, which had been chosen by Dad.

'*Oh, that my words were written! Oh, that they were inscribed in a book!*' it began, and I wondered what Dad would have said about the vicar's uninspiring cadences. Despite being a committed Christian, Dad was always highly vocal about the inadequacies of the various vicars and priests he encountered. I'm sure he would have enjoyed complaining about this vicar, unless he'd mellowed in old age. Did he ever sit where I was sitting now? Did Jeanie come with him? After all, church was where they'd met, at our family church in Chelmsford.

Come to that, where *was* Jeanie? Of course, I didn't know what she looked like now. I hadn't seen her for pushing forty years. She was always frozen in time for me as a spiky, bone-thin woman – think Wallis Simpson – with dark permed hair, shot through with a grey streak. I scanned the mourners in the front pews. She'd be in her early seventies now, and could easily be that white-haired woman with her head bowed. She was sitting next to a middle-aged woman who gave off an impression of elegance, even from the back. This was surely Jeanie's daughter Andrea. Pronounced An-dray-ah.

The last time I saw Jeanie and Andrea I was fifteen, and Andrea was only about seven or eight. My abiding memory was of her sitting on her bed, holding a book in front of her like a shield. The book – though why I had retained this detail, since so many far more important things had faded, I don't know – was a dull girl's comic annual called *Penny*. I pushed the memory away, and attended to the vicar, who was droning on about what a stalwart Dad was.

'Always ready to roll up his sleeves for the good of the community. He volunteered for the church food bank, at the youth club, acted as an unofficial deputy to our churchwarden, assisted the treasurer, organised the Christmas Day community meal for our homeless brethren...'

Brethren was a strange word. *Brethren*. You only ever heard it in a Christian capacity. Old English, I supposed. A plural of brother. I myself had brethren. I was in a church with my two brethren, in fact, and I wasn't doing too great. My heart rate was way faster than it should be, and I could feel heat prickling along my hairline. If you died during a funeral, what did they do, did they open the coffin and tip you in?

Denny whispered, 'Pearl?' in his oh-my-god-you're-not-OK tone, and I came out of my reverie to find that water was literally pouring down my face. Not tears, but rivers of sweat. I was used to unexpected sweats – I was a woman in my fifties – but this was full-on panic sweats. Jeanie was over there! Next to Jeanie's daughter! Two rows behind me were Eleanor and Greg, and somewhere here were their three children. *Christ!*

I was running out of breaths. I only had a few left. Denny turned to give me a tissue just as my hand moved towards him, out of my control. It swung up and knocked his sunglasses onto his lap, allowing me to see the panic in his eyes.

I stood up. 'Excuse me,' I whispered to Benjy.

'What the hell?' he hissed. 'Where are you going?' Then he registered my expression, and shifted his knees out of the way instantly. Though I was moving as quietly as possible, I sensed everyone looking at me, and even the vicar hesitated in his droning before resuming, '... and a devoted husband to Jeanie, and a dedicated dog owner to their spaniel Snoopy...'

As I hurried past their row, I caught Eleanor's eye. She sent me such a sympathetic look that I wished I could grab her hand, pull her along with me, have her raise my spirits like she always used to. But I rushed on alone, wrestling with the heavy door and managing at last to get out of the clammy, claustrophobic church.

I stepped outside, grateful for the fresh air, and leaned against the wall. I closed my eyes. There was a pounding silence in my head. Why had I thought I could do this? Come here, be with these people? What kind of first-rate idiot was I?

I heard a noise, and opened my eyes again, sensing that even here, I was being looked at. A brown-haired woman was standing in the churchyard, a sleeping baby in her arms. It seemed as if she'd been about to go into the church, but seeing me had stopped her in her tracks. She smiled uncertainly at me, and I tried to smile back. My breathing stuttered back into life. Then the church door banged open and Denny came barrelling out. 'Pearl! Pearl!'

'I'm here. I'm OK.' I held out my hand to him, and he pulled me into an embrace. I looked over his shoulder, and saw that the woman was no longer there.

As Denny held me, my breathing gradually slowed, and my heart settled back down to its usual pace. He stroked my hair, saying, 'I'm sorry, I'm sorry.'

'Why are you sorry?' I said. 'You told me repeatedly not to come here today.'

He was magnanimous. 'You thought you could handle it, and it was good to try. It was brave.'

'What shall we do?' I pulled away from him. 'They'll be out soon, and there will be the wake, and this wretched legacy I don't even want.'

I expected him to say, let's leg it; jump on a train, head straight back to Heathrow. But instead, he said, 'Look. We're here now. We might as well finish this thing off.'

I was impressed – and surprised – by his balls of steel. I knew he'd rather be literally anywhere else right now, because he'd spent most of the last week telling me so. He gripped my hand tight. 'We're nearly through it. Couple more hours, and we'll be on the next flight out.'

'Can't wait.' The quiet cottage and our orderly life in France felt unutterably precious right now.

The church doors banged open again, and people started streaming out. We stood to the side, and bore the curious glances from people we didn't know. Finally, the little white-haired old lady – definitely Jeanie – came out, clinging to her daughter's arm. Andrea was slim and smart in a well-fitting dark blue suit and matching heels, higher than people usually wore in real life. Though her expression was lofty, even regal, I could just about see the pinched, anxious face of the young Andrea superimposed over her grown-up face.

They looked at me, and I saw Jeanie hesitate. It took every ounce of courage I possessed for me to step forward.

'Jeanie, I'm Pearl. I'm so sorry for your loss.'

'I know who you are,' Jeanie said. In my heightened state I couldn't tell if her tone was hostile or friendly. 'I suppose you are coming to the wake?' She didn't add, 'to pick over the carcass of your unearned legacy', but I could hear it echoing in the whistling scaffolding of our conversation.

Shakily, my bravado with the taxi driver a distant memory, I nodded, my eyes on the ground. 'Yes, if it's all right...'

Eleanor materialised at my side. I smelled her scent before I felt her gentle hand on my shoulder. I wondered if it was the Issey Miyake perfume I had sent for her last birthday. How strange, yet how right, to have her next to me again.

'The White Hart, isn't it, Jeanie?' she said. 'We'll give Pearl a lift.'

'Don't feel any obligation,' Jeanie said. 'There's no need.'

It wasn't clear if she meant there was no need to come, or no need to give me a lift. Someone came over and started telling her how sorry they were, and Jeanie turned her back on us. I raised an eyebrow at Eleanor – even under these strange circumstances, Jeanie was being unexpectedly rude – and she whispered, 'Tell you later.'

Denny and I walked with her and Greg along the road to their car. 'Where are the children?' I said, the words meaty in my mouth. I couldn't bear wondering any longer when they were going to pop up. I'd managed so successfully to avoid seeing them in the church, it was as if I'd magicked them invisible.

'At school,' Eleanor said. 'No need for them to come to the funeral of some useless piece of shit grandfather they never knew.'

'Gracie's at *school*?' The words were out before I'd even processed them.

'Yes, sweetie.' Eleanor put her hand on my arm. 'She's in Reception.'

I stopped walking. How many kicks in the stomach would I endure today?

Greg turned round, having missed all this. 'What's the matter?'

'Go ahead, you two,' Eleanor said.

Denny hesitated, hovering.

'Go on,' she said, more forcefully, flapping her hand. She'd never been particularly tolerant of Denny's fussing around me.

'Go on,' I said to him, more gently. 'I'm OK.'

He gave me a look but turned and walked on ahead with Greg.

Eleanor waited until they were out of earshot, then said, 'What do you want to know?'

'Nothing. I'm OK. I hadn't registered that Gracie was five already, but of course she is. In February. I ought to have sent a present, I'm sorry.'

Eleanor waited for me to process it, her face full of kindness. What did I think? That Gracie would stay a baby? On an intellectual level I knew she would be growing up, but emotionally I'd not considered that she was old enough to be at school. To have a little uniform. A tiny backpack.

'You're pale as a sheet,' she said. 'I thought you were going to throw up in the church. Panic attack?' Eleanor knew me well.

'A little one. I don't know why I'm surprised. I thought I was prepared – we've had six weird days hanging out in a hotel getting used to the idea – but I'm still a bit overwhelmed to be here.'

'You always were the mistress of the understatement, my sweet,' Eleanor said. 'I thought so many times about coming to Hastings to see you, these last few days. You felt tantalisingly close. No sea between us! But you didn't reply to my messages, so I wasn't sure I'd be welcome.'

I side-stepped this. 'It was a weird little minibreak. We went for lots of walks. Greg did well to get the funeral organised so quickly.'

'That was for your benefit, love. He was very keen to make sure you were here; that you didn't get fed up waiting and run back off to France.'

'We nearly did, several times.'

She held open her arms, and I walked into them, let her fold herself around me. Her scent, her warmth, were so familiar, so missed.

'I know it's hard as hell, Pearl, but I'm so glad you're here. I've thought about you so much...'

'Eleanor! Pill!' We broke apart, and turned to see Benjy running unfitly towards us.

'Oh joy,' Eleanor said. I'm sure she was as tempted as I was to start walking fast in the opposite direction, but of course, we waited politely.

He lurched up, panting. 'Did you see that witch Jeanie?'

'She's a little old lady, Ben,' Eleanor said.

'Yeah, right. An old lady who looked at me like I'd murdered someone because I had the misfortune to be sitting next to this noisy dingbat.' He meant me. 'Didn't you see her turn round? I swear to god her head swivelled *all the way round* like an owl, and sent laser rays at Pill. Alas for her, Pill was a rapidly moving target, so I copped the worst of the damage and Barbara took the rest.'

'Where is Barbara, anyway?' Eleanor said, trying, I knew, to take the heat off me.

'Dropping Gina at the train station. We didn't think Gee-Gee should have to come to the wake – it's bad enough she's missed work for this shit. Barb'll come on after for the limp sandwiches and the thrillingly erect inheritance. Where's your massive limousine, Eleanor?'

'Just up here,' Eleanor said with no trace of emotion, a useful trait when dealing with Ben. 'Couldn't get parked any nearer.'

I wondered why Benjy didn't drive himself, then recalled that he lost his driving licence a couple of years ago. I was sorely tempted to pretend I'd forgotten, and ask him about his car to get back at him for calling me 'Pill,' my hated childhood nickname. But then I told myself firmly that I was a woman of fifty-two, not a child of nine.

As Greg steered their people-carrier into the street, Eleanor said to me, 'You know I said I'd tell you something later, when Jeanie was weird about you coming to the wake?'

'Oh, yes. What was that about?'

She twisted round in the front seat to look at me. 'She's unbelievable. Do you know, she got Andrea, pardon me, *An-dray-ah*, to phone Greg up last night—'

'Eleanor,' Greg said, his voice a warning.

'Jesus, Mary and Joseph!' Eleanor slapped her hand down onto the dashboard. 'There's enough BS floating around about who can and can't know things without us adding to it, Greg. Pearl's stayed for days to come to this, because you nagged her. The least we can do is—'

'All right, all right.' Greg held up a hand in submission. I could feel Denny, next to me, trying to disappear into the upholstery.

'I should think so,' Eleanor said. 'So *An-dray-ah* phones up, gives Greg an ear-bashing about your famous legacy. She says the lawyer won't tell Jeanie what it is until you've been told. Apparently it was in a separate note to the will, and Jeanie is losing her goddamn mind that you're going to get a secret fortune or their house or something.'

'Surely Jeanie's still living there?' I said. 'Anyway, if she knows what's in the will, why is she worried?'

'Maybe she's thinking that this legacy overrides the will?' Eleanor said, eyes alight with the drama of it all.

'Why would Dad leave me their house?' I said. 'It doesn't make sense.'

'None of this makes sense,' Benjy said. 'Why do *you* get the moolah? Dad didn't like you any more than me.'

'We'll find out soon enough,' Greg said, 'because Jeanie has insisted that the lawyer go through the details at the wake.'

'Oh, *terrific*,' I said.

'You know what?' Eleanor turned a mischievous look onto Greg. 'Let's drive past it.'

'What?'

'Their house, of course!'

'Eleanor...'

'Come on Greg, we're near their street, aren't we?'

'How do you know where they live?' Benjy asked. 'You've never been here, have you?'

'No,' Greg said, but there was something about how quickly he said it that made Ben and I flash a rare look of sibling complicity at each other.

Eleanor said, more firmly, 'We had a good old nosey at it on Google Earth. Rather nice, Pearl. A good size. I don't suppose you'd want to live in it but it would fetch a good price. Sell it back to Jeanie; that would be funny.'

I wasn't finding any of this particularly funny. I was still holding my breath about being in the car and in close proximity to my *brethren*, and most significantly to Eleanor, who was once my closest friend. It was all I could do to keep breathing normally.

Under Ellie's dogged insistence, Greg followed the satnav to Dad's street. I didn't tell them, of course, that I'd been here once before, in 1990. No-one knew about that.

The name of the house and street were etched on my memory. Hope House, Pendlebury Avenue. On all our memories, really, because we had all written, variously over the years, pathetic cards and letters to Dad that generally went unanswered. Benjy always said the name was short for, 'Hope This One's Better Than My Last Family'.

Greg pulled up opposite an unremarkable, if large, semi-detached house. I recognised it well enough to feel a faint echo of the fear I'd felt that day, sitting on the pavement, unable to move forward or back.

'Weird, isn't it?' Benjy said. 'Dad would have known this house as well as the back of his hand.'

Indeed, this house would have been even more familiar to Dad than the house we children grew up in. This was his home for more than thirty years, almost his entire married life with Jeanie. How bizarre to think that he was here, alive, little more than a week ago. For a fleeting moment, I railed at my own stupidity in not coming here until it was too late, until he was too dead, then remembered that it wasn't my choice.

'Dear Dad,' my letters would invariably start, 'I'm happy to visit you, any time that suits you.' Nine times out of ten he didn't reply but then, one day, there was a letter, which I opened so eagerly when I saw his handwriting that I ripped it.

Dear Pearl, please don't come, it's not convenient. Francis.

How fired up I was at that moment, how bold. It all faded, of course, right here, on the ground. I wondered if the kind boy who rescued me still remembered our encounter.

'Let's go, for god's sake,' I said, and perhaps there was something of that last visit in my tone because Greg instantly started up the engine and we screeched away. Denny put his hand on my arm. I gave him a feeble smile and whispered, 'I love you.' He whispered it back to me, and I took a full, proper breath for the first time this awful day.

15TH DECEMBER 1981

How could I have spoiled things so soon? I'm an idiot. J is a darling, my true love. It was one of the happiest days of my life when we were at last able to be together, and I can't wait until she is my wife. I feel terrible to have upset her so. I bought flowers but she put them aside. She said, you'll have to tell your children that plans have changed. We must discuss things as a couple, you can't make big decisions without speaking to me. She is right, of course; it was extremely thoughtless to invite them without talking to her first.

To not upset her further I rang G's Halls from a phone box. He twisted the knife in my heart. Said: Dad, great news I can stay longer at yours, my term doesn't start till 10th January. Told him straight that I was sorry, change of plan, we have to postpone the Christmas visit. I said it was my fault; I didn't discuss it with J before I invited you kids, we agree it's a bit soon for a long visit. OK, G said, a short visit then, couple of days. I said, even a short visit would be disruptive for A... This was the wrong thing to say of course, I knew it as soon as the words were out of my mouth. G said, disruptive for A? Oh, we can't have that, can we? I said I was sorry, I didn't seem to be able to please everyone. He said, glad it isn't me who has to tell PP and B it's all off.

We stayed on the phone, not speaking. Finally I said, we have to remember this is very early days for us all; we are still getting used to the many changes. I can see you in the new year. He said, it's fine for me, I'm away from home but PP has been doing everything for Mum, and counting on being away for a few days. I'll call her now, I said, and he hung up without saying goodbye. I stayed in the phone box a while. It was raining outside so no-one waiting thankfully. Couldn't face upsetting another person in the same day. How to explain it? PP and B are still children, not as young as A of course but...

J pleased I'd cancelled, kissed me, said it was the right thing, we're still finding our way. She said strong couples discuss every-thing, which is right of course. I mustn't be sad not to see the chil-dren at Christmas, I will keep them in my prayers, and find a good moment to discuss them visiting in the new year.

FIVE
PEARL

The White Hart was a neglected-looking hotel, the sort of place you wouldn't go unless there was no other option. The reception-ist directed us, with much 'sorry for your loss' head-tilting, to the Oak Room, where people were milling around a buffet table holding plates and cups. I thought fondly of a hot drink, wondered if they might rustle up a mint teabag, but we were barely through the door before Andrea came over to us, looking tense.

'Finally! Mum wants to have a receiving line.'

'Oh goody,' Benjy muttered in my ear.

We followed Andrea to the back of the room where Jeanie was waiting, looking, if that was possible, even less friendly than before.

I stood strategically on Benjy's left, which meant Greg, on his other side, formed a buffer between old and new family. I'd have appreciated the symbolism of this more if I wasn't feeling so strung out.

People drifted towards us, glad to have something more to do than circle unappetising plates of puff pastry.

'Awful business, so sorry,' an elderly man said, taking my

hands in his damp ones. 'I was your father's best man, first time round. Childhood friend.' His milky eyes were full of tears. 'Haven't seen him for many years, you know. He didn't want to.'

'I'm sorry,' I said, unsure what I was apologising for. Andrea, who'd been at the far end of the line with Jeanie, suddenly materialised at my side.

'Sorry for your loss,' she gabbled at me.

I wanted to say, 'well, it was hardly my loss, was it? I lost him years ago.' Instead, I mumbled, 'You too.' It was way more of a loss to her than me; Dad was actually *in* her life. She so resembled, physically, my memory of her mother at a similar age that I had to keep reminding myself that she was the daughter. Like Jeanie back then, she was skinny, uptight, the same Cruella de Vil grey streak in her dark hair.

Out of the side of her mouth, she said, 'Bit awks.'

'Sorry, a bit what?'

'Awks. Awkward. This legacy thing.' She gave a thin smile. 'Like a Victorian novel.'

She smiled at an elderly woman who took her hand and said how sorry she was. 'Thanks, Aunty Jo.' When the woman moved on, Andrea's smile disappeared, and she said in a low voice, 'Thing is, Mum's devastated.'

I wanted to say, 'well, sure, her husband's just died.' But there wasn't much mileage in playing dumb. And anyway, grown-up Andrea terrified me at least as much as I had terrified child Andrea.

I was saved from saying anything by Jeanie's voice whistling down the line: 'Andrea!'

'Talk later,' Andrea said, and hurried back to her mother.

Denny, who Eleanor had corralled into handing round cups of tea, escaped from his duties to stand next to me.

'Are you OK?' he said. 'What did Andrea say? Do I need to have a word with her?'

'No! Don't be daft. I'm sure it's possible to have a family

gathering without a fight.' He winced, and, too late, I realised he must think I was referring to Gracie's christening. 'Oh, I didn't mean—'

'Ssssh!' Greg said, as he kissed a random aunt. 'Do you need to be here, Denny?'

'I'm supporting Pearl,' Denny said.

Various other relatives of Jeanie's, and church friends of Dad's, filed past us. Some of them stopped to explain who they were ('Like we care,' Benjy muttered), and they looked at us curiously, this strange outsider family who were not any part of the life of the man they knew.

Barbara came along the line, unlit cigarette in hand. 'Darling, you really are quite the trooper for coming, did I say?'

'You did, Barb.' I realised I must be starting to relax a little, because her louche, out-of-time style made me smile. Feeling that same mischievous flicker from the taxi, I said, 'You'd look amazing with a long cigarette holder, like a forties film star.'

'Is that a compliment, darling, or a dig at my great age?'

'A compliment, of course.'

She raised her eyebrows at me, then moved on to Benjy, with much kissing and gushing on both their parts, though they'd been sitting together in the church half an hour earlier. Denny and I grinned at each other; I was glad he didn't let my careless comment about fights get in the way of a classic Barb moment.

'Pearl.' A man in his late sixties, with bright white hair, took my hand. 'Your father spoke so fondly of you.' I glanced across at Greg, assuming he'd introduce us, but he looked as blank as me.

'He did?' Poor fellow, he must have got confused. If there was one thing I was sure about, it was that my dad didn't speak of me fondly, or at all.

'I'm Hugh Sargeant, the churchwarden here,' the man said.

'Your father used our small office for his writing, and he and I got to know each other rather well.'

'I didn't know he wrote,' I said. 'Do you mean for the parish magazine?' Dad contributed endless articles to the church magazine back in Chelmsford; he was even the editor at one point.

'Oh yes,' Hugh said, eyes twinkling. 'Among other things. He was here several times a week.' He released my hand, and added, 'I'm really going to miss him. My sympathies to you and your brothers, and your step-sister.'

He moved on, leaving me reeling at the thought of Andrea being my step-sister. Well, I suppose she was, technically, but really!

When everyone had been thanked for coming, we dispersed to the buffet, where we stood awkwardly, holding small plates of sad party food. Denny ate a stuffed cherry tomato and looked like he'd never regretted anything more.

Greg came over, accompanied by a tall man in a very appropriate funeral suit.

'Pearl, this is Mr Claymore, Dad's lawyer.'

'Sorry for your loss,' he said, and I wanted to reply, 'I know!' but managed to thank him like a normal person. The room seemed to have gone a little quieter, and glancing round, I saw that pretty much everyone was looking at me and the lawyer with undisguised interest.

'How come everyone knows about this legacy?' I asked Greg.

'Benjy has a hell of a mouth on him,' Greg said, then had the grace to look slightly sheepish. 'I guess I did mention it to a couple of people on our side. I'm pretty sure Jeanie has told people, too.'

Now Jeanie herself came over, leaning heavily on Andrea's arm. She was frailer and more reticent than ever, and let

Andrea do the talking. 'Mr Claymore, thank you for coming. The sooner we sort out this business, the better.'

'Absolutely!' He told Jeanie that he was sorry for her loss. She nodded, only slightly more gracious than me on hearing this for the hundredth time.

'I've booked a room for us to talk through Mr Nichol's wishes,' Mr Claymore said, 'but the only person actually required to attend the reading of the legacy is its beneficiary, who in this case is Mrs Pearl Flowers. We can then bring the rest of the family in for the will reading proper, if you wish.'

'Required?' Andrea said, eyebrows up in her hairline. 'Legally, maybe, but morally, surely my mother, as the widow, should be privy to the discussion.'

'It's not really a discussion, as such,' Mr Claymore said. I admired the way he wasn't intimidated by Andrea, despite her eyes sending spiky daggers into his heart. 'The will itself is straightforward, with the bulk of his estate left to Jeanie. The legacy for Mrs Flowers is something more personal.'

'Thank god,' Jeanie breathed. It looked like Eleanor was right: Jeanie had clearly been afraid that the legacy would render invalid what she knew to be in the will. I too felt like thanking god – it would have been beyond horrendous to be given something massive. I felt my shoulders come down a notch.

'Is there any reason my mother and I can't be there to hear what Pearl's been given?' Andrea said.

'It's fine if Mrs Flowers agrees,' Mr Claymore said, and three pairs of eyes swivelled over to me.

How I'd have loved to say, 'I jolly well don't agree.' I did sometimes wonder how different my life would have been, had I been the sort of person who could say things like this, and not give a damn. But then I thought about the taxi driver I'd lied to, and felt a pang of guilt.

'Of course,' I said.

Mr Claymore led me, my brothers, Jeanie and Andrea to a private room, and we took seats round a large table. Benjy sat next to me and whispered, 'Listen, Patty Cake. You'll share this big prize, won't you? You'll think of your favourite baby brother who is a bit broke, won't you?'

'I'm pretty sure this is going to turn out to be bugger all, Ben.'

'Maybe. Hey, listen, wanted to tell you this weird idea about Dad. I've thought it for a while, since Gina—'

'As we're all here, I'll start with the will proper,' Mr Claymore said, and we turned our attention to him. 'I think Jeanie knows most of its contents already, from discussions with the late Mr Nichols.'

'I hope I do,' Jeanie said, faintly. I wondered if she was fazed by the word 'late' being used in relation to Dad. I certainly was. What with will readings, legacies, 'late', and Mr Claymore's undertaker-style suit, it was all so wretchedly Dickensian. Why was death like this, stuck in the nineteenth century? Even Mum's funeral – a humanist ceremony, at her request – was more from the past than the present.

'What do you mean, most of it?' Andrea said, on high alert.

'Well actually, there is a recently added coda,' Mr Claymore said, 'from earlier this year. I don't know if Mr Nichols had the chance to discuss it with you?'

'What does it say?' Jeanie's startled face spoke volumes.

'I'll read it shortly,' he said, 'but the substance of it is to provide bequests to his children and friends.'

Benjy raised his eyebrows at me excitedly. The word 'bequest' was even more thrilling to him than 'legacy'.

Mr Claymore took some papers out of his briefcase, gave a self-consciously theatrical cough, and started to read. 'Francis Nichols leaves his home and effects to Jeanie Nichols, less the money which is to be distributed as per the codicils to this will.'

Jeanie nodded, eyes downcast, and Andrea reached across

and took her hand. They must be so relieved that he didn't muck about with the house.

'He leaves to Andrea his much-loved dog, and hopes that she will look after him in her own house.'

Andrea's head jerked up. 'But Snoops lives with Mum?'

'Francis' wishes are clear that he should go to you,' Mr Claymore said.

'I expect he thought the walks might get too much for you, Mum,' Andrea said.

Jeanie took her hand away from Andrea and smoothed her hair. 'It's fine.'

'Can't imagine Dad being so into a dog, can you?' Benjy whispered, and I shook my head. Just add it to the million other things we didn't know about him.

Mr Claymore continued, 'Next, to each of his children, Greg, Pearl, Benjy, and Andrea, he leaves five thousand pounds, with his blessing.'

Benjy muttered something unintelligible, and slumped back into his seat. Greg looked resigned, and Andrea looked, well, I didn't know what her expression was. I didn't know what mine was either, because while it was five thousand more than I was expecting, I felt sorry for Benjy, who'd clearly hoped for a huge windfall.

'There are also two bequests of £2,500 each to two friends,' Mr Claymore said. 'And now we come to—'

'Who are the friends?' Jeanie said. Her cheeks were very red.

I got the sense that Mr Claymore was reluctant to answer, but his professional smoothness meant there was only the smallest hesitation before he said, 'Hugh Sargeant and Caroline Haskett.'

Hugh was the churchwarden I'd just met, of 'your father spoke so fondly of you' fame.

'We know Hugh,' Andrea said. 'But who's this Caroline?'

'I'm not able to provide that information, I'm afraid,' Mr Claymore said, leaving it nicely ambiguous as to whether he did or didn't know.

'Secret mistress?' Benjy whispered to me.

'And now we come to the item that Mr Nichols wished to be entrusted to his oldest daughter, Pearl Flowers.'

I'd never thought of myself as the oldest daughter, because I'd never felt any connection to Andrea, never thought of her as another daughter. But in my teens I spent an unhealthy amount of time wondering what her life was like. Andrea was the golden child who stole our dad; the one who got the best of him after he cut off ties with us. It was easy to imagine the marvellous times she had with him, sitting together in a fancy restaurant, both laughing, clinking glasses, her hair piled high in a sophisticated updo.

Now, sitting in the same room as Andrea, watching the tension roll across her face, I wondered how things really had been for her.

Mr Claymore lifted a heavy-looking hessian bag from the floor at his feet, and put it on the table. Benjy sat up straight and squeezed my knee. 'Here we go!'

'Mr Nichols leaves to Pearl his journals, which he kept for almost forty years.' Mr Claymore pulled the sides of the bag down slightly, revealing a tall pile of books, and took out the top one. It was an ordinary notebook with a hard-backed yellow cover.

Addressing me, he said, 'They cover the period from 1981 to 2018. I believe the final entry was made only a few weeks before his death.'

A chill ran down my spine. My dad's life, laid out, for the entire period that I didn't know him.

There was a short silence, then everyone except me started speaking.

Benjy cried, 'Is that *it*? This is what the fuss has been about? Some crappy *notebooks*? This is a joke, right?'

Greg put his hand on Benjy's arm in an attempt to calm him, and said, 'If Pearl doesn't want the responsibility, I'm happy to take them.'

Jeanie turned to Andrea and said, 'Did you know about this?'

Andrea replied, 'No, didn't *you* know?'

Benjy shook Greg's hand off and sat back in his chair. Under his breath, he muttered, 'Wow, well done, Dad, one last fucking annoying thing from you to cap off a shitshow of a life.'

Jeanie reached towards the diary in Mr Claymore's hand. 'I need to see them.'

'I'm sorry, Mrs Nichols,' he said. I think it was the first time he'd called her that, rather than Jeanie. 'Mr Nichols was very clear that they are for Pearl alone.'

'That's outrageous!' Jeanie was considerably more animated than the grieving widow who'd walked slowly into this room on her daughter's arm. 'This can't be legal. How did you even get hold of them? I'm his wife; these should have been left in our home. They are my property.'

'You didn't even know they existed till five minutes ago,' Benjy said.

Greg and I flapped our hands at Benjy – shut up! – and Jeanie sent him a look of pure hatred, but he just smirked right back at her. I'd forgotten how quickly he bounced from mood to mood; now he saw the notebooks' power to create discontent, he'd got over his disappointing share of Dad's cash. Andrea frowned at him, shaking her head slightly.

'What, And-ree-ah?' Benjy said, spreading his arms wide, revelling in mispronouncing her name. 'Your mummy's just upset cos it turns out Daddy didn't share everything with her after all.'

'What a terrible thing to say to someone who's bereaved,' Andrea said.

Jeanie stood up. 'You know we can't expect any better from someone like him, Andrea.'

'Oh yeah? Who is someone like me?'

'A waster, a loser, a moron.' Cold as ice, Jeanie enunciated every word. You had to hand it to her, she was cool under pressure. '*That's* someone like you.' She was now recognisable as the spiky-sharp woman I'd met forty years ago, who'd called me a *rude and scruffy child*.

'Benjamin, for goodness' sake,' Greg said. 'Do you have to get everyone riled up? As if things weren't fraught enough. Jeanie, please don't rise to it, and please don't insult him. It's not necessary.'

'Big brother's wading in now, Jeanie,' Benjy said. 'Better watch it or we will both be on the naughty step.'

Mr Claymore slapped his hand down on the table, making us all jump.

'People, please. I'm aware that emotions are running high. But there is no need for personal attacks. Mrs Nichols, please take a seat. I understand this is a shock, but the diaries are not legally your property. They weren't kept in the house. Francis stored the completed notebooks in an office in the church—'

'Oh!' Andrea cried, then clapped her hand over her mouth.

As if she hadn't interrupted, he continued, '...with instructions that they be handed over to my care, until such time as Pearl is able to take them.'

Jeanie sat down heavily, and Andrea put her arm round her. I surprised myself by feeling sorry for both of them.

'Well, look.' Greg straightened his shoulders, and Benjy nudged me again; we both knew well his older-brother-in-charge stance. 'What if Pearl is unwilling to take them?'

'Then my instructions are to destroy them,' Mr Claymore said.

I couldn't help feeling a frisson at the drama of it all.

'But Pearl could take them, then hand the responsibility to someone else,' Greg said. 'I'd be happy to, for sure.'

It was annoying that he kept saying this without asking me.

'Would they go on a bonfire,' Benjy said, 'or what?'

'May I look at a notebook?' I said. Mr Claymore handed over the one he'd taken out.

'Or through a shredder?' Benjy mused. 'That would take ages.'

'Do you know why he left them to Pearl?' Greg asked, which was, of course, the obvious question. Why me?

'I think if Pearl opens it, we will discover at least one part of the answer.' Mr Claymore smiled. He seemed to be actively enjoying this. Maybe it made a change from the usual boring will readings where everyone got what they expected.

My hands shook slightly as I opened the notebook to the first page. It was covered in writing, though not recognisably Dad's, because it was...

'What the hell?' Benjy said, leaning across to look. 'It's just a load of scribble.'

'It's shorthand,' I said, light dawning. It was forty years since I last used shorthand, but it was seared into my brain such that I could immediately read a line in the first paragraph. It said, *This isn't in the least what I wanted.*

'Dad knew shorthand?' Andrea said, and in those three words I heard the heavy weight of loss, of not knowing someone as well as you thought. Of secrets.

'Yes, when he was in his teens he didn't do very well at school,' I said, 'because of missing a lot through illness.' It sounded like something from the Victorian era, but Dad had complications following measles and fell behind with his lessons. 'His teachers recommended he skip the final year and go to secretarial college.'

Jeanie held out her hand for the notebook but I pretended not to notice.

'That would have been unusual for a man, back then?' Mr Claymore said, looking interested.

'I think so,' I said, realising that I didn't know much of this story. As a child I simply accepted it at face value. Had we had a relationship as adults, I would have asked him more about it. 'He went on to be a clerk, and that led to various promotions which is how he paid his way through college and got his teaching degree.' Dad's vision of himself was as an autodidact. Someone who'd been thwarted at school but had reinvented himself and finished his career as a well-respected headteacher.

Jeanie was still holding out her hand, and I was still pretending that I hadn't seen it.

'This, I understand, is one reason why the journals have been left to Mrs Flowers,' Mr Claymore said. 'Because she is able to decipher them.'

Unexpectedly, my eyes filled with tears. Dad loved and encouraged my early interest in words. He conversed in French with me, discussed the fundamental principles of Esperanto, showed me how to interpret cryptic crosswords and, when I was pretty young, no more than seven, he taught me shorthand. Not the old-fashioned Pitman kind he'd learned as a young clerk, which required fountain pens to make the all-important thick and thin line distinctions, but a more modern type called Teeline. He'd picked this up this during the early 1970s at journalism evening classes. I had a vague idea that he'd planned to retrain as a journalist. But other than writing articles for the parish magazine, I don't think this ever came to fruition. At some point in the late 1970s he became a headteacher, which I suppose made teaching seem interesting again.

For a while, he and I would communicate in Teeline's secret code. I remembered the thrill of it, of reading something neither of my brothers could understand. As late as my fifteenth birth-

day, the year he gave me the field glasses – a few weeks before
he left us – Dad put a shorthand message in my card. I didn't
remember what it said, now, but I remembered reading it. The
card that came for my sixteenth birthday, the first to come
through the post rather than waiting for me on the kitchen table,
didn't contain any secret messages.

'What does it say?' Jeanie said, craning over to try to look at
the pages.

'I'm not sure,' I lied. 'I'd have to refresh my memory about
how to read it; it's been such a long time.'

'This is ridiculous!' she snapped. 'She can't even read them.
There's no reason for Pearl to have these. I can easily get
someone to translate them.'

Pointing at the page, Benjy said, 'Doesn't this line say, "wow
my second wife is such a cow"?' And with that, the gloves were
finally off.

'Mr Claymore, do you see what we are up against?' Jeanie's
face was red with fury. 'I demand you intervene. These notebooks may contain material that my husband's former children
will exploit.'

'*Former* children?' Benjy said, laughing.

I glanced down at the page again, and read: *It would be
necessary to keep this...* Then there were several symbols I
couldn't read, followed by: *I have hidden so much.* What the
heck was in these diaries?

Andrea, glaring at Benjy, said, 'Mr Claymore, my mother is
understandably worried. Surely it's inappropriate for my
father's private journals to be in anyone's hands but hers?'

'I'm sorry,' Mr Claymore said, not sounding it. 'Francis'
instructions were very clear. They are to be handed to—'

'Give me that.' Jeanie snatched the notebook from the table
in front of me. I automatically reached out and grabbed an edge
of it, and there was a brief moment in which we were tugging at
it, like toddlers fighting over a toy. Then I thought, what am I

doing? Dad was gone, for the second time in my life, and this time he'd dumped a poisoned chalice all over me as an encore. I'd wasted years trying to work out what was going on in his head. What would it mean to go back to that now? Would there really be the answers I burned to know, or would it be a lot more uncertainty and pain? I let go of the notebook, and Jeanie, rather surprised, took possession of it.

'Mrs Nichols, this is unacceptable!' Mr Claymore said, standing up. All at once, he'd gone from being a beige fellow on the edge of our family business to looking as stern as a high court judge.

'You can't just take it, Jeanie,' Greg said, trying, as always, to be the voice of reason in the face of utter unreasonableness.

Staring Mr Claymore in the eye, Jeanie triumphantly, and with surprising strength, ripped the notebook in two, down the middle page. Unmoored from the flimsy staples, pages from the two halves fluttered onto the table.

'Oh, well *done*, Jeanie!' Benjy said, sitting back and grinning from ear to ear. 'Really handling this like a mature grown-up.'

In two strides Mr Claymore was next to Jeanie. He took the dismembered notebook out of her hand and swept up the pages. 'Disgraceful,' he said, angry spittle on his lips.

It looked like Jeanie would be needing to find a new family solicitor. She sank into her seat, and Benjy leaned towards her with a mock-serious expression on his face.

'Go on, Jeanie. You can tell us, we're all family here. What are the disgusting dark secrets that Dad's revealed in these books?'

'*Family?*' Jeanie said. 'You don't know the meaning of the word, you awful little man. Come on, Andrea. We don't need to sit here and be insulted.'

'That's right,' Benjy said. 'We can insult you just as well if you're standing.'

Andrea hurried round to her mother and helped her up. I

thought she looked embarrassed, though I didn't know her well enough to be sure. Jeanie was back to looking old and frail, the woman who ripped the diary someone else entirely.

They went out, and Greg and I stared at each other.

'I'm so glad I stayed for this,' I said to him, deadpan.

But his thoughts were elsewhere. 'I'd forgotten about you and Dad doing shorthand and stuff like that,' he said, his eyes misty. 'Do you remember you used to do crosswords together all the time, too? The hard ones in the *Guardian*?'

'I still do them now,' I said, and he and I shared a tiny moment, the older siblings silently acknowledging that there was a time, way back, when our dad was just our dad, fun and interesting, and full of love. Not a source of hurt feelings and broken hearts. Benjy was too young when Dad left to remember much about him, and anyway, he wasn't the sentimental type.

'You two are cute enough to kiss, you make me puke,' Benjy said, and ruffled my hair vigorously.

Unlike Andrea and Jeanie, Greg and I were so used to his stream of jibes that we barely registered them. When Denny and I first got together he was constantly astonished by Benjy's behaviour, until I explained that he had never really grown up from his role as infuriating little brother. I'd like to think he behaved better with his wives but his divorce track record would suggest not.

But now Greg, who prided himself on never reacting to Benjy's wind-ups, was properly annoyed. He yanked Benjy's wrist down from my hair. 'As if this day wasn't hard enough already. You're being a complete prick, Ben.'

'Your yogalates has really been paying off, tough guy,' Benjy sneered, trying to pull his wrist away, but Greg was strong, and it was held fast. Benjy jabbed at him with the other hand, and Greg grabbed that wrist too.

Mr Claymore coughed, to remind us that we had an audience to our embarrassing sibling squabble.

'Not sure this is helping hugely, Greg,' I said.

'Total overreaction,' Benjy said. 'I was only yanking your chain.'

'I can hold these spindly little arms all day if necessary,' Greg said.

I had to admit, I kind of liked him in this mode.

'I could get out if I wanted to, old man,' Benjy said, changing tack, 'but I don't want to.'

Mr Claymore had been busily putting the pages back into place in the torn notebook, and now he pushed it across the table to me. I opened it carefully to the first page, and read: *For all that I wasn't able to, I really hope that she and you...* but I couldn't read any more. Who was the 'she' here? Jeanie? Andrea? Who was 'you'?

'Will you pack it in now?' Greg said, in the voice of authority from Benjy's childhood. It still worked.

'Fine, OK, sorry,' Benjy said, and Greg released him. Benjy made a show of rubbing his wrists, and mouthed something extremely rude at him that luckily, I don't think he saw.

'So what do you know about this?' Benjy addressed Mr Claymore, trying to show that Greg hadn't got the better of him. 'Has Dad left the diaries to Pearl to piss Jeanie off? Because that's my reading.'

'I'm afraid I don't know.' Mr Claymore turned to me, clearly wanting shot of us. 'Do you wish to take possession of the notebooks now, or shall I have them sent to your home?'

'I'll take them,' I said.

He handed me the bag, which I heaved onto my shoulder. It was heavy, a literal burden. Cheers, Dad!

'I will have the damaged notebook repaired and sent to you by special delivery,' Mr Claymore said, holding out his hand for it. I passed it over, and he put it in his briefcase. It didn't feel possible for me to tell him not to bother, that I could sort it with some Sellotape.

Outside the room, normal life was going on, in so far as a wake was normal life. Denny was talking to Barb, so at least he was being entertained. He looked up when he saw me, anxiety all over his face, and mouthed, 'You OK?'

I started to head towards him, but alas, Andrea intercepted me, sidling into my path like a wraith. 'May I have a quiet word?'

Would this day ever end? 'Think we've all said plenty, to be honest.' I folded my arms, keeping a tight hold on the handle of the bag in case she tried to snatch it and make off in a getaway car.

'*Please*, Pearl.' She looked so strung out, I nodded wearily, and followed her to a table in a corner. When we sat down, I noticed that pretty much everyone in the room was rubbernecking, even if they couldn't possibly know yet about the recent drama. Eleanor, Greg, Benjy and Denny were all looking over at us with identical concerned expressions. It made me want to smile.

'We are objects of great fascination,' I said, hoping to warm things up a little.

'I have no idea what you mean,' Andrea said.

It was incredible to think that if Dad had wanted to merge his new family with his old one, she and I might have been close. I'd have loved a sister, of course, being the only girl between two brothers. But her brittleness would have probably been a barrier, anyway.

'Dad wasn't in his right mind, you know, near the end,' she said, getting straight to it. 'We think he had dementia. So we could challenge the bequest.' She coughed. Maybe she was feeling a bit 'awks'. 'You know. Legally.'

I kept my face calm. 'Yes, of course you could.'

'Oh.' She looked surprised.

'Andrea, I haven't seen Dad for thirty-five years.' I stared at my lap so as not to have to look at that cruel streak of grey in her hair. 'It's quite something, I don't mind telling you, to discover that he had been thinking about me in his last few months. I didn't realise he ever thought about me at all.'

'I get that,' she said. 'I just want to protect my mum.'

'What are you protecting her from?' I said, my voice low. 'What went on with our parents?'

'They were very happy, to the end,' she said, 'but their marriage was a private matter.' She grabbed my hand. Hers was dry and bony. 'I'm serious. Imagine how Mum feels, knowing that other people will be privy to the private details of her life. Dad wasn't thinking straight when he left them to anyone but her.'

Jeanie was sitting near the door, her hands over her face. A couple of relatives had their arms round her, saying presumably soothing things. I thought how awful it would be if someone I barely knew got to have Denny's secret diary – not that he kept one. Or maybe he did? Would I know, if it was secret? Jeanie didn't know about Dad's, after all.

'If you give me the diaries, not only will we drop the legal challenge—'

'You're talking as if you've already started one!' I had to laugh. 'Can you let go of me? I won't run away.'

She released my hand. 'But I also promise to answer in full and truthfully any and all questions you have about Francis.'

'How do you know I have questions about Dad?'

'You must have. You didn't see him for all those years. Don't you want to know what he did during that time, what he was like?'

I was taken aback. 'You'd be willing to do that? Really?'

'Desperate times, Pearl.' She glanced across at her mother. 'You'll get far more of the truth from me than the diaries. They're probably full of excuses, justifications – lies, even.'

I'd lived through so many years of not knowing what the hell was going on with my father, why he'd found it so easy to walk away from us. Now, like buses, two possible routes to the answers rocked up on the same day. Should I plough through Dad's opaque coded version, doubtless full of self-justifications? Or sit down with a living archive who could answer my every question? It ought to have been a no-brainer.

There was only one flaw, which was that for almost forty years, Andrea, the neat and tidy new daughter, had embodied the life I didn't have. She was already leaning towards me, as if planning to unhook the hessian bag from my shoulder. Her entitlement, her certainty that I would agree, that she would, once again, get to have the thing that by rights, belonged to me, shook me out of the mild trance I'd slipped into.

Denny appeared by my side, and as he sat down, I slid my hand into his. So many people had held my hand today, but his was the only one I actually wanted to hold. He squeezed it, comfortingly. He knew what this conversation, this day, was costing me. I could already feel the massive headache I'd get from opening these diaries, looking through the detritus of a person's life, a person who turned my own life upside down. A person who walked out when I was fifteen, who unfathomably withdrew completely from me, my brothers, his own friends and relatives.

And yet. Of all the bizarre, unfathomable things Dad ever did, the most recent was leaving these diaries to me. If I handed them over, I'd save myself a load of hassle. But it would be yet one more mystery that there would never be an answer to.

Denny's grip gave me courage, and I looked Andrea in the eye. 'For many years there was only one thing I wanted to know about Dad; why he cut off his children, and never spoke to us again.' I stood up. 'So, I'm looking forward to reading his take on that.'

'This isn't over.' Andrea looked up at me. 'They don't belong to you.'

'They do, actually,' Denny said, standing up too, 'and it is over.'

We didn't stay long after that. I saw Andrea and Jeanie looking over at me, but they didn't try to approach again. Benjy swaggered off, saying he and Barbara were going out to dinner and to splash some of his bequest around.

'You don't have it yet,' Greg reminded him.

'Boring as always, big bruv,' Benjy said, swaying slightly, holding an empty glass. 'Crap to see you, and you too, Daddy's Best Girl, keeper of the juicy secrets of the Fatherland.' He gave me a kiss on my cheek, the tenderness at odds with his words, and weaved across the room to the exit.

'Charming,' Greg said. 'You can see why he's such a hit with the laydeez.' His serious face on, he said in an undertone, 'Listen, it's insane for you to be lumbered with these. As if you didn't have enough to worry about.'

'Like what?'

'Well, you know...' He did a little facial mime that only a sibling could interpret. Shorthand in gesture form. He meant, *your unmentionable mental health issues.*

'Pearl, let me take them, it would be my pleasure to relieve you of this...'

Eleanor appeared, took a look at my face, and gave him a wifely shove. 'Leave her be, you eejit.' She put her arm round my shoulder. 'You did brilliantly today. I'm sorry it was such a bloodbath. What are your plans? Will you come back with us? I've made up the spare bed. We could get a take-out and have a funeral post-mortem, if that's not too macabre a phrase.'

I didn't need to look at Denny to know he'd be doing his best to keep his face neutral, to let me decide. But he would absolutely hate it, hate going to their house for the first time in all these years. If I was on my own, I might do it. I'd faced so

many demons today, why not one more? But Denny was my
priority now.

'I'm sorry, Ellie. Another time,' I said. 'We're heading back
to Heathrow now.'

'I *adored* seeing you, and it's been so long,' she whispered,
all big eyes. 'But you're still not ready for me, are you?'

I hugged her, not able to answer, trying hard not to cry at
the closeness of her.

Then, thank god, we were out of there, and in a taxi driving
fast away from my old life: just me, Denny and, in a tatty
hessian bag on the seat between us, the undiluted outpourings
of my estranged late father.

SIX

CARRIE

Mum definitely looked better today. There was more colour in her cheeks, and she grasped my hand so tightly I felt sure she must be getting stronger.

'It's so lovely to see you,' she said, as if it had been months, rather than a couple of days. Her eyes flickered over Emmie in the buggy, fast asleep, her cheek resting on her hand.

'Ahhhh!' Mum breathed in the sight of her. 'What a beauty. She looks just like you, when you were a baby.'

'You say that, but I can't see it.'

Mum wriggled into a slightly more upright position. 'So? Tell me everything! I've been on the edge of my seat waiting for you.'

'Edge of the bed, surely. Well, look. There isn't much to tell.'

'Really? But you said you'd gone.'

'I did go. I got as far as the church, then I came home again.'

'Oh, sweetheart.' Mum reached for my hand. 'I'm sorry I encouraged you to go, if it was so difficult. You had a wasted journey.'

'No, it wasn't. I was outside the church – I was late, took

ages to get to Rye – but I was fully intending to sneak quietly into the back. Then she came running out.'

'Oh my goodness!'

'We almost collided.'

'Heavens! Why did she run out?'

'Overwhelmed, I suppose? She looked like she was having trouble breathing.'

'Poor woman. How do you know it was her?'

'Her husband, I assume it was, came out after her and called her name. But to be honest, I already knew it was her, somehow.'

Emmie stirred. I loved the way she woke up: slowly, then all at once.

'Did you get a good look at her?' Mum said. 'What was she like?'

'Short dark brown hair, nice smile but thin and nervy. Her face was sad.'

'Ah no, was it? But then, she was crying, and it was a funeral.'

'I got the impression it was always sad.'

Mum patted my hand. 'Take care you're not just seeing what you want to see, darling.'

'Anyway, after that, I rather lost my nerve.'

'So you didn't talk to her?'

'No. That was enough for one day.'

Emmie was properly awake now. I unclipped her and pulled her onto my lap.

'Look, baby, it's Nana!'

Emmie reached her hands towards Mum, but it was tricky with all the wires. I shifted my chair nearer to the bed so she could reach more easily.

'Well, it's a good start,' Mum said.

'And a good finish.'

'Oh, now, Carrie...'

'No. That's it, now. Done. It was your idea, remember, not mine. That's enough.'

Emmie pressed her arm into Mum's face, and Mum fluttered her eyelashes against it, making Emmie giggle at the tickly sensation. Mum used to do that to me when I was little; a butterfly kiss, she called it.

A nurse came in to check the readings on the machines. She smiled at Emmie and said to her, 'Grandma's looking good, isn't she?'

'She does look better today,' I said. 'More colour.'

'That'll be the rouge,' Mum said. 'Paula, the other nurse, got me to put some on before you arrived, said I was so pale I'd frighten you.'

'Oh Mum! You don't have to do yourself up for me.' Damn, I'd really thought she looked better.

When the nurse went, Mum said, 'I know I'm being pushy, darling...'

'Yes, you flipping are!' I tried to keep it light, but I wished she would let it be.

'I'd feel so much easier in my mind if I knew you'd made contact.'

I sighed. 'All right. If it makes you feel better, we can talk about it again in six months.'

'I won't be here in six months, Carrie.'

'Don't say that! Of course you will...'

'I'm so tired, darling. I'm sorry.' Mum sank back into the pillow, looking far more exhausted than before. I kissed her, and scooped Emmie up. We weren't even out of the door before Mum was asleep.

A nurse stopped me at the desk. 'Dr Shah asked if he could have a word before you go. Do you have a minute?'

'Sure.' That sounded ominous. She took me into a small examination room, with a handy box of toys which Emmie started to 'sort through', which meant taking them out and dropping them on the floor.

The doctor came in after ten minutes or so, looking harassed, apologising for keeping me waiting. He chatted to Emmie and asked her about the toy she was holding. He was good with her, making faces and laughing, but when he looked up at me he turned serious.

'It's not good news, I'm afraid.'

My heart started thumping. 'But you said the last round of chemo might do the trick. I suppose it didn't?'

He took a chair opposite me. 'It didn't work the way we'd hoped. And now...'

'What will you try next?'

'That's the thing, Carrie. We don't think there's anything else that will have a substantial impact on the progression.'

'What are you saying? That's it? There's nothing else?'

'I'm really sorry.'

There was a silence. I looked at Emmie, sitting on the floor, babbling to herself. *Just you and me soon, babe.*

'So...' I said, finally.

'We think she might benefit from hospice care.'

'Hospice?' How had this spiralled so quickly? Less than a year ago Mum was still working, running her own home, looking after my baby so I could have a night off.

'We've identified a couple of places that could take her, and we can make the arrangements to transfer her quickly, but it needs your consent. And hers, of course.'

'She really can't stay here?'

'We can't do anything else for her, and...' He waved his arm, which I knew meant, 'she's taking up a bed that someone else could get proper use out of'.

'I couldn't have her in my house? Look after her myself?'

'Do you have nursing training?'

I laughed, despite myself. 'I'm in computing.'

'I think it would be very difficult, and she would be much more comfortable being somewhere that understands pain management.'

'OK.' I swallowed. 'If it's fine with her, it's fine with me.' Fine, what a stupid thing to say. How could it be fine, planning the end of my mum's life, this indomitable woman who was still, even though I was a proper grown-up, my whole world?

I drove home on autopilot. Emmie babbled happily along to the music I put on for her, which made an incongruously chirpy backdrop to my shell shock. I'd been so optimistic about Mum getting better, but now it seemed that I'd had my head in the sand. Mum's shrewd eyes had, several times, told me as much, but I'd been unwilling to accept the truth.

What was I going to do without her? She was my safe place, my home. What would it mean for that to disappear? I felt all at once not capable of being safely in charge of a car, and I pulled over haphazardly at a bus stop, my hands shaking. It was so unfair. Mum was scarcely in her sixties; she hadn't even had a chance to get to know Emmie beyond the baby years. I made a noise, an involuntary sob, and Emmie, who'd been improvising a bassline to 'Baby Beluga', stopped chattering abruptly. I swivelled in my seat to look at her. She stared back at me, and there was a strange moment when I wouldn't have been surprised if she'd said, 'Don't be upset, Mum.' But instead, she started jabbering along to the music again.

It was enough to snap me out of my wallowing, and I drove us the rest of the way home. I got Emmie out of the car and staggered along the pavement with her, feeling the full weight of her in my arms. I didn't notice that Henry from next door was out in front of his house, supervising Numa on a little scooter, until I almost walked into him.

'God, sorry!'

'No problem, I am loitering, after all.'

I watched Numa scoot along to the end of the street – only about fifty metres – and then scoot back.

'She's doing brilliantly,' I said. I couldn't imagine a time when Emmie would be able to do that. Numa, at nearly three, seemed infinitely older, though I could see how quickly they jumped from one stage to the next.

'I'm making sure she stays on the pavement, but she's definitely getting the hang of it.' He took another look at me. 'You OK? You look awful.'

'Ah, thanks. What every woman wants to hear. I've had bad news about Mum.' My voice broke on the word 'Mum' and I turned it into a cough.

Henry looked at me, his eyes worried. 'God, I'm sorry. Want to talk? I can bring Numa in now.'

'No, another time maybe. I need to get this one settled down.'

'Let me know if you ever need a hand with Emmie, when you have to do things for your mum,' he said.

'I will, thank you.'

'I mean it. Hey, Numa! Get back from the edge.' A combination of bravado on Numa's part, and a van driving too fast, sent Henry speeding off down the street, but she was fine, her front wheel barely coming into contact with the kerb.

I waved, and went into the house, and it wasn't until I'd got Emmie into bed that I allowed myself to cry.

11TH MARCH 1997

Called B to ask if I can stay this weekend. Knew it wouldn't be easy, I haven't seen him for so long, but A and C have their hands full with the baby, so I didn't want to bother them. G was busy. Couldn't pluck up the courage to ask you. I knew I could stay in a hotel but that feels too lonely, I hanker to see a friendly face. Other reasons, too, that I don't want to write down.

Tried several times, at last he answered. But he didn't understand what I needed, said I couldn't come this weekend as they had people staying but next weekend was fine. I tried to explain, it had to be this weekend. He got cross, swore. Said: you haven't been in touch for years, this is out of the blue. I'm not a hotel, you can't just turn up when you like. Tried to explain about J's 50th but he didn't get it, why should he?

Had to get off phone quickly so didn't really say bye, that won't help. Ended up booking hotel. Stupid to think it would be a chance to change things.

SEVEN

PEARL

Our cottage was Denny's pride and joy, the second greatest achievement of his life (marrying me being the first, of course). He started building it long before we met, intending it as a holiday home. He never expected to live in it full time.

But despite not knowing me when he planned the layout, there was a room upstairs at the front that seemed designed especially for me. We called it my study, though I didn't really have anything to study, except French. This was where I sat when I wanted to be quiet, to draw or read. The large window overlooked the wood, of course – all our windows looked out over the wood – and the dark green walls made the room feel like an extension of the trees outside. The shelves were filled with my books on art, nature and the French language, and the windowsill was cluttered with paints, brushes, and pencils in jam jars. I loved the way the sun shone through those jars, making rainbow prisms on the walls.

But my study felt a lot less like a sanctuary with the diaries in it. The hessian bag crouched in the corner like a toad, challenging me every time I came in. I couldn't quite bring myself to open it. In fact, I was finding it hard to settle to anything at all. I sat with a book or a crossword, taking nothing in. Everything felt off. I knew it wasn't jetlag after a two-hour flight but that's how I felt: blurry, out of sync.

The outside world was starting to creep in. As well as the diaries in the corner, there were the semi-regular messages from Eleanor. Going to England had opened that channel again – the English Channel, Denny called it, with a frown. But the most unwelcome intrusions were the daily voicemails from my new best friend, Andrea. By the time Denny and I got back from the UK there were already five, all variations on the same theme: *Pearl, this is Andrea. I need to talk to you. Please call.*

I admired her brevity as I deleted them. But the next day there were two more; the day after, the same.

We got into a little pattern: voicemail, delete, voicemail, delete. Denny advised me to keep my phone on silent, which made the calls easier to ignore.

But on the fifth day of this, when he and I were sitting in the garden after lunch and my phone started vibrating again, Denny reached for it.

'Don't answer!' I said.

'I've had enough of this. She's harassing you.'

'Wait! What are you going to say?'

'Tell her to sod off, of course.' He clicked the answer button. 'Hello? This is Pearl's answering service.'

I grinned. I rather liked Denny in bodyguard mode.

'Oh, hello Andrea, what a surprise,' he said, rolling his eyes. 'No, she's out I'm afraid. She often leaves her phone here, actually.' There was a long silence, during which he made all manner of tortured facial expressions. Then, 'I'm afraid that won't be possible, but I'll tell her you called.' He hung up, seemingly while she was still talking, and handed me the phone. Doing her voice, deep and rather breathy, he said, 'It's *imperative* she speak to you. *Urgent*, apparently.'

'Oh yeah? And what were you afraid wouldn't be possible?'

'You calling her back today.'

'How did she even get my number? Do you remember the old days, when people couldn't get hold of you whenever they wanted? If they called the landline and you weren't in, that was that. I miss that.' I pushed my phone towards him. 'Why don't you keep it for me?'

'Really?'

'Honestly, I've had enough of *people* for the time being.'

'OK, if you're sure,' he said. The moment he took the phone from me, I felt lighter, freer.

After lunch, I put on make-up and changed into a sunny yellow tea-dress, with a darker yellow scarf round my neck, tied in the French style. The late April weather was considerably warmer here than in the UK, and I didn't bother with a jacket. It was the first time, since we'd got back, that I felt ready to brave a trip to town. Denny looked relieved to see me in working mode, and I kissed him goodbye with something approaching my usual energy.

I had a rescheduled appointment with Mme Remard, my most regular client. When I'd called her from England to cancel, she did her best to be understanding, but ended the conversation by saying, 'It's fine, my dear, I just won't go out without a hat.'

I picked up my hairdressing case and stepped outside. I never tired of the wood, never stopped feeling lucky to have it on our doorstep. There were three clear paths into it from our front gate, as well as numerous overgrown tracks. The middle path was my usual route, my favourite. The path on the right went into the open part of the wood, where the trees were sparse. If it was a public wood, it's where day-trippers would lay out their rugs on the patches of grass, feast from picnic hampers and let their children run wild.

Today I took the path to the left, which was straight and smooth underfoot and led directly to the edge of the wood, and to what Denny referred to jokingly as 'so-called civilization': our town, Sévérac-le-Château.

I was through the gate in ten minutes, but Madame Remard lived on the far side of town, half an hour's walk farther on. On the way, I seemed to meet everyone I knew, all stopping to tell me they were sorry to hear about my father. Mme Remard only had herself to blame if this made me late, because it would have been her who'd told everyone. She was the town worthy, a self-appointed position.

I first met her in the post office not long after we moved out here. She discovered, via one of her impossible-to-deflect interrogations – in a past life she might have been big in the Spanish Inquisition – that I used to run a beauty salon. I did my best to explain that I wasn't available for any hair or beauty treatments, that I was here to rest and recuperate. But she pretended not to understand my hesitant French, and by the time I was more fluent, it was too late. The commitment to her roots was every week, rain or shine, and I didn't think I'd be able to get out of it until one of us died.

I rang the bell at her house, a huge and elegant home befitting her late husband's mayoral status, with a green tiled roof and wooden shutters. I'd never heard mention of any children, and though I knew she'd had a number of lodgers in the past, now there was just Vivienne, who ran the *tabac* in town. The two of them must rattle round in there. Vivienne had a whole floor to herself.

Madame Remard flung the door open with the energy and enthusiasm of a child.

'Madame Fleur! Thank god! My hair is a disaster!'

I followed her down the hall to her sitting room, designated as our styling room. She was a short, well-upholstered woman in her late seventies who would look like a perfectly ordinary older lady if not for the vivid mulberry hair. I was implicated up to my eyebrows in this folly because of course, I was the one who helped maintain its particular shade of 'cassis'. As I set out my tools, I felt the vestiges of funeral agitation finally start to dissipate. I was even pleased to see the *bichon au citron* pastries Mme Remard always put out for me. I'd made the mistake of saying they were delicious when she first served them to me, and it was far too late to tell her now that I hated lemon curd.

She sat in her chair in front of her ancient mirror, its heavy gold frame dull and tarnished, and I apologised for missing our last session. The roots were already showing in a way I knew she would hate.

'Pfft. I am lucky to have such fast-growing hair. And I wore this,' she said, pointing to an absolutely shocking hat sitting on her plump mahogany sideboard. 'Oh, Mme Fleur, the compliments I got!'

When I'd finished, she pressed the usual twenty-euro note into my hand. Since my brothers and I had sold Mum's house and salon I didn't really need the money, but I'd worked all my life and it was nice to earn. I headed back through town to the *tabac*.

Like Mme Remard, her lodger Vivienne was eternal. At thirty-four, she was young enough to be my daughter but she had a vintage style; with her hair tied up in a blue scarf, and her denim dungarees, she looked like Rosie the Riveter in the WW2 poster. She was serving two old fellows in flat caps when I came in, but left them to run over to me, crying, 'Ah, the wanderer returns!' and to give me a hearty kiss on each cheek. 'Sit, sit, I'll bring it.'

I took a table near the back, and watched as she pressed buttons and pulled levers on the coffee machine like an accordion player, the machine hissing and spitting at her command. Vivienne spoke little English, and I liked pretending to be French when I was with her, trying out my vocabulary. I also liked the version of myself that I presented to her: more worldly and witty than my usual buttoned-up, middle-aged English-woman self. She brought over our coffees, and asked about my unexpected UK stay. I glossed over it somewhat; our friendship was light and easy and I didn't want to tell her the whole of it – not the row Denny and I had in Hastings when I said I wanted to stay until the funeral, not the stress of all those faces from the past, not the awful scenes with Jeanie and Andrea. I managed to make a comic story out of the will reading and the diaries, but even so, she looked taken aback.

'This is so much to deal with,' she said, finally. 'You must not even know what to think.'

'I admit, I'm rather all over the place.'

'What do the diaries say?'

'I haven't read them yet.'

She raised her eyebrows. 'I wouldn't be able to wait even a moment. Imagine!' She put on a spooky voice. 'A message from beyond the grave!'

'That's scary!'

'I joke. The dead cannot hurt us.'

I didn't want to say that I knew my father could. The very effective plaster I had worn for so many years, which more or less covered over the wound of his abandonment, felt as if it was starting to peel off. He'd long been a complete blank, his behaviour inexplicable, his motives unknown. To find out, after all this time, what he was really thinking might be unbearable.

'So, you should read the diaries, no?' Vivienne sipped her coffee. 'Surely they will help you turn the page?'

Tourner la page. 'What page?'

'It is a metaphor, you know. Meaning to move on, to put the past behind you.'

'Ugh, you mean "closure",' I said in English.

'Closure?' She pronounced it 'clo-zure'.

'Like closing a door,' I said, miming it.

The bell rang, and a customer came in, an elderly man in a vibrantly checked three-piece suit, and we both laughed at the timing. 'Or opening a door,' she said, and stood up. 'Close the door, turn the page.'

Closure! I hated the very concept, and the word as well. Turning the page sounded a bit nicer.

After coffee, I took a whistle-stop tour of the *boulangerie*, butcher, and greengrocer, thanking everyone for their kind words of commiseration – that Madame Remard, honestly! – collected the post from Jean in the post office, and, weighed down with bags, headed back into the wood, feeling, as I often did on leaving town, that I had done enough socialising for a month.

I was halfway back to the cottage when I heard my phone ring. Heart thudding, because last time my phone rang in the woods it didn't go so well, I rifled through my bag. But I couldn't find my phone. I turned out all my pockets, and still it rang. I started going through the carriers, in case I'd absent-mindedly put it in one, and annoyingly dropped a cheese out of its wrapper onto the ground – Denny's favourite, too – but it wasn't there. At the exact same moment the ringing stopped I remembered that I didn't have the phone with me – I had left it behind with Denny.

I sat on the grass verge at the side of the path, surrounded by my strewn belongings, wondering if I was properly losing my mind. Then a man walked past. He didn't acknowledge me. He was in his forties, bearded and fat. His face was lined and weather-beaten. He had a rucksack over one shoulder and a leather strap over the other. It took me a moment to say anything, because I had never before seen a stranger in the wood, and my brain struggled to process his existence.

Trespassers were Denny's nightmare. After we moved out here, his first big project was to build a fence round the entire perimeter of the wood. He didn't properly relax until it was finished. The only entry point was a forbidding-looking iron gate, which he originally planned to keep locked, but I convinced him that wasn't necessary. We were already surrounded by trees and fences; I knew I'd feel trapped if we were actually locked in the wood as well. As a compromise, the gate was plastered with 'Keep Out' signs, and almost no-one, to my knowledge, had ignored them. Until now.

'Hey!' I called, and the man reluctantly stopped.

'Yeah?'

'Was that your phone ringing?'

'Yeah.'

'But you didn't answer it?'

'Who the fuck are you, my wife?' His words, which should have seemed rude, were actually rather droll in his Parisian accent.

'I thought it was my phone. It's the same ringtone.'

'Wow, we match.'

I got to my feet. 'What are you doing here?'

'*Excuse* me?'

I reminded myself that I did not like confrontation. What was I doing? But it was too late to pretend I hadn't said anything. Stammering slightly, I said, 'These woods are private. Didn't you see the signs?'

'Those signs are bullshit. I walk where I like.' His humorous face was quite at odds with his words. '*Arrache-toi*, lady.' *Clear off*.

'You're the one trespassing, not me.'

He laughed. 'Fine, I was leaving anyway.' He turned and went back the way he had come, towards town. As he rounded the bend I saw that the leather strap over his shoulder was attached to my field glasses. That completely knocked the stuffing out of me, and I sat down again on the verge. I hadn't seen the glasses since the day of Greg's call; I must have dropped them in the wood in all the confusion.

The glasses were the last gift Dad gave me before he left us. My fifteenth birthday present. I remembered my glee on opening them. They were tiny, designed to fit in a pocket, clean and sharp as a magnifying glass. I called them 'baby binoculars' which Dad found amusing. Not for the first time, I wondered if, in giving me something so precious, he had hoped to soften the blow of his leaving.

'They're called field glasses,' he told me, and I loved that term, loved the way it made them seem like a scientific tool. If you looked at birds through binoculars you were a hobbyist, an amateur. But someone who used field glasses was a professional. I might have liked to do something related to nature for a career. I had lots of options at school. I was going to do A Levels in Biology, French and Art, back when I thought I was going to do A Levels.

Everything was so bewildering and up in the air right now, and that stranger somehow having my field glasses was just one part of it.

I hastily gathered my shopping back into the bags, leaving the ruined cheese for pine martens to find. Thankfully, Denny was out when I arrived home, doing some preliminary work at the chapel in Rodez, which meant I could come down from my flustered state without him wondering what was wrong. I calmed my nerves with a mint tea, and looked regretfully at the hook where my field glasses usually hung. Then, with Vivienne's voice in my head ('clo-zure'), I went upstairs and looked at the hessian toad bag.

'All right then,' I said out loud. I tipped it upside down, and poured the diaries onto the floor. Most were similar to the one that Jeanie ripped, yellow with a thin, hard cover. Others were blue marbled exercise books of the sort I remembered using at school.

I sat on the floor and counted them. Nineteen. Most must cover more than one year, I reasoned, because nineteen wasn't enough for one per year. I picked one up at random. The first entry was marked March 1997. I was about to make a note of this date on the cover when some words caught my eye, my shorthand senses translating them automatically: *Called B to ask if I can stay this weekend.*

It took nearly an hour, and four read-throughs, before I got every word of this short entry. At this rate I'd still be translating the diaries when I was a hundred. Actually, I didn't get every word; I was very rusty and Dad's squiggles weren't easy to interpret, so some of it was guesswork based on the context, and to make it more difficult, everyone was referred to by their initials. He *really* didn't want anyone to know what he was writing about. Dad completely Fort Knox-ed this diary, and kept it in a safe place out of the house. Even then, he didn't commit everything to paper. '*Other reasons, too, that I don't want to write down.*' What on earth was he hiding? A long-term affair, maybe? He had previous, of course: Jeanie had been the other woman in my parents' marriage for at least two years before it all came out. I remembered Dad visiting me and my brothers a few months after he'd left home, and telling Greg, when he didn't think I was listening, that he'd had no choice, that he had fallen hopelessly in love with Jeanie. *Hopelessly in love* had sounded unpleasant to me ever since. Abandon all hope, ye who enter here.

This entry was a baffling account of trying to go somewhere during Jeanie's fiftieth birthday, assuming 'J' was Jeanie. It must be, and A must be Andrea.

Anyway, all that was small potatoes next to the real question which was: why was Dad trying to stay with Benjy (who must surely be the B referred to here) because it was his wife's birthday? There was so much to unpack. Firstly, I had no idea he was even in touch with Benjy at that time. Secondly, what was the deal with Jeanie's birthday – why did he want to be away for it? Thirdly, this throwaway couple of words: *G busy.*

Greg, undoubtedly, but how did Dad know he was busy? This was 1997, years after Dad had fallen out of our lives.

I had no idea what to do with these thoughts, so I employed my usual strategy for dealing with difficult things, and pushed them to the back of my mind, pending a later, unspecified time in which I would have the mental capacity to deal with them. I decided instead to put the books into chronological order, which took the rest of the day and was complicated enough to stop me thinking too hard about anything. I labelled each one with its dates, discovering as I did so that almost all of them covered two years, apart from the last three, 2015, 2016 and 2017, which each had their own separate book. Two were missing: the 2018 one, which was being repaired, and the one from 1987 to 1988.

I tried not to read anything as I flicked through them, but every so often something snagged my eye against my will. For instance, the first diary, from 1981 to 1982, had this upbeat entry from January 1982, a couple of months after he left home:

A brand new year for me and I hope it will be good for all of my family.

Yeah, it wasn't great for *all* your family, Dad.

From the 2017 notebook: *It's time to act, in fact it's long overdue, but even now I baulk at contacting Claymore.*

A sighting of the austere Mr Claymore! It took me quite a while to decipher 'baulk', mainly because it was such an implausibly formal word for someone to put in their diary. I wondered if the adult me would have found Dad pretentious. So here, he was instructing the solicitor about something. Maybe the late bequests to me, Greg and Benjy?

Then in 2001, this jumped out at me:

Desperately sorry to hear your engagement was called off, PP.

What the *what*? I put down the diary, my hands trembling. There could be no doubt that this referred to me, and my engagement to Kim, my long-term boyfriend before Denny. The month and year tracked.

Your engagement. What did this mean? Was he... addressing me directly?

21ST DECEMBER 2003

I asked after you as always, PP, and I hear that things are good, that you are seeing someone, an older man whom you met at French class. You always were good at languages, I remember. The boyfriend is building a house in France, how lovely.

8TH MAY 2005

Thrilled to hear that all went well with you marrying your French-class man yesterday. Sounds like a wonderful day, with you looking beautiful in pale grey.

EIGHT

PEARL

Desperately sorry to hear your engagement was called off, PP.

So I was 'PP'. Pretty Pearl? Pathetic Pearl? Previous Pearl?

But never mind that; what was this 'you' business? I picked up the 1997 diary and looked again at the entry where he'd contacted Benjy about staying with him. Both my brothers were mentioned – and then: *Couldn't pluck up the courage to ask you.*

Was I 'you'? It was starting to look that way.

And never mind *that,* because how the *hell* did Dad know about my engagement to Kim? Who told him? A shiver ran up my spine, and I thought of Mum, saying it meant that someone was walking over your grave. Mum... Surely it couldn't have been her, secretly talking to Dad behind my back? But that was impossible. They weren't in touch at all after he left. She didn't bad-mouth him, but she never completely got over him leaving her, and she rarely spoke of him. It couldn't have been.

But then... *someone* told him.

Throughout these nearly forty years of silence, Dad was absolutely not part of my life. There were long periods –

months, even years – when I barely thought about him. But it seemed that he was thinking about me. And now, he wanted me to know that he was thinking of me.

I looked again at the 2001 entry. 'Your engagement'. Dad was clearly addressing me here, it couldn't be anyone else. Was this why he had left me the diaries? Could they possibly be – were they actually – written *for* me?

I sat paralysed, torn between the need to know more and the need to push all this away forever, and I don't know how long I'd have stayed there had Denny not opened the door.

'Why are you sitting in the dark?' he said, and I was amazed to discover that it was early evening. He snapped on the desk lamp and took in the scene: me sitting, blinking, on the floor, the notebooks spread round me.

'Are you reading them, then?'

'No, I'm experimenting with a new kind of flooring.' I squinted up at him. 'How did it go at the chapel?'

'Good, thanks. Massive job, it'll take months, but they're lovely people. Thanks for collecting the post. This one's for you.' He handed me an official-looking letter which was from the UK. It was a letter from Mr Claymore that hadn't reached me in time for the funeral. It mostly contained information I already knew: that my father had requested I attend the funeral in order to receive the legacy, and the practical details of time and place. But at the end, there was one puzzling line:

Your father asked that I pass on this phone number to you, in case.

There was a UK number, with the reference: 'Roberta, PAC-UK'.

In case of what? Who was Roberta? Oh, god. It was yet another exhausting piece of this jigsaw puzzle from Dad that made no sense. I shoved the letter back in its envelope.

'Shall I make supper?' Denny said.

'Is it really that late?' I got up, my knees creaking. 'I'll do it.'

'Let me,' he said. 'You look exhausted.'

No way would I tell him he was right, that my head was throbbing. I didn't want him to know that the diaries were giving me grief. 'No, it'll be good to do something different.'

I left everything in a jumble, the notebooks on the floor, and went down to the kitchen. I usually enjoyed cooking, but tonight it didn't work its usual magic. I dropped a bag of flour on the floor, like a pantomime dame, and once I'd finished clearing that up, discovered that I hadn't put oil in the pan I'd left to heat up, so its underside was burned. I opened the back door to let in air, then sank into a chair and rested my head on my arms. Everything felt a bit much, right now.

When Denny came in, he took one look at the devastated kitchen and his pathetic wife, and said, 'Let's eat out.'

After the weirdness of the past week, it felt pleasantly normal to sit in our favourite restaurant, La Bicyclette Jaune, familiar menus in front of us. Not that we needed them, because we always ordered the same things: salmon with black rice for me, and steak frites for Denny. The head waiter, Gabriel, who greeted us by name, often tried to convince us to have the special, but we were creatures of habit.

'So... how are you doing?' I asked Denny, once we'd ordered. It was good – strengthening –to be somewhere other than inside my head. To sip white wine in a room full of other people.

'Fine...' he said, looking at me warily. 'Why do you ask?' We didn't normally do such formal check-ins with each other.

'I was just wondering, you know, how you felt being back there? England? You haven't said much about it.'

'Oh! Well, it was a lot harder for you than me.'

'Not really. You got stuck there for a week and then you had to face all my family in one big go.'

'They are a lot, aren't they?' He smiled, and raised his glass to me. 'But you know, no-one said... anything difficult or awkward.' His smile dropped, and he continued quickly, 'I'm just glad to be home, on our own. No drama. Other than mild phone harassment from Andrea.'

Thank goodness that was the only drama he knew about. The man in the woods, the revelations from the diaries... I'd keep those to myself. Poor Denny had been through enough. I said, 'You haven't really told me what you did while I was in the will reading. You just said you talked to Barbara.'

'God, well, you were in there for what felt like hours, and we could hear the shouting.'

'Really, you could hear that?'

'Easily. Then Jeanie and Andrea came storming out, faces like thunder, and they sat in a corner arguing with each other, and we all pretended we couldn't see.' Denny topped up our wine. 'Barbara was a tonic, as always. She's clearly hoping to become the third Mrs Benjy.'

'Fourth, I think,' I said, counting Benjy's wives in my head. 'I suppose Barbara isn't absurdly older than him.'

'Yes, Alice was a child bride, wasn't she? Anyway, Barb speculated for half an hour about whether Benjy will marry again, and the subtext was so heavy it gave me a migraine.'

Gabriel brought our food, and Denny smiled appreciatively at his steak.

'Poor old Barb,' I said. 'Why would she even want to marry him?'

'He makes her laugh, apparently.'

'He makes me laugh, too, but not in a good way.' I chewed some rice. 'Has Andrea called me again?'

'I don't think so, but I've put your phone away, out of sight.'

'She's probably given up.'

'Told you. Ignore these people, they go away.'

'You're right.' In a rush, I said, 'Denny, can I tell you my plan for the diaries?'

He busied himself with a cube of steak. 'I guess you'd better, because your main outlet otherwise seems to be throwing flour all over the kitchen and setting pans alight.'

I knew he'd prefer that I put the diaries away and never mention them again. He and I, our whole marriage, was all about finding a peaceful equilibrium. We sent ourselves off course a few years ago, before we moved here, but we'd been working back to stability ever since. Now the funeral and the diaries had set the pendulum swinging again.

'OK. I've nearly put them in chronological order, so that when I'm ready, it will be easy to translate them from the beginning.'

'You know you don't have to, though? Just because Greg or whoever wants you to. You can sling the sodding diaries in the fire pit and we'll put a match to them. Or we can pop them in your saucepan.'

'Funny. You burn one pan... I don't think Greg wants me to at all, actually. He keeps offering to take them himself.'

'Pearl, I don't want you to get hurt.' He scrunched up his napkin and threw it onto the table. 'You don't know what's in those diaries; it might be horrible and upsetting.'

I decided this wasn't the right moment to tell him that someone in my family had kept Dad up to date with the major events of my life. 'I know. If this was a film I would just drive to Montpellier and dump the bag in the sea.'

'In that case,' Denny said, 'I wish it was a film.'

It was only a little past nine when we got home, and I was no longer tired. The two glasses of wine had revitalised me.

'I'll put the diaries away,' I said. 'Then I can forget about them for a bit.' I went up to my study and closed the door, feeling as if I was doing something illicit. I picked up the next notebook, 2003–2004. I did truly intend to not read much more, but my wine-dulled senses baulked, as Dad would have put it, at being sensible, and I started scanning the pages for mentions of 'PP'. I still hadn't quite got my eye in with the shorthand, but just looking for those two little marks wasn't too difficult. It wasn't long before I saw one.

...you are seeing someone, an older man whom you met at French class.

I almost dropped the book. So Dad even knew about Denny! My god, this was beyond weird. *I asked after you as always, PP.* Who did he ask about me? Someone from our extended family? But who? No-one, not even the distant cousins, had ever mentioned being in touch with Dad; the received wisdom was that he'd cut ties with everyone.

It seemed as if everything I knew was wrong. I'd always thought that none of us had been in contact with Dad since the mid-eighties. But now I knew that at least ten years after that, Dad had called Benjy, asking to stay at his place. Could Benjy have been in touch with him in secret for all these years? This was certainly the sort of bizarre thing that he might do, but it was hard to believe that his barely hidden anger and pain about Dad weren't real.

Or what about Greg? When we did the drive-by past Dad and Jeanie's house, he reacted oddly when Benjy said, 'You've never been here before, have you?'. And he knew that Dad was in hospital, had enough of a rapport with Jeanie to persuade her into a quick funeral. But why the hell wouldn't he have told me?

There was so much here I didn't understand; none of it comfortable to dwell on.

The next diary, 2005–06, unbelievably contained a

mention of my and Denny's wedding! *Sounds like a wonderful day, with you looking beautiful in pale grey.*

There were only a handful of guests at our wedding, so that certainly narrowed it down.

I was thirty-seven when I met Denny, and juggling looking after Mum with running her salon in Chelmsford town centre. I had given up on the idea of meeting anyone. Boyfriends had come and gone, and none had been willing to take on Mum as well as me – not even Kim, who I went out with for six years. I didn't blame him when he finally broke off our engagement. He didn't quite say, 'It's me or your mother,' but that was the gist. He wanted us to travel, he wanted us to live together and, most reasonably of all, he wanted to rank higher than Mum in my priorities. I suppose things might have been different if we'd been lucky with trying for a baby, but that would turn out to be the thing that I was lousiest at of all.

But Mum and I, we were a package deal, and I was the only person she could tolerate looking after her. Eleanor, of course, refused to accept this. Once, she put me in a car without telling me where we were going. I'm pretty sure Kim was in on this scheme. She drove me to Seabrook Home, a lovely old manor house that had been repurposed to accommodate thirty residents; a place for ill people rather than the elderly. A rare space had come up, and it was mine – Mum's – if I wanted it.

'It's a no-brainer, Pearl,' Eleanor said on the way home, which I remember because it was the first time I'd ever heard that phrase. But Mum wouldn't look at the brochure, far less agree to be taken to see the place, and I didn't push her. It was easy for me to let it go. Looking after Mum was just my job, from the day Dad walked out until the day she died, and that was that.

I'd overheard Mum on the phone, talking to a friend at the

salon, the morning of Benjy's ill-fated first marriage. He was nineteen. 'Everyone leaves,' she said. She didn't know I'd heard her. Greg had gone years earlier, of course, and now Benjy. And before them, it was Dad who left, on a cold November day, and never came back.

I said to myself then, *I won't leave.* And I didn't. I was proud of that.

My routine was the same for years. Wake up at six a.m., get ready for work, get Mum up and in the bath. While she was in there I'd make her breakfast, then help her out of the bath, and leave her to get dressed while I went to Ivory Hair & Beauty. My work days were busy: I supervised staff, saw clients, dashed home to give Mum lunch and grab a sandwich, back to work, home for supper. She did very little in the day, other than read and watch TV, plagued by one illness after another, but in the evenings she and I would watch TV together. I cherished those times. We'd take it in turns to choose a film or programme and I loved to hear her laugh or get involved in a plotline. Her favourite film was *Meet Me in St Louis*, and towards the end of her life we watched it once a week, because she found it so comforting. I could still sing every word to 'The Trolley Song' if necessary, though what kind of emergency might require it, I couldn't say.

I knew it wasn't much of a life; my brothers told me often enough that I was sacrificing too much. I didn't see either of them step up to help, though, and I couldn't see a way out of it that wouldn't make Mum unhappy. Thursday evenings were the only times I could go out guilt-free, because our next-door neighbour came in and sat with Mum. After Kim and I split, I used the time to go to classes, mostly in art: life drawing, nature drawing, botanical painting. I loved it. Then, for a change, I took a French conversation class, and that's where I met Denny.

He took those classes very seriously. He wanted to get more fluent because, years earlier, he'd inherited a derelict cottage and woodland from his maternal French grandmother. His long-held dream was to rebuild the cottage. We got talking in the break, because we both recoiled from the grey instant coffee that was on offer. I rather liked the way his eyes crinkled when he smiled, and I definitely liked the feeling in my stomach when he looked at me. I felt that he really saw me. He wasn't seeing Pearl the hairdresser, or Pearl the carer, but Pearl the person.

At the end of the first class we both dashed out together, as soon as the tutor said she'd see us next week. I said, 'Got to get back for my mum,' at the same time as Denny said, 'Got to get back for my dad.' He and I were in the same boat – he was looking after his dad, who had MS. We started meeting for a decent coffee before classes, and as we got to know each other, we discovered a lot more in common than a desire to improve our French. Like me, he'd had a long-term relationship in his twenties that fizzled out thanks to his caring responsibilities. It felt quite natural when, six months after we met, he asked me to marry him. I thought he'd been sent from heaven. His dad was very ill, so we agreed to wait, though we were of one mind about trying for a baby straight away, but it didn't happen. We had a very small, low-key wedding two months after Denny's dad passed away. Everyone was teary that day: Greg when he walked me down the aisle; Denny when he said his vows; me when Denny gave an emotional speech at the lunch.

Denny sold his dad's house, and moved in with Mum and me. She was in her mid-seventies, and laid low by the dementia that would kill her two years later. She never quite got used to Denny being around, which I understood – for years, it had just been me and her in the house. Denny was rarely there, anyway, not wanting things to be awkward for Mum. He was mostly in France, building the cottage. We both thought of it as a holiday home, maybe our retirement place. But a few years ago, after

Gracie's christening, I realised how lucky we were to have somewhere to escape to.

There were ten guests at our wedding, and it was easy to rule most out of being the mole on the grounds that they had never met Dad. The only ones I knew for certain that had were Mum, Greg and Benjy. I started typing a furious email to my brothers, then deleted it. Instead, I ordered a book called *Brush up Your Teeline Shorthand* for eleven euros. I needed to think, not rush into anything. We'd achieved a reasonable *entente cordiale* at the funeral – I smiled whenever I thought of Greg holding Benjy's wrists – and it would be a foolish woman who'd easily trample over that. Perhaps this was Dad's plan all along for these diaries: to sow even more seeds of discontent than he managed in his wretched life.

I was so caught up in the past, thinking about my wedding, about Dad knowing about it, that the knock on the front door made me jump out of my skin. I assumed it did the same to Denny, given the shocked expletive that shot up the stairs. Not only was it very late, but we never got unexpected guests at our house. We didn't get expected guests either, come to that. We weren't the world's most sociable couple.

Nervously, I went downstairs. Denny and I locked eyes in the hall. There was a blurry shape through the glass window in the door.

'Who on *earth* is that?' he whispered.

By far the most likely visitor, I knew, was the person I'd seen earlier today in the wood, the bearded man, and my heart, already fluttering precariously, started thudding. He'd followed me here. Waited until nightfall. Kept watch as we left the wood to drive to the restaurant in Millau. He didn't break in then, while we were out, because he wanted us to be here. He was going to murder us in cold blood.

Or, I don't know, perhaps he just wanted to return my field glasses.

I started towards the door, but Denny pushed in front of me.

'Stay back, I'll go.' He grabbed his rifle out of the cupboard. He had never actually fired the thing; he only owned it in case of wild boar, and we'd never seen any in our wood. It seemed a bit over the top to answer the door with it, but this didn't seem to be the right moment to make that point. He approached the door, and I crept behind him. Our visitor knocked on it again, making us jump even higher.

'All right!' Denny yelled. He flung it open, and standing there, wearing a rucksack, an inappropriately smart suit and heels and a weak smile, was my father's wife's daughter.

An-dray-ah.

NINE

CARRIE

It all happened so quickly: from Dr Shah saying that Mum needed to be in a hospice, to them moving her to one, took scarcely more than two days. Mum was strangely sanguine about the move, but Dr Shah said she was becoming more confused now, as the cancer did its terrible work and the pain medication increased, so she might not have taken in where she was going.

I was teaching when they moved her first thing today, but went this afternoon as soon as my last class had finished. The hospice was nearer home than the hospital, and I kept reminding myself of this positive aspect on the way there. I was looking for silver linings, clearly. And I found plenty once there: pretty trees lined the drive; smiley staff greeted me warmly and seemed less frenetic than the nurses at the hospital; and Mum had her own room, a light and airy space with paintings on the walls.

She was lying on her back in bed, but she was awake.

'Hello, my sweet,' she said. 'Welcome to the Final Destination.'

OK. So she did know where she was.

'Loving the gallows humour.' I sat down and gave her my useless gifts: sweets, fruit, magazines; the usual. She pushed them aside, completely over all that.

'Emmie not with you?'

'No, she's with Iain.'

'Again!'

'Yes, amazingly! I hardly know what to do with all the free time.' I took Mum's hand, which seemed thinner than before, almost transparent. 'I wasn't sure about bringing her here; I didn't know what it would be like. It's surprisingly nice, though.'

'Thought it would be walking cadavers, did you?' Mum smiled. 'I did, myself. I cried all the way here.'

'Oh Mum. I'm sorry. I should have been here with you.'

'I was glad you weren't.' Mum tried to reach her water cup, which was literally an arm's length away, but she couldn't manage it, and I passed it to her. 'Thanks, love. So that's *very* promising, with Iain.'

'Is it?'

'I often thought, all that young man needs is a bit of time.'

I could see, in my mind's eye, Mum's vision for my future. It was one in which she no longer existed, but by her lights I was fine, safe, because I was with Iain, a proper family with Emmie. Mum was a dreamer, a romantic. I sometimes wished I could be more like her, and less pragmatic.

'You never know,' I said.

'So... have you thought any more about what we talked about?'

'Way to get straight to it.' My throat felt dry. I'd been hoping to avoid this topic. I took a small bottle of polish out of my bag. 'Would you like me to paint your fingernails?'

'No, I wouldn't. Caroline, listen.'

'Ooh, she's using my full name. It's definitely a code red.'

'I don't want to banter, I want to talk properly.'

'I'm sorry.' I slipped my hand back into hers. 'But, Mum, I'm not interested. You know my feelings.'

'Your feelings...' She closed her eyes and the silence went on for so long, I thought she might have lost her thread, or even fallen asleep. Then abruptly she said, 'Your feelings aren't as important as mine right now.'

'Wow!' I stroked the hair off her damp forehead. 'What are they teaching you at hospice school? Assertiveness?'

'Standing on the precipice here, you see things differently.' Mum looked so sad, I wished we could start over. 'I'm speaking up for myself, is all.'

'I like it. If it wasn't directed at me, I'd like it even more.'

'Will you please make contact? I know if you say yes, you'll do it. I trust you.' She squeezed my hand – at least, I think that's what she was going for, but she had so little strength it was like a butterfly kiss. Yet something of the intensity of what she was feeling travelled from that tiny movement into me, reminding me, as if I needed reminding, of the strength of our bond.

'I just don't know if I can bear it if...'

'What, darling?'

'If it's horrible? If I hear something I wish I hadn't.'

'I understand. I think you should call Roberta first. She's used to this sort of situation. And I'll be there to hear about it, hold your hand.' Mum smiled. 'Will you? Make the call?'

'I don't have the number.'

'I do.'

Oh god. She was never going to let this go. 'Do you really, really want this, Mum?'

'I really, really do.'

That's how ill she was – she didn't break into the Spice Girls' song. There was a time when wild horses wouldn't have been able to stop her doing that.

'OK. I'll call. I promise.'

'Darling.' Her eyes filled with tears. 'Thank you. My

gruntle is feeling very well.' She barely got through it, her voice cracking on 'gruntle'.

'You are a pushy old thing,' I said, and my own damp eyes mirrored hers. 'But luckily, you are also the best mum in the world.'

'Oh, get away with you,' she said, and smiled. It was wonderful to see a seemingly untroubled smile. Had my simple promise to make that call been enough to soothe her worries? In which case, I was glad, though I really, really didn't want to. 'I'm so proud of you, you know.'

'Aw, you're making me blush.'

'You've done such amazing things, Carrie. Teaching programming at the highest level, a brilliant career with all the perks.'

'You do love that subsidised crèche.'

'Responsible for bringing more women students into your department than ever before.'

'Well, it wasn't hard to improve on two, was it?'

'I've always been proud of you. From the moment I saw you, I knew you would bring great joy into my life, and you have.'

'Oh, Mum...'

Then, as if a switch had been turned off, she went to sleep. One minute she was praising me and smiling, the next she was lying still, her eyes closed. It gave me a horrible turn, because I thought... well, it was obvious what I thought. But then I saw her chest rise and fall, and let out a long, relieved breath. Doubtless the emotion and the strain of getting me to agree to her request had worn her out.

A nurse – were they nurses in hospices? – stopped me as I crept out of the room. 'I'm so glad you got here,' she said, smiling broadly.

'Well, yes, of course I'm here! I visited Mum almost every day when she was in hospital.'

'Ah, that's good. I just mean, she's very ill.'

I raised my eyebrows, thinking, I've got news for you, Nurse – everyone here is very ill. I said, 'She's only just arrived, though.'

'The hospital kept her in a long time, longer than I'd have thought. I imagine they were hoping she'd respond to something eventually.'

She seemed very upfront. It made me feel that I could ask direct questions myself. 'How long do you think...'

'I don't know.' Oh. Maybe not that upfront. She smiled again. 'Will you come tomorrow?'

Well, I blimming would now, Nurse Grim Reaper. The sunlight outside felt too much, made me disoriented, and I sat in my car for a few minutes staring blankly at the windscreen. I thought about what I'd agreed to. It wouldn't be for my sake. Any curiosity I'd felt had been laid to rest. It would only be for Mum.

At Iain's flat, he and Emmie were painting with their toes on a long river of paper, which was stuck to the floor with masking tape.

'Well Iain, you have genuinely amazed me,' I said. 'I had no idea that under that cool exterior was a children's entertainer waiting to bust out.'

Emmie wobble-ran over to me, her feet leaving red and purple paint marks on the wooden floor. I pulled her into my arms, and she immediately managed to transfer paint onto my jeans.

'It's different when it's your own, isn't it?' Iain said, standing up carefully onto a piece of paper. 'I never thought I'd like doing this stuff, but she's such fun.'

His trousers were rolled up to the knee and there was paint on his hands and face, but he was, nonetheless, genuinely attractive to me for the first time in about eighteen months. Mum's theory was that it was all about the timing; that Iain and

I would end up together. Daft, surely? I'd changed a lot since we broke up.

'Want a cuppa?' he said, and that familiar phrase, absent from my life for so long, because Emmie was too young to use a kettle, made me feel sentimental.

'Go on, then.'

He grabbed a stack of A4 paper and set one piece at a time down on the floor in front of him so he could make a pathway to the kitchen without getting paint on the floor. It was slightly futile as Emmie was now stomping round making cute little splodges everywhere, but it made me laugh.

'So was it grim there?' he said, as he filled the kettle.

'It was nice, actually. Everyone is very smiley.' I sat down at the table. We'd chosen it together from Ikea, but it was his now.

'I'm sorry, though. A lot to cope with.'

I had an urge to tell him about Mum's request, but I'd got used to not sharing things with him so I didn't. The silence between us stretched out oddly. He looked as though he wanted to say something, then carried on making tea instead. Emmie came padding in and I pulled her onto my lap. It was handy, having her as a buffer.

'Dada!' she said.

'Loud and clear.' Iain smirked triumphantly. 'She's said it loads today.'

'It was non-stop "Mama" yesterday,' I lied. 'Also she said that she wants to go into quantum physics when she's older.'

'So how's our house? I miss it, you know. All that space, and the garden.'

My poor old gritted teeth; would they make it through this conversation? I tried to unclench them, and said in as neutral a voice as I could muster, 'Well, if I remember rightly, it was your decision to move out.'

'Lovely neighbours, too,' he said, as if I hadn't spoken. 'I suppose you and Henry have been Brady Bunching it up, have you?'

'Can it be a bunch, with one kid apiece? Brady Bunch 2.0, sponsored by the Family Planning Association.'

I'd forgotten about Iain's mild jealousy of Henry. He was very popular, being a handsome single dad in a street full of single mums. He didn't seem in a hurry to make any romantic connection with anyone, though. I suspected he was still bruised from the end of his relationship with Numa's mother, who hadn't taken to motherhood and had moved to Scotland with a woman when Numa was tiny. He and I were not 'Brady Bunching' it, alas – I'd have to join a long queue – but we did have some very useful childcare/parcel acceptance/shopping arrangements which we both relied on.

'I could come and hang with Emmie sometimes in the house, when you're out,' Iain said. 'So she doesn't always have to be dragged over here.'

'I've hardly dragged her,' I said, 'but sure, if you like.' Maybe Mum was right, and he was trying, in his ham-fisted way, to reconcile.

My phone rang and I stared in disbelief at the caller.

'Oh god. It's the hospice.'

I answered it, my fingers already slick with sweat. I gripped tight onto Emmie with my other hand as a kind-voiced woman told me that Mum had just passed away.

It took me a long, sickening moment to process this enough to form a reply. 'But... I was there an hour ago,' I said, as if that would somehow make a difference. 'She only arrived this morning.'

'It was really peaceful. It seemed that she'd been waiting to see you, and then she let herself slip away.'

She carried on talking, and I could hear what she was saying, was even able to respond to the things she said about arrangements and doctors and so on. But after she'd said how sorry she was, and goodbye, and hung up, I held the phone to my ear listening to nothing, waiting for her to say it was a mistake; that it was someone else, someone else's mum; that mine was fine, she didn't even need to be in a hospice, really.

'Carrie?' Iain's voice came from somewhere far away.

'I think she's gone,' I said.

'The woman who rang?'

'No, my mum.' I laughed, though it didn't sound like my normal laugh at all. 'And the woman, too. Different sorts of gone.'

'Oh, Carrie.' Iain slid the phone out of my hand and took Emmie gently off my lap. The top of her hair was wet with my tears, which was weird because I didn't even know I'd been crying.

'What happened?' I said, looking at Iain in complete confusion. 'Did Mum really just die, in the hour since I saw her?'

'Jesus, I'm so sorry.'

'I wasn't there. I left her, why did I leave her? She died on her own.'

Iain put Emmie into the bouncy chair he'd bought for her. He put his arm round me, and said, 'Carrie. She wasn't alone. There were people who have been through this many times. They knew what to do.'

'They didn't know her, though! She only arrived this morning!'

If I hadn't have left, she surely wouldn't have died. Oh my god, I was such an idiot! All I'd had to do was stay there with her, and she wouldn't have died. 'I can't believe it. What was the point of moving her? Why did she...' I tailed off, realising that once she had managed to extract a promise from me that I'd make the phone call, she was able to quietly fade out. She'd been clinging on, waiting until I agreed.

For more than one reason, then, I wished with all my heart that I had not made that promise.

21ST FEBRUARY 1982

Disastrous first visit from PP. I honestly don't know what happened. I was so excited for half term, because G said he'd bring her for postponed Xmas visit. J said it was still too soon but I said to her, this is my new life and I want my children to be part of it. But maybe she was right. Awkward from the moment G and PP arrived. A was hiding in her room. J took PP up there, but scarcely fifteen minutes later they were down again, J saying PP had made A cry.

I tried to find out what had happened but PP said she wanted to go. I said what about staying, she had her overnight bag, but it was no good; she stood by the door, waiting for G to take her. When they'd gone, J took me in her arms, said she was sorry but it was clearly too soon to expect to join the two families, I should be prepared for it to be slow. I'm sure she is right.

TEN

PEARL

Denny and I stood in the doorway, gaping at Andrea.

'Hi,' she said, giving an awkward little wave. *Awks.*

'What. The. Hell?' Denny said, his voice scarily quiet.

'Well, if the mountain won't come to Mohammed...' Andrea's tone changed, and she pointed at Denny with a shaking finger. 'Is that gun *real?*'

Denny and I both looked at the rifle in his hands, as if wondering how it had got there.

'It's not loaded,' I said.

'Oh, well, that's fine, then.' Andrea waited for us to respond, then when we didn't, said, 'Er, it's not really fine, do you think you could...?'

'Yes, of course,' he said, returning it to the cupboard.

'Well?' I said, my arms folded.

'Look, you didn't answer my calls, so I thought...'

'For goodness' sake, Andrea! You can't just turn up unannounced.'

'I know. I'm sorry.'

'Well, good,' Denny said. 'Bye, then.'

'Please may I come in for a minute?' Andrea said. 'It's been quite a journey. There's one thing I want to ask, then I promise to leave you alone.'

'You should be leaving us alone already,' Denny said. 'If you had even the slightest idea what Pearl's been through...'

'Denny.' I put my hand on his shoulder, but I understood his anger. This house was our citadel, our private space, and none shall breach. The fact that Andrea, of all people, had somehow found her way here must feel like an attack on his very being.

'...all these years, the shit she's put up with, if you had any idea of it,' his voice was louder now, 'you wouldn't dare stand there, showing up uninvited with your bag on your back, your pathetic pleas, your—' He broke off, because Andrea was crying.

'I'm sorry,' she said. 'I'm really sorry.'

I felt awful, letting her stand outside in the dark. 'Denny love, why don't you go to bed? I'll handle this.'

Andrea looked up hopefully, tears streaked across her grubby face. How long had she been travelling to get here? How did she even track us down? Our house was hard to find because we didn't want to be found. Our unofficial address was 'Middle of Nowhere'.

'Go on,' I said to Denny, in my gentlest tone. 'We can't send her away without a coffee at least.'

'Thank you,' Andrea said, between little gasps.

'This is a terrible, terrible idea,' Denny muttered, but he nonetheless backed away, and went reluctantly upstairs. 'I'm leaving the door open. Shout if you need me.'

As soon as he was out of earshot, I whispered, 'Look here, Andrea, if you're here to slap me with a lawsuit like on the telly, the whole "you've been served" business, you can turn right round again.' I didn't want Denny to know about the legal threat Andrea had made at the funeral; that was exactly the sort of thing to make him regret putting the gun away.

'God, no. I don't think we do that in the UK, anyway?'

'We're not in the UK,' I pointed out.

'I swear, on my mother's life, that I'm not here to serve you with papers.'

'OK. Come in.'

I led her to the kitchen, and put the coffee on. She sat at the table watching me, her head propped up on her hands like a tired child. It was so weird, such a novelty, for someone to be in our house. I wondered what it looked like through her eyes.

'Those are lovely,' she said, and I thought she was pointing at our burnt-orange tiles. Then I realised she meant my little framed paintings, a series of birds and trees I'd done over the last couple of years. Every time I finished one, Denny made a bespoke frame for it, with tiny carvings in the wood.

'Oh, they're just my dabblings...'

'*You* painted them? They're amazing.'

'Thanks.' I got out two cups. 'So... you said you wanted to ask me something?'

'That's right. May I use your bathroom first? I can't remember when I was last near a not-disgusting loo.'

I directed her upstairs, and put together a plate of bread, cheese and leftover salad for her. Then I sank into a chair. Without her in the room, all the weirdness that she represented came flooding back. And-*ray*-ah, here, in my house. How on earth had this happened?

I first met her in early 1982, a few months after Dad moved out. Initially at least, he was keen for us children to be part of his new life. He sent letters and cards regularly, and encouraged us to phone him – less chance of him having to speak to Mum that way. Mum got teary very easily those first couple of years, and we sensed without being told that she didn't want to know about our contact with him.

Greg was eighteen or nineteen when Dad left, and old enough to have a relationship with him without Mum having to be involved. And one time, he offered to take me along too. We created a subterfuge about me visiting Greg at his university halls in Bristol. Benjy cried for hours that he wasn't allowed to come too – he completely fell for the cover-up – but Greg and I knew he would spill the beans. He was only ten, and I was fifteen, which was a world older at the time.

Dad and Jeanie hadn't yet moved to Rye. They were renting a house in London, and Greg drove me there in his beat-up VW Polo. He'd already been there once, he boasted on the way. What's more, Dad had visited him twice in Bristol, and he and Jeanie had taken Greg out to dinner. I was scared about seeing Dad with his new family, scared to meet Andrea. An-dray-ah, Dad had mentioned on the phone. I said her name in my head, over and over, so I wouldn't get it wrong. And I didn't.

But everything else went wrong. Jeanie was unfriendly, and we sat in awkward silence in the living room, my eyes drawn repeatedly against their will to the grey streak in her hair. Andrea was in her bedroom, and after I'd been given a glass of squash and a clagging walnut slice, Jeanie said she would take me up to meet her. I remembered she walked straight into Andrea's room, which surprised me because my mum always knocked on my door, even when I was very young.

Andrea was a pinch-faced little girl of seven or so, sitting cross-legged on her bed reading a book. She was very neatly dressed, in a matching skirt and jumper, with white knee socks and fluffy lilac mule-type slippers that I coveted instantly. Her hair was shiny and well-brushed, held back with a white Alice band.

Jeanie left us alone, and I stood there awkwardly. I asked Andrea what she was reading. Though she was half my age, I thought we could at least talk about books. Silently, she held up a *Penny* annual which I assume she'd got for Christmas. I told her I preferred *Misty*, with its scary ghost stories. Being so much older than her, I probably got a bit show-offy. I sat on the bed and gave her a blow-by-blow account of one of the scariest *Misty* stories, and by the time I finished she looked rather alarmed. Temporarily puffed up with teen bravado, I said, 'So how do you like living with my dad?' and she replied, 'I liked my real daddy better. You can have yours back now.' That shut me up, because it was of course so exactly what I wished would happen. But only one of us was young enough to think it might. My bluster melted away and I burst into tears.

Jeanie came barrelling in (I wondered now, was she listening at the door?) and said, 'What on earth is going on?' I clammed up, and she grabbed my arm and shook it. 'You can't come in here, making a silly fuss, upsetting everyone. You'd better go home now, tell your dad you want to go. It's for the best.' Still holding my arm, she led me downstairs, muttering under her breath that I was a rude and scruffy child.

The visit didn't last much longer. I know that I didn't say another word, for fear of saying the wrong thing, but I couldn't remember leaving, only sitting in the car going back to Bristol, Greg irritated because it seemed I had messed things up. After I cried, he bought me a McDonald's to make up. It was the first time I'd had one, but I couldn't eat much of it because my stomach was so clenched.

That was the only time I met Andrea. It was pretty much the last time I saw Dad, too. He made two visits to Chelmsford after that, to see me and Benjy, both that same year. He met us in the local park so he wouldn't have to come to the house. And that was it.

I was propelled back to the present with a jolt as the grown-up Andrea reappeared. Even though I knew she was here, it was still a shock to see her, and I hope I sufficiently covered up my startled 'Oh!' with a cough. She smelled of my soap, and her face looked considerably cleaner than when she'd arrived.

'Is this for me?' She pointed at the plate of food I'd made for her, and started shovelling bread into her mouth. 'Thank you so much. I haven't eaten for hours.'

Her hands and wrists were badly scratched up, and the jacket sleeve of her right arm was streaked with dirt and torn. Now her face was washed, I could see there were scratches on that, too.

'Did you get lost in the wood?'

She winced, embarrassed. 'I don't know how long I was wandering around in there. I fell over, look.' She showed me a long scratch on her shin. 'Tree root. Thank god I ran into the ranger.'

'Ranger?'

'The bearded guy living in the woods, with the binoculars? I think he said ranger but my French is so rusty.' I didn't have time to think about what this meant before she put down the bread and burst into tears again. 'I just miss him so much.'

'The *ranger*?'

'Dad!' she wailed. 'I miss him every minute of every day.'

'Of course you do.'

I turned away and got busy pouring our coffee. The child in me wanted to yell that he was my dad first, that he would still *be* my dad if she hadn't taken him off me. Doctor Haywood would probably approve of how easily I was able to inhabit my child-self, seeing it as an important way of dealing with the pain of my father's abandonment, but at times like this it wasn't ideal. I needed to be able to access a more adult mindset in which I felt bad for Andrea, because for almost our whole lives, he was way more her dad than mine.

It was like she was following my thoughts, because she said, 'You're the last person I should be saying this to. You missed him for years.'

As at the wake, when she'd known I might want to hear about Dad's life with her, I was touched by her empathy. 'Yeah, well, on the plus side, that means I don't feel particularly devastated now.' I put a cup of coffee in front of her very gently, to compensate for being so blunt, then sat down. 'So, how did you get here?'

'With great difficulty. I suppose you don't get many spontaneous visitors?'

'You're the first.'

'That tracks. It started off easily enough. Plane to Rodez, taxi to Sévérac-le-Château...'

'You got a *taxi* from the airport? How much was that?'

She shrugged. 'Hundred and fifty euros.'

'My god, for that I'd expect to keep the cab. The bus is eight euros.'

'I just wanted to get here. But the driver wouldn't take me further than the edge of the wood.'

'He can't, there isn't a road.'

'So how do you drive here? How do you get deliveries? Letters?'

'We don't.'

'You *don't*?' She looked around the kitchen as though seeking confirmation. 'Maybe it's nice to be so hidden.'

'We like it. So, go on, the taxi?'

'The driver said I couldn't go in the wood because it was private. He actually got out of the car to read me the signs on the gate. I had to persuade him I knew you. Then he asked some random woman who was walking past, and she said she thought the house was in the middle, so if there was a path I should follow it to a junction, then take the right fork. Or a left one, I don't know. It was like following instructions in Alice in fucking Wonderland.'

'And you got lost?' I always thought of the wood as small

and manageable, but I suppose that was because I knew it so well.

'Immediately. I'd still be out there now, terrified, bleeding to death probably, if I hadn't met the ranger.'

'We don't...' I stopped. 'A bearded man, you say?'

'Yes, quite large. Wearing a lot of clothes.'

'Parisian accent?'

'How the hell would I know?'

'And he told you where the house was?'

'Yes, he drew me a map, look.' She took a paperback novel out of her bag, and on the back inside cover was a neat, accurate little diagram in black pen. So the trespasser with my field glasses knew where we lived. That led me to another thought.

'How did you even know our address? My phone number?'

'Dad had them.'

My cup was halfway to my mouth and I was so startled I missed, and spilled coffee onto my top. 'Blast!' I jumped up and got the cloth. Yet more things Dad somehow knew about me.

Denny came thundering down the stairs. 'Pearl! You shouted! Are you OK?'

'Yes, fine. Spilled my coffee, that's all.'

He shot a filthy look at Andrea, as if she'd chucked the coffee at me, and went out again.

I turned my attention back to her. 'Well done on finding us, but I'm afraid you've had a wasted journey. I've already started translating the diaries.'

'Got very far?' She didn't sound quite as casual as I think she intended.

'Not very. So, where are you staying, the hotel in town?'

'Er, well, it's so late. I was thinking I could stay here tonight...'

The thought of her in our spare room! 'Gosh, no, that's not possible, Andrea. I'll walk you back to town. The hotel is very nice, I believe. I'll call them now. Would you like another coffee before we go?'

'Do you have anything herbal? I've had so much coffee today, my veins are pure caffeine.'

'Fresh mint tea?'

'Perfect. Thank you.' She picked up her rucksack. 'Can I just use the bathroom again?'

'Sure. You can leave your bag.'

'Oh, I need it. Sanitary protection, you know.'

When she'd gone up, I rang the hotel and booked her a room. Then I went to my herb patch by the back door and snipped a few sprigs of mint. I stood for a moment in the dark, breathing in the delicious herb smells that were always stronger at night. I took the mint into the kitchen, washed it and put it into an infuser. It wasn't until the water was almost boiling that something clicked in my brain, and I sprinted up the stairs three at a time. The bathroom door was wide open, because of course, she wasn't in there; she was in my study, cramming diaries into her rucksack as fast as she could.

She whirled round guiltily as I stormed into the room. 'Uh, I couldn't find the bathroom.'

'You already used it, you silly, lying cow.'

I grabbed her rucksack and turned it upside down. The diaries poured out in a tangle of clothes. We both stared at them for a moment, then Denny walked in, assessed the scene instantly, and, with a muttered, 'For crying out loud,' took hold of Andrea's shoulders and marched her out of the room.

'My bag!' she called.

I quickly checked there weren't any diaries still in there, bundled her clothes in, and followed them downstairs.

Denny opened the front door and she stepped outside. I shoved her bag at her, then stepped back into the hall. I didn't want her to see that I was trembling.

But she was trembling too. 'I'm so sorry. I don't know what I was thinking.' She was pale as a sheet, her eyes huge with astonishment at her own behaviour.

Coming here, making a silly fuss, upsetting everyone.

'You should be sorry,' Denny said. 'We allowed you in our house and you immediately betrayed our trust.'

'I'm so, so stupid. I didn't even tell you the thing I came all this way to say.'

'It looks like you had a fair attempt at the thing you came all this way to do, though,' Denny said, gesturing at her rucksack. 'You blew it.' He started to close the door.

She said, her voice higher than normal, 'Christ, it's almost midnight, and I don't know how to get back.'

'I'm sure you'll manage; you got here, right enough,' he said.

'Denny, Pearl, please! I know I'll get lost. I only made it here with the help of—'

I realised she was going to mention the so-called ranger, the bearded man, and I had to stop her, had to prevent Denny finding out that we had an intruder in the wood. He already had more than enough to cope with.

'I'll walk you,' I said, stopping her mid-sentence.

'Oh god, *thank you*.'

'No Pearl, let her go.' Denny grabbed my hand. 'She's already taken complete advantage...'

I pulled out of his grasp. 'I'll be back in half an hour. I'll see her to the hotel.' I picked up my torch from the hall table. 'Otherwise she'll just get lost and turn up here again. Or get eaten by wolves, and I can't have that on my conscience.'

'Christ!' Andrea said, looking round wildly for wolves.

Denny stared at me.

'It's the right thing to do,' I said.

'Fine,' he snapped, and slammed the door.

Andrea and I looked at each other. 'I'm really sorry,' she said. 'He's cross with you now, because of me.'

'You keep apologising, and then you keep being a pain in

the butt.' It was quite cathartic, saying that. I started walking along the left-hand path, spitting words as I went, her trotting beside me. 'Andrea, you turned up here, as if we have some kind of relationship.' Fast walking, or heightened emotion, was making me breathless. 'You expect to be let in, you expect to be allowed to stay, and then you try to steal something that belongs to me. It's shocking behaviour, really it is.'

'They belong to my mum,' she said quietly.

'They do *not*.'

'How on earth do you know your way in the dark?' She hurried to keep up in her silly shoes.

I didn't reply, and we walked on in silence. How strange it was to be taking this familiar route with anyone other than Denny. The beauty of the woods was hidden at night; you couldn't see much other than the dark outlines of trees either side of us, and the small section of path illuminated by my torch.

At last, breathing heavily with the effort of walking quickly, Andrea said, 'Pearl, please believe me, I'm genuinely sorry. I don't want you to think I came here to take the diaries.'

'Of course that's why you came.'

'It really wasn't, I swear. I had no idea they'd be lying around on the floor, did I? It was honestly just a stupid impulse when I saw them. I really regret it.'

There was a noise, probably a barn owl, and she let out a cry.

'Oh my god, it's really spooky.' She moved so close to me, I could feel the fabric of her jacket against my hand. 'Do you like living here, in the middle of nowhere? Don't you miss civilization?'

'What I like most about the wood,' I said, with heavy emphasis, 'is that it usually keeps civilization away.'

'I don't know how your ranger can bear to live out here. I'd be terrified.'

I wrestled with not wanting to give anything away, and wanting to know what the hell was going on with the bearded man. 'What makes you think he's living in the wood?'

'Well, he has a tent, a fire pit, those are kind of giveaways. That's how I found him; I saw his tent. At first I thought he was a homeless person. He looks rough as a goat. I was scared, but not as scared as I was of being lost and eaten by wolves.'

'There aren't really wolves round here. They're mostly higher up, on the east, in Jura.'

'That's such a comfort.'

'He's only out here temporarily, while the peregrine falcons are nesting,' I improvised. 'Normally he lives off the estate.' I'd have to go and see him off the premises pronto, before Denny got wind of it. Andrea turning up at our house, and a stranger living in the wood – he'd blow a gasket. He'd blow every gasket. 'So, go on, you might as well tell me. What did you come here to ask?'

'To offer you payment for the diaries.'

'No thanks. As I've said repeatedly, I'm keeping them.'

'Not to hand them over. I mean, I'll pay you to provide me with an exclusive translation.'

'Meaning what?'

'That I have the only translation, and you can't share it with your brothers, or anyone, till I've decided what parts to embargo.'

'Isn't that censorship?'

'Well, that's not how I see it,' Andrea said. 'I'm only trying to protect my mum.'

Thank goodness, we were finally at the gate. Had this walk ever taken so long? 'Here we are.'

Andrea stopped, and put her hand on my arm. 'Well?'

'I'll have to think about it.'

She took a step closer, and I could feel her breath, unpleasantly warm, on my face. 'If you're going to translate them anyway, you might as well earn good money. I'll pay. A lot. Thousands. What's to think about?'

I recognised in her tone the same certainty as when she'd confronted me at the funeral, the expectation that I'd be easily rolled over. I wondered where that idea had come from.

'I've thought about it, and the answer's no. If you go straight ahead for five minutes you'll hit the main street.' I hustled her through the gate. 'The hotel's off that, second left. Hotel des Vignes.'

'Really? That's it? *The hotel's over there.*' She stared at me, an incredulous expression on her face. 'We've known each other for more than thirty-five years, Pearl.'

'No, we've known *of* each other for more than thirty-five years. It's not the same thing. You don't know me at all. For instance, you don't know that I'm not in the least motivated by money.'

'Is there nothing I can say to persuade you?'

'You might have had more of a chance if you hadn't tried to steal them.'

'How can I steal something that rightfully belongs to my mother?'

'OK. Andrea, one more time for the cheap seats in the back. Dad. Left. Them. To. *Me.*' It was the first time that I'd really said that out loud, the first time I'd owned the notion that he'd written them for me. My conviction clearly hit home, because unexpectedly, she nodded. Her usual ramrod straight posture slumped, and there was an unreadable expression on her face.

'You're right.' There was a crack in her voice. 'Bye, Pearl. Sorry for bothering you.' She turned and walked slowly up the dark street, leaving me feeling not triumphant, as I ought to, but guilty. I thought about calling her back, but to say what? I hadn't changed my mind.

I returned to the soothing, shrouding woods. How could Andrea think we had 'known' each other all these years? As if the simple passage of time was enough, without any effort on either side.

I was some way along the path when my torch picked up a faint light-coloured shape off to the side. I followed a rutted path towards it, stepping carefully over the bumpy tree roots underfoot. The branches got increasingly tangled just above my head, but I was rewarded as I approached a tiny clearing, by the sight of a humble homestead. The shape I'd seen was a thin light-grey tarpaulin; it was thrown over branches and propped up with sticks to form a makeshift tent. Close by it were the glowing embers of a fire. I marvelled at Andrea's ability to reach this, before remembering how covered in scratches she'd been. Then my torch picked up the bearded man, lying on the ground in a sleeping bag outside the tent, and I nearly cried out. Thankfully, his eyes were closed. I took a tentative step closer and he let out a long whistling snore that made me jump back. What the hell was I doing, approaching an unknown man in the middle of the woods at midnight?

I turned to go, and almost walked into my field glasses, hanging on a tree branch. I looped them off and slipped them into my pocket, feeling the comforting familiar weight of them. Then I paused, and hung them back on the branch, without quite knowing why. I hastened away to the safety of the cottage, not looking back.

ELEVEN

CARRIE

I unlocked the door, stepped into the tiny hall, and then... stood there. It was so quiet, I could hear the clock ticking in the living room. I'd been into Mum's flat a number of times since she went into hospital, so I knew what it felt like when it was empty. But this time, the emptiness and the silence were different. This was the first time I'd been here that I knew she wouldn't ever be coming back.

I steadied myself, then went into the living room. It was tidy, as she'd left it. There was a month left on the lease and then someone else would move in. I didn't think I'd have an attachment to it. It wasn't my childhood home, after all. Mum moved here after Dad died, wanting something smaller and easier to manage, though I think it was more that she couldn't stand being in the house without him. I knew how she felt – I couldn't stand being here without her. I kept expecting her to pop her head round from the kitchen, with that big smile of hers, asking what I wanted to eat.

I packed up her clothes, in the spirit of doing the hardest job first. They still smelled like her, and I cried pretty much the whole time I sorted through them. Most of them went into boxes for the charity shop. Mum was much bigger than me, both height and width-wise, a fact she loved mentioning – 'My dress could fit two of you, Carrie!' I kept aside some of the nicer things for her friend Ruth in the flat next door, and a cream jumper for me which I'd always liked, and which had shrunk in the wash to my advantage. I also kept all her silk scarves; she was mad for them and had quite a collection. Emmie might like them when she was older.

That done, and tears, so I thought, exhausted, I flopped onto the armchair I always sat on, and looked across to the sofa, and her empty space on it. The tears turned out not to be exhausted. I swapped seats to the sofa instead, so I didn't have to look at her absence, and that's when I noticed the blue cardboard folder on the coffee table. It had my name written on it in Mum's familiar handwriting, underlined twice. Inside were various documents relating to me that had somehow remained in her possession: certificates from school, my old students' union card, some birthday cards. There was also an envelope which bore the legend: 'Important – please read, Carrie!' Inside were Mum's birth and marriage certificates, and two other pieces of paper. One was a short note, written rather formally in the same neat writing as my name on the folder, saying that she wanted to be cremated. It then detailed where she wanted her ashes scattered:

By Dad's grave.

In the sea at Severn Beach.

Somewhere exotic that I have never been before.

A big city (bigger than Bristol).

Somewhere that is special to you, Carrie.

Well, that was quite the homework assignment. Not in the least bit devastating, nope, that was simply dandy. I sat with it for a few minutes, trying to think of somewhere that was special to me, other than this flat, which was considerably better than thinking about Mum's ashes. Then I wiped my eyes, and turned to the second piece of paper. This listed three phone numbers, for Francis, Roberta and Pearl. Underneath, Mum had put three kisses. One for each of them, perhaps.

You'd think, wouldn't you, that a note about where your mother would like you to scatter her ashes would be the pinnacle of emotional anguish that notes could possibly bring. But the phone number note knocked it into second place. Because I realised that Mum had left these notes for me before she went into hospital. Before we had any conversations about any of this stuff. Before Francis died, even. She was thinking, already, as she packed her case and went to hospital, that she might not be coming back. She left her affairs in order.

The days after Mum died I trudged round in a daze. Getting out of bed felt like a major achievement. But I had to dress myself and Emmie, feed her, call people who needed to know, listen to a lot of sad people on the phone, play with Emmie while my mind was elsewhere, make more food, give thanks for children's TV so I could have a cry without Emmie seeing, make yet more food, get Emmie in the bath, read her a story and put her to bed.

Iain took Emmie on Sunday so I could get on with tidying Mum's flat, but I couldn't stop thinking about Emmie while I was there, and how she wouldn't remember Mum when she was older. It felt like a physical pain. How would I explain to her what Mum was like? No matter what I said, how descriptive I was, how many photos or videos she saw, Mum would always be someone she was told about, not someone she knew. She wouldn't even remember the butterfly kisses. Emmie scarcely had any significant important people in her life, other than me. Iain's parents lived abroad. And while Iain was around now, who knew how long he'd stay in this current engaged mode?

There was an obvious solution to Emmie's lack of grandparents, but I couldn't bear the thought; it felt so crass. 'Oh dear, one's gone, I'll just replace her.' Ugh. I knew I should talk about it, try to sort out my feelings, and it wasn't even that there was no-one to talk to. I had plenty of friends, good friends, who kept checking in on me. Henry knocked every day with a friendly smile and a small gift: a flat white from the coffee shop, a homemade cinnamon bun, a toy for Emmie that Numa had outgrown.

But I didn't feel able to talk to anyone about it, about the promise I'd made to Mum. I'd never made any secret of my origins. My friends all knew I was adopted, but they also all knew that I never wanted to do anything about finding my birth family. I'd only be doing it now for Mum, because I'd told her I would. And for Emmie, for the chance – pretty slim, realistically – that she could have another involved adult in her life. Were these good enough reasons?

Sometimes it seemed that they were, and on Sunday night after Emmie was in bed, I picked up the phone and dialled the first few digits of Roberta's number, before cancelling the call. It was, surprisingly, Iain who broke through my jumbled thoughts. I took a couple of days' bereavement leave so I could finish the flat and make funeral arrangements. He was a godsend, taking Emmie to and from the crèche. On the second afternoon of this, we met in the park for me to take Emmie home for tea, and though I'd intended to go straight away, I was so tired, and Iain's eyes so kind, that instead, I sat down on a bench and had my four millionth cry of the week. Emmie, oblivious, sat on the grass playing with Iain's keys.

He sat next to me, and made soothing noises. He didn't put

his arm round me – physical things between us were a bit awkward – but he showed willingness to listen. So I told him what Mum had asked me to do, about the three phone numbers I'd found waiting for me in her flat. I even told him I'd tried to call Roberta, the mediator at PAC-UK, but lost my nerve.

'What's to think about?' He shrugged. 'You promised your mum you would do it. So do it.'

'But what is it I'm saying? What am I asking for?'

'You're not asking for anything, Carrie-cat. Call the mediator person, ask her for the best approach. She knows your mum wanted you to make contact. See what she suggests.'

When Iain and I were together, I was never sure if his intensely logical approach to problems was because he was far cleverer than me, or far stupider. Sometimes, when we were getting on well, I was convinced that he was a genius at cutting through all the noise to get to the heart of the issue. But other times – particularly in the final throes of our relationship – it seemed that his clarity was purely because he was unable to think through all the possible consequences of an action.

I still didn't know if he was worth listening to. But his suggestion did have the benefit that doing something would be better than doing nothing. And it would stop me feeling so guilty that I hadn't yet kept my last promise to Mum.

Emmie gave Iain his keys back, and he pretended to have lost them by putting them behind his back and making a confused face. She bellowed with laughter, the world's most joyful sound.

I gave him a grateful smile. 'I wish I could see things as clearly as you.'

'Well, what's the worst that can happen?' he said.

'She might be horrible.'

'The mediator?'

'No! Obviously not. *Pearl*. She might be mean, or a drunk, or crazy. She might have hated me her whole life. I might symbolize the darkest time she went through. I might have been a product of violence, or assault. She might not want to know me.'

'Yes,' Iain said gently. He pretended to find the keys and put on an exaggeratedly surprised face that Emmie copied immediately, adorably. 'Or she might be nice. She might have always wondered about you.'

'I guess so.'

'Here's a suggestion. Why don't I take Emmie back to mine and give her supper? That gives you a couple of hours to relax, and maybe make that call.'

'Really? That's very kind.'

'No worries. If you don't do it, you'll always wonder,' he said. 'And look at it this way. You've lost both parents, you careless woman. But here's a chance to get another one. Most people don't get that opportunity.'

'Interesting take, Iain.'

I got up, then stooped down to kiss the top of Emmie's head. 'Want to go back to Dada's?' I said, and she babbled delightedly and waved her fists around, which we both took to be a 'yes'.

He smiled. 'If it was me, I'd do it fast, not think any more about it. What's that thing from *Hamlet*, 'twere best to do it quickly?'

'*Macbeth*. Hopefully this will be less of a tragedy.'

He turned his attention to Emmie, and I started walking to my car, glancing back to see him carefully putting her into the buggy. It was the first time I'd spent with Iain in ages that my teeth didn't ache from gritting.

TWELVE

PEARL

I had a disturbed night, waking several times in a cold sweat. If it wasn't confused images of Andrea climbing in through the window, a rifle slung across her shoulders, it was Denny yelling at me about spilled flour which had got in between the pages of the diaries. He hadn't yelled at all in real life, of course, but he wasn't at his friendliest last night when I got back from walking Andrea to town. To have let *that woman* across the doorstep was bad enough, he said, but to have gone out of my way to escort her to safety after she *stole* from me... well! He politely enquired if I had completely lost my mind.

I wanted to tell him that I felt sorry for her, but knew such a confession would have him fearing even more for my mental wellbeing. I apologised, and we were friends again by the time we finally went to bed.

Late nights did not suit me, and as the watery dawn sunlight filtered through the curtains I felt sleep-deprived and grumpy. Denny, always up with the lark, was already out for his usual pre-breakfast walk. I made strong coffee, and he looked glad of it when he got back. Late nights didn't really suit him, either.

'You know,' he said, cradling his cup in both hands, his voice unnaturally jolly, 'I think we'd both better stay here today, in case that lunatic Andrea comes back.'

Had he too dreamed of her climbing in through the window? But staying in would mess up the plans I'd formed for today, during my many wakeful interludes in the night.

'Actually, I want to do some outside painting,' I said. 'The trees are budding so beautifully. And I'd like to get my phone back.' This morning would be a good opportunity to ring my brothers, away from Denny's hearing, and interrogate them about who had a secret relationship with Dad. I could always pretend to lose the signal if it got too stressful.

'I don't know if that's such a good idea.' Denny got up and started washing up last night's dishes with extreme care. I knew, the way you did when you were married, that it was so he didn't have to look at me. Over his shoulder, he said, 'Andrea called you several times last night, after you'd left her in town.'

'You didn't expect her to give up, did you?' I said. 'I just won't pick up.'

'You will. I know you. You're too nice.'

'Denny, I know you've enjoyed being my fancy secretary.' I held out my hand. 'But it's time to give me my phone back.'

'My god. I won't be able to relax until that woman is back in England.' He shook his head. 'I don't know how you can, to be honest, Pearlie!'

'Don't "Pearlie" me. Right. Fine.' I chugged down my coffee. 'I'm going out. I need fresh air more than I need my phone.'

'I'll come too,' Denny said, following me into the hall, drying his hands on a towel. 'I fancy a walk.'

'You've just been for one!' I stared at him. 'What's going on? Andrea is hardly going to ambush me in the woods, is she? She's in a state herself, the poor thing.'

'OK, listen.' He stood in front of the door, his face grave. 'This isn't only about her. Please don't freak out, but there's someone camping in the woods.'

'What?!' I squeaked. Luckily, Denny misinterpreted my shock.

'I know, I can't believe it either. Don't worry, I'm sorting it.'

'Why do you think someone's camping?'

'I've had my suspicions for a few days, and this morning I found a fire pit, still warm. And some belongings scattered about. Including...' He reached into the back pocket of his jeans and pulled out my field glasses.

'Oh!'

'These are yours, aren't they?'

'They look like mine...' I took them and turned them over in my hand. 'I lost them a few weeks ago.' It was a relief to be able to tell the truth. 'This person must have found them and borrowed them.'

'Borrowed?' Denny shook his head. 'Weird way of putting it. I suppose they're also "borrowing" our wood. Anyway. I'm sure they're not there right now, but I don't want you going out on your own until I've got rid of them.'

'How are you planning to do that?'

'I've got a couple of ideas. For one, I'm going to go back this evening, when they'll likely return to their fire, and give them a friendly warning.'

'With your rifle.'

'I won't use it, Pearl. It's to show I mean it, that's all.'

'And what if they're armed? Or there's more than one of them?'

'Seems unlikely that someone who has to steal binoculars would have a gun.'

'They're field glasses,' I said, more sharply than I intended, and Denny looked surprised. While he was on the back foot, I said, as though we hadn't just had this conversation, 'Right, I'm off then.'

'What the hell? Didn't you hear me? There's a potential madman out there!'

'I think there's a potential madman in here.'

'Pearl!'

'Denny, you've always been an absolute rock. Always there for me to lean on. But I keep trying to tell you: I'm stronger now. I get stronger every day, thanks to you. I'm strong enough to face some poor frightened homeless person. I've dealt with Andrea, I went to my father's funeral, I saw all my family, and I didn't fall apart.'

'Not quite all. You didn't see the children.'

I thought of Gracie, no longer a baby, a child in school uniform, and I swallowed. 'No. But you know what? I'm ready to. I'm ready to call Eleanor, get to know Gracie before it's too late. Before I lose her, like I've lost Gina, and the other nieces and nephews.'

'You didn't fall apart, no.' Denny took my hand. 'You did really well. But it was difficult.'

'Hell yes, it was difficult! It was awful. But that's life, isn't it! Life isn't always easy. I need to get back out there. I need to take risks. I'm starting to suffocate under all these layers of cotton wool.'

Wow. I did not know that speech was coming. Nor did Denny.

'You mean I'm suffocating you.' He leaned against the wall, all the fight gone out of him.

'I want to be less cautious. I feel like I'm emerging from...'

'Fine, Pearl.' He shook his head. 'I'd prefer you don't go out without me, but it's up to you, of course. Do what you have to do.'

Had he ever said that before: do what you have to do? Keen as I was to get out, to warn the 'ranger' to vamoose, I couldn't bear leaving Denny upset. His over-protectiveness was sometimes annoying, but I knew it came from a place of love. I leaned against him, and said, 'I'm not going anywhere until I know you're OK.'

He put his arms round me. 'I'm OK. I still see you as my fragile little flower, and I know I shouldn't.'

'Aww.' I kissed his cheek. 'I'm tougher than you give me credit for.'

'Just wait a sec.' He went into the kitchen, and moments later, came back with my phone. It was ice-cold, so cold I almost dropped it.

'What the hell, Denny?' I tossed it from hand to hand, trying to warm it up. 'Did you put it in the *freezer?*'

'I couldn't stand hearing it ring any more.'

'You know there's a perfectly functional off button, right?'

'I just wanted it out of my sight. I saw the freezer, and I thought...' He looked so contrite that I started laughing.

Thankfully, the screen sprang into life, none the worse for its Arctic sojourn. 'Look. I'll keep it in my hand, your number open on it, so I can press it if anything happens.'

'All right. Don't confront anyone. Walk away quickly, but don't run.'

'You're making the camper sound like a bear. They don't usually use field glasses.'

'Just... please be careful.'

'You too. Don't put anything important in the freezer while I'm out, now.'

I kissed him again, picked up my art kitbag for authenticity's sake, and went out. As soon as I was out of sight of the cottage, the thought of the ranger staring down the barrel of Denny's rifle sent me running along the middle path to give him fair warning. But there was no sign of him. Maybe he'd got wind of Denny and cleared out.

I retraced my steps, and walked along the town path, scrolling through the calls on my still-chilly phone to find Andrea's number. She answered straight away.

'Oh, thank god!' she cried. 'I thought I'd blown it, that you'd never speak to me again.'

I reached the gate in a flash, compared to last night's long march. 'Look, do you have time to meet before your flight?'

'God, yes.'

I told her how to get to the *tabac*, and made my own way there. Vivienne looked up as I pushed the door open, and smiled broadly.

'Here she is, the dark horse!'

I walked up to the counter. 'I am?'

'You never told me you had a sister.'

'Goodness, she's not my sister. You know that. I have two brothers.'

'She calls herself your sister,' Vivienne said, starting to make my coffee. 'She was in here first thing, telling me all about it. I could barely understand one word in ten. I think she said that she had tried to steal something from you, but that can't be right? Her French is shocking.'

The bell over the door rang, and Andrea came in.

'You'll get another chance to fail to understand her now, then,' I said.

'If you nod twice, I will throw her out,' Vivienne said, pushing my cup towards me.

I ordered a coffee for Andrea and slid into a seat opposite her.

'Thanks so much for meeting,' she said. She looked slightly less intimidating than usual. Her hair was loose and her make-up sparse. 'I'm sorry again for turning up unannounced.'

'And for trying to steal the diaries,' I reminded her.

'I'm not actually sorry about that.' She smiled. 'Joking. I am really sorry. I didn't want to upset you. It was very out of character.'

'I'll take your word for that. So, when are you going home?' I knew, from Dad's 1997 diary entry, that her husband or part-ner's name began with a C. Dad had mentioned them having a baby then; she must have been quite a young mum. The child would be in his early twenties now. 'I suppose your husband will be wanting you back?'

She looked confused. 'My husband?'

'Sorry, I don't know his name. Begins with a C?'

Her face cleared. 'Are you thinking of Colin? We divorced more than fifteen years ago.'

'Oh. Sorry. But your husband now, or your boyfriend, isn't he expecting you home?' I was being nosey, I knew. I was interested in her home life, all of a sudden. 'Or your... I think you have a child?'

Very fast, the words tumbling into each other, she said, 'Yes-James-he-lives-abroad-in-Australia-he-couldn't-get-time-off-work.'

'Australia, gosh, you must miss him.'

'Yes.'

In the ensuing silence I stared at the table, wondering whether to make her the offer I had in mind. The *tabac* tables were a mottled matte silver, with bright orange plastic round the edges. Old-fashioned. They made me think of France long ago, when I was a child. Day trips to Calais with Mum, Dad, Greg and Benjy. Francs, cheap *prix fixe* menus, scalding hot chocolate, people carrying paper-wrapped baguettes under their arms.

Vivienne put a coffee down in front of Andrea, interrupting my reverie.

'Everything OK, Pearl?' she said, managing not to wince at Andrea's accent as she thanked her.

'Fine, thanks.' I had to hold myself back from doing a double nod, just to see what Vivienne throwing Andrea out would look like. When she'd gone, I braced myself, ready to speak. But Andrea's unhappy face stopped me in my tracks.

'I like it here,' she said.

'Oh, well, thanks! I do too. It's very...' I stopped, because silent tears were falling down her face. For someone I'd thought so poised, even statue-like, she sure did cry a lot.

'I miss Dad like a physical pain. He really looked out for me. I don't know what... I don't want to go back.'

'Gosh, don't you?' I tried hard to imagine what it felt like to be in her shoes. 'It must be so hard at home, with you and your mum both grieving.'

She didn't respond, just sipped her coffee, her eyes boring into me.

'Are you worried about something?'

She looked away, and I followed her gaze, but there was nothing much to see; a couple of other customers, and Vivienne leaning on the counter scrolling on her phone, pretending she wasn't looking at me and my 'sister'. I took a punt. 'Or someone? Your boyfriend?' Her eyes flickered, and in a rush of sympathy, I put my hand on hers, but she pulled away.

'Give it up with the boyfriend, already.' She fished in her bag for a tissue, and dabbed daintily at her nose. When she looked up, whatever had been on her face a moment ago had gone. She'd closed down, put the difficult thought back in its box. I knew that look. I was an expert at that look. Heck, I *invented* that look.

'I'm only worried about my poor mum's reaction, coming back empty-handed,' she said. 'It's hard being the only child. You wouldn't understand.'

'I do understand!' I felt the prickly stirrings of irritation. 'You think I don't know what it's like to feel responsible for a mother? Heavens, Andrea! I lived with mine till she died. Nursed her for the last few years of her life. You think my brothers were any help? Don't get me wrong, I loved her to bits, I'd do it again in a heartbeat, but you're not the only one who's had shit to deal with, you know?'

I sat back, stunned. Where had all *that* come from? It was clearly a day for saying what was on my mind.

Andrea's eyebrows were raised almost to the top of her head. 'Wow, Pearl. You really think...' She stopped.

'What?'

'Actually, never mind. Can I smoke in here?'

'What? No, of course not.'

'I thought the French were cool about smoking in bars.' She took out a packet of cigarettes, a French brand.

'It was banned years ago.'

'They let me last night, in the hotel.'

'Surely that was out on the terrace?'

'Oh, I suppose it was outside, now I think of it.' She tapped a cigarette out of the box, and for one startled moment I thought she was going to light it. But she just fiddled with it, rolling it between her fingers.

'Since when do you smoke?'

'Since last night.' She grinned. 'Well, I smoked once or twice in my teens but Mum...'

She stopped, and I finished for her, 'Found out?'

'Yes.' She looked down at her hand, at the cigarette. 'Made me give up.'

'Well, it is a dangerous habit.'

'That's part of the appeal, don't you think? Flirting with death.'

Who was this woman? I'd thought she was my *bête noire*, my nemesis. Daddy's Best Daughter. The steel-eyed princess in the fluffy mules. But that perfect image of her I'd always carried round in my head did not at all fit with her trying to steal the diaries, crying all over the place, randomly starting to smoke, and being all teen-nihilist about it.

There was so much I didn't know about her. 'Do you live with your mum?' I asked.

'House opposite.'

'Wow, that's handy. How did you manage that?'

'I'm an estate agent, Pearl. I waited till one came up in the street. I did live farther away when I was married, but it was difficult, having to keep driving backwards and forwards all the time. Mum's glad I'm so near.' She drained her cup and stood up, her face bleak. 'I suppose I'd better be going.'

I felt even sorrier for her than I had last night, when she cried on our doorstep. She'd had my father, yes, but now she'd lost him as comprehensively as I had. And while I'd had years to process my loss, hers was still red-raw.

'Wait a minute, Andrea. I wanted to tell you that I *will* give you and Jeanie first look, when I've translated the diaries. Exclusive, like you said.'

She sat back down immediately. 'You will?'

'I'll show you before I show my brothers, or anyone.' I owed Andrea and Jeanie precisely nothing, and my brothers would kill me if they knew. But actually, I didn't owe my dear brethren anything, either. All those years when it was just me and Mum, where were they? Andrea, on the other hand, hadn't actually done anything to me. Sure, she got to grow up with my dad, but that wasn't her fault, or her choice.

She dropped the unsmoked cigarette into her coffee cup. 'Pearl, you have no idea what this means to me.' She clasped my hand, and I let her, though hers was clammy.

'To be clear, I'm not promising to redact anything,' I said. 'I'll show you the translation first, but after I've given you time to read it, I'll pass it on to my brothers and I'm not going to remove anything unless there's a really good reason for it. Understand?'

'All right. I don't need to tell Mum that part.' She nodded slowly. 'So, how much?'

'How much, what?'

She laughed. 'How much do you want to be paid?'

'I already told you. I don't want your money.'

'Well, what—'

'I want what you mentioned at the funeral,' I said in a low

tone, feeling ridiculous. It sounded like a line from a mafia movie.

'I can't hear you, Pearl. You do have a quiet voice. Mum used to call you Little Miss Mouse.'

What a mean nickname. I wondered if Andrea really thought it was about my voice, rather than the more likely explanation that I'd been so easily pushed around that time I visited them. I looked past her, to Vivienne, who smiled encouragingly.

More loudly, I said, 'I want you to tell me the truth. Anything to do with my dad's life that I want to know, you have to answer honestly.'

If I was going to allow myself to plunge into Dad's story – if I was going to be forced to see the world as he saw it, through his diaries – it would be useful to get a second opinion, even from someone as biased as Andrea.

'Of course. Do you already have something in mind?'

I opened my mouth to say, 'Yes, tell me, Andrea, were either of my brothers in touch with Dad?' I'd been planning to ask this from the moment I walked in here. But something stopped me. Instead, I said, 'Why do you think Dad kept the diaries at his church?'

'I have absolutely no idea, sorry. Probably because there was a quiet room for him to write in.' She looked at her watch. 'If I leave now, I can get a flight back tonight.'

I didn't know her, not at all. But I did know what someone looked like when they didn't want to do something.

'Why don't we get another coffee and sit outside? Then you can smoke if you like,' I said.

'My flight...'

'You look like you want to miss it.' When she didn't answer, I called over to Vivienne for two more coffees, and we took them outside to the green metal tables in front of the *tabac*. It was a fine place to sit, soak up the May sunshine and watch people come and go across the square. Andrea put on her sunglasses and took out another cigarette. I could see from the inelegant way she held it that she really had only taken it up in the last twenty-four hours. I had a dozen questions about that, but I kept quiet.

'I can't stop thinking about Dad, you know,' she said.

'I'm sure.'

'I was thinking this morning about when he got Snoopy, our dog. I'd wanted one for years, and Dad told me I could share him. We used to walk him together, most days. He was a wonderful father.' She saw my eye-roll, and said, 'Shit. Sorry. That was insensitive.'

'I'm trying very hard to be glad for you. I wish he could have been a wonderful father to me. Actually, before he left, he was a pretty good dad. It's not easy to remember that, though.'

She puffed smoke into the air, and we were silent for a while, preoccupied with our separate thoughts.

'Remember when you came to our house in London, when we were kids?' she said abruptly. 'I'm sorry I made you cry.'

'God, don't be daft. It wasn't your fault. We were both so young.'

'I don't think I had any idea what was going on, really.'

'I didn't, either.'

'I owe you, honestly. To let me have first look at the diaries, you don't know what that means to me.' She sent a puff of smoke into the air. 'Ooh, I did a smoke ring nearly!'

I laughed, and said, 'What is it you think is in them?'

Andrea's Jackie O sunglasses obscured most of her face, so I couldn't be completely sure that she'd heard me. She didn't answer, anyway. Instead she said, 'Dad encouraged me to keep a diary, you know.'

'Did he?'

'He said it was a great way of processing your thoughts, like talking to a sympathetic, non-judgmental friend.'

I thought of her at the wake, her startled 'Oh!' when Mr

Claymore said where Dad had kept the diaries, and realised that of course, she had known all along about their existence. But she hadn't known where he'd hidden them.

'Did you look for the diaries, after he died?'

'Yes. Turned the house upside-down when Mum was out,' she said. 'Can't believe I didn't think of looking at the church. He was there all the time.'

'It sounds like you're the one who really wanted the diaries, more even than your mother.'

She looked at me thoughtfully. 'Smart of you. Yes, I want to know what's in them. Find out Dad's take on, well, everything. Mum would probably prefer not to know.' She blew another 'smoke ring', then said, 'I'll get the morning flight. I fancy another evening on that hotel terrace, with some nice French wine. I deserve a couple of nights off.'

She stood up, grinding her cigarette with her heel, and put a fifty-euro note on the table. Lucky Vivienne.

'Thanks, Pearl. I really am grateful, you've been so kind.' She held out her hand, and we shook formally, like business associates, then she clicked away on her heels. I shook my head; she was an enigma and no mistake.

I made my way back to the wood, my head swimming with her hints and half-confessions that didn't add up to anything coherent. I was so completely in another place that it took me quite a lot longer than it should have to realise that I was pushing at the gate without getting anywhere. I took a step back, and to my astonishment discovered that there was a padlock on it. Of course – this was doubtless one of Denny's 'ideas' for dealing with the trespasser in the wood. He'd grabbed his chance to fulfil his dream: lock the wood, keep the outside world away even more effectively. How utterly maddening. I rang him, but it went to voicemail. I left a terse message, then stared at the padlock. It was heavy duty, not the sort I could pick with a hairclip, not that I had a hairclip on me. Or knew how to pick locks.

I glanced round to make sure no-one was witness to my forth-coming foolishness, then I threw my bag over the top of the gate and started to climb. The gate wasn't particularly tall, maybe two and a half metres, but it was old and rusty and the higher part didn't have much in the way of footholds. Plus, I was fifty-two. The last time I climbed anything, the Bay City Rollers were in the charts.

It was surprisingly all right on the way up, but then I got to the top and stupidly, looked down. Wow, it was a really a long way off the ground. I was hit with a wave of dizziness. I closed my eyes and clung on tight. The moment passed, but when I opened my eyes, I was still on top of a high gate with no clear way down.

'Help!' I said, but very quietly, because I didn't really want anyone to hear. I tried to assess the height of the drop realisti-cally. If I jumped, would I be more likely to break my ankle, hip or kneecap? As I considered my options, my phone rang. This wasn't the ideal moment for a chat, but I answered it in case it was Denny.

'Pearl?'

Greg. Great. Sure, he was certainly on my list of people to talk to, but perhaps not right now.

'Yeah, hi Greg,' I said, all casual. 'I'm, er, kind of in the middle of something, can I ring you back?'

'No you bloody well cannot! Do you know how many times I've called? Why does bloody Denny always answer your phone? I've spoken to him more often than my wife this week!'

'I promise I'll ring back...'

'No way, you're always fobbing me off. I need to talk to you about the diaries.'

I slipped slightly, and gave a startled scream.

'Sorry, Pearl, don't get upset. I know you probably don't

even want to think about them yet. I don't mean to "trigger" you or whatever the phrase is, but I'm convinced it's far too much of a burden for you. I'll pay for someone to translate them. It's not right asking you to delve into all that crap of Dad's, not fair on you when you're already vulnerable...'

'Is that what I am?' I got a better grip on the gate.

'That came out wrong. Just, you know. You've got a lot on your plate.'

I was so high up I wondered if I could see the roof of our house, but I couldn't; it was probably too far into the wood, too surrounded by tall trees. 'You needn't worry about me. I've already started reading them.'

'Oh, yes? Er, well done! What are they like?'

'They're very interesting. There are a few things I don't understand, of course.'

'That's the shorthand, I expect. It must be years since you—'

'The key thing I don't understand, Greg, is how Dad knew so much about my life, when he hadn't spoken to me for almost forty years...'

There was a noise below me and I leaned forward to see what it was – a bad idea, as I was already rather unstable. I clung on grimly with my one hand, and as I righted myself into a less wobbly position, I saw that there was a person on the wood side, walking towards me. I'd so hoped to avoid having any witnesses.

'Damn it!' I said.

'Oh my god, what's wrong?' Greg said.

'Talk later.' I hung up and shoved the phone in my pocket.

The man, the so-called ranger, reached the gate and looked up with an amused expression. 'So I'm not the only one thwarted by the gate being locked.'

'I wanted to check out the view from up here,' I said airily. 'Very nice.'

He held up his arms. 'I'll catch you.'

'You will?'

He shrugged, looking slightly more laid back than I'd like under the circumstances. 'Sure.'

I supposed I couldn't stay up there forever. Without thinking too much, I jumped off the gate into his arms. He was strong and hairy, and smelled of wood smoke, as well as another scent, more chemical, that I couldn't immediately identify. There was an uncomfortable moment when we were physically much closer than I think either of us wanted to be, then he gently set me onto the ground.

'Thank you,' I said.

'No problem.' He gestured to the gate. 'Do you know when it will be unlocked?'

'I'm sorry. My husband put it on to keep you out. I have to warn you that he's going to come looking for you tonight, and won't be very friendly if he finds you.'

'I don't have much chance to leave now,' he said, gesturing at the gate.

'That is a good point,' I said. 'I'll try to do something about that, OK? And then you can go.'

He nodded, and walked off the path into the trees; in moments he had disappeared. I headed back towards the cottage, and was halfway there when my phone rang again. Probably Greg, or Denny? But it was an unknown number. I answered, feeling impatiently ready to give a cold-caller a very hard time, pumped full of unspent adrenaline from my bizarre morning. 'Yes?'

'Oh, er, hello, is that Pearl?' It was an English woman's voice.

'Yes, what is it?'

'Er, gosh. Is this a bad time? Sorry to bother you...'

'Whatever it is, I'm not interested. I haven't been in an accident that wasn't my fault, I don't need any new windows. You people, honestly!' What was the point of having an unsmart phone if I was still going to get pestered like this?

'I'm sorry, I'm not trying to sell you anything. I'm, er, I'm connected to you. God, what I mean is...'

'Who is this?'

'Sorry. I'm Carrie. Caroline Haskett. What I'm trying to say is, Francis wanted me to contact you.'

'Francis, my father?' I stopped walking. Caroline Haskett... the name rang a bell.

'Yes, he wanted me to make contact, and my mother, she's...'

'What's this about, exactly?' I remembered where I'd heard that name: one of the friends Francis left money to. Hugh Sargeant, the churchwarden, and Caroline Haskett.

'It's, er, this sounds silly, sorry.' She coughed. 'I'm your, er, god, I don't know how else to put it. I'm your, er, daughter.'

3RD NOVEMBER 1982

Terrible, upsetting day.

The phone rang when we were eating supper. J answered, said I was busy, hung up. Told me it was PP, that she'd been calling all day and needed to learn she couldn't get her own way about everything all the time. I said, actually she hasn't really had her own way about very much lately, has she? J not pleased! She is quite the firecracker, not always the easy-going woman I met at church.

I went to the phone, but to my shock, J pulled the socket out of the wall and took the phone upstairs to the bedroom. I followed, asking what she was playing at. She said I was at my former family's beck and call and it had to stop. That we had been together almost a year and I was still putting them first. She got properly angry, shouting, said what with going to see G in Bristol all the time (for the record, twice), and speaking to B and PP on the phone, I was not there properly for her. She put the phone in the wardrobe, said I could call tomorrow. I was angry but she was really crying. I knew she felt second best even though that's not what I think at all. I was concerned for A, who ran up to her room when the shouting started. I went up later to see if

she was all right, and brought her plate up to her, though J told
me just to leave her be.

I finished supper though I had lost my appetite, and all the
time I worried about PP. It wasn't like her to call so much, she
was always very contained. J coaxed A down to watch their soap
opera, and I said I was going for a walk. I went into town, to the
phone box outside Boots. Unfortunately Ivy picked up. Not my
day. Hung up. Waited five minutes, tried again. This time it was
PP, thank god. Soon as she heard it was me, she started crying.
Took a long time to get it out of her.

Long story short, she is pregnant.

She kept saying she wanted an abortion. I of course was
horrified at the thought of my little girl in this terrible situation,
but tried to be practical. I asked a lot of questions but I was none
the wiser about whether the boy in question knew, nor how many
weeks pregnant she was. When I asked why she wasn't getting
help from her mother she couldn't really answer, but putting
together the little she said, I got the impression that Ivy had
rather let herself go, mentally and physically. I had no idea Ivy
was in such a state, disgraceful to fall apart like that with children to look after.

PP said she wanted me to go to the doctor with her, to give
my permission, but I knew I couldn't promise. It would be so
difficult to arrange. And abortion! All abortions are tragedies,
that's the Church's teaching. I said she should talk to a doctor
about her options but she said she had to go.

I stood in the phone box until a woman knocked on the glass
and told me to get out as she wanted to use it.

THIRTEEN

PEARL

My phone was pressed hard against my ear, my fingers taut and strained. I focused on a small twig on the ground.

'I'm sorry, what did you say?'

The woman said, 'God, maybe I should have called Roberta after all.'

'Who did you say you were?' The twig had a tiny pink bud on it.

'My name's Caroline. Carrie. Well. Your, er, daughter. Sounds weird saying it. Don't worry, I don't want anything, it's only—'

I hung up, and turned my phone off. It took several tries because my hands were shiny with sweat. Instead of deep-freezing my phone, I ought to smash it with a hammer and bury the pieces in the wood. I bent down and picked up the twig. If I put it in water, the bud might open.

I got home. I don't remember walking there but I must have done, and I must have put on the kettle because it startled me when it whistled. I took a cup of mint tea into the garden, sat on a lounger and stared up into the sky.

My name's Caroline.

A pair of eagles were lazily circling, looking for prey. Their mournful calls made me think of seagulls, of long walks by the sea when I was a teenager in Bristol. The eagles were beautiful. I thought they might be circaète Jean-le-Blanc, but I'd been neglecting my bird studies lately. I followed their trajectory, thinking how I could draw them, plotting the lines and arcs in my head. I couldn't say how long I'd been doing that when Denny hurtled in, hair askew, bringing me back to reality.

'I've been phoning and phoning!' he cried.

'You and everybody else,' I said. 'Look at those birds, won't you? Stunning.'

'You said in your voicemail that you were locked out!'

'Indeed I was.' I picked up my tea, but it was stone-cold.

'I thought you were staying in the wood! Painting, you said! I didn't mean to lock you out!'

'I guess you did mean to lock me in, then?'

'No! Well, yes! Not really. Oh, god! I only wanted to keep the trespasser and Andrea out, and keep you safe.' He sank down onto the chair next to me. 'Why didn't you tell me you were leaving the wood?'

I'm Caroline. I'm your daughter.

'I didn't know I had to, Denny.' I looked back up into the sky. One bird had disappeared, but the other was still making lazy circles through the clouds. 'I had no idea I needed your permission.'

'You don't! I'm so sorry. How did you even get back in?'

'Climbed the gate.'

'*Climbed the gate?!* You could have broken your neck!'

'I did try to call you.'

'I couldn't find my phone this morning, I was all at sixes and sevens after that sodding Andrea.'

'Tried the freezer?'

'Not funny.'

'You're not going to like this, either. I met sodding Andrea in town.'

'For god's sake!' Denny slapped his hand down on the table, and I had to grab my cup to stop it spilling. 'After she plundered your belongings like an animal!'

'Plundered?! Is she a pirate?'

'This whole insane circus has to stop. I hate to think what this is doing to your state of mind.'

Thank god he didn't know the true state of my mind right now. 'You shouting at me isn't all that great for it, either.'

'I'm sorry.' He took a breath, and in a quieter voice said, 'Pearl. I don't want to always be the one to remind you about your nervous breakdown.'

'And I don't want to always be the one to remind you that Doctor Haywood told the other doctor off for calling it that. He said that "nervous breakdown" is not a helpful term for emotional distress.'

'Whatever you call it, they both said very clearly that you should try to avoid stressful situations.'

'They did, but they also put a time limit on it. Remember? They said "for the next few months". In December it will be six years.'

He looked away.

'They didn't mean for the rest of my life. I'm doing well.'

Shimmying over the gate, leaping into a strange man's arms, facing Andrea eye to eye. Going to my father's funeral, seeing Eleanor, asking about Gracie, and not needing a fortnight hiding under my duvet to recover.

My name is Caroline... Well yes, apart from that, I was definitely doing well.

'You are doing well,' he said, staring at the ground. 'Way better than me.'

'Ah, Denny.' I reached for his hand. 'I'm sorry. Have you thought any more about—'

'I don't need to see anyone, I've told you.'

'I just think it would help. Even a few sessions. It really helped me. It would be good for you to have someone to talk to other than me.'

'It's not my thing, that's all. I don't need to talk to anyone else.'

I stood up, too restless to sit any longer. I wanted to be on my own. 'Can I have the padlock key, please? I'll get a copy made in town.'

He stared up at me. 'I don't think...'

'Denny, I'm telling you, you don't need to worry about me.'

'I do worry, I will worry, worrying is what I do.' He handed me the key, then turned away.

For the second time today I took the town path. How quickly my well-established routines had been upended. All it took was for my crazy father to die and start messing me about from beyond the grave.

It was annoying having to unlock and relock the gate, and I was determined that once Andrea and the ranger were safely gone, I'd convince Denny to remove it. Jean in the post office cut two spare keys for me, then I walked past Andrea's hotel. I got as far as the door, then I thought, for what purpose? With *that* phone call, everything had shifted, and Andrea and my father were no longer top of my panic list.

Back in the wood, I made my way to the ranger's tent, but there was still no sign of him. I found an old envelope in my bag, and scribbled on it: *This is for you. I recommend a change of venue for the next couple of nights.* I signed it: *your grateful friend who you caught.* I put the spare padlock key in the envelope, and left it in the entrance of the tent. After a moment's thought, I put the field glasses in there too.

. . .

Another night of stressful break-in dreams. This time it wasn't Andrea coming through the window, but a young woman with long mermaid hair. I knew exactly who she was. Denny went into the spare room at some point, which I realised when I woke up with a feeling of doom at four thirty a.m. At breakfast he told me I was flailing around and nearly knocked him out of bed. He called me 'slugger' and I managed a feeble smile.

'What were you dreaming about?'

'I can't remember,' I said.

'Those sodding diaries,' he muttered as he put a large coffee in front of me, 'stirring everything up.'

He was right. They were stirring up everything I thought I'd known. Reminding me of things I'd forgotten, revealing something hidden, offering a new take. It was a history lesson with two differing perspectives: mine and Dad's.

Today I was drawn, lamb to the slaughter, to the earliest volume: 1981–1982. Where else would I go? *I'm your daughter.* There were doubtless plenty of painful things in these diaries, spelled out in Dad's scratchy, merciless shorthand. But this was the big one. The time when, hopelessly young, several months pregnant, and at my wits' end, I called on him for help.

I read as far as his justifications for not being there for me in my hour of need, then stopped. It was hard to connect that time, the sick uncertainty of it all, with the woman's voice on the phone. *My name is Caroline.* How jealous Jeanie was of his previous marriage! It sounded just awful, and I felt a rush of sympathy for Andrea, running upstairs to hide when the arguments got too much. I suppose Jeanie was insecure. She and Dad weren't married at this point, after all; the divorce didn't come through for several years. Maybe Jeanie was scared he would go back to Mum. Well, she needn't have worried – she won that one.

I put the diary aside and googled the organisation mentioned in the lawyer's letter, the one Dad wanted me to have the number for: PAC-UK. I already knew what I was going to find, but even so, their homepage still hit me like a brick. *PAC-UK: Specialist advice and support for all affected by adoption.*

So Dad had been in touch with them, and through them, had made contact with...

I went downstairs in search of emergency coffee. When it was brewing, Denny came in, safety goggles perched on his head, drawn by the aroma.

'Been reading the diaries again?' he said, in the tone he'd adopted whenever we spoke of them, which made it sound like I was doing something shameful. It *did* feel a bit shameful, rootling through someone's past, even if most of that past turned out to be my own.

'They're extremely compelling,' I said, reaching for a levity I wasn't feeling. '"One should always have something sensational to read on the train." Oscar Wilde.'

He studied me thoughtfully. 'OK, Oscar. Well, I'm off to the chapel now, taking some of the wood over. Don't, er...'

'Don't spend all day morbidly reading the diaries? Blast! That was my plan.'

When he'd gone, I turned on my phone and then, almost before I'd decided I was going to, pressed Greg's number. It rang twice, and Eleanor answered. 'Pearl! How lovely.'

If I could have got away with it, I'd have hung up there and then; her husky Galway voice made me sad. I blurted, 'Is Greg there?'

'He's in the shower. I picked up when I saw it was you. Can I help, my love?'

I closed my eyes at the affection in her gentle voice. She was beyond kind when things went wrong between us. I would probably never know everything that she did for me.

'Ellie, I need to ask him something... maybe you don't know about it, about Greg and my dad, but I've been reading the diaries, and Greg—'

'I'll get him.' I heard her put the phone down on a table. Oh-*kay* then! While I waited, I thought about PAC-UK. Roberta must work there, be some kind of intermediary. Dad had mentioned her in the diaries, and so had... I was on the verge of hanging up and calling Roberta instead when I heard hurried footsteps down the line, then Greg, breathless as he snatched up the phone.

'Pearl?'

'Are you standing there in a towel? This can keep for another time.'

'It can't. Talk to me.'

I made a conscious effort to slow my breathing. 'It's either you or Benjy, and I think it's you.'

'What's me?'

'One of you was in touch with Dad for years. Maybe the whole time. One of you kept Dad informed about what was going on with the rest of us.' I could hear myself echoing back as I gabbled. 'In some ways it's such a Benjy-type stunt – you know how impossible it's always been to understand what the hell goes through his mind. But he can't keep secrets to save his life. And anyway, he didn't try to take ownership of the diaries. You did. Repeatedly. So I think it's you. Tell me it's you. Tell me it's not you.'

'Yes.'

'Which yes? Yes, you were in touch with Dad?'

'Yes. I'm sorry.'

The silence went on and on. Though I'd already guessed it must be him, I was still thoroughly shocked. I thought about his several attempts to 'relieve' me of the burden of the diaries. He must have known he'd be all over the pages, spilling my secrets to our father. He must, realistically, have expected this call.

'What do you want to know?' he asked, finally.

What did he *think* I wanted to know? I wanted to know *why* he was in touch with Dad after he treated us so badly, but even more than that, I wanted to know why the hell he had never told me. Why he'd lied to me for all these years. Why everything felt like one lie after another.

I started with something slightly easier. 'When did you last see him?' I said. 'Before he was in hospital, I mean.'

'God! He never wanted to meet. Probably nearly ten years ago.'

'What did he look like then?'

'Old. Not how you'd remember him. He was about seventy. Knackered. Thinning grey hair. Jeanie was away somewhere, and he and I met in London. He was not the full shilling, to be honest. Restless and uncomfortable. I wondered if he was ill. I bought him lunch. He asked after you and Benjy a lot.'

All at once, the energy that had propelled me this far went out of me, like air out of a punctured balloon. For my entire adulthood, I'd thought we were all estranged from Dad, but it turned out that was a lie – Greg had been a double agent for more than thirty years. It was actually only me and Benjy that Dad was estranged from. Or maybe he was mates with Benjy all along too, and it was just me. Old muggins. Always out of the loop.

I needed to get off the phone, stop listening to this liar. I had more important things to deal with. Like the fact that *my daughter* had called me.

'I'll talk to you another time,' I said.

'What? Hey, Pearl, wait—'

I ended the call and turned off my phone.

Another restless night, half-dreams of betrayals and break-ins. In the morning, I put the diaries on a shelf and turned my back on them. After a glance at my emails and phone messages – Greg devastated, Eleanor conciliatory, making it clear that she knew about this all along, the traitor – I ignored them too. Let them sweat. I focused on my neglected appointments book for the rest of the day, and in the early evening, Denny and I took a very pleasant walk in the woods, arm in arm, looking out for blossom and new growth. Mercifully, there was no sign of the ranger, as I'd now come to think of him; Denny hadn't found him the other night and assumed that he'd been successfully locked out.

I turned off thoughts of the outside world. I allowed myself to think of Caroline, but that was all, and I promised myself I wouldn't contact her until I was in the right head space. It was all too much, right now. Denny and I both kept things light, as we had learned to do in times of stress, and if I looked up a few times during our evening meal to see his worried eyes on mine, well, I was used to that.

On Friday morning I decided to do some painting before my appointment with Mme Remard. Art was part of the mental wellness routine Dr Haywood had devised for me, along with daily walks in nature and keeping to a regular routine. I only had five or six sessions with him before we left for France, but the things he said had really stayed with me. I took the middle path to my favourite place, noticing with pleasure that the canopy of leaves overhead was thicker, the trees bursting into their spring glory. I sat down against the broad beech, and painted the tree trunks opposite me in watercolours, detailing the moss growing up them, the whorls in the bark. As I worked I started to feel properly calm instead of fake calm, and could feel myself come slowly back into focus. My brain loosened, not thinking about anything at all. Just the trees, birdsong, and my brush, dipping in and out of the water pot, in and out of the paint.

I wasn't sure how long I'd been there before I sensed a

change in the air, something different, and I slowly surfaced to register a chemical smell. Chlorine. I looked up, and saw the ranger walking towards me.

'Thanks for the padlock key,' he said. He sat on the ground opposite me. 'I was worried about being trapped in here.'

'I'm sure you could climb that gate, no problem.'

He laughed. 'I am not fond of heights myself. And I am bulky.' He indicated his body, and I saw that Andrea's initial impression of him was right: he was wearing a lot of layers. 'There's a lot of staying still when you live outside, chills you to the bone, so I wear all my clothes at once.'

I noticed that his hair was damp. 'Have you been at the pool?'

'Yes, I go every morning. It's good exercise. And I like to keep clean. I am not a hobo.'

I smiled, because he looked exactly like a hobo, with his long damp hair and his shaggy beard.

'Thanks for the warning about your husband.' He pointed to my painting. 'You are an artist, I see.'

'Oh, not really. I enjoy it, it's therapeutic.' I put my pad down. 'Where have you been staying?'

'The park on the far side of town. Not such fine accommodation as here. I'm back now.'

'Sooner or later he'll stumble across you again, or at least your tent.'

'I'll take it down each morning. I have an excellent hiding place.' He smiled. 'I'm good at not being seen. And you two, you are the most regimented people in the whole of France. Maybe the world. You each go the same ways on the same days, like clockwork.'

'Oh! I had no idea you were watching us.'

'Really? A fellow camps in a private wood for three months, you think he won't keep tabs on the owners?'

'You've been here three *months*?'

'Until you started messing with your pattern, it was easy to stay out of your way.' He looked at me steadily. 'I'm grateful for your warning, and for the key, but why are you helping me?'

'Well, because I...' I stopped. Why *was* I helping him? I really wasn't sure. I only knew there was something about him that struck a chord with me. Of course, I couldn't say that. Instead, I said, 'You helped me when I was stuck on the gate. I'm just repaying the favour.'

'I know the woods are private. You are a lucky lady, to own land. I'd stay forever if I could. But don't worry, that's not my plan.' He blew air out in a long stream. 'I am almost ready for my next move.'

'Is that move difficult?'

'The most difficult of my life.'

'So do you have to do it?' I leaned forward eagerly, hoping he'd say no, that we didn't always have to face the difficult things that awaited us; that it could be just as courageous to turn away. The phone call was burning inside me. 'You could avoid it.'

'Of course I have to do it.' He stood up, his habitual half-smile no longer there. 'We have to do the hard thing, even if it takes us a while.'

I glanced at my watch. 'Oh no, I'm going to be late.'

'You're going into town?'

'Yes, I've got an appointment.' I hastily gathered up my things.

'I've found a quick route to the gate from here. You want me to show you?'

'Oh! Yes, please.'

He set off, quite fast, zig-zagging through the overgrown scrub.

'Are you going into town too?' I asked, panting a little, following behind him.

'No. I only go in first thing to the pool, when no-one else is about.'

The pool didn't open until ten, I knew; he must be breaking in in order to swim. I think he realised I'd worked this out, because he hurriedly said, 'Where is your appointment?'

'At the big cream villa on the edge of town.'

'The Remard house, with the dark green shutters?'

'That's the one.'

He walked even faster. I was beginning to wonder if it was actually all that sensible to be alone in the wood with a strange man, when he turned a corner and to my surprise, I saw that we were almost at the gate. Before I could thank him, he disappeared back into the trees, and moments later I heard my name called. Turning, I saw Denny some distance off, waving. My heart beating – that was a close call – I waved back and waited for him to catch me up.

'How was the painting?' he said, as we walked to the gate together.

'Good. I'll show you later. Where are you going?'

'Need more oak planks.'

I wasn't sure who saw first that the padlock was unlocked and hanging open.

'What the hell?' Denny said, unhooking it.

Keeping my face neutral, I said, 'Oh! I'm so silly, I must have not locked it yesterday.'

'I've been out since then, though,' he said. 'Last night, remember, to get the beeswax out of the van.'

'Oh, perhaps you forgot to lock it, then. Easily done.' Oh god, I was gaslighting him.

He frowned, turning the padlock over in his hands. 'That was careless of me, I'm sorry.'

'Well, don't worry,' I said, hoping he didn't see the sweat breaking out all over my face. 'I'd better go, or I'll be late.'

He kissed me distractedly, and I walked away, attempting a

light-hearted stroll. When I turned back he was still looking at the padlock. Damn! I'd have to tell the ranger he needed to find the courage for his next move sooner than he'd planned.

After the morning's excitement, it was nicely calming to stand in front of Mme Remard's gilt-edged mirror and comb her hair through. I was so grateful to her for always being the same that I ate more of the dreaded *bichon au citron* pastries than usual. Yep, still awful. Vivienne came in, hoping to wheedle a quick fringe trim.

'Your sister, have you spoken to her lately, Mme Fleur?' Mme Remard said, looking at me in the mirror. 'Vivienne says she burgled you, is that right?'

Poor old Andrea, forever tarred as a thief, in this ornate room at least. 'Not really,' I said. 'No, I haven't talked to her but I have been in contact with my older brother. He and I have been estranged for a while, which made us both sad.' I didn't mention that we now seemed to be re-estranged, but even so, there was a ripple of puzzlement in the room.

Vivienne, frowning, said '*Etranger?*' which meant 'stranger'. She'd misheard my use of '*estrangé*'; surely it was a French word? But when I looked in my dictionary later, I realised I'd made it up.

I substituted a literal translation: 'Err, *quelqu'un qui a perdu le contact avec sa famille.*'

Vivienne and Mme Remard exchanged a look in the mirror, and Mme Remard said, 'You must be sad about not having seen your father for so long, and now he is gone?'

'I don't know. I suppose I've been wondering...' I put down the comb, because I was aware that both sets of concerned eyes were on me. To avoid meeting them, I began mixing the dye. 'Well, my father walked out on us when we were children. But I've discovered that my older brother kept in touch with him. And I feel...'

'Cheated?' Vivienne said.

'Not exactly...'

'You wonder if you made a mistake in allowing the separation to continue,' Mme Remard said, so kindly that one or two of my welling tears spilled over.

'Yes,' I said. 'I didn't realise I had a choice about that, but Greg clearly did.'

'We don't all have the same choices.' Mme Remard waved away my advancing tint brush, and got slowly to her feet. 'Come with me.'

'Adeline,' Vivienne said, but Mme Remard shook her head.

'It is good to talk about these things, yes?'

Puzzled, I followed her out of the room, and walked behind her as she clambered laboriously up her huge staircase. I'd not been up here before, and was interested to see that the first-floor hall was lined with silver-framed photographs. Mme Remard stopped at a picture of a handsome young man with cropped hair and a broad smile, wearing graduation robes. The boy looked like Mme Remard: the slightly too-large chin, the lively brown eyes. He must be her son, but I didn't remember her ever mentioning him.

She said, 'It was not long after this picture was taken, a year, maybe two, that he left.'

'Where did he go?'

'Ran to Paris with a foolish woman who should have known better.' She lowered herself slowly, and with a fair amount of grunting, into a sitting position on the top stair. Her back to me, she said, 'He was twenty-two then. Next week he will be forty.'

'And he hasn't been back?'

She waved a hand, still not looking round. 'Serge was a smart boy. Graduated with special honours, you know. Scientist. After university he taught at the school here, and was preyed on by the deputy principal, a married woman, older.' Mme Remard extracted a tissue from her sleeve, and spat into it. 'Evil woman.'

'They ran away?'

'I told him not to ruin his life, that she was looking for an escape from her dead marriage, but he was in love, of course. Furious that I didn't approve, said I was ruining his life. Oh dear.' She used the tissue to dab her eyes. 'He took only one bag. I thought he would come back. But no. And then, when his father died, I wrote to the address I had for him, but he and the woman were no longer there.'

'Did you try to find him?'

Vivienne came up the stairs, and sat a few steps lower than Mme Remard, twisting round to see us. 'Oh, we looked everywhere!' she said.

'Vivi and I went to Paris,' Mme Remard said. 'We walked every day for a month, hoping to see his face.'

'Every night we went from bar to bar, never stopping.' Vivienne stretched out her hand and Mme Remard patted it.

'Oof,' Mme Remard said, struggling to get up, accepting help from Vivienne and me with old-school dignity. As we walked down the stairs, she said, 'I'm sorry it is too late for you and your father, as it is too late for Serge and me.'

'It's not too late for you and Serge,' Vivienne said.

'Oof,' Mme Remard said again, an all-purpose word, which this time meant, 'Don't be a sentimental fool.'

I finished doing her roots, then trimmed Vivienne's fringe, working as quickly as my standards would allow. I felt all at once oppressed by the stuffy house and its dusty layer of secrets, and was glad to leave. Vivienne walked out with me, heading for her shift at the *tabac*.

'That was incredible,' she said. 'Adeline never talks about him.'

'I'm sorry if I upset her. I feel bad, raking all that up.'

'No, she's right; it's good to speak of it now and then.'

'Did you know him? Serge?'

'Everyone knew him. He was gorgeous. When he got the job at our school, oh, us girls nearly died.'

'Was he a good teacher?'

'Who knows? You'd have to ask one of the boys.' She smiled dreamily. 'I planned to ask him to dance at the end-of-year dance.'

'Your teacher?!' I said, mock-shocked.

'Ach, I was sixteen and leaving school, he was only a few years older.' She shook her head. 'But of course, by then he'd already run off with that ball-breaker, Mme Odee. Scandal of the year.'

'Oof,' I said.

I made my way back through the wood, going the new way the ranger showed me this morning, cutting in and out of the trees. Rather to my surprise, I found myself back at my canopy in record time. I sat against the tree, watching the sunlight dappling on my arms while I worked up my nerve. Then I took out my phone. Two difficult conversations with two people I had hung up on.

I looked through my recent calls, and once again, my finger hovered over a certain number. But my heart immediately started racing unpleasantly. I thought about Mme Remard saying, 'We walked every day for a month, hoping to see his face,' and promised myself that I would not put it off for too much longer. But for now...

'Pearl! Thank goodness.'

'Sorry I hung up before, Greg. It's all a bit...'

'No need to apologise. I'll tell you anything you want to know.'

'There's only one thing I want to know. Why?'

'Why was I in touch with him?'

'Duh, yeah, and why didn't you, I don't know, mention it, maybe?'

'OK. That's two questions.' As ever, the pedantic big brother. 'The why is easy. I loved him, Pearl. I had a great relationship with him. When he left, you and Benjy were still kids...'

'I was fifteen! I had a great relationship with him too.'

'But I was eighteen, and we were kind of starting to be grown-ups together, you know?'

I heard him put his hand over the phone, presumably to talk to Eleanor, but that never worked on mobile phones, and I could hear him say, 'Fuck. Cancel them.'

'Sorry,' he said, less muffled. 'I'm back.'

'Who are you cancelling?'

'Oh, some random couple who were coming over to buy Gracie's old toddler trampoline.' He laughed. 'Eleanor's being such a told-you-so.'

'About the trampoline?'

'She always said I should try to tell you again.'

'Tell me what, again?'

'That I kept in touch with Dad.'

'What? You *didn't* tell me at all.' I shook my head, furious that Greg would lie to me even now. 'You never said a word.'

'I did, Pearl. I only told you once, and that's on me. Ellie always said it wasn't enough, but I did tell you.'

'The hell? When did this alleged revelation take place?'

'Long time ago. Twenty-five years, a little more, perhaps. Where does the time go? At Ben and Alice's wedding.'

At the words 'Ben and Alice's wedding', something stirred at the back of my brain. Damn it to hell, I think he *was* telling the truth. I couldn't remember what happened, not exactly, but I could feel a tiny edge of something, an image of a glass of wine and then, like silk, it slipped through my fingers. The entire wedding day was fragmented in my mind; it was an awful day and I was certainly drunk enough to have missed something important. It was probably the most drunk I had been in my life.

'Pearl, give me a second, my boss is on the landline. I'm meant to be working at home,' Greg said. 'Please don't go anywhere!'

It was meant to be a happy occasion but Benjy's bride was too young. I was only twenty-five myself, but next to seventeen-year-old Alice, I felt like a stately matron. Alice was, of course, visibly pregnant – what other possible reason could there be for this wedding? My whole life was crowded with fecund women; Alice was just the first. Bless her, she looked happy enough, far too young to guess what was coming down the pipe: a life stopped in its tracks before it had got started, her youth turned upside-down by baby Gina, a hopeless husband in Benjy. She wouldn't be smiling so beatifically, hand cradling her stomach, if she'd known about the years to come – Benjy's drinking, Barb always interfering, the bitter divorce, a rotten second marriage. Poor Alice did not get off to a flying start.

Benjy was barely twenty himself, and probably he would now admit what was obvious then to Greg and me: that he was only marrying so he didn't have to live with me and Mum any more. Mum hadn't been particularly sympathetic about their shotgun wedding, but I, who had also been pregnant too young, stood up for Alice. Mum did her best but she was in a bad mood all day.

Alice's mother, Barb, went to the other extreme. She was in her early forties then, newly divorced, and flirted wildly with all the men. The highlight – lowlight? – of the evening was when her dress ('A bra would ruin the line, darling') came open during a particularly vigorous dance routine with a boorish college friend of Greg's.

To think that this wedding from hell could have been even more fraught had Dad been there. Benjy did send him an invitation, but his RSVP said he'd only come if Jeanie was made welcome, and as none of us could imagine Jeanie and Mum in the same room, Benjy had to turn him down. I'd always assumed that put the finishing touches to Benjy's relationship with Dad.

'You were holding two drinks, a glass of wine and a G&T...' Greg said, coming back on the line, and the faint silk flicker slid back into my grasp. I saw myself standing by the buffet table, disco lights flashing round the walls, lighting up people's faces so that they looked like terrifying caricatures. I was watching, as was everyone, Barbara's white pointy breasts, unfettered by underwear, bouncing as she danced. I still didn't know to this day whether she realised her dress was undone. The music was loud enough to cover up the laughter and comments, and thank god, Alice was dancing with Benjy at the opposite end of the dance floor and hadn't noticed that everyone was gawping at her mother. A bit grim, being only the second most watched person in the room when you were the bride.

I was holding two drinks, Greg was right, and they were both mine, because I knew that getting really hammered was my only way through this day. I didn't remember what Greg was saying, only that it was about Dad, and I wished he would stop trying to talk to me about Dad. I was too drunk, too miserable, to listen. Benjy was the first of us children to marry, and Dad should have been there; I was devastated that he wasn't. There was a gap in the memory, then I remembered walking away, holding someone's arm, saying I didn't want to hear about Dad any more, ever again.

If I felt like a stately matron at twenty-five, what was I now? Whatever I was, I was way too old for any more lies.

'You're right, Greg,' I said. 'I remember you telling me something, but I walked away.'

'Well, you didn't merely walk away.' He laughed. 'You were

plastered. You had two drinks on the go all night, I don't know why I thought that was a great moment to talk to you. Probably I was scared to do it when we were both sober. Anyway, you kept shutting me down. I swear, I tried, I really tried to tell you that I was in contact with Dad. But you kept saying, "Don't speak to me about him, I don't want to hear about him ever again." When I tried once more...'

'Got to admire your persistence,' I said, belatedly embarrassed by the stubborn rudeness of my younger self.

'I know! I wish I hadn't, because this last time, I managed to blurt it out, and you looked at your two drinks, trying to work out which one you wanted the least, and then you threw one in my face.'

'Did I really?'

'It's hardly the sort of thing I'd forget. It was red wine.'

'Oh no!'

'I had to throw that shirt away.'

'God, I'm sorry.' A weird thought crossed my mind. 'Did you tell Dad about it?'

'About what?'

'Benjy and Alice's wedding, Barb's boobs, me throwing the drink?'

'Er, yes, probably...'

It occurred to me that I could seek out Dad's account of this event, and see if it matched Greg's version. The diaries were an actual time capsule, a historical record, not just of Dad's life, but of mine too. Then I remembered that it would still be Greg's version of what happened, through the lens of Dad's take on it.

'OK,' I said. 'So, as you say, it wasn't an ideal moment to tell me, was it?'

'No, and Ellie said I should tell you again.'

'Lots of times!' I heard Eleanor shout.

'Lots of times,' he repeated dutifully.

'And again when the fecker died!' she yelled.

'And again when—'

'I can hear her, Greg.'

'And she said it before the funeral, and then again when the diaries came to light...'

'Did you know Dad kept the diaries?'

'No. I was as surprised as Jeanie. And a bit worried about what he said about me.'

I could put him out of his misery and say that so far he'd come out of them pretty well. But I wasn't ready to be nice. I said, 'Let's get this completely straight. You were in touch with Dad the whole time? From when he left Mum, to when he died?'

'Not the whole time, no.' He exhaled. 'There were long periods – months, years even – when we didn't speak at all. Particularly in the last few years. And look, you need to know this: even though I was sometimes in touch with him, I don't pretend to understand why he allowed us all to drop out of his life.'

'Not all of us.' I brought a bit of much-needed Benjy to the conversation. 'He didn't drop you, the golden boy.'

I could almost hear him count to ten, exactly the way he did when Benjy wound him up. When he spoke, it was in the calm, quiet tone of someone who was trying to rise above everything. 'It was always me who kept the contact going. Not Dad. Whenever there was silence between us, it was always me who got in touch. Otherwise, I knew he would have let it go, like he did with you and Ben.'

'I honestly didn't think he wanted to hear from me.'

'He did, I assure you, very much, but he knew he had no right to want that. He never stopped asking about you.' Greg sighed. 'I didn't mind crawling back to him each time, but you wouldn't have been willing to, and I don't blame you.'

'You think I'm unforgiving?'

'No, I think that you just have a strong sense of what you are and are not willing to accept.'

I rather liked this take.

'So if Eleanor kept saying you should tell me, why didn't you?'

'I suppose I was scared.'

'Of *me*?'

'You know when we moved in with you?'

This felt like a swerve. He meant the time, early in their marriage, when he and Eleanor were between houses. They moved in with Mum and me, taking up temporary residence in Greg's old bedroom. That three or four months was the brightest period in all my decades of living with Mum. Eleanor and I had always got on well as sisters-in-law, but during that time we became best friends. Thanks to her, I briefly got my life back because she helped out so much.

Greg said, 'We got really close then, and I didn't want to mess things up. Me keeping in touch with Dad felt like a grubby little secret.'

'What's Benjy said about it?'

'Haven't told him yet.'

'Golly, let me know when you do, I'll get the popcorn in. You *are* planning to tell him, aren't you?'

'That depends on you.'

'On me, why?'

'On whether you think it's obvious from the diaries that I was in touch with Dad.'

'You're kidding, right? Pretty much everything Dad's written about is us. If he's got anything much to say about his lovely life and his lovely second family, I've yet to see it. And it's pretty obvious that everything he knows about us comes direct from you.'

'Ah, damn it.'

'Tell you what, maybe don't worry about it, then when you

die, Ben can find out the truth from your own diaries.' This was Benjy-level sarky for me.

'Oh, *Pearl!*'

'Oh, *Greg!* He's as entitled as you and me to see the diaries, you know that.'

He let out a long, weary breath. 'I'll find the right moment to tell him.'

I bit my lip, so as not to say, 'ah, why don't you leave it another thirty years, sure it was good enough for me'.

I was starting to get cold, and got to my feet. 'Well Greg, it was enlightening talking to you.'

'Pearl, we'd so love to see you again soon...'

'I'll be in touch,' I said. 'Send my love to Eleanor. By the way, I've agreed to let Andrea look at the translation before you and Benjy. Bye, then!'

I could hear Greg spluttering as I hung up.

Well. There you had it. Confirmation that everything in my life that Greg had been witness to, Dad had also been witness to. Benjy's, too. Greg had passed everything on behind our backs, to a man whose key fatherly impulse was to put an emotional distance the size of the Champs-Élysées between us.

Yep, this would take a bit of unpacking. I shook my head at my own charmingly understated irony, and started walking stiffly back towards home, shaking the life back into my legs. A few hundred metres along the path there was a whiff of chlorine, and I stopped and looked around. Through a tangle of trees I saw the ranger's tent; he'd found a new place for it. I pushed through the branches, and saw him sitting on a tree stump, his back to me. I stepped closer and snapped a twig on the ground.

'*Oh la vache!*' he said, jumping to his feet. 'You startled me.'

Something that had been percolating in my tired, confused brain since I saw the photograph at Mme Remard's house now came to the boil. I studied the ranger's face. Yes. Take away twenty years and a massive beard, a mess of hair, and it could easily be.

'Hey, Serge,' I said. 'You forgot to lock the padlock today.'

He looked at me, his eyes burning into mine, then turned back to his fire pit. 'That's not my name,' he said.

I stood there a moment longer, but he didn't look up, and it wasn't until I was nearly home that I realised I should have asked him, in that case, what his name actually was.

FOURTEEN

CARRIE

'Your phone's ringing,' Iain said.

'I'm aware.'

'It's got a funny code, starts with thirty-three. Is that abroad?'

'Yep.'

'Shall I pick it up for you?'

'Don't touch it!' I whirled round from the chopping board, knife in hand.

'OK! OK! Don't stab me!'

'Sorry.' I put the knife down, and dried my hands. 'Just leave it, please.'

'What's Mummy like, Emmie-wemmie?' Iain said in a silly voice, and she banged her hands appreciatively on her high chair.

The phone stopped ringing. 'There,' I said.

'Is there a foreign boyfriend you'd like to tell me about? Who you'd prefer not to sweet talk in front of me?'

I felt my face start to colour, infuriatingly. I turned my back on him and resumed chopping onions. Casually, I said, 'It's Pearl.'

'Pearl as in your birth mother?'

'She lives in France.'

'Shit on a brick, you went ahead with it! You never told me. Well done!'

'It's not well done at all. I rang her, she hung up, it was horrible, and now she keeps calling.'

'What does the mediator say?'

'Oh.' I focused my attention on a small piece of onion that could definitely benefit from being smaller. 'I didn't actually ring her, I jumped straight in with Pearl.'

'I'm intrigued by our role reversal, Carrie-cat. For once, I'm the sensible one, and you're the dive-right-in one.'

'Yeah, well, I totally repudiate the person I was when I did that.'

'Why don't you turn the phone off?'

'I can't. I'm waiting for the letting agent to call about Mum's flat.'

'All right then, why don't you talk to her?' Iain said, and when I didn't reply, went on, 'So, she was useless when you rang her, but you probably caught her on the hop. By the way, that onion is now down to its constituent atoms.'

'It's really *annoying* that you're being so sensible.' I scraped the onion shrapnel into a pan, and turned back to look at him. 'I don't like this role reversal.'

'Told you.' He sat up straight and put on a 'grown-up businessman' face. 'I'm mature now.'

I was still none the wiser about why he was back in my life. Part of me was starting to wonder if Mum had been right, that all he needed was time. That perhaps he did now regret how hopeless he'd been when I got pregnant. The person who said, back then, that he wasn't 'ready to commit to being a family', that he was 'too young' to be a father at thirty-five – thirty-five! – and who lounged around playing video games while I went to antenatal appointments, was unrecognisable as the person who sat here now, patiently handing Emmie bits of carrot and wiping her face. And a tiny part of me wondered if it wasn't only Emmie he felt more warmly towards.

Whatever. I was just grateful to have him around. Not only did he stop me missing Mum quite as much as I would have otherwise, but he was of practical help too. He'd looked after Emmie a lot these last weeks, including having her during Mum's funeral, because I didn't want her to see me ugly-cry. It was fun to hang out, the three of us, being the family I once thought we would be. I knew that somewhere, Mum was looking down, that quietly pleased expression on her face. She'd never really quite got why I finished things with Iain, but that was because I hadn't told her everything about our last few months as a couple. She once said that having a baby – me – had brought her and Dad closer together, and I don't think she would have understood how it had set Iain and I further apart.

When I was seven months pregnant, Iain announced that he would be in Lanzarote with his mates on the birth date, was that a problem? And when I said it was indeed something of a problem, he claimed that by being absent, he was doing me a favour, that I didn't want him in the hospital, 'staring at the business end', that I'd only be worrying about him during labour instead of myself. It was his final, most blatant rejection of parenthood since I first showed him the pregnancy test and he asked if I planned on keeping it. He didn't take the initiative and leave me, I knew, because he absolutely hated being the bad guy. He saw himself as a fine fellow, loved by all, and couldn't bear to be thought of by his friends as someone who left a heavily pregnant woman. But being thrown out by one, who he could perhaps depict as a ball-breaking tiger mom who insisted on doing everything her own way, well – that would play well with his group. His relief when I finished things was deeply unflattering, so if you'd told me then that less than two years later he'd be my main confidante, I'd have laughed.

I turned the heat down under the onions and cracked eggs into a bowl. It made me foolishly sentimental to be cooking onion omelette for him again. It was always our favourite quick meal when we were together.

My phone started ringing again.

'Same number?' I asked.

'Yep.' Iain looked at me. 'Take it this time?'

'I'm in the middle of cooking.'

He picked up the phone, and before I could even register what he was doing, answered it. 'Hello, Carrie Haskett's phone.'

'No! NO!' I mouthed furiously, waving my arms at him, little flecks of egg flying off the wooden spoon.

'Yes she is,' he said, grinning at me, the little shit. He held out the phone, and whispered, 'Go on. You might as well do it now than have it hanging over you. 'Twere best done quickly, right? I'll finish cooking, and be here to debrief.'

'I'll fricking debrief you, that's for sure. With a large blunt implement.' I took the phone and went into the bedroom, closing the door behind me.

'What,' I said sullenly, reverting to being a teenager.

'Caroline? Oh, thank god. Thank you for answering.' Her voice was deep, hesitant.

'I didn't, my stupid ex did. I'm about to hang up.'

'Please don't, not yet, please let me apologise. I'm so sorry for not being able to talk when you called. I don't want to make excuses but you really caught me at the most bizarre moment, I'd just jumped off a gate...'

'What?'

'Sorry, I'd got stuck up a gate, not a small one, a really tall one, and a strange man rescued me. Well, he isn't strange, in that I sort of know him but he is kind of a homeless man and a bit odd. OK, this isn't very relevant, I was in a bit of a state and... are you *laughing*?'

'I am laughing.' I sat down on the bed. 'I haven't laughed for quite a while. Thank you. This is absolutely not how I expected this conversation to go.'

There was a short, startled silence, then Pearl started laughing too. 'I'm glad, if you're glad.'

'So,' I said, thinking that I was in it now. 'If you're not too busy with gates and homeless men, do you want to meet?'

'Yes,' she said immediately.

'I thought perhaps you wouldn't. After you hung up last time, well, I had a bad few days after that.'

'I'm so sorry.'

'I've only just lost my mum...'

'Oh my god, Caroline, I had no idea...'

'It's Carrie. It seemed like the universe was giving me a good kicking. Pow! Your beloved mother's died. Bam! Your birth mother doesn't want to know. To lose two mothers in the space of a couple of weeks sounds like the sort of unfunny joke Oscar Wilde would make.'

It was a lot to throw at her, I knew that. But I also knew that there was no merit in pretending to be nice. She was either in, or not. I wasn't in the market for a half-assed response.

'I am so sorry, Carrie,' she said. 'I appreciate you giving me a chance. And I appreciate a fellow Oscar Wilde fan. Shall I come to you?'

'No!' Ugh, that she wanted to come here, walk into my life after thirty-five years!

'Sorry. I was only thinking to make it as easy as possible for you.'

'You're in France, right? Francis told my mum. So, let's meet in Paris. I've never been there.'

'If you're sure... when?'

'I'll text you. I've got to go.' I hung up, quickly, before the tears started.

There you go, Mum. I did it. I spoke to her. I wish I could tell you for real. You said you'd be there to hold my hand after I called, but you weren't.

While I'd been clearing out Mum's place I'd found it easy to talk to her there, have a bit of a cry, but I couldn't do that now the flat was emptied and ready for the next tenant. I could go to Dad's grave, I supposed, where I'd scattered some of her ashes, and talk to her there. But I knew what she'd have to say about that, if she was here. *Bit morbid, Carrie love.*

Back in the kitchen, Iain had finished the omelettes, made a tomato salad and buttered some slices of sourdough bread. Emmie was sitting on the floor near him, playing with her coloured wooden stacker.

'I'm sorry,' he said, his mouth full. 'Do you mind that I started?'

'I can't quite believe that's what you're apologising for,' I said, sitting down. My omelette was almost cold, but I ate it anyway.

'I know, I'm an impetuous fool,' he said. 'I was trying to get our old dynamic back – you know, me being impulsive, you being sensible. Anyway, it was obvious you wanted to talk to her, and it doesn't suit you, playing games.'

'I wasn't playing games. I was trying to avoid being hurt.'

'She can't hurt you, not unless you let her.'

'I've said I'll meet her, in Paris,' I said.

'I think that's great.'

Emmie burst into a string of babbling that included her favourite words, yargh and dada.

'Emmie thinks so too.' He poured me a glass of wine. 'Will you take her with you?'

'I suppose so. I hadn't thought.'

'Be a lot easier on your own though, wouldn't it?'

'Are you offering to have her?'

'Yes, of course. A whole day, Emmie, you and me, what say you?'

Emmie looked up at the sound of her name, and said clearly, 'Yes.'

Iain and I looked at each other. 'Flipping heck!' he said.

'She's started saying a lot more recognisable words. She said "today" this morning, and "doggie" when we were in the park.'

'Doggie!' Emmie said.

'She's so clever. Aren't you, Emmie?' Iain pulled her onto his lap. She laughed and tried to pick up his plate. My heart ached at the sight of them together. I never thought Emmie would have this, a father who cared about her.

'Then yes, thank you, if that's a genuine offer, I will leave her with you. Would a Saturday work for you? I can drop her round before I go.'

'Brilliant, let me know when.' He snuggled his cheek against Emmie's. 'There's something I wanted to ask you. I don't know what you'll think. It's about sharing custody.'

'Umm...' What the hell?

'Just think about it. You don't have to answer right away.'

Letting Iain take charge of Emmie, since he'd proved himself more than capable of looking after her properly – that was one thing. Allowing him to come back into her life, share raising her, make decisions about her – that was quite another.

'Why do you want to?' I said.

'Ah, I was such a fucking idiot.' He stretched his hand out across the table and, warily, I took it. 'These last few weeks, I've seen how much I missed out on.'

How long had I wanted to hear this? I looked into his brown eyes, the same colour as Emmie's. 'You *were* an idiot. But how do I know you won't be again?'

'I've grown up a lot since we split. You know I have.'

'Do I? I've only seen a change recently. Before that, when you came to see Emmie, you were in and out in five minutes. Couldn't wait to get away.'

'Babies, mate,' he said. 'You know I don't really get babies. But now she's this little person! Talking, and playing, and so cute.'

'She's not a toy, Iain.' I took my hand away. 'I'm not wild about babies, myself, but I didn't have a choice. It wasn't possible for me to walk away.' I was going to say, 'mothers can't walk away' but then, look how easily Pearl walked away from a baby. Instead, I said, 'I don't understand why you've gone from nought to sixty so fast.'

'I've realised what I'm missing, is that so hard to understand? My mum keeps going on about it, how lovely Emmie is, what a twat I am.'

Iain's mum, a lovely woman, had come to my place to see Emmie a few times, but she lived in Guernsey so it was quite a journey. 'It doesn't make you sound as mature as you think, if your reason for wanting to be involved is because your mum told you to.'

'That's not it at all.' He smiled. 'I just want to try, in a tiny way, to make things up to you. I know I was useless when you were pregnant, and when Emmie was little. I want to be more present. Please think about it.'

I was relieved when the doorbell rang, for the few seconds on my own it gave me as I walked down the hall. All these might-have-beens, floating tantalisingly within reach. Was I really going to Paris to meet someone who had made a clear decision not to be part of my life more than three decades ago? Was I really considering trying again with my daughter's father, who at best was inconsistent, and at worst, a total flake? Had I really just lost my mother, the one I would normally have asked for advice?

I opened the door to Henry, who looked a bit stressed, Numa in his arms.

'I'm so sorry,' he said. 'I know it's getting late. Can you possibly...?'

'Yes, of course. Come here, sweetheart.' I took Numa from him. What a weight she was. In little more than a year and a half, Emmie would be this big.

'You're an absolute star. I've been asked to do a last-minute revision session for a group of my students; they've got an exam tomorrow and will pay double-time. I can't afford not to.' Henry had a whole raft of hustles, including maths tutoring. I'd recommended him to some of my own programming students who needed to sharpen up their skills, and they said he was amazing.

'Hey, Henry,' Iain said, coming into the hall. 'Good to see you, man.'

'You too,' Henry said, less enthusiastically, because he'd heard plenty of my complaints about Iain in the early days of new motherhood.

'I'd better shoot,' Iain said, and he kissed my cheek over the top of Numa's head – the first time we had kissed in well over a year. 'Let me know about Paris.'

I stared at his departing back as he walked down the road, feeling flustered and confused. Henry said, 'Paris, huh? Very romantic. Well, I'll be back in ninety minutes. She's eaten and everything. Is that OK?'

'Perfect. I'll read her and Emmie a story or something,' I said, and trailed back into the house. I realised he must think I was going to Paris with Iain. How affectionate did Iain's kiss look, exactly? In fact, how affectionate was it?

'Nu!' Emmie said on spotting her, which was the first time she had ever acknowledged Numa. Emmie was nearly two years younger, and though that wouldn't always seem such a huge gap, I hadn't expected they'd ever be proper friends. But they immediately huddled on the floor together and started playing some weird game with spoons. My mind was too full to do anything useful, so I just sat on the sofa watching them, wondering what on earth I'd agreed to now.

26TH SEPTEMBER 1990

Couldn't believe my eyes. Heard people talking outside, looked out of the bedroom window, and there was a young man crouching down speaking to a young woman. Knew straight away it was PP. Haven't seen her for almost ten years, but G sends photos occasionally. Anyway, I'd have known her anywhere. Knew straight away that my letter had brought her.

For some reason she was sitting on the ground. I couldn't hear what she was saying, and didn't dare open the window in case it alerted her. I wondered if the man was her boyfriend? A very pierced and punky-looking fellow. He pointed at the house, and I jumped back, though I knew I couldn't be seen. I wondered if he was encouraging her to knock. But then he helped her up and they walked away. I couldn't believe it. Was she really not even going to try?

I ran downstairs. Of course, J got there ahead of me. Where are you going? It's not your usual time for a walk, I'll come too. And so on. Not for the first time, I thought that if I had a dog I could go out more regularly even if I didn't have church business. Managed to get past her but she came after me, still asking what was I doing, was I planning to meet someone? She grabbed hold of my arm but I pulled away, saw PP getting into a car, too far away to shout. I ran but the car pulled out, an old beige Cortina. I saw the number plate, ran after it to the end of the street, but couldn't keep up and they were gone. Tried to remember the plate, said it over and over in my head.

But in the kitchen J was holding my diary, not this one but the previous one, 1987–88. She had taken it out of my desk drawer. What is this secret code? What have you been saying? By the time we'd thrashed this out, I'd forgotten the number plate other than it ended in an X.

[Half a page crossed through here]

FIFTEEN

PEARL

It was only when a waiter glided past and dropped a fresh paper napkin in front of me, with a classic Parisian-waiter sneer, that I realised what a mess I'd made of the previous one. It was a white pile of a thousand tiny pieces. I hastily gathered them onto a side plate, then put my hands on my lap, out of the way of any other innocent items I might inadvertently destroy. It was so hard to keep still, harder yet not to drink my wine down in one go and order something stronger. Her train was meant to have arrived thirty minutes ago.

'I've never been to Paris, and I don't speak French,' she'd said, unreassuringly, in one of her texts. Seeing her name come up each time we exchanged updates about times and places made my heart thud. I sent her step-by-step instructions to find the brasserie, chose it because it was literally opposite the Gare du Nord, but still had visions of her wandering lost and confused round the streets.

I could scarcely believe I was here. That this morning I had kissed Denny goodbye, left the cottage, got on a train and then a plane. That now I was sitting in the Brasserie Terminus Nord, watching the door. I caught a glimpse of myself in the mirror on the opposite wall, and for a moment, saw myself as a stranger would see me. As Carrie would. A woman in her fifties, tightly belted into her coat. Brown hair, haircut more stylish than the face, frown lines between her eyebrows, cheeks starting to sag a little. Overall impression: stressed.

Every time the door opened my heart rate sped up. Some of the people who came in were women of about the right age, on their own, but none of them were looking for someone. And then she came in, and I knew her immediately.

Because I'd seen her before.

I stood up, and she came over: a slim brown-haired woman in a dark blue peacoat, her expression as uncertain as mine. I couldn't keep my breath on an even keel, and of course, telling myself not to think about my breathing only made it worse. She looked tired, worried, wary. The shape of her face, nose and eyes were uncannily like mine and Benjy's. She had black eyeliner flicks, expertly applied. Her hair was straight, even straighter than mine, and neatly tied back, with caramel high-lights and a blunt-cut fringe that suited her. I didn't know if we were going to hug, or kiss, and when she stood, awkwardly, on the other side of the table, and didn't make any move, I didn't either.

'Carrie, thank you for coming,' I said. She smiled, a small fleeting smile, and sat opposite me.

'Where's your baby?' I said. Blurted, really. I realised I'd been counting on her bringing it.

She looked confused. 'How do you know I have a baby?'

I'd heard her voice on the phone of course, but nothing had prepared me for the impact of it in real life. That was my daughter speaking, in that soft Bristol accent! My *daughter*!

'I saw you with him. Her?' I said shakily. 'At my father's funeral.' I thought of the moment I'd seen her, when I ran out of the church. A woman outside, holding a baby. She and I locking eyes. Denny coming after me, calling my name.

'Oh! Did you know then that it was me?'

'No.' It would feel silly, manipulative even, to tell her that actually I'd felt a connection with her in those few seconds. 'Were you intending to go to the funeral?'

'Sort of. Francis – your dad – he was really keen for me to come, for some reason. But when I saw you, I kind of lost my nerve.'

The penny dropped. *For some reason.* I finally realised why Dad had wanted me to attend the funeral, so much so that he made a big deal about an interesting 'legacy' that I had to receive in person. Of course I didn't really need to be there to get the diaries – they could have been sent to me – but I did need to be there in order to see Carrie. *She* was what he meant by his legacy: trying to make right what he'd failed to do when I was pregnant with her. Ah, Dad. Was it a foolish and self-aggrandizing gesture, or something lovely? I had no idea.

'She's with her dad,' Carrie said, and I blinked, confused about whose dad we were talking about. 'Emmie, my daughter,' she clarified.

'Oh! That's nice.' I knew absolutely nothing about Carrie, and any question I formulated I immediately dismissed, feeling that it was too prying. The waiter came over and Carrie pointed at my wine. I ordered one for her and another for me, slightly staccato because of the good ol' breathing difficulty.

Nonetheless, Carrie said, 'You're completely fluent!' She looked impressed.

'Oh, not really. I'm getting there.'

'You sound properly French. How long have you lived here?'

'Nearly six years.'

'What prompted you to move?'

'Oh, we just fancied a change.' This sounded exactly like the brush-off it was, and I sought desperately for something to add. 'Things were a bit... well, we were a little tired of the UK...'

She stared at the table, and I wondered what she was thinking. It had been her idea to meet; she had suggested Paris, she had travelled farther than me to be here. But now she was actually here she seemed slightly hostile, as if she had been forced to come. But that might just be her normal manner. I didn't know.

She didn't say anything more about why I'd moved here, so I asked questions instead. She answered everything politely but with the minimum amount of words necessary. How was her journey? Fine. What work did she do? Computing researcher and tutor at Bristol University. What were Emmie's age and temperament? Fourteen months, lively and fun.

In an attempt to escape interrogation mode, I told her how sorry I was about her mum. She said she still couldn't believe it, that she regularly started dialling her mum's number before remembering. I thought that might thaw things but another awkward silence followed, cut mercifully short by the arrival of our wine. I quickly knocked back the remains of my first glass, and when I put it down, I saw that Carrie was observing me intently.

'Our eyes are the same shape and colour.'

'Yes!' I was delighted that she'd noticed. 'My brother Benjy's, too.'

'Emmie's are the same shape, but brown, like Iain's.' She took a large gulp of her wine. 'Dominant gene.'

Her hand holding the glass was like mine, the fingernails identical. For how long had I wanted this, dreamed of this: to see features of my own reflected in my child? This wasn't how I had imagined it happening, and, stupidly, I hadn't anticipated it, or built up to it at all. And with her little girl, there would be more. I was here now. In for a penny, in for a pound.

'Do you have a photo of Emmie?'

'Millions.' She smiled again, another fleeting smile that lit up and faded like a sparkler. She handed me her phone. 'This is her, yesterday.'

I stared at the picture of the toddler, beaming at the camera, holding something made of orange plastic. Lego, perhaps. Her hair, in two tiny bunches, was the colour of Carrie's, but the wavy kink at the temples was all mine. I could feel exactly how I would paint her, the colours I would use, the brush strokes.

My granddaughter.

'She's beautiful.'

'She's really fun,' Carrie said. 'Her language is exploding.'

I wanted to say, 'I'll teach her French,' but let the words stay buried. I handed back the phone and attempted a steadying breath, but there were still no steadying breaths to be found.

'What did you look like when you were a baby?' I said.

'I don't know. All babies look the same, don't they? Like Winston Churchill.'

'Or when you were a little girl?'

'I looked all different ways. There were a lot of years of being a little girl.'

I deserved that. I'd missed all the little girl years. 'Carrie,' I said, determined to push through, 'I'm really glad you called me. I was wondering – why did you?'

'Mum wanted me to.' She looked directly at me. 'I personally never felt the need.'

Well, that helped explain the sense of reluctance. 'No, I understand that...'

'My parents were brilliant. I always felt very loved.'

'I'm so glad, that was what I always hoped for...'

'Did you?' She took another gulp of wine, then spread her hands on the table, as if bracing herself. 'Look, Pearl, to be honest, I'm not completely sure why I'm here. I have wondered, most of the way here, if I'm actually in my right mind. I'm grieving, I know, and trying to do what my mum wanted. But I'm not shopping for a new mother, and if I don't want that, then I'm not sure how this works.'

'I completely understand. I'm absolutely not offering

myself up as a replacement, I wouldn't even think of that. I am here for whatever you want,' I said, 'even if that turns out to be nothing.'

This was clearly the right thing to say, because her expression softened slightly. 'OK. Thanks. I had thought, because Francis was quite pushy with my mum, that it was coming from you.'

'God, no. Not at all. The first I knew of it was you phoning me, which was why I was so useless, so flustered. I'd no idea he was in touch with your mum. He and I weren't in contact at all, hadn't been for many years.'

'Mum told me he'd cut people out of his life.' She raised her eyebrows. 'Was it because you had me?'

'It started around that time, sure, but you weren't the cause. He left our family, and things were already rather strained when I was pregnant with you, and he...'

Carrie finished her glass of wine and looked round for the waiter. 'I'll need another one of these, I think.'

'Sorry. I got a bit heavy a bit fast.'

'No, I want to know. Heavy is the key element today. I was expecting it. I just think it would help to have another drink while you tell me.'

I gestured to the waiter.

'Mum never made a secret of me being adopted,' Carrie went on, in a rush. 'She told me my birth mother was too young to look after me and wanted me to go to a loving family. Mum made me feel special, chosen, all the things you're meant to do with an adopted child.'

'She sounds wonderful.'

'She was. But when I was an annoying teenager, I told Mum I wanted to find my real parents.'

'Ouch.'

'She and my dad were fine about it. To my face, anyway. They contacted the adoption agency, and they gave us my mother's, er, your name, but told us that you hadn't left instructions saying you'd be happy to be contacted.'

'I'm sorry I didn't do that, I didn't know...'

The waiter brought over two more glasses of wine which gave me a moment to regroup. Carrie managed a '*Merci beaucoup*' that made Andrea sound like a native. She saw me smile, and said, 'Ugh! Was it bad?'

'It was very good,' I said.

'I know you're lying.'

When the waiter had gone, I said, 'I didn't even know I could leave my contact details. No-one told me. I'm sorry.'

'They helped me put a note on my file saying I'd be happy to be contacted by my mother or other people from my birth family. And they made suggestions for how I might go about trying to trace her. You. Mum and I went a little way down that road, looked for a marriage certificate, or birth certificates of your children, but there wasn't anything.'

'I didn't get married till I was quite old,' I said, 'almost forty, and I didn't, well, didn't have other children.'

'That's one of my questions answered,' Carrie said. 'I wondered if there were any half-siblings out there.'

'No, we wanted them, tried, just lots of miscarriages, and things.' I managed to say this in an outwardly calm way, floating along the top of my breath like a surfer on a wave.

'I'm sorry to hear that. Anyway, other things took over, and after a while, I forgot about it. Mum and Dad were my parents, and that was that. Then at the start of this year, I think, Francis got in touch with my mum, via a caseworker at PAC-UK. Mum rather than me, because it was her contact details that were at the agency.'

'I'm starting to work out why he got in touch,' I said. 'I'm getting to know him a little now through his diaries. He left them to me, weirdly. I was reading one on the way here, in fact, on the plane. I'm slowly piecing together what his life was like after he left my mother. I think...' I stopped, wanting to say out loud to someone what I'd discovered about Dad's marriage to Jeanie. How every new diary entry confirmed that Jeanie was difficult and controlling. The entry I'd read on the way here, in which it turned out that he had, after all, known I was outside his house that time, back in 1990, raised more questions than it answered, and none of them pleasant ones.

But this absolutely wasn't the right place, nor the right person to share my suspicions with. Instead, I said, 'It had a page that he'd crossed out. Very intriguing, particularly as it came right after the only time I ever tried to see him when I was an adult.'

'Can I have a look?'

I took the notebook out of my bag and showed her.

'What on earth is this written in?'

'Shorthand.'

'You speak French and shorthand? Is there no end to your linguistic capabilities?' She examined the scrubbed-out part. 'Wow, he really didn't want anyone to be able to read this, did he? Mum said he sounded rather nervous, paranoid even, when they spoke on the phone.' She tilted the page. 'There's a method one of my colleagues developed for the university library to read old faded texts that have been written over. You scan it at high res, then put it into editing software, and do some filtering, basically find the difference between the scribble and the paper, increase the contrast... what?'

'I'm staring at you in undisguised admiration,' I said. 'What an incredible thing to know about.' I didn't add, though I was thinking it, how beautifully animated her face was as she spoke about her work. The slight air of hostility had quite disappeared. 'I don't suppose you'd consider asking her to have a go, would you?'

'Oh!' She looked rather shocked, and I saw that I'd overstepped, proposed a level of engagement she wasn't ready for.

She put the diary on the table. 'Well, I'm not sure she's got time...'

'It's OK, I shouldn't have asked. It's probably nothing anyway, he most likely simply made a mistake and crossed it through.'

'But you don't think so.'

'Well, no. There are enough hints in the diaries for even a dunce like me to understand that his marriage was pretty tough.' I put the diary back in my bag. 'I feel like he's left me a series of clues, and this is one of them. It's the last entry in which he refers to me by name, or by initials, anyway. After this, he addresses me directly, as "you". So something changed at this point.'

Carrie reached for her glass, and said, 'I don't know how much he told Mum about his life. He was ill, and she was sympathetic because she was, too. She hated the thought of leaving me on my own. That's why she wanted me to call you.'

'But you didn't want to?'

'Well, not at first.' She sipped her wine. 'But I realised that now I have Emmie, there are a few things I ought to know. Where I come from, my genetic heritage, that sort of thing. Because it impacts on her.'

'Of course.' I sat back. My panic-state was giving way to something less high-alert, and I could breathe more easily. 'What would you like to know?'

She laughed. 'Ever since we arranged to meet, I've been thinking, finally! At last I'll get to find out who my father is. But I'm not sure I want to know, after all.'

'Gosh! I had no idea this was a big secret. Did they not tell you at the adoption agency?'

'Apparently no-one knew; it wasn't written down anywhere. It's not on my birth certificate, and Francis didn't know.'

'Oh, I never would have told him! It's not a very exciting answer. He was called Simon, and—'

Carrie held up her hand. 'Can you stop just a minute, Pearl?'

'Of course!' I waited while she turned away. It was a chance to look at her properly, without her gazing back at me with those cool blue mirror-image eyes.

'I've imagined all the worst scenarios over the years,' she said, her gaze fixed on the other side of the room. 'Rape, violence, a predatory older man, a teacher, incest... if it's something awful, it's probably better if you don't tell me.'

'It wasn't anything like that at all. He was a boy my own age and—'

'OK, thanks.' She looked at her watch. 'You know what, I'd better go. There's a train in half an hour.'

'Oh!' I felt side-swiped. 'I didn't know you were going back so soon.'

'Well, it's the first time I've left Emmie with her dad. I ought to—'

'Shall we have a quick walk first? It seems a shame, that on your first visit to Paris, you don't get to go more than a few yards from the station.'

'Well, all right.'

I left some money on the table and we went out together, a little distance apart. I saw that we were the same height, and wondered if she noticed it too.

I'd have liked a nice sunny backdrop, Paris at its prettiest, but it had been showering on and off all day. Though it was currently dry, the sky was dark and threatening, the pavements wet.

Denny and I had taken a couple of short breaks here, and I remembered this area a little. I said, 'We're near the Sacré Coeur; it's scarcely more than a kilometre. At least you can say you've seen a Parisian landmark.'

'OK, I'll get the train after this one.'

We walked in silence, and I racked my brains for a neutral

topic. Did Carrie really need to get the return train so soon? Or was it more that she'd got overwhelmed when we started talking about Simon?

'What will Emmie be doing with her dad?' I asked, hoping to see again that lively, confident expression I'd glimpsed earlier when she was talking about more comfortable topics. I wondered if Carrie and Emmie's father were a couple; it didn't sound like it, if this was his first time alone with the child.

'He's good at playing with her,' Carrie said. 'Big kid himself. I expect they'll go to the park. Oh my god, there's a Five Guys! That's so weird.'

'Paris has all the chains. I take it you're not together?'

'No, but he wants to be more involved.'

'That's good. Isn't it?'

'Maybe. I did really like him, before.' Carrie stopped at a small windswept stand, selling tourist trinkets. 'I guess if he wanted to try again, I'd be up for it. It's pretty lonely, being a single parent. I've got great neighbours, and Mum helped a lot, of course, but now...' Decisively, she picked up a snow globe containing a tiny gold Eiffel tower, and paid an absurd ten euros for it before I could stop her. 'For Emmie,' she said.

We carried on walking, turning onto the Boulevard de Magenta.

'What was it like, then?' Carrie said abruptly. 'You and Simon?'

'Well, we were in the same class at school, and he was lovely.'

'Oh, thank *god*!'

'I'm so sorry. All these years you've been thinking you had this...'

'Horrible origin story?' she finished for me.

'Exactly! Origin story. I like that.' I thought back, excavating layers of soil, trying to remember things I could tell her. 'It was very sweet. He was a really nice boy. Jewish. Liked rock music. He was good at languages, we had that in common.'

'So I'm half Jewish! That's very cool.'

'Yes, and half lapsed C of E on my side, I'm afraid, which is slightly less cool.'

Simon's name sounded rusty to my ears; I hadn't spoken it out loud in more than thirty years. He was forever preserved in my mind as a laughing boy with dark floppy hair, leaning over my desk. Our first kiss, at the bus stop, tender and soft. Of our one night together I remembered little, hazy as it was with alcohol, but despite everything that happened afterwards, I had only good feelings about him.

'We sat next to each other in class, held hands on the way home from school, very innocent. We got drunk at a party. My first ever party with booze. Neither of us had got drunk before, or done, er, you know.' I smiled, embarrassed. 'We went out a bit after that, to the cinema and whatnot, but when I discovered I was pregnant I stopped talking to him. I feel bad about that to this day, because he never knew why.'

'Didn't he see you, at school though? With the, er...' She mimed a pregnant stomach.

'Oh. God.' Here came the less-good feelings. A familiar tightness started forming in my chest. 'Well, this part is less sweet. Are you sure you want me to...?'

'Go on.'

'I think it would be handled differently now, but I basically dropped out of school. No-one seemed to suggest there was any alternative.' How best to phrase the next part? There was no reason for Carrie to know how hard I'd tried to get out of being pregnant. 'My parents had only recently separated, and my mum was in a bit of a state, so I was looking after her a fair bit anyway, and responsible for my younger brother...'

'You were a carer. That must have been rough.'

'We didn't call it that then, but I guess I was. Anyway, long story short, I left school before I started to show, and went to work at Mum's hair and beauty salon. The women who worked there were lovely. One or two of them had been through a similar thing at a young age. Then later on, my brother Greg found a place for me at a mother and baby unit in Bristol, where he was studying.'

The unit was designed for what were called 'unmarried mothers', women who were planning to give up their children for adoption. There was so little I cared to remember about my few weeks there. Being away from Mum and Benjy, the hard bed – still the hardest I'd ever slept on – which I took correctly to be some kind of punishment. The night-time tears of the other girls, the helpless pain of labour, the baby being taken away after a few minutes. I tried never to dwell on it, hadn't thought about it properly for so long. And the interminable, unbearable hollow homesickness in my stomach – ah yes, *that* was where I first had that feeling.

The tightness increased round my chest, and I stopped still for a moment, my hand on my heart, trying to slow my breathing down. The last thing I needed right now was a panic attack. Though, when would a panic attack be welcome? What exact circumstances would those be? Despite myself, I smiled, and Carrie, who'd been looking at me worriedly, smiled back.

'So *that's* why I came to be in Bristol.' She pulled a scarf out of her bag and wrapped it round her neck. 'That sounds fricking awful, Pearl, I'm sorry. Surely you must have thought of an abortion?'

How could she say it so calmly? That was herself she was talking about! I felt angry for a moment that she could be so casual about it. Then it passed; I had absolutely no right to be angry with her. I had no rights over her at all.

'I expect it crossed my mind,' I said, feeling tired right down to my toes, 'but it was all a very long time ago.' We turned into the Rue Livingstone.

Casually, as though not caring about the answer, she said, 'What was Simon's surname?'

'Lewison. Will you look for him?'

'Doubt it. Don't want to give him a heart attack, if he never knew about me. I'll probably just do a little light googling.' Carrie breathed out heavily. I wondered what the impact of all of this was on her. She seemed to be taking it incredibly well, but I didn't know whether this *savoir faire* was usual or if she was putting on a good show for me. I wanted to stop, take her by the shoulders, say, 'are you OK?' More than that, I wanted to put my arms around her, pull her close, ask her to say again what she had said on the phone. *My name is Caroline. I'm your daughter.*

'So you never saw him again, then?' Carrie said, and it took a moment to understand who she was talking about.

'I did, once or twice after I'd come back from Bristol, but we avoided each other. Poor lad. I imagine he thought I'd gone off him.' I remembered encountering Simon in the high street a few weeks after my return, and darting into a shop to avoid him. I caught a glimpse of his face as I turned away, and the confusion and hurt etched on it was as eloquent as a declaration. I felt, then and now, that I'd done everything wrong. Hurt people, behaved irresponsibly, made the wrong decision at every turn. I imagined Carrie thinking that of me, too.

We didn't speak again until we went into the Square Louise Michel, with its postcard view of the Sacré Coeur high above us, as white and flouncy as a wedding cake. A tourist cliché, I knew, but for good reason. If you'd never seen it before, it was breath-taking.

'Oh, will you look at that!' Carrie cried. She took out her phone. 'Pearl, let's get a selfie.'

I stood next to her on the steps, the Sacré Coeur behind us, and she put her arm round my shoulder and clicked away.

'I'm not very photogenic,' I said, flustered by the physical contact between us.

'Not at all, look.'

We both silently pondered the photo, which, its two faces side by side, revealed exactly how alike we looked.

'Tell you what,' she said, breaking into my thoughts, 'I *will* ask my colleague if she can get a reading on that diary.'

'Really? You're sure?'

'Absolutely.' She held out her hand, and I took out the notebook and gave it to her. This pleased me hugely, because it meant we'd have to meet again.

'OK, don't freak, but I'm going to do something a little crazy,' she said. She rummaged in her bag, and brought out a small padded envelope. A wicked smile crept across her face. 'Just going to put some of Mum's ashes here.'

'Good lord!'

She knelt down by a flower bed, and started scraping a hole in the soil. 'It's mad, but she asked for some of them to be scattered in an exotic place that she'd never been to before. She wasn't very well travelled, so I'm pretty sure she never came here.'

She dug a little more, then, after looking round to make sure no-one was watching, tipped some ashes from the envelope into the hole. I knelt beside her and helped her cover it over with earth.

'There you go, Mum. The start of your Paris adventure.' She took a photo of the place the ashes were buried, then stood up and brushed herself down. 'Thanks, Pearl. Sorry to pull you into weird gothic stuff.'

'I'm honoured to be part of it.'

'Hey, let's do another selfie, you need one on your phone.'

'Oh! I can't.' I showed her my phone. 'It only has a rudimentary camera, and doesn't do selfies.'

She laughed. 'Cute! A flip phone. You don't see them very

often. You've got an absolute ton of missed messages, did you know?'

'It's fine, they're from Denny, that's my husband,' I said. 'I've been wondering if I should get a more modern phone. Be a bit more connected.'

'I like this one. It suits your style. Hang on and I'll send you the photo.' She sat down on the steps like tourists the world over, like tourists around us were doing now, and fiddled with her phone. 'Do you not need to call Denny back, then?'

'Oh, it's OK. I told him I had lots of appointments today, and would be back late. He's probably trying to find out what time.' I turned off my phone, so as to not have to think about Denny, but when I looked up, Carrie was staring at me, a strange expression on her face.

'You didn't tell your husband you were meeting me.'

'Oh. No.'

'He doesn't know about me.'

'No. I'm really sorry, I haven't—'

Carrie stood up. 'Wow, Pearl, my expectations were pretty low, but fucking hell. You never left your name for me to trace you: OK. You never told my birth father about me, well, bit weird but you were young, OK. But you didn't tell your *husband* about me? Aren't you scared he might find out? Did you die a little inside when I contacted you?'

I could feel my knees buckling at the force of her sudden anger. How had it gone from zero to sixty so quickly? One minute we were sharing a personal moment with her mum's ashes, the next she was furious with me. 'No, not at all, I'm so sorry, it's complicated, I can explain, Denny and I, we've...'

'It's fine.' A tear rolled down her face and she brushed it away. 'It was my fault. I come barging into your life, don't know anything about you... it was a fucking stupid idea. I'm sorry, I don't know why you should have thought about me during the last thirty-five years at all. I do *not* know what I'm doing here.

Let's forget the whole thing, I'm certainly happy to.' She started walking away.

'Carrie, please, wait.' I ran after her, grabbed her arm. 'That came out wrong. I haven't told Denny but I was planning to, right after I saw you. I just needed to wait for the right moment. I lied to him a long time ago and...'

'Please don't.' Carrie shook my hand off. 'I want to get my train.' She looked absolutely stricken. I could see it was the bewildered anger of an abandoned child, anger I had been prepared for but that she had given little sign of initially. Yet it clearly had, after all, been very close to the surface.

'At least let me walk you back to the station.'

'It's fine; I know the way.' She walked off, fast, and I stood watching her, wondering how I had made such a mess of it.

It was evening when my plane got in to Rodez airport, and I was too flattened to face the bus journey. I took a leaf out of Andrea's book, and got a taxi. To hell with the expense.

I knew I should go straight home, and quickly – Denny had left so many messages – but I had an overwhelming urge to see Serge first. To tell him I had done the hard thing and it hadn't gone well, so what now? At the gate, I was puzzled to find that the padlock was missing, the chain hanging down empty. Denny must have removed it. Perhaps he'd accepted that it was more hassle than it was worth.

I went into the wood and breathed in the familiar night-time smells and sounds, glad to be away from noise and people and lights. I made my way back to the last place I'd seen Serge's tent, but there was no sign that he'd ever been there. Maybe I had misremembered. Then my torchlight swept across a plastic sandwich bag nailed to a tree. I went over to investigate, and saw that it contained the gate padlock and the spare key.

I tried to tell myself that this was a good sign, that Serge had no more need of the wood, that he'd gone to do what he needed to do. But when I took the padlock out, there was a scrap of paper wrapped round it, which I unfolded to read the single word: *Désolé*.

Sorry.

I walked wearily along the path to the cottage. The wood felt less magical without Serge there, somehow. I'd liked the thought of him sleeping under the stars, as if he really was the ranger and was guarding the wood. Serge coming back, searching for the courage to confront his past, had given me the impetus to confront my own, but it hadn't worked out for either of us. Maybe he was right to run away. Sometimes it was better, perhaps, to admit that you weren't ready – might never be ready – to face up to something.

I certainly wasn't ready to face anything when I got in, other than a wash and a mint tea before collapsing into bed. But Denny was waiting for me in the kitchen, and I saw straight away that I would have to face a lot more before the night was over.

'Thank god,' he said. He looked gaunt with anxiety. 'It's getting dark.'

'Oh, yes, I did so many dye jobs today, you know how they overrun.' I kissed the top of his head. 'Two lots of highlights as well! Took forever. I didn't even get time to check my phone.'

'What's happened to your nails?' He was staring at my hands, and when I looked down, I saw that they were dirty as a schoolboy's. My cursory wash in the loos at Gare du Nord hadn't shifted the Sacré Coeur soil that sat under each fingernail.

'Just hair dye.' I put the kettle on the stove. To avoid Denny's eye, I focused my attention on a parcel lying on the table, addressed to me. 'What's this?' I started to open it.

'I collected the post this afternoon. It's from England.'

Inside was a familiar type of yellow exercise book. 'Oh,' I

said, and my overriding emotion was exhaustion. 'It's the repaired diary, the one Jeanie ripped.'

'Pearl, where were you today?' Denny's voice was deathly quiet. How I'd love to pretend that I hadn't heard him.

'You know where, seeing clients, dealing with the backlog from when we were in England...'

'When I went in for our mail, Jean said he'd seen you this morning. At the airport.'

Oh, god. I went to the shelf and took down a cup, my hands shaking.

'He was collecting his cousin. He thought you didn't see him. He said, but of course he can't have got this right, that you were at the Air France check-in.'

'That's a new side-hustle for Jean, alongside cutting keys: spying for the secret police.' I went to the back door. 'I'm getting some mint.'

In the garden I leaned against the wall and breathed in the herb-scented air. I could run now, jump the low picket fence – an absolute cinch compared to the gate I'd climbed. I could run through the wood, start a new life somewhere else. Get a new name and identity. Put all this churning, complicated, aching stuff behind me.

I picked some mint and went back into the kitchen. Well Pearl, I said to myself, you are in it now.

'I'm sorry,' I said.

'You're sorry? That's it?' Denny whirled round. 'I've been literally going out of my mind! I was sure Jean was mistaken, and that it was just someone who looked like you, so I went round to the clients you'd mentioned, and of course, none of them had seen you. You didn't answer any texts, I left I don't know how many voicemails. And the padlock was gone from the gate. God knows why you took it off – to give me something extra to worry about, perhaps?'

'I'm really sorry I scared you.' I stood behind him and put

my arms round his neck. That familiar, much-loved smell of his: part soap, part wood and sawdust. I could feel him shaking.

'I've been imagining the absolute worst. First I thought you'd left me, maybe there was another man. Then I thought, far worse than that, what if you were in some kind of trouble, that someone was after you, and you'd been too scared to tell me, so you ran away?'

I'd never thought of myself as someone who might run away, but the alternative fantasy life that I'd pictured in the garden made me wonder. Like Serge, would I run when things got too difficult? In fact, some people – Eleanor's wry smile swam into my mind – might have thought I *had* run away when things got difficult, five years ago.

'I was so relieved when you walked in. But please, don't lie to me any more, Pearl. Where did you go?'

'Denny, you have to believe me. I wanted to tell you, but in my own time.'

'Tell me now, please.' He sounded choked up.

I sat next to him. Had his face ever looked so sad? Yes, once. The best thing was to tell him quickly, rip the plaster off.

'I went to Paris. I went to meet my daughter.' The words 'my daughter' felt unfamiliar, sticky on my tongue. Also beautiful, precious, the most extraordinary words in the world.

'I'm sorry. What did you say?'

The kettle started shrieking, and I stood up to turn it off, poured water messily into a cup. My back to him, I said, 'My daughter.'

'I'm so confused. What daughter? What do you mean?'

All in one breath I said, 'I had a baby at sixteen and gave her up and she just got in touch and I'm sorry.'

There was an unbearably long silence. I sipped my tea but it burned my tongue. Served me right.

Then Denny laughed. Not really a laugh. His face was dark red, making the lines at the sides of his eyes stand out more than usual. '*Sorry?* We've been married thirteen years, Pearl. Five and a half years ago we—'

'Denny...' I sat down, and forced myself to look at him. I couldn't bear to see the pain on his face.

'We had a... had a child together.' His eyes were wet. 'And never once... not once, did you tell me that you were already a mother.'

'I wasn't a mother. Not at all. I barely even saw her when she was born. It was one of the hardest times of my life.' I couldn't say it was the hardest, because what he and I had been through supplanted it. Quietly, pleadingly, wanting beyond anything for him to believe me, I said, 'Denny, I swear to you, I never talked about it. I never knew what had happened to her.'

He moved, as if he was going to reach for me, take my hand. 'That must have been terrible.' For a moment, he was focused only on what I'd been through, not the pain I was causing him. I was sure that I'd be able to make him understand.

'No-one knew,' I said. 'Only my brothers, because they were there at the time, that was all...'

He sat up straight, a new thought clearly having hit him for six. 'Oh my god! That doctor knew! The one who talked to us when you were in hospital.'

When Denny and I lost our baby, the doctor came in to talk through what had happened, what might have gone wrong. She sat on my bed, held my hand.

'We don't really know,' she said. 'Stillbirth is not uncommon, maybe 1 in 200 births. There are sometimes clear causes but often not. You're a little older, that might have played a part, but we don't know. I'm so sorry.' She was gentle and kind. Then she said, 'I understand you've had several miscarriages.'

'Yes,' I said, 'three with Denny, and two with Kim, my previous partner, all in the first three months.'

'And one live birth,' she said, looking at her notes, 'when you were much younger.'

'No,' Denny said, 'that's not right.'

'No,' I echoed, 'that's not right.' I gripped my arms so tightly that later I saw there were marks on my skin, actual tiny bruises in the shape of fingertips.

The doctor looked at me, and said, 'I'm so sorry, I misread it.' Later, when Denny had gone, she came back, and asked if I wanted to talk. I cried my heart out, and she held me.

'I'm such an idiot,' Denny said now. 'I assumed she'd got your notes confused with someone else's.'

'I should have told you then. I wish with all my heart I had. It's just... for most of the time it's locked away, always has been. Months go by without me ever thinking about it.'

'But all those times with us.' He spread his arms out, a gesture of incomprehension. 'The pregnancies, the miscarriages...'

'I just... didn't know how to tell you. It felt so cruel, unfair, to tell you that while we were trying so hard and getting nowhere, I casually gave a child away years ago.'

'I'm sure it wasn't casual, was it?' His eyes were full of empathy, which felt extraordinary under the circumstances. I remembered Peaches at the salon once saying how she'd never heard of a male carer before Denny, and that the world would be a better place if more men were like him. How proud I was when she said that, how lucky I felt.

'No, it wasn't. It was incredibly painful. You called yourself an idiot,' I said, 'but I'm the idiot, to think that I couldn't have told you about it.'

'I so wish you had. I think I've always shown that you can trust me. Finding out now, only after you've been backed into a corner, makes me feel... well, I don't even know how I feel.'

'Can I tell you now? Do you want to know about me meeting her? Carrie? She showed me a photo of her child. We have a grandchild out there, Denny. A little girl, like...' I stopped, because this was the hardest thing. We never said her name out loud, and my voice cracked before I could get to it: a name so familiar inside my head, so impossible and strange outside.

Denny looked so sad, I moved towards him to put my arms round him, make it better. But he stood up. 'I don't know, Pearl. I think you have a grandchild. And I'm glad for you. But *I* don't.' He went to the door. 'Going to bed.'

I listened to him going upstairs, slowly and heavily, as if he weighed a hundred tons. I let my head sink onto my arms. I wished I could go back in time, even just a day. Before I met Carrie, when a relationship with her still seemed possible; before Serge ran away; before I lied to Denny.

I stopped myself from going after him. He needed to be alone. I opened the repaired notebook, the ideal thing for my flattened mood. Dad's final diary, from earlier this year. I remembered reading some snippets of the first entry at the wake: an account of a phone conversation he had with Roberta at PAC-UK in January this year, a few months before he died.

For all that I wasn't able to, I really hope that she and you can find a way to make up for lost time.

Now I knew that the 'she' was Carrie, and the 'you' was me. Well, sorry, Dad. It looked like your last wish just wasn't going to happen. I trailed upstairs, one step at a time. Maybe Denny was still awake. I could crawl into his arms, murmur my regrets, comfort him and be comforted in return. But he was in the spare room, the door closed between us. I brushed my teeth and started to wash the dirt out from under my nails. But then I stopped. I didn't want to remove this physical reminder of seeing Carrie, of a shared moment before things went wrong.

I got into our empty bed. The sheets were cold, and I ached all over, my limbs tired from the stresses of an unfamiliar day. I didn't usually feel my age, but tonight I could easily imagine what it would be like to be an old woman with aching knees and stooped shoulders. I hugged myself, feeling the absence of Denny's arms as a physical pain. Did him sleeping in the spare room just mean he was angry for now, or did it mean he was through with me, with us? I closed my eyes, telling myself that sleep was the only answer, that things would look better in the morning. But I knew I was kidding myself.

My first conversation with Linda, the adoptive mother, was awkward, even though I followed the structure of the PAC-UK script Roberta sent me. L naturally wary, said straight away that she had not yet told Caroline she was speaking to me, didn't know if she would, hated to upset her, was waiting to see how it went. Well, that put me on my best behaviour! She said C had a lot going on, a single working parent with a small baby. Plus she, Linda, was ill and felt that C was in denial about it. I sympathised, said I would leave it with her if/how she talked to C.

After we said goodbye I felt sure that it was the end of the road. Wished I could talk to A about it but I don't want to burden her. She has enough on her plate now she lives so near us again, is at J's beck and call. I always hoped she'd be able to stay away, even after her marriage ended, make her own life. But once James went to live with his father I know it was hard for her to keep away. James was made of tougher stuff than A, was always telling her to stand up for herself.

I called Roberta to tell her what Linda had said. She was optimistic, said not to make any assumptions, let some time pass.

Roberta is a young woman with all the time in the world, how I envy her! I do not have that luxury.

But she was right, because today she rang. Thank god I was out walking Snoops and able to answer. She said Linda had called to say that there were more things she wanted to know from me. But after that, she would find the right moment to speak to C, would give her my contact details and yours too. Roberta seemed to think this was extremely positive so I knew I had to be content with that. I suspect that I probably won't get to speak to C but that doesn't matter as long as you do.

Asked Roberta if she knew C's baby's name but she said she didn't, would ask Linda for me. Keep thinking about the 'small baby'.

SIXTEEN

CARRIE

I had too much time to think on the Eurostar. I couldn't concentrate to read, but I couldn't sleep either. *Mum, I did what you wanted. But it didn't work out.* Too much water under the bridge. Too much unknown past.

I texted Iain, telling him that I should be back in Bristol by seven p.m. Then I flicked to the selfie I'd taken of Pearl and me. It was crazy how similar our faces were, our blue eyes and brown hair. We were the same height, too. I could see exactly how I'd look when I was older, not that she was vastly much older than me. It was a good look. I liked her style, slightly out of time, her pixie cut and her belted raincoat, channelling Audrey Hepburn. There was a time, in my teens, when I would have killed for such a photo: evidence of a genetic connection to someone, another person in my life who looked like me. Mum and I were physical opposites. She was busty, large-boned, and fair-haired, much shorter than me. Our only similarity was the blue of our eyes, and even then mine were darker. But when Emmie was born, that satisfied my need for such a connection. She had so many of my mannerisms, and our eyes were different coloured versions of the same eyes, her smile a carbon copy of mine.

I put my phone in my bag, and found that I still had Francis' diary that Pearl had given me. Damn. Well, I'd send it back to her with a note saying that my colleague couldn't interpret it. There was no need to prolong contact. It was too messy and complicated, there was too much baggage. Pearl gave birth to me, but she wasn't my mother. I didn't know who the hell she was, or who I was when I was with her. The important thing was that I'd kept my promise to Mum. She'd asked me to meet Pearl, no more than that, and I had. That was more than enough.

Mum wanted some of her ashes scattered in a big city, and though Paris could count as that, it felt like cheating to use it for two categories. Anyway, there weren't many bigger cities than London. The Big Smoke, Mum always called it. I calculated that I just about had time before catching my connecting train. The map on my phone directed me to a tiny square three minutes from Paddington, and in a quiet corner I put some of Mum under a chestnut tree. I whispered a few words, then rushed back to the station and, miracle of miracles, caught the train I was aiming for.

As we pulled into Bristol Temple Meads station, I realised that I was an hour earlier than I'd told Iain. In the chaos of the day I'd forgotten that I'd put my watch forward in France. I flopped into a cab, deciding to go to Iain's flat anyway. I would just call him if they weren't in.

I always liked Iain's street. Being here reminded me of the early casual-dating phase of our relationship. He'd lived in this same flat above a Turkish deli when I first met him, and had rented it out when we bought our house together. My all-time favourite baker was on this street, a Greek place which sold amazing filled doughnuts in every flavour. Iain's barber was a few doors along, and there was a good second-hand baby clothes shop where I always found something nice for Emmie.

It was early evening and still warm. People were buzzing about, laughing and talking, standing outside bars and cafes, rather like the streets I'd walked through in Paris just hours before. I smiled as I told the driver where to pull over. I decided that when I collected Emmie we could get a juice at the stand on the corner. Maybe Iain would come too. Would it be the worst thing in the world if Emmie spent more time here? If I did too?

As I got out of the cab, I saw a couple with a baby standing outside the deli; it took me a few moments to realise that it was Iain and a woman I didn't recognise. The woman was taller than Iain, with long yellow hair, and she was holding my Emmie in her arms. I watched the driver rifling around in his little bag for my change, and it seemed to be in slow motion.

'Don't worry about it,' I said, moving away.

'Well, thanks very much, love,' he said, surprised – I clearly didn't look like someone who tipped eight quid for a twelve-quid journey.

He drove off, and I stood where I was, on the opposite side of the road to Iain and his shiny new family. He was resting a hand on the empty buggy so they'd either been out, or were going out now. The woman said something to him, and he gestured towards the flat. Then she looked down at Emmie in her arms and kissed her cheek, and I was across that street in two seconds. The woman saw me approaching first, but obviously didn't know me; there was a split second when she frowned, confused, because I was coming too close to them. Emmie twisted in her arms and said, 'Mama!' and I don't even know how the changeover happened but then I was holding Emmie, her warm hands tight round my neck, my heart thumping as if I had been running.

'Oh, you're the mummy!' the woman gushed. 'I'm Melody.

Thank you so much for lending us your gorgeous daughter. Yes, you are gorgeous aren't you! Yes you are!'

She chucked Emmie under the chin and Emmie laughed, the traitor. I held her tighter to me and breathed in her smell but there was an overlay of unfamiliar perfume on top. Or not so unfamiliar perhaps, as I realised I had smelled it in Iain's flat. I'd assumed it was one of his many products – he liked his products, the shaving stuff and the colognes and the fucking hair stuff. I couldn't wait to get home, get Emmie in the bath and wash her with her baby lotions that smelled pure, of nothing.

'You're early,' Iain said to me, and in those two words were a whole dictionary of lies. I knew without being told that they'd spent the day together, that Melody was meant to be long gone before I returned. They'd been saying goodbye when I arrived.

'Iain said you've been to Paris!' Melody said. 'That is so cool!'

'How did it go?' Iain said, his concerned face on.

'Fine.' Like I would ever tell him anything important again. 'How was Emmie?'

'Oh, we had such a fun day!' Melody said, utterly oblivious to, well, everything. 'We went to the park, didn't we, Emmie, for a picnic! We had little sandwiches and Emmie had a few crisps – she loves them, doesn't she? Then we fed the ducks and she went on the swings, and we went to the shops, and I got her such a cute top. Then, after a nice long nap at the flat, we played games and watched TV, and I made her pasta shapes with cheese for tea. She ate it all up, and then we went back to the park again because Emmie can't get enough of those ducks, can she?'

'She likes ducks,' I said, in a voice I barely recognised. My teeth started to feel painful, the way they often did around Iain.

'Well, I'd better get going. Lovely to meet you, Cassie.'

'Carrie,' I said. Carrie was the name of the mother of the child you pretended was yours all afternoon.

'Of course! Sorry!' She kissed Iain on the lips, and then went to kiss Emmie. I pulled away, just enough for her to step back but not enough for her to know if I was doing it deliberately or not.

'I'll see you tomorrow,' Iain said, and she went, and then it was just the three of us.

'Carrie, I'm sorry, I know that was a bit weird...'

'It was certainly a bit something.'

'You should see Emmie with her. Melody really loves kids.'

Emmie was becoming heavy and sleepy in my arms, but I didn't want to put her down. 'It would be good,' I said, 'if you'd told me my daughter was spending the day with someone I don't know.'

'I was going to tell you about Melody,' he said. 'But you were upset about your mum, and everything.'

Iain's sudden desire to be back in our lives finally made sense. I tried not to blush at the thought of how I'd allowed hope to override my natural scepticism. He was just using Emmie as a prop, a way to make him look like a well-rounded, decent guy, without doing any of the hard work of actually being well-rounded and decent.

I shifted my weight to accommodate Emmie, who was now properly asleep. 'Are you really interested in shared custody? Or is it something you think will impress Melody?'

'What?! How can you even ask me that?' Iain spluttered, but he couldn't quite meet my eye. He was unlucky that I'd had so much experience of what he looked like when he was lying. I suppose that made me unlucky too, if you thought about it.

'Well, I'd better be going.' I took the buggy out of his hand and walked off, pushing it in front of me, not wanting to put Emmie in it in case someone had a notion to take her away from me. I didn't look back.

'It's you and me, kid,' I whispered to my beautiful child. 'Just you and me.'

Roberta and I were on the phone for half an hour. She asked a lot of questions about you, your life now, most of which, to my shame, I did not know the answer to. These were things Linda had asked her to find out. But I did talk about things you and I had liked to do together when you were a child. I told her about how good you were at languages, the fun we had with shorthand, writing coded messages to each other. Do you remember we had a phase of learning Esperanto, too?

And crosswords, of course. I loved doing them with you. I remember the first time you got a difficult clue by yourself. You were about ten. It was after church, and we were sitting outside in the sun waiting for someone, I think to bring me pages to type up for the parish magazine. I spent a lot of time waiting for copy, ah, the life of the amateur journalist! I'd given you the cryptic crossword from my newspaper to look at. You worked away at it quietly, then said, 'I've got one!' You had, too. 'Wild animal in capital city' was the clue. The answer, of course, was 'Manila'. How proud I was!

I probably rambled on rather. Poor Roberta! She was very

polite, said she would pass the information on. Right at the end of the call, she said Linda had said it was fine to tell me the name of Caroline's baby. It's Emily Ruby Haskett. They call her Emmie for short. Beautiful.

9TH MARCH 2018

Bleak news from the doctor today. I don't know what happened to my life, and now it's almost over. It will always be my biggest regret that I wasn't a proper father to you and Benjy. I wasn't much better with Greg but at least we kept in touch. I don't delude myself that I can make it up to you. I'm amazed, to be honest, that you kept writing to me for so long after I let you down, well into your twenties. When you wrote in 1990, asking if you could come and see me, I wrote back saying, don't come. I need to tell you that I didn't mean it. My hands were tied. I hoped you knew it wasn't really from me, that I just wrote what I agreed to write, because I signed it with my name, rather than 'Dad'.

I think you did realise, because you did come. But then you ran away before we spoke, and I was too late to stop you. I don't think my heart ever mended after that. If you only knew the hundreds of times I started to write, picked up the phone. But it was easier to let you go. I made my bed, I had to lie in it. It's too late, too much water under the bridge now, to say it wasn't my wish to be separate from you. I should have been different, better.

I didn't lead the life I wanted. I should have been a true Christian instead of a church-goer, the two are not the same.

But at least now there's something I can do for you, to make the smallest reparation for the time when you asked for my help and I didn't give it.

The fun we used to have with shorthand! It's such a useful skill, though I hear that student journalists aren't taught it any longer, what a shame. When you need to make notes quickly, or don't want someone to know what you're writing, there's nothing better. When I started keeping my diary properly for you, after that missed visit, I hoped we would look at it together some time, so you'd know that I was always thinking of you, even when we were apart. I give thanks to God that I didn't know then that would never happen.

So, dear PP, I wrote these diaries for you. Please share them with your brothers. I know A would like to see them too, but I will leave that in your hands. She would have greatly benefitted from having you three as siblings, but again, I made a pig's ear of all that. I worry about how she will manage after I've gone, but that is my cross to bear, not yours.

I'm sorry I can't leave any of you much money. I did not manage to hold onto much, other than an account that my friend at church, Hugh, kept in his name for me.

But when you come to my funeral to collect the diaries, as I hope you will, you will find that I have left something else for you. Something more interesting and important than money, or my witterings. Someone else, not something. Of course, it's up to you to decide whether you continue the connection I began. I hope you decide to. I hope it more than anything. But whether you do or don't, at least I've given you the choice that was taken away from you, when you were very young.

I should never have left you to cope with so much alone. I should have stood up for what I knew to be right, however diffi-

cult and however bad the consequences. I have tried to tidy up the mess I made while you are still young enough to benefit. I would like you to be able to say of me, nothing in his life became him like the leaving it.

SEVENTEEN

PEARL

The cottage, which used to feel decadently big for two, felt claustrophobic when those two people were trying to avoid each other. I hadn't started out wanting to avoid Denny. On the contrary, I'd tried numerous times to talk, kept telling him how sorry I was. But he didn't want to talk. I understood, at first. I'd kept this huge thing from him, and he was entitled to feel that I'd betrayed his trust. If the shoe was on the other foot, and I found out that *he'd* had a child without telling me, I'd of course be equally devastated.

But days went by, and still he kept out of my way. He slept in the spare room, took his meals at different times, and spent far more hours than usual in his workroom, the buzz saw going so continually that I suspected he was leaving it on so it sounded like he was busy. After a while, I took to making it easy for him by removing myself. I offered more client appointments than usual, and when I wasn't working, I went for long walks, continued my drawing series of the trees, and painstakingly translated the diaries.

I was surprised how poignant and touching I found the diary entries from the start of this year, knowing Dad was right at the end of his life. How sentimental he became in his old age, all that business about us doing crosswords. Fancy remembering me solving that clue! The shorthand here was wobbly and uncertain, maybe because he was becoming more ill, or just because he was old. I ran my finger under the words, remembering how he'd take my hand when teaching me, running it along lines of shorthand. Our heads bent close together, both delighted when I recognised a word. If you'd told me then, when I was seven or eight, that there would come a time when he was not a part of my life, I wouldn't have believed you.

I saw three clients this morning, but was in no hurry to get home. Instead, I made my way to my favourite place, and rested against my tree. The wood felt empty without Serge in it. There was a time when I had just accepted, if not necessarily agreed with, Denny's take on things. I'd understood his belief that we should keep the wood to ourselves, fortify ourselves into our own little private fiefdom with a fence and gate. And I'd understood his gentle encouragement to protect ourselves from the world in other ways, too.

But now Denny and I were out of sync. He still hadn't said anything about Carrie at all, hadn't asked how it went, how I felt. I would have asked him, had the roles been reversed. I was desperate to talk about her, but apart from Denny-the-Silent, there was only one person I could imaging telling, taking advice from. I opened my phone and looked at Eleanor's number for a long time. But there was already a heavy weight, like a cartoon anvil, hanging above my marriage. Calling Eleanor, telling her about Carrie, about my problems with Denny, would mean I was ready to bring it crashing firmly down.

My hand scrolled to Carrie's number. I'd thought every day, every hour, about contacting her. To say how sorry I was for how our day in Paris ended. To ask if we could try again. Every time, instead of pressing the call button I would put the phone away, find somewhere to lie down and weep. The last time I cried like this I was in a hospital bed, a kind doctor listening patiently as she held my hand. As then, everything felt completely hopeless. And this time, I didn't even have a kind doctor to lean on. I had no-one. My husband, who had for so long protected me from people's expectations, had pushed me away because I didn't live up to his. My best friend and I had a chasm between us that I didn't know how to close. My daughter – so weird to think of someone with that designation – had reached out to me, and I'd failed to grasp her hand. She was lost, then for a short shining moment she was found, and then I somehow contrived to lose her again.

Even my father, who I thought couldn't possibly affect me any more, had come crashing back into my life to tell me that he did really love me after all, that he'd always been thinking about me. *So, dear PP, I wrote these diaries for you.* And I had let him come crashing back, had run to him when he was ill, then laid myself wide open for more hurt, with a front-row seat to the inside of his head for forty years.

For what purpose, Dad? All those wasted years when we could have seen each other, supported each other. And all I'd had to do, it seemed, *à la* Greg, was keep trying. I tried once, and for some stupid reason, I didn't try again. Frankly, it was no wonder Denny was furious with me. He was furious about the wrong thing, perhaps, but it turned out that I was an absolute champion, across the board, at letting slip through my fingers all the people I should have loved and clung onto the hardest. They had a part to play, too; I wasn't so self-flagellating or self-important to think all these breaches were entirely my fault. But there was no denying that each seemed to follow a similar pattern, and all starred Little Miss Mouse, who passively let events wash over her as though she had no more say in them than in the turning of the tide.

I looked down at the drawing pad on my knees, and saw that my tears had soaked into the drawing, smudging lines and buckling the paper. I wiped my eyes. *Come on, Pearl, get a grip.* I needed something, or someone, to shake me out of this. And as I had that thought, I knew there was one person who wouldn't judge me, who'd face me head-on, not turn away. Well, he might judge me actually, but not in a way I cared about in the least. And he certainly wouldn't let me wallow in self-pity. I picked up my phone again.

'Hey Chicken Licken,' Benjy said. 'Has the sky fallen in?'

'Huh?'

'You never phone me. So, must be something pretty savage. Go on, I'm ready for a laugh.'

'It's not going to make you laugh, I'm afraid. There hasn't been a load to laugh at lately.'

'You had a front seat at the world's most hilarious will reading, how can you say that?'

Even with Benjy, I needed to build up to it. 'I wanted to update you about Dad's diaries.'

'Wow.' He sounded genuinely surprised. 'That's good of you. What are they like?'

'Very weird. Dad's relationship with Jeanie... well, it sounded awful. He was really afraid to upset her, tiptoeing round on eggshells the whole time.'

'*Jeanie's* really weird on her own. What did she call me at the funeral? A loser, a waster. Me! I'm the exact opposite.'

I side-stepped this. 'The weirdest part is how closely he followed what was going on in our lives. He knew pretty much everything about us.'

'Seriously? How come?'

Thinking about the diary entry from the nineties, when Dad rang Benjy, I said, teasingly, 'I was going to ask you the same thing.'

'Me? Why the hell would I know?'

'He mentions talking to you a couple of times...'

'He does? Well, yes, Inspector Clouseau, I did, but literally only a couple. And only for a minute each time, at most. I certainly never told him a single thing about me, let alone you...'

'It's all right, Ben. I'm just yanking your chain, as you might put it. Turns out he was in touch with Greg all the time.'

'I thought that was only for the first ten years or so.'

'What? I didn't even know that. No, they were in touch right to the end.'

'He's such a shit, isn't he?'

'Greg?'

'The "he" works for both of them.' There was a pause, then Benjy said, faux casual, 'So what does Dad say about me?'

'I've mostly read the bits that relate to me,' I said, in the upfront way you could only admit to a sibling. 'But he has mentioned you a fair amount. He was full of regret at the end that he hadn't been around for us.'

'Ah, I don't know why I care. I can't even remember what he looked like.'

'My image of him is stuck in the 1980s, but Greg said the last time he saw him, around 2009, he was a tired old man with thin grey hair.' My voice quavered a little as I said this. 'Like in the photo on that order of service.'

For no discernible reason, Benjy put on an American Deep South accent. 'Don't go getting all maudlin now. Daddy, he be dead, all right? You can't go do nuttin' about that.' Mercifully, he reverted to his usual voice. 'So your shorthand must be in good shape now. Do you understand it all?'

'Most of it, though he refers to pretty much everyone by their initials which makes it slow-going.'

'Christ, could he be any more cloak and dagger? It's already in code!'

'And my name is weird, he always calls me PP instead of just P. I honestly don't know...'

'Wow, you really can't remember what that stands for? You're getting Alzheimer's, old woman.'

'Wait – you know what it means?'

'Don't you remember about Dad and *Peanuts*?'

'Peanuts? Huh? The, er, salty nut?'

'Peanuts are a legume, not a nut, dumbo.'

'OK, I have completely lost my way in this conversation, Ben.'

'*Peanuts*, the comic book. You know, Snoopy, Charlie Brown, all that. Dad loved them.'

Peanuts and Good Ol' Charlie Brown. I was whooshed into a memory I didn't know I had: all of us in the kitchen, Christmas time, cold outside, the windows misted up with heat from the stove. I'm stirring something in a pan, Mum's leaning over to look, Benjy is drying dishes, Greg's sitting at the table reading a book. Dad calls us in to the living room. 'It's on!' he says, excited, and we all run in to watch *A Charlie Brown Christmas.* I sit next to Dad and watch him as much as I watch the show, fascinated by how captivated he is.

Connected to this was a flash image of a bookcase in a small room, squashed behind the door. You had to close the door to access it. I said, 'Didn't he have some of the books?'

'He had loads, those little paperbacks that were, like, twenty-five pence each. I have them now.'

'You do?'

'Well, somewhere. In the loft at Barb's house, I think. *Peanuts* was our thing, my and Dad's thing. God!' Benjy almost yelled this last word. 'I'd repressed this, you know? He had such a weird mix of books in the box room. *Peanuts* next to *Moby Dick* and *The Once and Future King* and *The Joy of Sex*.'

'He used to call that room his study,' I said, and the breath went out of me as if I'd been punched in the stomach. Thank god Benjy wasn't here in person to see me register that I had exactly the same thing, without realising who I was imitating, or even that I *was* imitating: a box room that I called my study, which was lined with bookshelves, books mixed up in no order. Denny always said he didn't know how I could find anything.

'Yeah,' Benjy went on, mercifully unaware of the contortions my mind and body were going through, 'he liked talking about those cartoons in a boring grown-up way, layers of meaning, spiritual symbolism and blah blah bullshit. I just thought they were funny. "You fathead, Charlie Brown."' Benjy laughed. 'I used to say that all the time. Barb still says it to me sometimes.'

Wishing Denny and I were on good enough terms for me to report this conversation, I drank an imaginary shot at the mention of Barb's name.

'So why am I PP...?' I started to say, and then I remembered at the same time as Benjy answered, and as I remembered, I wondered how it could ever have slipped my mind. It was so weird, wasn't it, the things that stuck and the things that faded over the course of half a century? But this shouldn't have faded; I loved that name.

'You were Peppermint Patty, of course.'

Dad always insisted I was like her, though I'm sure we all knew that I wasn't. Patty was brave, brash and funny. Young as I was, I knew I was more like Marcie, Patty's sidekick, the shy one with big glasses who called Patty 'Sir'. Another Little Miss Mouse. I assumed Dad chose Patty for me, because who wanted to be Marcie?

But Benjy remembered it differently. 'It was because you liked mint.'

'It was?'

'God, yes, everything had to be mint. Mint Aero, mint sauce, After Eights. You were the only one who liked mint ice cream.'

So there it was. The whole time Dad was absent from my life, he referred to me in his private thoughts by the affectionate nickname he bestowed when I was tiny. The frozen image of him as uncaring and uninterested that I had retained for so long was starting to crack. Underneath was another Dad: a troubled, unhappy man carrying hidden layers of softness and memory and regret.

'You still there, Patty Cake? Hey, where do you think I got Patty Cake from, if you hadn't remembered Peppermint Patty?'

'I don't know. I never thought about it.' How many more things were there I had never thought about?

'So, are we done?' Ben still had the attention span of a flea. 'Is that the end of this week's hike down memory lane?'

'Not quite.' My grip tightened on the phone. 'Listen, I want to tell you something.'

'Ooh, your voice is even more Radio Four newsreader than usual. I am *braced*.'

'My daughter rang me.'

'Your *what*?' There was a moment's pause, then Benjy, who always had a quicksilver mind, even if he never cared to deploy it in a constructive manner, said, 'Oh my god, are you *kidding*? The *baby*?'

'I met her. In Paris. She's called Carrie.'

'I can't believe it! What's she like? How old is she? Must be in her mid-thirties? Hey, is she hot?'

Maybe this was why he hadn't been my first choice to tell. 'She's beautiful, Ben, and can I remind you, she's your *niece*.'

'Are you going to see her again?'

'I don't know. It didn't work out terribly well.'

'Shit, Pill. You need to sort that out. Don't lose her again.'

'That's surprisingly heartfelt, coming from you.'

'Yeah, messed-up families are my jam. Why'd it go badly?'

'She was upset that I'd never told Denny about her.'

'You didn't? Oh, Peppermint Patty, you *fathead*. Bet he's well pissed off.'

'You could say that. We're still at the silent treatment stage.'

'I'm sorry.' Benjy sounded sincere, for once. 'That's properly rough. You were only a kid yourself. I remember how fucking awful it all was. Didn't Mum send you away? Positively medieval. Want me to talk to Denny for you?'

I felt the tears start again, and blinked them back. Imagine a kind word from my annoying little brother setting me off! I sniffed, and realised there was a familiar smell of chlorine. I looked up, and Serge was standing in the clearing, looking at me uncertainly.

'It's OK. Thanks, Ben. I have to go. By the way, she has a baby.'

'You're a granny! Love it! The role you were born to, you old bag.'

'I'm younger than Barb, your favourite girlfriend.'

'Ha ha, there's that terrific Patty Cake sense of humour.' He hung up.

Serge and I looked at each other.

'So,' I said. 'Running away didn't work out for you, right?'

He glared down at me. 'What the hell do you know about it?'

'I know about running away.' I craned my neck to look at him. I would have liked to stand, but my legs were shaky. 'I wish I didn't, but I do.'

'This is your shit, not mine.'

'Serge, she misses you every day.' I stared at the ground, so I didn't have to see his face. I could feel the tension coming off him like heat from a fire. Finally, when I wasn't sure I could bear the silence any longer, I heard him sit down.

'I'm a mess,' he said. 'How can I go to her like this?'

He was in poorer shape than when I'd last seen him: his hair and beard longer and more straggly than ever, his clothes dirtier. But he ought to know that his appearance wasn't what mattered.

'How can you *not* go to her? Haven't you been planning this for months? You stayed here for ages, waiting for the right moment.'

'It's still not the right moment. You know what, if your fucking husband wasn't going to kick me out, I could stay here till I was ready.'

'You'll never be ready. It will never be the right moment. There's no such thing. There's just the times that you didn't do it, and the time that you do.' I knew I was talking to myself as much as him. The times I didn't act – I'd lost count of how many there were of those.

'I've tried to keep my clothes presentable,' he said, 'but it's hard. And my hair and beard make me look like a homeless man.'

'You are a homeless man.'

'Fuck you.' He got up again. 'I don't know what I thought, coming back here again. I nearly made it to Paris.'

'I can help you,' I said. 'I know what your hair used to look like.'

'So?' He spat on the ground. 'You're not a fucking hair-dresser.'

I opened my case so he could see the kit – the scissors, combs, clippers, rollers, all neatly stacked in place. 'I am a fucking hairdresser.'

'A woodland fairy hairdresser?' He stared at the case, then his eyes slowly travelled to my face. 'Who. *Are*. You?'

I stood up, my legs no longer shaky. 'My name is Pearl Flowers. I am a trained beautician and hairstylist. I love children and I nearly had children and I lost them. I know what that feels like. I maybe know a little of how Mme Remard feels. She is an old lady, now.'

'I saw her one morning when I was leaving the pool,' he said, quietly. 'I only knew it was her because her hair is still that crazy colour.'

'I'm her colourist.'

'Of course you are.' He shook his head. 'Nothing surprises me today.'

'I can't do anything about your clothes,' I said. 'Removing a few layers will help. But I can certainly do something about your hair.'

He hoisted his bag onto his shoulder. 'I can't, I'm sorry. I can't walk up to that house, and knock on the door...'

'I'll come with you.'

He closed his eyes, and I waited.

Finally, he said, 'Why did you give me the key to the gate?'

His eyes were still closed, so he couldn't see me shake my head. How the hell could I explain it? I didn't understand it myself. I just recognised, when I first saw him, something of myself. Hiding in a safe space, waiting to feel brave enough to break out. In limbo. Like him, it had taken me a long time to be ready to move on, but I knew it was coming. I had allowed Denny to hide me away in a safe place, and it wasn't his fault that I didn't want that any longer.

Carrie thought I was fluent, but I didn't have the French to say all that; I scarcely had the English. 'You needed the key,' I said simply, 'like you need a bloody haircut.' I pointed at a tree stump. 'Sit down.'

Serge opened his eyes, and stood still, his bag on his shoulder. The moment slowed down. Stay? Or go? I knew it was stupid; it made no sense to conflate my own destiny with this man, this stranger. But I didn't want him to go. I didn't want him to leave his mother wondering what had happened to him for the rest of her life.

I raised my eyes away from his, and stared at a tree covered with small pale leaves. The sunlight was filtering through, and if I moved my head very slightly, it shimmered off the leaves, making them look like gold. I tried to memorise the exact shade, so I could capture it in paint later.

An eternity went by, then I heard him drop the bag onto the

ground. He sat down on the tree stump, and I put the cutting collar round his neck, getting to work quickly before he changed his mind. The clippers' battery was low, so I couldn't use them, but you could get as neat a hairline with scissors, if you knew what you were doing.

For a while I cut without either of us speaking, no sound but the swish and snip of my scissors. His hair was thick, very dark brown, almost black, with a few threads of silver, and at least three inches too long in every direction. It was strange working outdoors, rather nice, and the slight breeze whisked the snipped hair away, no need to sweep up.

He broke the silence, finally, as I tilted his head down to get to the nape. 'Thank you.'

'Not anywhere near done yet.'

'You know what I mean.' He coughed, and when he spoke, his voice was thick. 'What did you run away from?'

'Same as you. My old life. My family.'

'They didn't love you?'

'Oh... no, they did. They do. That's not what...'

'Not the same as me, then. I ran away from people who didn't love me, back to my mother, who does. You've made a mistake.'

'It's not as simple as that, it's...' I stopped, because I didn't know what it was. 'You don't know anything about it.'

'I know exactly as much as you show, which is a lot.'

I moved round and started trimming the side. 'What do I show?'

'Some kind of trauma. Not properly recovered. Hiding from it rather than confronting it.'

'You picked all that up from seeing me walking around the wood?' Thank god he had no idea the effect his brutal summary had on my heart rate. I concentrated on slowly combing out the front of his hair, releasing a waft of chlorine. 'So, what should I do?'

'I'm not a shrink, am I?'

'I don't know. You might be? I don't know what work you do. I don't think skulking around in private woods is an actual career – or at least, I can't imagine it pays too well.' I heard myself deflecting the darkness of what he'd said about me with silly chat. 'The woman you helped to find our cottage, my, er, sister...' – how odd that sounded, but I had to face it: Andrea was my sister – 'thought you were a ranger.'

'Ha, wish I was. Back in Paris I was a research chemist.'

'What happened to the girl you ran away with? The teacher?'

'Wow, you know my tragic backstory.'

'Adeline has a photo of you on the wall. You haven't been forgotten.'

'My photo?' His shoulders shuddered, and I moved the scissors away so as not to mis-snip. 'I thought she would never want to see my face again.'

'On the contrary. It's on display. Vivienne, her lodger, still remembers you.'

'Who did you say?'

'Vivienne Legrain. She was at the school when you taught there. She manages the *tabac*.'

'I remember Vivi Legrain, all right. She was beautiful.'

'She still is. I'm surprised you never saw her in town.'

'I was never there except in the early hours, at the pool, and the twenty-four-hour garage for food. Didn't want to be seen. How incredible that Vivi still lives here. All these people who stayed, who never moved away, I used to pity them. Now I envy them.'

'It's a wonderful town. I'm lucky it's taken me to its heart, an immigrant. I've made some amazing friends.'

'You're white, of course, the right sort of immigrant.'

'That's very cynical.'

'I am a cynic. But all right, there is more to you than that.

You put crazy colours on old ladies' hair, you are quiet and elegant, you speak superb French. Of course they would love you.'

There was a long silence, during which I tackled the hair flopping over his forehead, putting in small layers for a better shape.

Abruptly he said, 'The teacher and I lasted precisely six months.'

'I'm so sorry.'

'She tired of my youthful ineptitude very quickly.'

I stepped back, partly to see how I was doing – pretty good – and partly to see his face – pretty rueful. 'Why didn't you come back then?'

'I left with an embarrassingly hubristic fanfare. The young are so stupid, aren't they?'

I resumed cutting on the other side. 'They can be.'

'It was all right. I made a life there. Met other girls.' I heard the smile in his voice. 'Lots of other girls.'

'Did you marry?'

'Sure, why not? Married twice. Divorced twice.'

'Kids?'

'Yes. They don't like me much. You are good at deflecting the conversation away from yourself, aren't you?'

'I've nothing to tell.'

'On the contrary, my friend, you have a lot to tell. And you asked what I think you should do. I have an answer for you.'

I didn't think I wanted to hear his answer. 'I'm just going to trim the beard so it's not so wild.'

'Should I keep it permanently?'

'Maybe not, but I don't have the equipment with me to give you a clean shave. Once you're settled in your mother's house, I'll do it when I come to colour her hair.'

'If I'm there.'

I stood in front of him to snip the straggly ends of his beard.

'You should do the same thing you told me to do,' he said. I could feel him looking up at me, his gaze intense. 'Face the thing you don't want to face, bring it out into the open. Tell the people you need to tell, then put it to rest.'

I shivered. Someone walking over my grave. 'How do you know I—'

'We all have something like that.' His voice was gentle. 'A narrative we need to change. Baggage we need to offload.'

I stopped cutting to wipe my eyes on my sleeve.

'Hey.' He pulled a surprisingly clean tissue out of his pocket and handed it to me. 'You'll be all right.'

Would I? The narrative I wanted to change felt impossibly ingrained. How would I even start?

I cut for a few more minutes, then stood back. 'That'll do.' I gave him my folding mirror.

'You're a miracle worker. I look ten years younger.'

I took the collar off, and brushed down his shoulders. 'Let's go.'

'You want us to go now? To my mother's house?'

'If there was ever a right moment, though we've established that there isn't, this would be it.'

Serge stood up. He looked rather handsome. Now the hair was off his face, it was much easier to recognise the young man from the photograph. 'Quick then, before I change my mind.'

We cut across Serge's shortcut at the top of the wood to get to the town path. Once we went through the gate, he started talking, fast. 'I could give you plenty of reasons why I left but I just... lost my nerve. Every time I thought about her face when she opened the door to me, I thought I would be sick. Actually, I was sick a couple of times.'

'Being scared is nothing to be ashamed of.'

'When I realised you knew who I was, I left. Hitched, had a few uncomfortable rides, slept in some rough places, and got most of the way to Paris, and then...'

'What?'

In a rush, he said, 'I realised I still had your field glasses.' He stopped walking, fished in his pocket and handed them to me. They were more battered than they had been. But they were still, I realised with a start, my dearest possession. My hand trembled as I took them back.

'You could have posted them, of course.'

'I didn't think of that.'

We were almost at Mme Remard's house when we met Vivienne.

'Hey, Pearl,' she said, then did a double-take. '*Serge Remard?*'

'Hello, Vivienne. Been a long time.'

She looked from him to me, then back again.

'You've got a hell of a memory for faces,' she said.

'So have you,' he said, smiling down at her.

I said, 'Serge wants to say hi to his mother.'

'How is she?' he said. 'I'm a little scared.'

'This is a hard thing to do alone, but much easier with friends,' Vivienne said, and she offered him her arm.

The three of us stood outside Mme Remard's house. Vivienne leaned against Serge on one side, already claiming ownership, while I was on high alert on his other side, because I knew that he might yet run.

'I can use my key, if you prefer,' Vivienne said.

Serge shook his head. He turned to me, his eyes wide and panicked. 'Pearl, this is definitely the right moment?'

'It absolutely is.' I lowered my voice. 'And you're right about me. My own moment is fast approaching.'

'Then I must do this, I suppose, to show you that it can be done.' He smiled, and I saw the resolve return to his face.

'It certainly can be done,' Vivienne said, and she kissed his cheek. It was perhaps that, more than any pep talk, that galvanised him. He stepped forward, and knocked on the door.

We seemed to wait there for hours, though it was probably less than a minute, and I imagined Serge dying a thousand deaths as we waited. I didn't dare look at him, could feel the anxiety radiating off him. But finally Mme Remard opened the door, and stood gazing at the three of us. Her confused eyes flickered across our faces, before they fixed on Serge, and she put her hands to her mouth. There were a few seconds, our breaths held, during which every possible worst-case scenario flashed through my mind. Would she scream? Slam the door? Say she didn't know him? What if he was, in fact, an imposter?

And then she said, 'My son,' and he stepped forward and embraced her.

It was the second time in a month that I had been present as a long estrangement came to an end. I hoped this one would be more successful than mine and Carrie's. I squeezed Vivienne's hand, and wondered what would have happened if I'd made it right up to Dad's door, that day of the panic attack, nearly thirty years ago. Or if he had managed to reach me before I got into the boy's car. Would we have walked towards each other? Would he have held me tight, as Mme Remard was doing now, her hands gripping Serge as though she would never let him go? Or would it have been awkward and uncomfortable, as difficult as Carrie and I parting by the steps of the Sacré Coeur? Would it have brought about a new beginning, or a more definite ending? It wasn't hard to picture Jeanie standing in the doorway radiating hostility, Dad caught in the middle, eternally incapable of reassuring either of us.

But he had done his best, posthumously, to repair our estrangement, and it was time to silently thank him for it. And time to unclench, to try to think of him with more compassion. Well, fine words, Pearl. It was going to have to be a work in progress, like a painting being added to, a little at a time. I wouldn't manage it all at once, not with all the years of hurt to take into account. But I would work on it.

So: Dad and me, Carrie and me, and Serge and his mother. Three estrangements down. One more to go.

'My beautiful boy.' Mme Remard finally released Serge, though she kept hold of one arm as though afraid to let him go completely. 'Thank you,' she said to Vivienne and me, 'for bringing him back to me.'

'It was Pearl,' Serge said. 'I wouldn't be here now if it weren't for her.'

'It was a happy day for all of us when Pearl came to live here.' Mme Remard kissed my hand. Then she turned back to Serge. 'Come in, my son, come in, let me make you something to eat.'

He sent a last grateful look at me, then followed his mother into the house.

'My god!' Vivienne said, her mouth wide open in an O. 'I have always said that you are a dark horse! How long have you been friends with Serge?'

'Never mind that – did you see the way he looked at you, Vivi?'

'You think so? Maybe I will go in and give Adeline a hand.' She winked at me, and went into the house.

I stood a moment, thinking. Then I turned back towards the wood. Time to face up to things I didn't want to face. Tell the people I needed to tell.

EIGHTEEN

PEARL

'Ready to go?' I said, putting my head round the door of Denny's workroom.

He was sawing something on his workbench, and looked over his shoulder at me, frowning. He didn't turn off the saw, or flip up his goggles. 'Go where?'

'For Sunday lunch at La Bicyclette Jaune, of course.' I sounded more confident than I felt.

'You really want to?'

I took a breath. 'Yes, I do. We've barely seen each other all week.'

'OK. I'll finish this bit, then I'll get ready.'

It was the longest sentence he'd said in days. I took courage from that, and when I went into the kitchen I took courage too from the twig I'd put in water on the windowsill, its bud open in a cheering white blossom. You had to take your courage where you could.

We walked through the wood in silence, a distance between us where once we might have held hands. Denny gave the unlocked gate a meaningful stare, but once in the van things felt easier. It helped that we didn't have to look directly at each other.

'Thanks for agreeing to come,' I said.

'No, you're right. We should talk.' He steered the van onto the tree-lined road that would take us to Millau, and said, 'So, do you want to tell me about it?'

'Which part? The recent bit, or my torrid youth?'

'God! I don't know. Start at the beginning, maybe?'

I wasn't sure where the beginning was. Was it the fateful party? Was it earlier than that, when I started seeing Simon? Or was it earlier still, when Dad left?

Yes, it was there.

'After Dad left, I kind of dropped most of my social life. But when term ended, my friends insisted I celebrate with them. Practically dragged me. Well, even the most Goody Two-Shoes fifteen-year-old needed to break out some time, so I went. Did all my year's partying in one go. Drank too much, danced too much. Had sex with my boyfriend once, boom – I got pregnant.'

Denny glanced across at me, and there was a moment of accord between us, in which we both silently acknowledged the awful irony. One time, when you didn't want to get pregnant, you did. Then, as an adult, you tried hundreds of times, but nothing.

'What did the boy say?'

'I never told him. I told Mum, but she couldn't get her act together in time.' My heart fluttered as if I was back there, young, pregnant and alone. Mum holding me in her arms, saying, 'Don't worry, something will come along,' and me saying, 'But you can help me *now*,' and her just saying, 'Shh, shh, we'll be OK,' as though she was soothing a crying baby. The letter I'd written, saying Mum gave me permission to seek treatment, that she would accompany me to my appointments, lying unsigned on her bedside table.

'That's appalling. How could she be so negligent?'

This was strong stuff from Denny. But I was there, and he wasn't.

'Listen, she was a ghost, that whole year or two after Dad. She couldn't look after herself, let alone me and Benjy. She clearly had serious mental health issues, though I didn't have the words for that at the time. She would sometimes not get up at all for several days. I dropped all non-essential things, including art club, so I could keep everything going. I took over the salon, started keeping the books, paying the wages. And at home, it was me who made sure Benjy had a packed lunch for school, that he did his homework, that he cleaned his teeth.'

Denny shook his head in disbelief. 'Where was Greg in all this?'

'At university. I didn't tell him I was pregnant, didn't want him to think he had to come home, maybe lose his place. He was the first in the family to go, and he'd worked so hard to get there. But I learned all about hard graft, too. I worked my arse off for months.' I could feel tears starting to come, and blinked them away. How foolish to choose now, after so many years, to cry about this stuff.

'I'm so sad that you never told me all this, about how much you were left to manage things at home.'

We arrived at the restaurant, and as we walked from the van, he reached for my hand. It was the first physical contact between us for days.

Gabriel, our friendly waiter, gamely listed the specials as always. And as always, Denny listened patiently, then started to order our usual meals.

'Actually, I will have one of the specials,' I said, and I wasn't sure whether Gabriel or Denny was more surprised. 'The *soupe au pistou*, please.'

Gabriel reeled away – presumably he had just lost a long-standing bet – and I sipped some water.

'I fancied a change,' I said, to Denny's questioning face.

'So, what did your father say about all this in his diary?'

'He was silent on the important news that I ordered soup instead of salmon and rice.'

'Ha ha.'

'He mainly did a lot of hand-wringing about why he couldn't do anything for me.'

'You did ask him for help, then?'

'I asked teachers, Mum, Dad...' I stopped. Until I told Carrie about this episode in my life, I'd never brought my adult sensibility to bear on it. Now the shutters had been raised, I saw how outrageously lacking in support from grown-ups I'd been, during the biggest crisis of my life. I told a teacher I was pregnant, and all she did was say, 'tell your mum, and here's a helpline number'. The helpline was the same: 'Tell your mum.' No-one said what to do if you did tell your mum but she wasn't able to help. Looking back, I admired, from a long distance away, the tenacity to get help that led me to call Dad. Every time I rang him I got Jeanie, who was quietly obstructive, but still, I persisted.

'So what did Francis say?' Denny asked.

'That he would talk to Mum. But I don't know if he did... He sent money, though. It arrived in a brown envelope. There was no card, only a note that said, "From Dad" and two hundred pounds, wrapped in elastic bands.'

'That absolute unfeeling arsehole,' Denny cried.

'I suppose he thought it would cover baby expenses.'

Denny stared at me. 'Pearl, it was money for an abortion.'

My pulse, already high, burst into overdrive, and my heart started thudding so hard, I could feel it vibrating through my entire body. A heart attack. I was going to die, here, in my favourite restaurant, with the other diners watching, and Gabriel saying, 'I *knew* she shouldn't have changed her order.' I reached for my water glass but I couldn't seem to get near it. I was dimly aware of Denny's terrified face looming in front of me. I couldn't hear him but his mouth was opening and closing. I couldn't catch my breath. I was going to black out... I closed my eyes, and scrolled through Dr Haywood's techniques for calming down. I pictured my favourite place, the canopy of leaves, sunlight sparkling onto my jacket, smooth broad tree behind my back, field glasses in my pocket. I was not going to die, it would pass; it always passed. I thought of the boy with spiky hair and nose-piercing, crouching next to me, telling me I was having a panic attack. I counted my breaths: one, two, three, four, in; one, two, three, four, out. I told my arms to relax, then my shoulders, then my chest, then I worked my way down...

'Pearl, are you OK?'

The normal restaurant sounds came back into focus: forks clinking, people talking. My breathing and heart rate started to stabilise, and I opened my eyes. Denny gave me my glass and I sipped some water, then smiled weakly at him. Gabriel brought our food. I took a few slow breaths, and watched the steam rise off my soup. 'Pearl, your face is white,' Denny said. 'I think we should go home.'

'I'll be all right now.'

The money from Dad... Denny was right, of course. I'd never before connected the dots. I forced myself to think back. I told Dad I was pregnant, thinking he would turn up and rescue me, but of course, he didn't. Now I could see that his relationship with Jeanie was already difficult, that if she wasn't keen on him keeping in touch with his children, she would hardly be OK with him accompanying me to an abortion appointment. And anyway, he was clearly horrified by what I was asking for. But later, he must have changed his mind. Or at least realised that I needed help, even if he couldn't be there. So he did the next best thing. In his ham-fisted way, he *was* trying to help, trying to give me what I asked for. I thought he hadn't heard me, but he had.

And now I saw, with the clarity that only hindsight could

bring, that if he'd stepped up properly and been there for me in the way that I asked, I wouldn't have sat opposite that beautiful woman in the Terminus Brasserie and looked into her familiar eyes. There wouldn't be a child now with little pigtails and a quizzical smile, shaking an overpriced snow globe from a Parisian street trader. An abortion would have been the right thing for me at the time, but paradoxically, it wouldn't have been the right thing for me now. Life could be very complicated sometimes.

'Do you want the end of the story?' I said.

'Only if you're up to it, darling.'

My panic attack had scared Denny. He was looking at me with considerably more fondness than he'd managed for a while.

'There's not much more. I dropped out of school. When Greg came home for the holidays and realised what was going on, he took me to a clinic, but it was far too late for anything other than adoption. I don't remember discussing the possibility of me keeping her. She was placed with her new parents an hour after her birth. I never did my exams, cancelled my A Level place at college, took over Mum's salon.'

'Pearl, I...'

'And I never told you all this, Denny, because I never told anyone. Yes, the birth was on my medical records, but that was the only place it existed, for me. It was as if it happened to someone else. The old Pearl, she died that night in the maternity unit when her baby was taken away, and I've scarcely given her a thought since.'

We stared into each other's eyes, making me think, oddly, of our courting days. His eyes were the colour of the grey winter sea in Bristol, the first place I saw Carrie.

'And now look.' I took out my phone, showed him the selfie she'd taken of us. 'The baby grew up.'

He examined it for a long time. Finally, he said, 'She looks so like you.'

I took a mouthful of soup. It was delicious.

'It's incredibly hard to find out this whole part of your life,' he said, 'a huge part, that you kept from me. I feel so sad that you didn't trust me with it.'

'That's not it at all, Denny. It was nothing to do with not trusting you. I simply didn't have the words for it. It was the most painful thing that ever happened to me.' He raised his eyebrows, and I said, 'The second most painful.'

My phone rang, and I glanced at it, intending to turn it off. But it was Carrie. I hadn't heard from her since Paris. My poor over-strained heart jumped into my mouth.

'Better take it outside,' Denny said, looking round at the quiet, well-behaved restaurant. We, in our fifties, were the youngest people here by some distance.

I pushed my chair back and walked out into the courtyard.

'Pearl?' Carrie was crying. She sounded frightened. 'I'm so sorry to bother you. I didn't know who else to call.'

'What is it? What's wrong?'

'It's Emmie. She's sick. We're in the hospital. I'm really scared. I dialled Mum's number, but of course... I'm such an idiot! Then I was going to call Iain, but he... I...'

'I'm on my way,' I said.

NINETEEN

CARRIE

Lately, Emmie had seemed to me to be getting quite big. Not as big as Numa, of course, but when I carried Emmie around, it felt that her feet were dangling quite a long way down my legs.

But asleep in the hospital bed she looked tiny, scarcely bigger than when she was born. The room was hot, and to facilitate the wires that were stuck on her body, she was naked apart from a nappy, which made her look even littler. Her usually lovely creamy-pink skin was mottled and red.

It was, I supposed, a twisted kind of blessing that Mum wasn't here to see her like this. But I couldn't bear that she wasn't. I had to sit here, terrified out of my wits, without Mum by my side to comfort me. Even if she'd been in the hospice I could have spoken to her, told her what was happening. And let's face it, she'd probably have tried to get out of bed to join me. I imagined her pushing back the covers, swinging her legs to the floor, saying, 'I have to go, Carrie needs me. Can you call a taxi?'

Mum didn't know Emmie was ill, she didn't know we were here, she was never coming back. Was I really going to lose both of the people I loved most, in the space of six weeks? I must have done something horrendous in a past life to deserve this.

The nurse who'd been writing on Emmie's chart put her arms round me. My damp face pressed against her shoulder and I could hear myself wailing, 'I want my mum,' from somewhere far away; I didn't have control over it. She patted my back, said, 'I'm sure she'll be here soon,' which made me cry even harder.

I'd already seen a lot of nurses, because one came in every twenty minutes to check Emmie's vital signs. Each time, I scanned their expressions for clues. This one had looked quite animated at first, but had lost her smile after charting the various readings.

I pulled myself out of her arms, my insides hollow. 'How is she...'

The nurse put her professional smile back in place. 'She's comfortable. Please don't worry. The doctor will be here shortly. We're doing everything we can.'

I wanted to grab her sleeve, shout, 'Are you, though? Are you sure you're doing *everything*?' But she was gone before I could ask any of the questions tumbling round my head: Is Emmie better or worse than when we were rushed here in an ambulance, her body limp, me clinging onto her clammy hand? Has she deteriorated? The doctor who said it looked like meningitis – is he usually right, or wrong? Do babies generally recover from meningitis? If you were a betting woman, what chances would you give us?

You only have time for one more question, Carrie.

All right. Here it is. Is my baby going to die?

When the doctor came in, a brisk woman about my own age, I blurted it out. I actually said, 'Is she dying?' Surely saying it out loud would make it less likely.

'You poor thing,' the doctor said, which wasn't a proper answer. She looked at the charts, then started taking the measurements all over again.

The silence between my question and her response went on for something in the region of five years. Finally she looked at me and said, 'She's very poorly.'

'What does that *mean*?'

'She hasn't had time to respond to the antibiotics yet. And we won't have the results of the blood tests for a little while.'

That didn't answer my question either, but I felt like I couldn't ask it again. Taking pity on me, she held my hand and said, 'It's so worrying for you. We don't know yet. It all depends on how she responds in the next day or two.'

'Is there anything I can do to help her?'

'Simply being here, that's the most important thing. We're checking her three times an hour but if you notice any change in between times, call us in.' She went to the door, and said, 'You're doing really well.'

But I wasn't. I was doing very badly.

When Pearl walked in a few hours later – scarcely any time at all, it seemed, since I'd called her – I didn't hesitate, just flew into her arms. I was never more relieved to see someone in my whole life. Before she arrived I'd been staring at Emmie until my eyes were dry and hot, not wanting to blink in case I missed any of the vague changes the doctor had alluded to. Every so often my acidic stomach lurched when I thought about what might be coming my way, and once I was actually sick into a carrier bag. I needed someone to be with me, to take me away from my worst thoughts, and Pearl stepped up. I would never forget that.

She held me tight and stroked my hair, and it didn't matter that we'd only met once before and that it hadn't gone so well, or that we knew almost nothing about each other. It wasn't the eternal, known-it-all-my-life hug that Mum would have given me. But it was the next best thing.

When we broke apart, Pearl looked at Emmie, lying on the bed like a frog, on her front with her legs bent up on either side.

'The poor little thing. And poor you. What do they say?'

'The most likely thing is meningitis. They're not sure yet if it's the bad kind or the less bad kind. They knocked her out with a sedative when we arrived so they could put her in the scanner and set up an antibiotics drip.' Under Pearl's sympathetic gaze, I kept talking, in a strangled voice I barely recognised. 'She was floppy and had a high temperature, then I saw the rash and called 1 1 1. They sent an ambulance. We're just waiting, now.'

Pearl took my hand. 'I'll wait with you.'

We sat on either side of Emmie's bed, watching her, and the hours blurred into each other. Pearl fetched me sandwiches I couldn't eat and horrible vending-machine coffee that I glugged down, asked doctors questions they couldn't answer, and held me when I cried. Which I did pretty much every twenty minutes, after each visit from a nurse: they came and went, adjusting wires and checking Emmie's pulse and temperature with gentle hands. My thorough survey of their faces revealed that not one nurse looked happier after checking her than they did before.

I'd thought I was used to hospitals, Mum having been in one for so long. But nothing had prepared me for this, for the depth of the helplessness I felt sitting there, unable to do anything. I was so used to doing things for Emmie. What was the purpose of a mother, if she couldn't help save her child?

'I'd give my right arm to swap places with her,' I told Pearl.

'Me too.' She reached across the bed and squeezed my hand. 'I'm sorry this is the first time I'm seeing her, but I'm sure I'll get to meet her properly soon. Tell me about her.'

I knew she was geeing me up, talking about a future in which she would meet Emmie, but I was grateful for it, for the chance to talk about normal-times Emmie, not suddenly-very-ill Emmie.

'Oh, she is brilliant. She likes everything. Apple rice cakes, and bananas, and chocolate cake. She likes cuddling, and she adores the ducks in the park. She likes music, especially reggae, and her favourite song is "Baby Beluga".' I tasted tears on my lips, and brushed them away; I hadn't even known I was crying. 'She's funny. She makes me laugh, she does these hilarious facial expressions. She loves Iain, damn it, so I suppose he'll be stuck in my life forever. Her first word was "Dada", annoyingly.'

'Does he know she's here?'

'No. I've been meaning to call him. I know I must. But he was a bit of a shit last time we spoke.'

'Shall I call him for you?'

'You'd do that?'

'Of course.'

'No. I ought to do it. A bit later, maybe.'

The doctor who came in for the afternoon round was harassed and busy, and got ready to leave as soon as he'd checked Emmie's notes, without saying anything. I was too wrung out, already too institutionalised to speak up, but Pearl stopped him as he got to the door.

'Do you know any more, Doctor?'

He looked surprised, as if he hadn't noticed there were people here other than the patient. I didn't blame him; there were black smudges of exhaustion under his eyes.

'We're still not sure,' he said. 'It's very concerning. But her temperature's come down a little, and some other responses aren't quite consistent with bacterial meningitis.'

'What are the other possibilities,' Pearl pressed on, 'if it's not meningitis?'

'I'd rather not speculate, but most are less worrisome than meningitis, if that helps.'

'Yes, it does. Thank you.'

He went out, and Pearl smiled at me. 'That's something, isn't it?'

'Thank you for asking. I wish I was the praying kind, don't you?'

'I am praying, in my head. Just not to God. Why don't you pray to your mum?'

I pressed my nails into my palms, to try and stop myself from crying. 'Do you think she can hear me?'

'I don't know, but I think it would be comforting to try.'

Mum had been so insistent that I get in touch with Pearl. Had hung on, fatally ill, until she extracted the promise from me. She'd wanted me to have someone who'd be there for me when she couldn't be. She hadn't known, of course, how quickly that would be needed. Mum couldn't be here, but she had sent her proxy.

'Who are you praying to?' I asked Pearl.

'The patron saints of Fairness and Not Being Evil.'

I let out a strange snort, half sob, half laughter. 'Isn't that Google's motto?'

'Whoever they are, they'd better be listening.'

I sipped my nasty cold coffee. 'Pearl, I haven't even asked. Where will you stay tonight?'

'Oh, there will be a hotel nearby. Don't worry about me. Are they letting you stay here?' She pointed to the pull-out camp bed.

'Yes. Marvellously comfortable, if I was only three feet tall and weighed one kilo.'

'Well look, I'll stay till you want to sleep, OK? And I'll come back in the morning.'

Tears clouded my eyes. 'Why will you?'

'Because there's nowhere else I'd rather be.'

'Did Denny mind? You dropping everything to be here at such short notice?'

'He was fine.' Pearl hesitated, then said, 'We're not in a great place, to be honest.'

'Because of me?'

'No! Well, not directly. It's because I never told him about you. He's still adjusting to it.'

'God... it's a lot to adjust to,' I said. 'I did wonder, you know, in Paris, how it was that you hadn't told him.' I was sure she remembered only too well that it had been a little more than wondering on my part. My angry reaction, looking back, felt really over the top.

'I know it seems weird. Worse than weird, probably. Like I was trying to pretend you didn't exist?' She gave a sad little smile. 'But honestly, all I can tell you, which is what I told him, is that it felt like part of my life I'd closed the door on forever. I never told anyone.'

'I thought perhaps you were ashamed of me.'

'Of you? No, never. I was ashamed of myself at the time, though I don't know why. Simon and I really liked each other. Bit stupid not to use contraception, but you know – we were very young and it was not premeditated.' She smiled. 'The fact is, things were tricky between Denny and me even before I was lucky enough to find you.'

Emmie let out a long, shuddering snore, and we stared at each other. It was an encouragingly healthy sound. I stuck my head out of the door and called a passing nurse in. 'She snored!'

The nurse checked Emmie over. 'She's in a really deep sleep,' she said.

'That's good, right? Isn't it?'

I wanted her to say that it was very good, but she looked at the chart for a long, silent moment before saying, 'Let's hope so.' She went out, looking downbeat, and my brief optimism drained out of my veins.

Pearl said, 'Sleep can be healing, can't it?'

We looked at Emmie. Was she sleeping so deeply because she was getting better, or was she slipping away?

As if she guessed what I was thinking, Pearl said, 'Why don't you sing to her?'

'Oh, I don't know...'

'That song you said she liked. So she knows you're here.'

She had a point. I hadn't really even talked to Emmie since we got here. Embarrassed – no-one would ever go out of their way to hear my singing voice – I started quietly singing the chorus to 'Baby Beluga'. I kept my eyes fixed firmly on Emmie, feeling very self-conscious, but after two rounds of the chorus, Pearl began to sing too. Her voice was exactly as tuneless as mine, and she didn't know all the words, just joined in with the ones she'd learned from me and lah-lahed the rest. I felt a warm wave of emotion towards her, and looked up at her, but she was gazing at Emmie, tears in her eyes.

When I couldn't face singing any more, I said to Pearl, the way I might to Mum, 'Talk to me.'

'Yes, of course. What about?'

'Anything. It will take my mind off... I need to listen to something outside my own head.'

'Erm... I've gone blank! Shall I recount the plot of the book I'm reading?'

'God, no. Tell me about Denny, what he said when you told him you were coming here.'

'Oh! Not much. We were in a restaurant when you called, and I told him I had to go back to the house, grab my passport and go. He wasn't sure I should.' She made a face. 'He said I'd only just met you, I oughtn't go dashing across countries on a whim. We went back home without saying much, I packed a bag, and then he drove me to the airport, also without saying much.'

'I'm so sorry if coming here has made things difficult at home.'

She sat up straight. 'You know what, I think it's good. It's forced us out of a static place. There are a lot of things we haven't talked properly about, not just you. It'll either herald a new dawn of openness, or something less cheesily positive.'

She stopped, seeming to have run out of things to say.

'Tell me about when you had me,' I said, thinking only about keeping the airwaves filled with distracting conversation, but then I felt awful. I owed her big time for being here, especially after I was a sulky cow in Paris, but it seemed all I was doing was encouraging her to talk about painful things.

But she leaned forward eagerly. 'Absolutely. What do you want to know?'

'Well... I've always wondered, how come you chose adoption? I know you were very young and didn't feel you could look after me, but not every fifteen-year-old would go through with the pregnancy. Was it for religious reasons?'

'Well...' Pearl frowned. 'You're sure you want to know this? I don't come out of it very nobly.'

When I nodded, she said, 'OK. I did try to get a termination. But I couldn't get it without a parent's permission.'

'Seriously?'

'Yes, back then, if you were under sixteen...'

'It's different now, I'm sure. God, some things have really changed for the better.'

'But Carrie, if I'd been able to, I'd have had it, like a shot, and we wouldn't be sitting here having this conversation.'

'That's true. I wouldn't be here if it weren't for the draconian sexual health laws of the 1980s. But I am still very much pro-choice.'

'I am too. Phew! I'm relieved that you aren't upset that I tried to get one.'

'My god, Pearl, this breaks my heart. You were so young.'

'It feels incredible to be telling you this,' she said. 'Cathartic.'

'I'd have done exactly the same, by the way. I wasn't ready for children till I was ready for Emmie, and even then, it felt like a massive step.'

'It is. Raising children is a huge responsibility.' Pearl pressed her hand to her cheek. 'One I wish I'd had.'

'Careful what you wish for,' I said, aiming for wry lightness and missing, 'you could end up sitting in a hospital praying to gods you don't believe in.'

A nurse came in and we fell silent as she did all the usual checks on Emmie. As she held her wrist to check her pulse, Pearl said, 'How is she doing?'

'She's stable.'

When she'd gone out, I said, 'Medical staff always say that. "Stable". What does it mean? God, I'm so sick of hospitals.'

'I'm not wild about them myself,' Pearl said.

The silence that followed felt unbearably oppressive, and I searched frantically through my mind for what we'd been talking about before the nurse appeared. 'So, did you have counselling, back then?' I asked, rather abruptly. 'Before you gave me up?'

'What, in the eighties?' Pearl laughed. 'We'd not heard of counselling. I had some sessions with a psychologist a few years ago. But I didn't even mention you. I should have.'

I wondered why she hadn't, and what she'd talked about instead. What had she seen a psychologist for? I found myself imagining what my life might have been like if Pearl had kept me — something I'd never really thought about, other than during my brief rebellious stage. I knew that if she'd been able to have an abortion, she probably would have. It was too impossible to think about that; you couldn't really imagine a world in which you didn't exist. And she'd ultimately chosen adoption. But what if, when I was born, she'd kept me? What would my life have been like? I suppose we'd have lived in her mum's house, in Chelmsford. Perhaps her mum would have helped look after me. Or maybe Pearl would have had to move out, into a council flat perhaps. I knew being a single mum used to carry quite the stigma, but did it still then, in the early eighties? I wasn't sure. She'd have been a young mum, more friend than parent. We might have had cosy times together, sharing the same tastes in music and television, swapping clothes and make-up. Or maybe she would have resented me, the person who had upended her life. Maybe money would have been tight, maybe there would have been a series of awful boyfriends coming and going. My imaginings couldn't picture me having with Pearl anything like the stability I'd had with Mum and Dad, who'd been desperate for a child their entire marriage and who never once made me feel anything less than a hundred per cent wanted and loved. Pearl seemed solid and capable, but what would she have been like at sixteen? If she'd taken me on, would she be a completely different person now, having trodden such a different path?

'So,' I said, coming out of my thoughts with a crash, 'did you make the right decision, giving me away?'

She closed her eyes, and I silently cursed myself. Why did I keep sending challenges her way? I mean, I knew why on one level: she gave me away! That never really stopped being anything other than what it was, a fundamental loss. But she was *here*. She'd shown up, at last, when I needed her.

'I'm sorry, I'm sorry,' I said. 'That came out so rudely.'

'No,' she said softly, shaking her head. 'It's such an important question.'

Since Mum first brought up the idea of me reconnecting with my birth family I'd thought a lot about what it was like for me to grow up without Pearl, but not thought at all about what was like for her, growing up without me. When she opened her eyes, the eyes that were so like mine, I could see the loss of it, just for a moment, etched across her face.

'It was the right decision at the time, but maybe now I wish I had done it differently. Done everything differently.'

Another nurse came in, and we fell silent. They seemed to be coming in even more regularly. That was surely not a good sign? This was a new nurse, who gave us a beaming film-star smile as she made for Emmie's bed. I made a bet with myself that the smile would not still be there in two minutes. She went through Emmie's markers, then looked at me, her face serious. I won the bet, damn it.

I resisted – barely – the urge to grab her arm. 'What's going on?'

'It looks like there's a big change in her respiratory rate,' she said. 'So big that I need to check it with the doctor.'

'What does that mean?' Pearl said, but the nurse was already out of the door.

Pearl and I stared at each other, across the bed. All at once, I was certain that Emmie would never open her eyes again. I could scarcely remember what she was like awake; it seemed I'd been watching her sleep forever. I would never again listen to her babbling, hold her hand as we walked towards the duck pond. All the tears I hadn't yet shed started pouring out.

'I've not known Emmie very long, little more than a year, but I don't remember what I did before she came into my life. I don't know what I'll do if she's not here.'

Pearl came round to my side of the bed and put her arms round me. 'It doesn't matter that you haven't known her for long. Even if you'd only known her a day, it would be the same. She's your girl.' She looked down at Emmie. 'Come on, little one. You can do it. You have a mummy here who adores you.'

'I really do,' I said, trying to stop crying. If I was sick of hospitals, I was even sicker of tears. I leaned heavily into Pearl's warm arms, and she held me tight. 'I wish you'd seen her when she was awake.'

The nurse came back in, accompanied by the doctor from earlier. He looked even more exhausted now, if that was possible. The nurse showed him the chart, and he examined it carefully, and together they took various measurements again. Pearl and I watched, our breaths held.

Finally he said to the nurse, 'You're right, there's been a steep increase. It's almost up to normal levels. Let me check her oxygen.' They fussed round Emmie for a few minutes, then they both turned to us. The nurse's megawatt smile was back. It seemed, all at once, as if the sun had come out.

The doctor looked twenty years younger. 'I think we may be out of the woods.'

'Really?'

'She'll sleep a while longer yet, but I'm cautiously optimistic. We'll keep checking but everything is going in the right direction.'

I wanted to hug Doctor Knackered, but he didn't look as if he would welcome it. The nurses kept coming and going, but now most of them smiled as they worked. I could feel myself very slightly unclench, and I even ate a bite of a sandwich that Pearl brought me. She and I starting talking more easily. She asked about my work, even enquired what my PhD was about, and I talked at some length, though I was conscious that she had likely glazed over from the first few words. She was very interested that I taught in a university, and said how she had wanted very much to go to college but it never happened. She asked if it was where I had met Iain, and I was about to tell her about that, when I sat up straight.

'Oh shit! I still haven't called him. I can't face it.'

'Let me do it. I want to help.'

I gave her my phone, open to his number, and she went outside. I watched Emmie, her body rising and subsiding with her breaths. Perhaps she was dreaming. I wondered what about. *Mum, thank you for looking after us.* I pictured her up in the sky, in a place which looked rather like the living room in her flat, everything arranged how she liked it. She was sitting on a sofa, her feet up on a stool, the newspaper in her hand, reading glasses halfway down her nose. She smiled at me. *You're in good hands, Carrie love.*

Pearl came back in and handed me my phone. 'He was very worried, asked lots of questions, and said he'd come tomorrow morning.'

'Yes, clearly *very* worried, dropping everything at once to race over here.'

'Well, I suppose it's getting late?'

'It's barely eight p.m.' I shook my head. 'He lives a few miles away. You were in a different country and you came.'

'I was glad to.'

The sky outside darkened, and still Emmie slept.

'I can't imagine her waking up, now,' I said speculatively. 'If she does, it will be a lovely surprise.'

'My mother used to say I was a pessimist,' Pearl said, 'but pessimists are often pleasantly surprised, unlike optimists, who are often disappointed.'

There was a knock at the door, and to my surprise, Henry came in.

'Oh!' I jumped up and hugged him. 'This is so kind of you.'

'Well I should damn well think so too,' Pearl said, almost growling.

'This isn't Iain,' I said, looking from Henry's confused face to Pearl's frown. I could feel a laugh bubbling up inside, a lovely feeling. 'Pearl, this is Henry, my friend.'

'A very good friend, to come at this time of night,' Pearl said, her face softening.

'I heard from Jenny down the road. I left Numa with her and dashed over. I was worried you'd be on your own.'

'No, this is my, er... Pearl, she's a family friend.' It was too confusing to call Pearl my mum, because Henry knew my mum had just died. He'd even come to the funeral. I'd have to explain another time. Anyway, it felt too weird to call her that. I hoped she didn't mind.

Henry sat on the arm of a chair while I told him what had happened, listening attentively, wincing at every turn. His eyes kept turning to Emmie, and I knew he was imagining how he would feel if it was Numa in the bed. 'I saw an ambulance leaving the street when we were coming back from the park, but I had no idea it was you and Emmie in there. You should have called me.'

'I didn't want to bother you.'

'I want you to bother me.' He said this in an unexpectedly intense way, and quickly added, 'You'd do the same for me.'

A different doctor came in to check Emmie's markers, and the three of us fell silent as we watched her work.

'She's been asleep so long,' Pearl said. 'Is that OK?'

'It's a little longer than we'd like,' she said. 'But lots of repair going on, hopefully. I'm sure the sedative will wear off soon, maybe in the night, and we'll have a better idea of where things are. You all ought to get some rest yourselves.'

'I'll leave you to it,' Henry said, after the doctor had gone. 'I just wanted to tell you that we are all thinking of you and Emmie. And to bring you this.' He handed me a delicious-smelling paper bag. 'Cinnamon buns. For strength. Lovely to meet you, Pearl.' He flashed his beautiful smile, and then he was gone.

'Well!' Pearl said. 'That's a thoughtful and handsome young man, who seems very keen on you.'

'He's just a friend.' I opened the bag and offered her a bun. 'He has a lot of women friends.'

'I bet he does, if he cooked these. Delicious.' She smiled. 'I can stay as long as you want, but do you need to sleep? You look exhausted.'

'I better had, in case she wakes up before morning.'

We hugged, and Pearl went, and I got into the uncomfortable camp bed. I hoped she could find a hotel room quickly, but my brain was too full to worry about it, and my eyes too heavy to keep open.

12TH DECEMBER 2012

Answered my phone in the hotel restaurant, bad form I know but it was G. J told me not to take it but when I shook my head, she waved me outside, smiling at the nice couple sharing our table. I knew it must be baby news.

G was crying. I felt sick, the food I'd eaten heavy inside me. Looked at the ocean in front of me, ice-blue, all the sadness it must have seen.

Your baby was a girl. Tilly. Beautiful name.

G said E tried to see you but you sent her away. G seemed shocked by this. Not me. Wished I could tell you I understood. They are best friends though, he said. And, we don't know what to tell the children about Tilly, he said. They will be devastated; we don't want them to think it might happen to us. He said, D is sleeping in the hospital next to PP but today he came to ours for a shower. He was a shadow, not really there.

I didn't realise I was crying too, till a hotel maid walked past. She touched my arm, a kind touch, what a lovely thing. Asked, could she get me something, I shook my head, said I was OK. It made me cry more, a maid I didn't know offering such kindness. I kept telling G I was so sorry. I didn't tell him it felt like it was my fault, for not being in the country. It wasn't about me.

I couldn't face the restaurant, went straight up to our room and got into bed. J so angry when she came in, I put the covers over my head but she pulled them away. Said, I didn't know where you'd gone, you left me on my own, so horribly rude. I told her the news but she was brisk, said, 'it happens', and she put my wallet, phone and room keys in her bag so I couldn't 'wallow on my phone', she said. I'd hidden twenty euros in my jacket but I didn't have anywhere to go anyway.

Later, when we were walking up on the levadas, she said oh, one of your children always has to have some drama or other. There was mimosa everywhere, fluffy yellow buds like cotton, it made me think of when the children were little, cotton buds I suppose.

I know how difficult J finds anything to do with my first family. She is very insecure, which I always thought would improve with time, but it has not. Even now, after we have been together more than thirty years, she still thinks I will put other people first. I have been patient, more than patient, I have allowed my relationships with my children to wither on the vine, my brother, my friends, all have gone. But still it isn't enough, still she wants to keep me from anything that isn't to do with her.

I felt so angry. Your child died, PP, and my wife was only afraid that this would take me away from her. I looked over the edge of the hill and thought how hurt one would be if one fell. Killed, probably. I could not tell you even now if I was thinking of myself, or her. There was a moment when I could have done something, my rage a kind of insanity, blurring my vision.

Finally I remembered how to swallow my anger, as I have needed to do many times. I calmly said I knew I wasn't there to hold PP or B but always felt I could, if they called on me. This time I was too far away to help. I knew it would be taken wrong. J said, oh what a silly superstition and what an insult too, said *she knew I was blaming her for the holiday that I hadn't wanted to take. I thought about you all the way there, PP, a long way – we walked and walked – and all the way back. I made a promise to myself, though I am old and most everything is too late, to make amends to you in some way.*

17TH MARCH 2013

G not answering. Sent text, gave him some times he could call me. Deleted it straight after. Walked Snoops to the harbour but J came too. Knew he'd call then and sure enough, felt phone vibrating in my pocket. No more chances to call him back. Worried something happened at the church. Knew you would likely be struggling.

23RD MARCH 2013

Six days after Gracie's christening, Fates finally aligned. G called when I was out with Snoops and we had a good half-hour talk. I could imagine how fragile you were, my poor dear. It was apparently fraught but manageable until near the end when little O said innocently, 'Where is your baby?' Though if you ask me, and I didn't of course say this to G, he and E should have briefed that child; it's a terrible thing to have to explain to a child of six, but given the situation, I really think it would have been wise to tell all the children not to mention anything. Anyway, what's done is done, sadly I am in no position to tell G or anyone what to do. I wasn't there. I couldn't help you this time any more than I could help with your troubles back when you were a teenager; that will never stop being my number one regret.

    G said you went white as a sheet, and before anyone reacted properly D was there, shouting, and he pushed O so the child went sprawling, banged her knees on the hard stone floor. Everyone in the church was looking. I don't know who I feel sorriest for, just awful. I expect the vicar did nothing, proving yet again my thesis on how hard it is to find a man of the cloth who is not a hapless fool. Every church I have attended has suffered greatly in this regard, the few good ones have a price above rubies. D bundled you out, yelling like a common sailor. What a terrible show for poor you, PP.

The hardest part for G – and for me – was seeing the warm, close friendship between you and E in pieces. I have never met her but by G's account she is a lovely person. Whenever I felt low, I'd think that I must have done something right, if you, G and his wife could be so close, so supportive of each other. That thought has long been a source of great comfort to me. It's depressing to think of this breach and I hope you can some time find a way back to her, to both of them.

Called B back, finally. He'd called weeks ago. He didn't want to talk about the christening. He was odd, said if I needed help I could turn to him. Before I could say anything I heard the front door opening and hung up.

TWENTY

PEARL

I found a Premier Inn ten minutes' walk from the hospital. I felt bad for Carrie spending another night on that rickety-looking bed, but knew if that was Tilly in the hospital, I'd have slept on the floor or standing up, if I thought it would help.

I sat up in bed and got out the diary I'd brought with me, the one I'd been skirting round from the moment they came into my possession: 2013–14. It was utterly bizarre to discover that Dad knew about Tilly, and to read his strange account of that horrendous time through Greg's lens. That Dad somehow felt responsible for Tilly's death because he wasn't in the country, wasn't there for me, felt self-important, but also amazingly touching. How connected he felt to me, and I never realised! How awful things were between him and Jeanie. How cruel she seemed. In his telling, she was the barrier between him and the rest of the world, terrified of losing him, of him loving others more than her. What a dreadful state of affairs, what a toxic marriage. I wondered if there was a way to ask Andrea about it.

. . .

Eleanor and I were so thrilled to be pregnant at the same time, barely six or seven weeks apart. She already had Theo and Olivia, of course, but she'd always wanted a third. I loved nothing better than hanging out at her and Greg's place, lying toe-to-toe with her on their lumpy kitchen sofa while Greg and Denny cooked, working out plans for our joint christening. A massive affair it was going to be, with all her Irish relatives.

We both knew we were having girls. Eleanor had an early fixation with the name Roisin, but eventually got too bothered by the likelihood that none of us 'heathen English' would be able to pronounce it, and Gracie became the front-runner. My niece Olivia, who was going through a dinosaur phase, suggested I call mine Diplodocus. She and Theo would sing songs next to our bellies so that their future sibling and cousin could hear them.

Looking back, this felt like someone else's life, not mine. The whole thing was covered with a smug golden glow. I really thought this was how things would continue: a sprawling, joyful family that lived in and out of each other's houses. That our children would grow up together. Tempting fate, to be so happy.

I was in a haze of grief and medication for a long time after Tilly's birth, and fragments of memories were all that remained. I couldn't handle Eleanor being around; seeing her, eight months full, with two healthy children already in the world... well, maybe some saintly bereaved women could stand it, but it was too much for me. Every time I thought of her telling one of the kids off, or rolling her eyes about something annoying they'd done, the unfairness of it slapped me in the face.

Unfortunately, my recollection of Gracie's christening was crystal clear. Eleanor had cancelled our joint christening, and was having something much smaller for Gracie. I'm pretty sure she wasn't expecting me to come, and Denny certainly wasn't – the fuss from him! – but I got out of bed and put on a dress and even some lipstick. I hadn't had my first appointment with Dr Haywood yet, though it had definitely been mentioned in the hospital, that I should talk to someone. But at the christening I was still shattered, peeled away. I shouldn't have gone.

In my addled state, I felt obligated to show people that I was all right. Of course, no-one was fooled by my cracked smile. I held it together all the way through the ceremony, shedding only an appropriate number of tears, Denny on one side of me, Gina, Benjy's eldest, on the other. But at the do in the church hall afterwards, I was counting the minutes until I could leave and crawl back to bed. I knew I was close to losing it. And then a little hand slipped into mine: lovely Olivia, no longer my youngest niece now that Baby Gracie had taken that spot. Denny was, for a rare moment, not by my side. He'd gone to get me some sandwiches, pointlessly, because I was barely eating.

Olivia and I smiled at each other. It was the first real smile I gave that day. I loved her like she was my own, and I knew she loved me. She stretched up, and whispered in my ear, 'I don't understand where your baby has gone, Auntie Pearl.'

It was a perfectly reasonable thing to say. I didn't under-stand where my baby had gone, either. I don't know if Eleanor or Greg had tried to explain what had happened to her, or if they hadn't known what to say. It wouldn't be like Eleanor to dodge something difficult, but on the other hand, she herself had just given birth.

But reasonable or not, it stabbed me in the heart. As in a film, when the camera suddenly rushes fast at someone, every-thing went into abrupt sharp relief. The outside sounds stopped. I could only hear myself crying, my breathing awry, and from a hundred miles away Olivia saying, alarmed, 'Auntie Pearl?' Everyone was turning in our direction, and in slow-mo I saw Denny drop a plate on the floor and run towards me. To get to me he had to push through several people, and one of those was Olivia, and she fell. It wasn't on the hard church floor, Dad, unlike in your second-hand account; it was on the industrial blue carpet of the church hall. Not much better, maybe, but certainly a softer landing than you were imagining. She hurt her knees, that was all. Denny certainly didn't push her on purpose. He didn't even see her, she was just in the way of him reaching me.

But the optics, as political pundits like to say, were pretty bad, and that was before Denny, his arms protectively round me, started shouting. The shouting was in response to Greg quietly telling him to not make a drama on Gracie's special day. If Denny had responded equally quietly with, 'you insensitive bastard', it would have been fine. It *was* really insensitive of Greg. But by yelling, it seemed that he wasn't aiming only at Greg, but at all of them.

I knew Eleanor didn't blame us at all, for any of it. She sent so many messages later that day – and in subsequent days and weeks – saying that Olivia was completely fine, that it was all a misunderstanding. Later messages even blamed herself for having the christening at all. But I just couldn't face her, or any of them, after that.

What a terrible show for poor you, PP. Fine understatement there, Dad. After that we went away, at my insistence, to our safe house in France, far from anyone or anything who could hurt me. From then on, it was just Denny and me.

Neither of us expected the move to be permanent. And I could never have imagined Denny's delicate handling of me would last so long. That feeling of him holding his breath, never completely sure that I was going to be all right, was always there between us, had been there for more than five years.

I slept surprisingly heavily, and woke early. Other than a 'no change' text from Carrie at six a.m., I had no messages. Nothing from Denny. On the way to the hospital I picked up some decent coffee and croissants from a chichi café. I told the friendly barista that the second coffee was 'for my daughter,' purely so I could say that pleasurable phrase out loud. He smiled politely.

Incredibly, at eight a.m. Emmie was still asleep. Carrie herself had slept fitfully. 'Like Mum always said, hospital is no place for a decent night's sleep.' I thought Emmie's skin looked less red, though didn't say so for fear of spreading false hope.

'I'm going to ask them for some of that sedative they gave her; I've dreamed about her sleeping through like this,' Carrie said. After the intensity of yesterday, I knew her well enough to see through this bravado, and sure enough, she turned away so I wouldn't see a tear slide down her face.

She was grateful for my offerings – 'Proper coffee!' – and had a little more colour in her cheeks after eating the croissant. Nurses bustled in and out, and they all seemed to think Emmie's sleep of the dead was perfectly normal.

Carrie and I took up our positions on either side of the bed, but we'd scarcely finished checking in about our respective nights when there was a knock on the door, and a young man came in, who I guessed was Iain.

'Sorry I'm so early, I'm on my way to work,' he said. He leaned down and kissed Carrie's cheek.

'Hardly early, I've been up since five.'

He looked at Emmie. 'How is she?'

'It was touch and go yesterday. They think she's going to be OK. But she's been asleep almost a whole day.'

'Well, that's good, isn't it? Healing?' He looked at me, seeking support, and as I didn't want to have to force Carrie into another awkward introduction, I said, 'Hi, I'm Pearl.' I was about to add the 'family friend' line she'd used with Henry last night, but she jumped in.

'My mother,' she said, in that firm, no-further-questions style of hers I hadn't seen since Paris. I smiled shakily at her, honoured beyond words to be given that factually correct but undeserved title.

'Lovely to meet you,' Iain said, shaking my hand. He had nice manners. And he was good-looking; I could see why Carrie had been attracted to him. But I could also see that nothing would make up for him not showing up in a crisis.

He pulled a chair over to the bed, and said, 'Look, she's waking up.'

'What?' Carrie swivelled round and, sure enough, Emmie was starting to stir.

'Un-fucking-believable,' Carrie said. 'I put in a forty-eight-hour vigil here, and all you've got to do is rock up.' But she was clearly too thrilled to be genuinely cross.

Emmie came to, in a lovely slow surprised way. She was absolutely beautiful, her big brown eyes the same colour as Iain's.

'Hello, baby girl,' I whispered.

She was still lying on her front, but swivelled her head to see who the people in the room were. She didn't seem unduly fazed by the wires attached to her, or by being in a strange place. She smiled when she saw Carrie, rolled over and tried to sit up, but got in a tangle with the wires and started to cry. While Carrie soothed her, I fetched a nurse, who soon had Emmie settled and drinking a bottle of milk, so hungry that she wasn't bothered by her temperature being taken.

'She looks a lot better, don't you think?' Carrie asked the nurse.

I crossed my fingers against this foolish Greg-style optimism jinxing things.

'It's a great sign that she's eating,' the nurse said, 'and her temperature's almost normal.'

'Is it still likely to be meningitis, do we think?' Iain asked.

The nurse smiled at him, the seemingly doting father. 'The

doctor will confirm that, but I have to say, it doesn't look like it to me.'

When the nurse had gone, Iain got up. 'Well, that's excellent news.'

My eyes met Carrie's, and I sent her a silent message of sympathy and support that I felt certain she would understand. She said to Iain, 'Well, see you some time. Say hi to Melody.'

He looked at his watch. 'Yeah, already late. Give Emmie a kiss from me. Nice to meet you, Pearl.'

'Ugh,' Carrie said, when he'd gone. 'Remind me to choose more carefully, won't you, next time I think about procreating.'

I laughed. 'I'll do that.'

We returned our attention to Emmie, who was watching me as she drank her milk.

'She's fascinated by you,' Carrie said, stroking Emmie's leg.

'Is she? I'm not particularly fascinating. Hey, Emmie. I'm your, er, grandmother.' I looked at Carrie, feeling awkward. 'Is it all right to say that? God. Sorry. I'm not trying to—'

'I know. I know you're not.' Carrie shook her head. 'Emmie is pretty short on grandparents all round, so it's a relief to know that, whatever happens, she has a new one in you.'

I admired the way that Carrie, sleep-deprived and still knee-deep in anxiety, could so clearly and articulately state her position. I loved her ability to speak up for herself. She was much bolder than me, my daughter; just look at her! She'd worked her way up in a male-dominated field. She wanted a child, her partner let her down, so she stepped up to raise her daughter on her own. She travelled to a funeral where she didn't know anyone, so she could see what she thought of her birth mother. I was tremendously glad she hadn't inherited my Little Miss Mouse-ness.

But maybe boldness wasn't inherited so much as learned? Taking my cue from her, I spoke as confidently as I could.

'I plan to be around for Emmie for the rest of my life, if

you're willing. But I want to be around for you, too. Do you remember when we first saw each other? Well,' I corrected myself, 'the second time. The first time you won't remember.' I thought of the grey Bristol Channel, and the endless walks I took along it when I was pregnant here. I ought to visit it before I left, see it in happier times. 'But at Dad's funeral, I felt a connection between us when I saw you outside the church. Even though I didn't know who you were.'

We smiled at each other, and then the doctor from the day before came in, the one Carrie called 'Doctor Knackered'.

'Ah, clever Emmie. She looks so well!'

'She needs a nappy change,' Carrie said, wrinkling her nose.

'You can do that in a minute. I'm going to detach her from most of these.' The doctor was already efficiently and gently unsticking wires. 'Well, I don't know what all that was about, but it wasn't meningitis. We'll keep her in for a couple more hours, but all the signs are that she's over it.'

'What was it?'

'My American colleagues would likely call it a "fever of unknown origin". Babies get so many weird rashes and high temperatures. It might have been caused by a virus – could have been anything, or nothing. Aren't I right, Grandma?' The doctor smiled at me, bringing me in, assuming a knowledge I didn't have.

But I just smiled and nodded. I was the grandma, now.

When Emmie was discharged, it seemed both very natural that I should go home with them, and also one of the more bizarre things that had ever happened to me. In the taxi I sat in the front, listening to Carrie give directions; this person who was both intimately connected to me, and yet really, still a stranger. She had formed no significant part of my thoughts or conversations for decades, and yet, she had always been with me. I felt like I was looking at the scene from outside, a glib documentary voiceover narrating it: *here is the birth mother, reconnecting with her daughter after thirty-five years, a second chance for both of them.*

Carrie and Emmie lived in a sweet little terraced house with a decent-sized back garden, in what looked to be a nice part of Bristol. She pointed out Henry's house next door.

'I didn't think your generation could afford houses,' I said, as we settled into the neat, sun-filled kitchen. My eyes took in every detail, in case this was a one-off and I would not be invited here again.

'Iain and I bought this together, and he still makes a small contribution to the mortgage. Mum used to help out a bit, too. Emmie and I are low maintenance. As long as we have enough rice cakes for her, and enough Cool Doritos for me, we're fine.' Carrie put the kettle on, then said, 'Oh my god, I have had a year's supply of coffee in two days. I know it's only lunchtime but would you like some wine?'

'That's very French of you, wine at lunch. I'd love some.'

She took a bottle of white out of the fridge, stepping over Emmie who was happily playing at our feet with some toys.

'Incredible, the way they bounce back,' Carrie said. 'Mum used to tell me this whenever I worried about some new thing that was wrong with Emmie, but I always forget, every time.'

I watched Emmie, storing up memories of her for later, imagining the pencil strokes I would use. Without thinking, I said, 'I can't wait to draw her.'

'Oh, do you draw? I'd love a picture of her, could you do one now?'

'You don't know if I'm terrible or not.'

'It doesn't matter. My birth mother's drawing of my child? That would be a pretty cool thing to have.' She fetched paper and pencils, and after a few steadying gulps of wine, I began to sketch Emmie as she played with the colourful discs of her wooden stacker, fast pencil work, capturing her spirit as much as her likeness.

'Oh my god, that's fantastic, I had no idea you were so talented!'

'That's sweet of you to say, but I'm honestly not. I love drawing and painting but I haven't studied it since school.'

'Were you going to study art?'

'Yes, probably. But hairdressing is what I ended up with.'

'Hairdressing is artistic, isn't it?'

'It can be, I guess.' I laughed, remembering a short-lived experiment at the salon in my twenties, when I'd done rough sketches of customers to show them what they might look like with the hairstyle they'd chosen. You could do that with computers now, of course. Anyway, I stopped doing it because people got upset that they didn't match up to the idealised results of the drawings.

'So what do you do, with all your artwork?'

'Oh, not much. The best ones we hang in the cottage. Denny makes wooden frames for them...' I stopped, a little choked up thinking about the way Denny backed the drawings onto cream card as carefully as if they were Cézannes. How he painstakingly hand-cut the exact right size of wood, and delicately carved something relevant to the drawing into each one.

'You're a funny mix, Birth Mother,' Carrie said. She had finished her glass and was pouring another. 'You're talented, but so low-key, like you're trying to fade into the background.'

I opened my eyes wide at this slurred assessment.

'I don't mean it to sound rude. I might be a little drunk.'

'I'd love to be as confident as you.'

'Bossy, right?' She grinned at me.

'Not at all, though I thought we were in favour of bossy women now. I mean, I love how clearly you express yourself. I should be more like you.'

'You seem more confident when you're talking French. That might be because I don't understand it, of course.'

'Do I?' I wondered what that implied for when I wasn't talking French. 'My dad's wife apparently used to call me Little Miss Mouse.'

'Wow, what an annoying nickname. If that's what people thought, no wonder you rebelled.'

'I didn't rebel, alas. I was a good girl, did everything I was told to do.' How satisfying Emmie's soft, round legs were to draw. I shaded in the sides of the ankles, pleased with the effect.

'Er, hello? Getting pregnant with me?'

'Oh. No. That wasn't a rebellion. Not at all. It was a... well, I can hardly say "mistake" when you're sitting in front of me – what a glorious mistake, at the very least! – but no, it wasn't what you think.'

She smiled at me, a smile very like my own, her lips pressed together, one side curled up, the other down. An ambiguous smile, Eleanor used to call mine. 'Tell me what it was, then. Tell me what happened.'

'You already know. We were tipsy at a party. I don't know why I didn't think about getting pregnant. It took me two missed periods to realise...'

I thought about Simon asking if he should borrow a condom from his friend, the sexually active friend all nice boys have. And I said there was no need, that I was on the pill. I didn't know now – did I know then? – why I lied. Was it embarrassment? Or was it really, floating under the surface of my consciousness, an act of rebellion?

'Maybe you're right,' I told Carrie. Maybe I had rebelled without realising, had once or twice let Peppermint Patty override Little Miss Mouse. There was no point now, trying to remember how I felt back then. So much of it had disappeared forever that Carrie might well have as good, if not better, a take on it as me. I looked at her, at that face so unknown and also so known. The extraordinary nature of genes. It wasn't simply that her smile went up and down like mine, but that the impact of the smile on the shape of the cheek, the crinkling of the eyes, were the same. And when Emmie smiled, there it was again.

'Do you ever wonder what would have happened, if we'd stayed together?' Carrie said.

'Of course. Do you?'

'It would have been like *Gilmore Girls*. More friends than mother and daughter, only sixteen years apart.'

I laughed. 'I might have been really strict.' What *would* it have been like? My life would have been much harder, for a while, but then, probably more fulfilled. Interesting. Different.

'Why did you never try to find me?' she asked, then winced, clearly regretting it immediately. 'Sorry, that came out a bit full-on. Too much wine. I just meant...'

'It's OK, I want to talk about that. Though I don't know if I can explain in a way that will make sense. I just never felt like I had any rights over you at all. The thought of seeking you out, bursting into your life, it felt totally inappropriate, like I would be an intruder. I had no expectations you'd want to hear from me.'

'I did,' she said. 'But I understand why you might have felt that way.'

'That's really kind of you,' I said, and then: 'I had another baby after you, Carrie.' I didn't know I was going to say it, I hadn't intended to. I couldn't look at her, so I looked at the top of Emmie's head. Children's hair was so gorgeous, shiny and healthy. 'I lost her, too.'

'I'm so sorry,' Carrie said softly. 'You mentioned miscarriages before...'

'We did have miscarriages. But Denny and I also lost a baby at full term. Stillborn.'

'Oh, Pearl. Christ, you've really been through it, haven't

you?' She moved her chair next to mine, and put her arms round me. I closed my eyes. 'When was this?'

'Five and a half years ago. End of the line for Denny and me being parents.'

'What was she called?'

I'd read her name in Dad's diary, only last night. I could do this. I could say it out loud. I opened my mouth, closed it again.

'I'm so sorry,' Carrie said, her voice husky. 'Maybe she didn't have a name. You don't have to...'

'Matilda.' I said it with a small enough hesitation that she might not have noticed. 'Tilly for short.'

'That's gorgeous.'

'I like names like that, ones you can shorten to something pretty. Yours is like that too, of course.'

We held each other for a little longer, and it felt perfectly natural. When we broke apart, we each took a steadying gulp of wine. Emmie looked up and said, 'Mama!' and Carrie pulled her up onto her lap. Emmie sat facing me, playing with her mum's fingers and giggling to herself. The lovely sight of her, a healthy child again, not a sick one. Some children made it, thank god, even if some didn't.

'Was it after you had Tilly that you moved to France?' Carrie said quietly. 'Did you move because of her?'

'Sort of.' It was strange to be thinking about this again so soon. Last night's dreams were full of Eleanor, always in a different room to the one I was in, always out of reach. 'I've made so many mistakes, Carrie.'

'God, haven't we all!'

'I was so tense for the first few months of pregnancy. But once I got past that, I actually managed to relax. I was really excited, because Eleanor – my sister-in-law, my best friend – was also pregnant. We had so many plans. But after Tilly... well, everything was very difficult. I was ill, you know, mentally.' I winced, remembering yet again those months, the rawness of it back after seeing it in black and white in the diary. 'Eleanor and I fell out, and it seemed pointless staying here after that, there was nothing to tie Denny and me here.'

Emmie started grizzling, and Carrie said, 'Please can you hold her a minute? I'll get her a snack.'

'Oh, I can get it...' I said, but Emmie had already been passed to me, and was curling in towards me, her hunger temporarily forgotten in the novelty of a new lap to sit on. She attended to my watch, running her stubby fingers round the bracelet, and I sat as still as I could. I hadn't held a child in my arms since my niece Olivia, years ago, and my muscles felt stiff and uncertain. How warm and weighty she was, how smooth her skin.

'You OK?' Carrie said, handing Emmie a breadstick.

'Fine! Of course.'

'It's just that you're crying.'

'Oh. Am I? How silly.'

We smiled at each other, and I risked moving one hand so I could wipe my eyes.

'You know what she likes?' Carrie said. 'Butterfly kisses. With your eyelashes?'

I leaned in to Emmie's face – she was gnawing on her bread-stick – and fluttered my lashes against her cheek, making her laugh and wriggle delightedly.

'We were talking about names before,' I said. 'Yours, Tilly's.' It felt easier to say it, this time. 'Dad – Francis – in the diaries, he said... Is he right that Emmie's middle name is Ruby?'

'It is. I always loved your name when I was growing up,' Carrie said. 'It was the main thing I knew about you. I wanted to give my daughter a gemstone name like yours, to remember you by.'

I didn't say anything. There was no need, because I could see from her expressive face that she knew exactly how precious a gift this was.

'What will you do now?' Carrie said, after a while. 'Are you going home?'

'Yes, and no,' I said.

'I am too tipsy to process that.'

'I'm going to stay in the UK for a little while. I have a few things to do.' I felt a bit tipsy too. 'Denny and I love each other, but we could use some time apart. He needs to decide what your existence means for me, and for us. He needs to see that I won't break into little pieces if he isn't always five paces behind me, waiting to catch me. And I need to work out what I want my life to look like.'

'I hope you can fix things, if you want to,' Carrie said, and as she leaned across to look again at my half-finished sketch, she stroked my cheek, a gesture at once so childlike and motherly that I had to turn away, so she needn't see any more of my tears.

I went to the park with them, to see the famous ducks, and when Emmie looked tired – 'How can she be tired after that epic sleep?!' Carrie exclaimed – we went back to their place. She put Emmie down for a nap, and she looked tired too, so I said I would head off.

'Oh! I meant to give you this,' Carrie said, as I stood outside her door, a cab waiting for me. She handed me Dad's 1990 diary. 'I forgot to tell you, what with everything else, that my colleague managed to translate the scribble. Or not translate exactly, we can't read shorthand, but she got a clean version of the marks. We were lucky because there was a good contrast between the pen Francis used to write the diary and the pen he crossed it out with. My colleague said that suggested he crossed it out at a different time to when he wrote it.'

'You mean he thought better of leaving it in, later?'

'Looks like it.' She showed me the page, which was messy, the shorthand marks blurred, but there was a separate piece of paper in which someone had painstakingly transcribed a copy of the marks.

I thanked her, and there was a brief, hesitating moment in which we weren't sure whether the other wanted us to hug. It was one thing, in the hospital, life and death, but another in the cold light of day. Then she stepped forward, and I held her for a long, wonderful moment. I got into the cab, and she waved as we drove away: the tall, beautiful daughter who strode so confidently through the world. Some part of me, broken for decades, felt like it was starting to mend.

On the way to the station, I read through the diary entry that Carrie's colleague had translated. I thought I'd shed enough tears already today, but it turned out I had a few more for Dad, and the seemingly impossible situation he found himself in. I had no doubt he had loved Jeanie madly. After all, he turned his life upside-down for her. A *coup de foudre*, they'd call it in my adopted country. But she, paranoid about losing him, showed just how desperate she was, the day I tried to go and see him. Things finally fell into place about why he'd let his children drift away; he was simply terrified about what she might do. He must have felt so trapped.

If I'd discovered this a few weeks ago, even a few days, I would have been furious at his weakness, at Jeanie's manipulation. But now, I just felt sorry for them, and sorry for myself.

I put the diary away, and called Denny. He answered on the first ring.

'Are you OK? How's the little girl?'

'She's fine.' I made my voice firm and sure. 'I'm about to leave Bristol, but I have some other things to do.'

He said quietly, 'When will you be back?'

I looked out of the window, at the UK rushing by, taking me every minute closer to home. I said, 'I don't know.'

26TH SEPTEMBER 1990 (CROSSED-OUT SECTION)

J so upset. Never seen her like this. She said she couldn't understand what had got into me – keeping a diary she couldn't read, in a secret code, running after a woman I thought was PP. Said she'd seen the woman, she was nothing like PP. She got me doubting myself.

I told her I didn't use shorthand to keep secrets, but it made no difference, and maybe that was fair because I was lying. I do use it to keep secrets. She put the diary in the sink and set light to it with the gas lighter. We were both shocked at how the fire roared up. I tried to turn on the tap but she pushed me away. Let it burn.

When the book was ashes, not salvageable, I gave J some home truths, threatened to leave, and she ran upstairs, locked herself in the bathroom, saying she would cut her wrists. It took hours to get her out of there, I had to stay very calm and gentle. I bandaged up her wrist. It was not a deep cut but it was terrible to see. She was sobbing and remorseful in my arms. Made me promise I'd never leave, never say anything about leaving again, not keep a diary any more. Afraid to set her off, I agreed to everything. And I will keep the first two, on my honour. But I made an unbreakable promise to myself to keep a diary, long before she asked me not to, and I cannot change that.

I promised myself that that one day I will sit down with PP and B and show them my diaries, talk through the years we weren't together, so they know I always held them in mind. I will not stand by and see my past erased. Tomorrow I will find a safe place to keep the diaries.

When A got back from college later all was as normal in the house. She said there was a funny smell in the kitchen and J said she had burnt toast.

TWENTY-ONE
PEARL

And so I went home. I always knew I would, one day. I knew it every time I looked at the open plane ticket Eleanor sent me last year, for the forty-fifth birthday party I didn't attend. I knew it long before I stood outside Mme Remard's house and watched her face as she held Serge tight. I knew it for sure when I drank wine in Carrie's sunny kitchen, and remembered a different time in another sunny kitchen. A woman sitting opposite me who knew me as well as anyone, who always had my best interests at heart, who I ran away from.

Eleanor opened the door and wrapped her arms around me.

'Oh sweetie,' she said, 'I've been expecting you.'

'You have?'

'Yes, for the last five years.'

'I wasn't here for your last birthday,' I said. 'I didn't want to miss this one.'

'You're early, it's not for another few days,' she said, holding me tight. I breathed in waves of Issey Miyake, the scent of home.

My life was non-stop reunion scenes these days. Enough to say that this one was the most straightforward, with a ridiculous amount of apologising and 'there's nothing to apologise for' on both sides.

You couldn't stand on doorsteps forever, of course, and finally, we let each other go, and she led me inside.

Greg was in the kitchen, and when he saw me he cried out, 'Ohhhh!' and jumped up, sending his chair flying, and hugged me so hard I thought my ribs cracked.

There were huge question marks in his and Eleanor's eyes, but they didn't press me, or ask where Denny was. Ellie made mint tea and sandwiches, like old times. How I'd missed sitting in this kitchen with its copper pans and light-grey tiles, the tea on tap. It was a place I had spent some of the happiest days of my life. And then there were the children. They were on half term and came noisily in and out, and all of them seemed delighted to see me, even Gracie, who didn't know me. My heart contracted a little, because this was what a five-year-old girl looked like. She gave me a shy smile when told who I was, and I smiled back, and I meant it.

Olivia, old enough to remember our last meeting, took a little time to thaw, but soon she and Theo were talking to me like proper friends. How tall and grown-up they were, at eleven and seventeen.

When the children went off to various friends and activities, I told Ellie and Greg about Carrie. Greg was astonished to learn that Dad had made contact with her, via her mother. But his astonishment was nothing next to Eleanor's, because it turned out that Greg had never told her about my teenage pregnancy. She was visibly shocked to discover that this happened to me when I was younger even than Theo, and retrospectively furious with Greg for his absence during those early post-Dad months.

Eleanor had often got irate in the past about my childhood,

how I seemed to have no choice in abandoning school and taking over Mum's business, but she was really on a roll now. 'My god, I always knew that you were comprehensively shafted by all the adults in your life. But lookit now! I didn't know the half of it! Your father dumped the care of your family on you, your ma fell apart, and your older brother left you to it, and yes, some offence intended, Greg – you were almost a grown man. And then, when you *finally* asked for help, every man Jack of them was as much use as a chocolate teapot!' She was completely steamed up about the events of almost forty years ago, and I loved her for it.

I was beginning to realise that getting pregnant so young had left me with a long-lasting feeling that I always messed things up. It would be a good idea to have some more therapy soon. But even without it, I knew things were starting to shift. I was getting better at acknowledging the things I did well, and lately there were several: I was there for Carrie when she needed me; I helped Serge reconcile with his mother; and I held out my arms to Eleanor.

I interrupted her long rant to ask Greg why he hadn't told her about my pregnancy. He was experienced at riding out Eleanor's impassioned diatribes. He smiled at her, and said calmly, 'Because you told me never to tell anyone, and I never have.'

'I can't believe neither of you ever told me!' Eleanor said.

'I never told Denny, either,' I said, and she gasped.

'Oh, no! Does he know now?'

'He certainly does.' I turned to Greg. 'I'm sorry I gave you a hard time about not telling me you were in touch with Dad. I did exactly the same, not telling Denny about important things in my life.'

'It's OK,' he said, doing his magnanimous-older-brother face – how I wished Benjy was here to call him out on it. 'And Ellie, don't be too mad with me. I wasn't quite as useless back then as you think. I took Pearl to Bristol, made the arrangements with the adoption agency.'

'What if Pearl had wanted to keep the baby?' Eleanor asked.

'She made it really clear she didn't want to,' Greg said. He turned to me. 'You were adamant. You said that once the baby had gone to its adoptive parents, you never wanted to think about it ever again.'

'Jesus, did I?' Clearly, I hadn't been Little Miss Mouse about everything.

'So, what is Carrie like?'

'Greg, she is wonderful. I can't take any credit for her, but her amazing parents have brought her up to be smart, and clever, and confident, and kind.'

'I can't take this in,' Eleanor said. 'It's a head fuck, all right. You have a thirty-five-year-old daughter.'

'And a granddaughter.'

'Jesus,' Eleanor yelled, knocking over her tea, 'what the hell is going on?'

'My last few weeks have been a bit strange,' I said, mopping up the table with a cloth. 'I've found out a lot about myself that I didn't know. Some from Carrie and some from Dad's diaries.'

'Do you know yet why he wanted you to have them?' Greg said. He tried to sound casual, but I knew it must have nagged at him all this time. Why me, rather than him?

'I think he had a few reasons. He felt he hadn't totally ruined things with you, because you were still in contact, however sporadic. And with Benjy, he might have felt that there wasn't enough connection there for him to be forgiven. But with me... well, I was reminded, reading them, that he and I were really close when I was growing up. He certainly wanted to try to make amends for not being there when I was pregnant. And I think he wanted me to understand him better, understand what he did and why he dropped out of our lives.'

'And do you?'

'Yes. His marriage to Jeanie was terribly difficult, perhaps almost from the start. But it was impossible for him to admit that, I think, for a really long time.'

'Does he say that in the diaries?' Greg asked.

'Not directly. But there's a section he crossed out,' I said, 'about a time when he got angry and threatened to leave, and Jeanie made a suicide attempt. I think, after that, he was always trying to protect her, to make sure she didn't tip over the edge.'

'A terrible thing, to hold killing yourself over someone to get your own way,' Eleanor said. 'He'd have been tiptoeing on broken glass ever after.'

'Did he never say anything to you, Greg?' I said.

'No! Never. But I suppose... there were hints. Once he got a mobile phone, it was very clear that I should only use that, never their home phone. But even when I called the mobile, he often wouldn't answer, or would text me to call back at a specific time when he was out walking the dog.' Greg looked thoughtful.

'I'm pretty sure he got the dog partly so he had a legitimate reason to regularly leave the house,' I said, 'and that's also why he was so involved in all the church activities.'

Eleanor put her hand to her mouth. 'Ah god, you're making me feel sorry for the poor bastard.'

'There's something I wanted to ask Benjy about. There's an entry from the late nineties, when Dad didn't seem to be in contact with you, and he wanted to stay with someone. He rang Benjy. It all sounded a bit weird.'

'Let's ask him now,' Greg said. He got out his phone.

'Put it on speaker,' Eleanor said.

'Hey, loser.' Benjy's voice came out loud and clear.

'Hey, rat-face,' Greg said, momentarily slipping into child mode. Eleanor and I rolled our eyes at each other, the years of not seeing her falling away with every minute that passed. 'We've got Pearl here with us...'

'Wow, what did you do, kill Denny and put her in the trunk of your car?'

'And we're on speaker,' I said.

'Hey Pill, got a pass card finally?' Benjy said, unabashed. 'It's feast or famine with you. Didn't we talk, like, three days ago?'

Greg said, 'We wanted to ask you something about Dad and Jeanie.'

'Talking of controlling partners,' Benjy said.

'Hey, you!'

Greg held up a finger – not now – and said, 'Go on, Pearl'.

I stored 'controlling partners' away for the time being, and said, 'Ben, do you remember that time, about twenty years ago, when Dad called to ask if he could come and stay with you for the weekend?'

'Oh yeah, what a hot mess. Course I remember, it was pretty much the only time he ever called me. Hey, is this in the diaries? Fame at last. Yeah, completely out of the blue; I hadn't spoken to him in years, unlike some of his brown-nosing sons, naming no names. He was in a right old state, think he'd been crying, for fuck's sake. Wanted to come and stay at the weekend. Random, right? I said we couldn't, we already had Barb staying. He sounded so gutted I almost felt sorry for him, thought maybe he wanted to make amends, too little too late but anyway, you know I'm a forgiving kind of guy.'

The three of us exchanged smiles.

'So I said, not this weekend, but come the one after. And he said it had to be this weekend because that's when Jeanie's fiftieth birthday was, and she was miserable about it, and wanted him out of the house.'

'Why?'

'I don't fucking know, do I? He said she didn't want to see his face. I assumed they'd had a row. Anyway, I said, "I'm not running a hotel, you can't call me after a hundred years and tell me you're turning up." And he went all quiet and said, "Sorry to bother you" and hung up! I was spitting feathers for days after that one – you can ask Alice. Well, I wouldn't bother actually, but anyway.'

'So he never got in touch again?' Greg said.

'Nope, that was my one shot, apparently. Anyway, years later, I was watching a documentary about abuse, keeping Gina company – she had to watch it for her social work course – and it occurred to me that if Dad had been a woman and made that call, I'd have realised straight away what was going on. He was asking for help. But I didn't make the connection back then. I just thought he was being infuriating as always. I was watching this programme, going like, Ohhhh fuuuuck, Gina will tell you.'

'Oh my god,' Ellie said.

'Yeah, and so after watching that, I rang Dad. It was about five or six years ago, I dunno, and it took him *days* to call me back. Maybe weeks. And he sounded really stressed, he said, "I can't be long." I said, "Dad, if you are in trouble and want somewhere to go, I am here."'

'Christ, Ben, why didn't you tell me?' Greg said.

'I didn't know I had to check in with you whenever I fart, Big Boy. Nothing happened, anyway. He didn't say anything, he hung up. I was actually going to tell Pill about this at the funeral, but we got distracted by more exciting events. Anyway, that was it, the last time he and I ever spoke.'

We were silent, then Ben said, 'You still there? I gotta go. Oh, by the way, I have news. I'm getting married again.'

'Congratulations!' we all said.

'Invitations will be in the post. Email, anyway. Lovely lady, Kelly-Anne, met her on the apps a few months ago. Gorgeous. Only thirty-two. The ol' boy still got it.'

'I give it six months,' Eleanor mouthed to me, then said out loud, 'It's not Barb, then?'

'Ellie Bellie, stop trying to make me and Barb happen. Right guys, thanks for the latest instalment of My Little Dysfunctional Family, see you later.' He hung up.

'That's the most sensible conversation I've ever had with Benjy,' Greg said.

'Fancy him inviting us to the wedding – he didn't bother with the previous two or three,' I said.

'I don't completely get what happened with your father and Jeanie,' Eleanor said. 'If she was scared of him leaving her, why was she so keen for him to get out of the house that weekend?'

'I don't know,' I said, 'but perhaps by that point, she knew he wouldn't leave her. Couldn't leave her. In the later diaries she seems to have given up being nice to him at all.'

'Ah, god love him,' Eleanor said. 'I feel wretched for him now.'

'Me too,' I said. 'The more I piece together about his life, the sadder it seems. But Greg, you saw him occasionally. Do you think he was actually contented, and I've been letting my imagination run away with me?'

'Wish I did.' Greg stood up and took a bottle out of their enormous built-in wine rack. 'He always seemed ill at ease and strung out, to be honest.'

'Oh great. I was hoping you could come up with some comforting redemption.'

'I guess that's what Dad was hoping for, when he made contact with Caroline's family.' He fetched three glasses. 'And he did manage that, so would that do for your redemption purposes?'

'I suppose so.' I thought for a moment, then sat up straight. 'Hey, what did Benjy mean, about Denny being controlling? Is that what you all think?'

'No!' Greg said, unconvincingly. 'Hey, let's have some wine.' He unscrewed the bottle's lid and poured wine into our glasses as though he was in a race.

'Well, maybe a little, sometimes,' Eleanor said, ignoring

Greg frowning at her. 'We know his heart is in the right place. He wasn't like that before... you know.'

'It wasn't just his idea to move to France,' I said. 'It was a joint decision.'

'Of course it was,' Greg said, handing me a glass.

'In fact, I was the one who pushed for it,' I said. 'I was the one who...'

'I know, love. It was impossible to be around us,' Eleanor said quietly. 'And the children.'

'Yes. I'm sorry. But something's shifted, and I don't feel like that any more. I've really missed you all. I'm sorry I froze you out.' I gave a little hiccough of a sob, and they both moved towards me, but I batted them away. 'I'm OK.' I raised my glass. 'To the fourth estrangement,' I said, and they dutifully repeated it, though they didn't have a clue what I meant, and we clinked glasses.

'I really must get the spare room ready for you,' Eleanor said, sipping her wine. 'You look about as knackered as I feel.'

'There's one more thing I'd like to talk about,' I said, 'because I'm not sure what to do. Andrea.'

'What about her?' Greg said, but Eleanor knew what I meant.

'Jesus,' she said. 'That poor woman.'

TWENTY-TWO

CARRIE

'Go on, then,' Henry said. 'Make a wish.'

He was talking to Numa, of course, whose birthday it was, but I decided he was also talking to me, and silently complied.

Numa did the same, screwing up her eyes in concentration, then blew out the three candles on her cake, spraying it with enthusiastic spittle, and we all cheered. She ran off with a group of toddlers, and I hitched Emmie higher up my hip. She was a bit overwhelmed and clingy, being around all these big kids. I watched the other mothers circling as Henry cut the cake, handing him plates, laughing at everything he said. One dabbed a non-existent crumb from his mouth with a pink napkin.

I shook my head when I was offered cake – Numa having sprayed on it made it seem slightly less appealing – and took Emmie out into the hall, where things were quiet. I sat on the stairs with her on my lap, and fed her little bits of carrot and crisps from my plate. She snuggled into me, sleepy and warm, and I sneaked my phone out of my pocket. During the singing of 'Happy Birthday' I'd heard it ping with Pearl's special text-tone. It was a photo she'd promised to send me, of her and Eleanor, my aunt, who I was looking forward to meeting.

Presumably taken on Eleanor's phone as it was a selfie, the two of them were smiling fit to burst, above the message: *Eleanor and I can't stop talking about you. Joyful.*

I was smiling myself when I realised that someone had come out into the hall, and I looked up into Henry's face. 'Can I join you?' he said.

I shifted along and he sat next to me. His arm was so close to mine, I could feel the heat coming off it. I would only have to move a few centimetres for us to be touching. For the first time in years I felt rather tingly. It was lucky that people couldn't hear your thoughts, because mine would have made Henry blush. Unaware, he glanced at Emmie, whispered, 'She's asleep.'

I didn't need to look down to confirm this; I could feel from the lovely weight of her that it was true. She seemed to double in heaviness when she was asleep.

'She's been through a lot lately,' he said. 'You both have.'

'We really have. I'm planning to take her for a little holiday next month.' I was going to use some of the money Francis left me, but I wouldn't book till I knew if we could go to a certain part of France. I didn't know when, or even if, Pearl would be going back there. But the wood she lived in sounded just right for the last place for Mum's ashes. *Somewhere that is special to you, Carrie.* It wasn't special to me yet, but I had a feeling it was going to be.

'A holiday, that sounds lovely. Numa and I should join you.'

I looked at him calmly, while my brain furiously tried to work out what that meant. Did he mean they should come on holiday *with* us? Or only that they should do the same and take a break of their own? The first interpretation was crazily close to my birthday cake wish. How long his eyelashes were; how excellent they'd be for butterfly kisses. The thought of being on the receiving end of such a kiss ratcheted the tingling up to such high levels that I actually shivered.

'Are you OK?' He put his hand on my arm and I almost lost it.

'Yes, fine,' I said automatically, as warm confusion flooded my brain. 'It's a lovely party. Numa's so thrilled.'

'Yeah, I'm really looking forward to calming her down later, after all the excitement and sugar.' He grinned, then circled back to the previous topic. 'So will Iain be going with you on holiday?'

'Oh! No. God. Iain and I are completely done.'

'That's a relief.' It was his turn to stutter. 'I mean... If you are relieved, then I'm relieved. But if you're sad, then, god, what am I trying to say?'

I thought about Pearl saying she admired my confidence, the way I stated clearly what I wanted. Mum used to phrase it differently – *when Carrie puts her foot down, there's no budging her* – but I knew she admired it too. And so, a mother on each shoulder, urging me on, I said, 'I think you're trying to say that we should coordinate getting babysitters soon, and go out for a meal.'

I couldn't pretend it was easy to say. But I was glad to have said it, no matter how he replied. Luckily, he looked delighted.

'Hell, yes, thank god, that is exactly what I've been trying to say, for some time.'

Numa came running out into the hall, and grabbed Henry's hands. 'Dada! Come on! Pass parcel!'

Henry got up, pretending that she had been able to pull him. 'You're so strong,' he told her, and to me, he said, 'Don't go anywhere.' He disappeared into the noise of the living room. I tightened my arms round Emmie, leaned my head on hers, and tried to stop myself smiling.

5TH APRIL 2013

Some happy news at last! So proud of A: senior division manager! She's worked hard, and it hasn't been easy. Since James chose to do his last years of school in Australia with Colin, I've been concerned about her. I know she misses him terribly. She has been a light in my life for more than thirty years. She said I don't need to look out for her but I see things more clearly than her. She has fewer defences than me, and wears herself out being there for her mother.

I finally managed to persuade her not to move back in with us. Not that I wouldn't love her to, but it wouldn't be good for her. Today she told me that instead she will buy the Jenkins' house opposite us. I think it's a bad idea, still far too close, she won't be able to keep the distance she needs. But better than her moving in. She said she could take Snoops whenever he gets on J's nerves, which is a very good idea. Selfishly, it will be lovely to have her close by again.

TWENTY-THREE

PEARL

When Andrea walked into the restaurant, orderly and composed in her neat suit and heels, I saw how mistaken my original impression of her had been. She wasn't imperious at all. She was stressed and on high alert, her face stretched into that haughty position from trying to keep control.

'Thanks for coming all this way,' I said as she sat down. 'I was honestly more than happy to come to you.'

'It's fine.' She smiled. 'I enjoy my little jaunts to godforsaken places. Least I didn't have to stumble through a foreign wood this time.'

'By the way, they have a nice smoking area out back. I checked.'

She looked at me like I was mad. 'I don't smoke.'

Oh. OK. 'So, what will you have? My treat.'

'I'm not hungry,' she said, looking at the menu.

I ordered a Caesar salad and a coffee. After a moment, Andrea said she'd have the same. When the waiter had gone, she leaned forward conspiratorially.

'You said on the phone you've got something for me?'

'Yes. I haven't typed up much of the translation yet, but I

wanted you to have this.' I handed her an envelope. 'It's a short section from the diary a few years ago, when you got made a senior manager at work.'

'Senior division manager.'

'Dad was very proud of you.'

She hesitated. 'Should I open it now?'

'If you like.'

She took out the sheet of paper and started to read. Hiding behind my coffee cup, I watched her. About halfway through her face softened, and I guessed she had reached: *She has been a light in my life.*

When she put the page down, her eyes were shiny. I thought of that neatly dressed little girl in the fluffy slippers, hiding in her bedroom.

'He really loved you,' I said.

'It took us a few years to get used to each other,' she said, 'but I really loved him too.' She took a sip of coffee, trying to compose herself. 'I'm sorry he wasn't in your life, but I was always grateful he was in mine.'

'It's clear, from the diaries, that he was grateful for you, too.'

The waiter brought our salads, and while he was setting out napkins and water glasses, I consciously shrugged on my confident persona, the one Carrie said I had when I was speaking French. This was not going to be easy.

'Dad mentioned James in that entry, and I was just thinking, it must be hard for you, him so far away. When did you last see him?'

'He visited a couple of years ago.' She fiddled with her coffee cup. 'He doesn't like it much over here. His father gives him all the sun, sea and freedom he wants.'

'And do you visit him there?'

'Oh... no... well, it's hard to get away.'

I could hear my old self when she said that. Kim, or Peaches, or Eleanor asking why I didn't go on holiday. *It's hard to get away*. Not that Mum had ever asked me to look after her. I chose to stay, to prioritise her. I wondered what had happened with James, how he had ended up living with his father. Had he, as a teenager, tired of the family dynamic? Felt compelled to put a large distance between him and his mother and grandmother?

We ate for a few moments in silence, then, trying to sound spontaneous, unplanned, I said, 'Andrea, you remember our arrangement? That I could ask you anything about your life with Dad?'

'Yes.' She put her cutlery down. 'What has he said?'

'It's not really about what he's said.' I gestured with my fork, trying to model casual eating and chatting behaviour. 'I was just wondering... how things were for you? At home?'

'What do you mean?'

I concentrated on spearing a crouton. Quietly, I said, 'It seemed, from what I've read, that Dad was quite concerned about you.'

'Oh, you know how he fussed.'

I didn't know, but I said, 'So things, uh, are OK?'

'I have no idea what you're talking about. Of course they are.'

Her expression was unchanged. Maybe I'd got it completely wrong. 'I'm glad,' I said. 'These are hard times, aren't they, after the death of a parent.'

'I'm doing all right.' She picked up a piece of bread, then put it down again. 'So do you have a rough idea of when I might get the translated diaries?'

'It's going to take a while. There are twenty of them, after all. Probably a year.'

'A year!'

'But I can give them to you one at a time, if you like.'

'Yes, that would be great.'

I mustered up the nerve say the next bit, which Eleanor and

I had worked through together. 'I'd like to ask one thing of you, when I give them to you.'

'What's that?'

I took a breath, and said quickly, 'That you don't show them to your mother.' There. Did it.

'Excuse me, *what*?' Her eyes drilled into me.

'It's obviously up to you. I can't stop you. But...' All in one big blast, I said, 'Dad went to great lengths to keep the diaries from Jeanie. He stored them out of the house, though they were written in code. And even then, he crossed parts out.' I almost faltered under the frightening intensity of her gaze, but pushed on. 'He was very determined that she should not be able read them. Remember, if I hadn't taken them, they were to be destroyed. And I'd like to try to honour his clear wish, and just give them to my brothers, and to you. He did really hope that I would share them with you.'

During the silence that followed, I moved food around on my plate, and listened to the sound of my heart thudding. It was one of the longer twenty seconds of my life.

Finally she said, in a low voice, 'But what would I tell her?'

I went cold. Perhaps I hadn't got it wrong, after all. I sneaked a glance at her. She was staring at her plate, her lips pressed together, a tear glittering like a crystal on her lowered lashes.

'You could always say I refused to give them to you? Blame it on me?'

Andrea shook her head. 'I don't know. If I have them, she, well, I don't think I could hide something like that.'

'Or I could keep them for you? You could come to see me and read them there? Then it wouldn't be a lie, you really wouldn't have them.'

She opened her eyes wide, and the crystal tear rolled out onto her cheek. She immediately brushed it away. 'Well. You're mighty keen for me to come back to your little French hide-away. Short of company, are you, out there in the sticks?'

Unnerved, I put a piece of chicken into my mouth, which was too large to chew elegantly. 'I kind of am,' I mumbled indistinctly. 'It would be nice to get to you know better.'

'I don't need new friends,' she said.

I took a sip of coffee to wash down the chicken, and said, 'But you might need an old sister.'

She pushed her chair back abruptly, and the couple at the next table looked over in surprise.

'You think you know me. You don't.'

'You're right. I'm sorry. I don't want to upset you. Maybe I've misunderstood Dad's intentions for the diaries. Maybe I've even misunderstood what he's said in them. They paint a picture of a difficult home life, and—' I coughed, embarrassed, 'a difficult marriage. But maybe he was exaggerating, or even making things up. You can tell me I'm wrong, and I'll accept it.'

Andrea rolled her eyes, and looked round the restaurant as if seeking confirmation that I was certifiably insane. But she didn't say I was wrong.

This was perhaps my only chance, so I ploughed on, 'After Dad died, you told me you turned the house upside-down, looking for the diaries. Why did you? Were you going to hide them?'

'I didn't want them to fall into the wrong hands.' She dropped her voice. 'Not that it's any of your business.'

And I would have left it there, had I not seen the same expression cross her face that I saw at the funeral, when she was threatening lawsuits, and looked across at her mother. *Desperate times, Pearl.*

I gripped my hands together under the table, and said, 'I'd like to help, if I can. Dad was worried about you, and—'

'I've had enough of this.' She stood up, grabbed the page I'd printed for her and ripped it up, throwing the pieces onto the table. It made me think of Jeanie at the wake, ripping the diary down the middle. 'I don't have to stay here and listen to this bullshit.'

The couple next to us were doing their best to keep their own conversation going, but I could see it was impossible. It took all Carrie's borrowed boldness for me to keep going.

'No, you don't have to stay,' I said. 'With me, you are a free agent. Any time you ever need help, please know that I will do anything I can. I wasn't there for Dad, he never asked for my help, but I am here for you. Any time, night or day, you can call me.'

Her face was as white as the tablecloth, and gaunt with the strain of keeping calm. She stared down at me, and I was pretty sure that the people next to us were holding their breath, as I was. For a wild moment I didn't know if she would scream, or cry, or slap me. I gripped my hands even tighter, feeling the nails digging in.

At last, she said, 'You don't know *anything* about my life.' Her voice cracked in the middle, and she turned and walked out.

I unclenched my fingers and tried to pick up my water glass, but my hand was shaking too much to hold it. The woman at the next table said, 'Are you all right, love?'

'Yes thanks,' I said. 'Bit of a tricky conversation.'

'She looked absolutely haunted,' the woman said.

I shakily made my way back to Eleanor and Greg's. I'd only been here a few days, but I had my own key, my own room, and my own fledgling relationships with my nephews and nieces. Plus a new understanding with Greg, and most significantly, a renewed friendship with Eleanor. The two of us had gone out the previous night to celebrate her birthday, and had drunkenly said a lot, perhaps too much, about what we meant to each other. The present I gave her was a drawing I'd been secretly working on since I got here, of her three children together. They'd kindly all sat for me in secret, one at a time, for fifteen minutes each, or, in Gracie's case, five as it was all she could sit still for. It was rough, but Eleanor loved it, as I knew she would. I wanted to tell her that Denny would make one of his custom frames for it, but I knew I couldn't make promises on his behalf, not when things between us were so uncertain.

Ellie was waiting for me now when I staggered in, reeling from the encounter with Andrea. She dished out tea and sympathy, and when I'd told her the whole thing, said, 'You can't rescue someone who isn't ready. But one day, she might be, and when she is, she knows where you are.'

'Why do I feel like you're also referring to non-Andrea situations?'

She smiled. We'd always had our own kind of shorthand, Ellie and I, a way of cutting through the noise to the meaning underneath.

'All right,' I said. 'I'm ready to be rescued.'

'I'm here,' she said. 'What is it you need?'

'I need to talk about Tilly,' I said.

'Good.' She put her hand on mine. 'I'd like to hear you talk about her.'

'I think about her every day, Ell. But not about who she'd be now, a child the same age as Gracie. I think of her as I saw her in the hospital, tiny and perfect. I feel like I don't know where she's gone.'

'Ah, sweetie. Do you and Denny ever talk about her?'

'Never.'

'Do you have any things to remind you of her, around the house?'

'No. I threw everything away. Even the beautiful cot Denny made. And I don't know what happened to the photos they gave us at the hospital.'

'Denny gave them to me.'

'He did?' I stared at her. 'When?'

'Last time he was here. When you were still in hospital and he came here for a shower. That was probably why he came here, rather than go to your place. He said, "Can I leave this here?" It was the folder of photos. He didn't want to look at them. I said I'd keep them safe for you.'

Denny wouldn't leave my bedside after Tilly died, and I didn't want him to. But finally, one of the nurses discreetly mentioned that he was in need of a wash. I was allowed to use the hospital showers but of course, he wasn't. I'd never known until now why he went to Greg's, rather than ours, which was nearer.

'Do you still have the photos?'

'Of course! I'll get them.' She started to get up.

'It's OK. I don't want to see them yet. Soon.'

'So you don't have any mementos of Tilly? Do you commemorate her birthday?'

I shook my head.

'Have you ever visited her grave?'

'No. I know it's in the Writtle Road cemetery but I'm not sure where.' I covered my face with my hands. What kind of person didn't know where their child was buried? For five years it had been on my mental 'to-do' list to call the cemetery and ask for details of the grave. But I never did.

'I know where it is.' Eleanor's gentle voice came to me from a long distance away. 'I'll take you.'

I took my hands down from my face. 'How do you know?'

'I go every year, on her birthday, and leave some flowers.'

I looked at her, this amazing person, who always had my back, even when I turned mine on her. 'Eleanor...'

'Because Denny asked me to.'

'He did?'

'He rang me. Just once. Almost a year after you moved to

France. He said he was sending some money, and wondered if I'd be willing to buy flowers for Tilly's birthday. I said of course, I'd be glad to. And he said please could I do it every year. So she'd know that she hadn't been forgotten.'

I couldn't trust myself to say anything, and Eleanor put her hand on mine.

'It's OK, love. I do it because I knew you would, if you'd been here.'

'It's way beyond the call of duty.'

'I don't agree. You lost Tilly, but so did we all. Me, Greg, Gracie, the older kids. We all lost her.'

'I know...'

'And so did Denny.'

I squeezed her hand. I'd sunk into a dark place after Tilly died. I was offered therapy, support, practical and emotional help. I was told that I was traumatised, that I should not be hard on myself or try to do too much. But Denny went through the same loss and no-one really acknowledged it. Not even me. No-one told Denny he might have had a nervous breakdown. No-one asked him how he was feeling. No-one except Ellie.

After Tilly, I knew Ellie was there, flitting between the dark shadows of my medicated half-life that went on for days. I remembered her sitting in the chair by my bed, sometimes silent, sometimes quietly chatting or reading to me. I remembered her talking to Denny, too, and holding both our hands, letting us sit with the sadness, letting us rage and cry and say whatever we wanted, not trying to solve anything for us, just being there, where we were at. Containing us.

And I remembered telling Denny I didn't want her to come any more. That her pregnant belly was too hard to look at. It never occurred to me until this moment that I wasn't the only one she was looking after, not the only one I hurt by sending her away.

By the time of the christening, I hadn't seen her for weeks, and I'd never seen Gracie at all.

'Eleanor... the christening...'

She took a breath, but didn't say anything.

'Denny didn't mean to push Olivia, you know.'

'Jesus, Mary and Joseph, of course I know that, love!' Eleanor said. 'It was simply an unfortunate set of circumstances, all forgotten now and...'

'I know Greg thinks he did, though.'

'No, not at all. Sure, he might have thought that at the time. Not that Denny pushed her deliberately, exactly, just wanting to lash out at us. I won't BS you, he did think that. But I told him, over and over, Denny was only trying to get to you, to protect you.'

I started crying properly. It came out of nowhere, great hard-to-muffle sobs. 'Denny would never hurt anyone.'

'I know, darling. I know. Greg knows that too, has known it for a long time. It's all right. Ah, don't cry now. You'll set me off.'

I couldn't reply – too busy blubbing – but it felt like a lot of pent up angst was coming out with the sobs, and I let it run its course.

'I have a theory,' she said after a while. 'It's called the Extreme Denny Hypothesis.'

'What is Extreme Denny?'

'The version he became after Tilly died. The Denny who covered you in bubble-wrap. The one who carried you off to that Grimm's fairy tale cottage in the middle of nowhere so nothing could ever harm you again.'

'He was trying to protect me.'

'Yeah, but he was also trying to protect himself.'

'How do you mean?'

'Denny is, I think, like a lot of blokes. He doesn't have many friends. Hell, Greg has one friend and they basically do nothing but slag each other off.'

'Denny doesn't have any, really. He has acquaintances, but not anyone close.'

'Except you. He adored his dad, and he adores you, and he would have adored Tilly. That's pretty much the sum total of his attachments. Now his dad and Tilly are gone, and he only has you left. My theory is that he's terrified of something happening to you. Everything he does is designed to avoid such a possibility.'

'I've never thought about it like that.'

'Perhaps even—' And she laughed. 'Do forgive me, won't you, for giving it all the Doctor Freuds. But maybe the guilt he felt over Tilly, that he wasn't able to help her – is he channelling that into looking after you?'

I didn't want to tell Eleanor that I thought he'd had a breakdown. I knew it wasn't the right term, but it was a good description nonetheless. But what she said made sense, even without that knowledge.

I nodded. 'You missed your calling, Ell. Psychotherapy doesn't know what it's lost.'

'Ach yes, will you lie down on that couch now?' She smiled, then said quietly, 'I don't love the way Denny's gone about hiding you away in your fairy cottage, Rapunzel, but I do understand it.'

She let me sit with that for a few moments. Finally, I said, 'I should call him.'

'Yeah, that sounds like a good idea.'

This afternoon, I took a walk into town, past my old salon. Peaches had kept the name: Ivory Hair & Beauty. When she bought me out, I told her she should rename it after herself, but she said it had strong brand awareness. And it was clearly doing well. It was freshly painted and when I peeped in through the window I saw that it was full of customers. I saw Peaches, standing by a chair with a client. Her head was thrown back and she was laughing, which made me smile, because that's how I always pictured her. I stepped away quickly, because I didn't want anyone to see me. I wasn't in the right frame of mind for any more reunions, but I was glad to see a bustling, thriving business.

As I walked on, my phone rang, and my heart gave a happy leap when I saw it was Carrie.

'How are you?' I said. 'How's Emmie?'

'She's good. Everything's really good.' Carrie laughed. 'You'd never think she had been at death's door; she's so full of energy and bonkers chat. Whole sentences now, and some of them almost make sense. How's things with Eleanor?'

'Really great. I'm staying with them for a while.'

I turned into my old street, and made my way to the house I lived in almost my whole life. The new owners had pulled up the straggly shrubs in the front garden and planted a cherry tree. The front door was painted a lovely dark blue.

'And Denny...?' Carrie said, tentatively.

'That's a work in progress.'

'I'm putting together a photo album for you, by the way. Of me at various ages. It feels a bit, uh, narcissistic, but you said you'd like to see them...'

'Oh my god, yes, I really would! Don't stint, put in as many pictures as possible. If it runs to two or ten albums, so be it.'

She laughed. 'Will do. Sorry, I have to go. Henry and I are taking the girls to the park. Shall we meet again soon?'

We hung up, and I looked at the house, thinking of all the different ways I had lived there. With Mum, Dad and my brothers. Then without Dad. Then without Greg, then Benjy. Just me and Mum, for a long, long time during which, looking back, I did little more than tread water. A brief glowing period when Greg and Ellie stayed with us, but other than that, it wasn't until Denny moved in that things began to improve. And, after

Mum died, Denny and I lived there alone for a while. And we were happy.

I heard birdsong, and looked up to see a lone blackbird on the roof. It was male, with an orange beak. I got the field glasses out of my bag and watched it for a while. When it stopped singing, it sat so still that I could easily plot out its shape in my head, for a future sketch. I thought of the eagles circling overhead, high up in the blue sky of Sévérac, the day Carrie first phoned me. Then a door slammed along the road, and the bird flew away. Feeling lighter than I'd done for a long time, I walked back towards town.

On the way, I called Denny.

'I'm sorry,' he said, before I could say anything.

'So am I.'

'It's been nearly two weeks. I really miss you.'

'I miss you too.'

'Would you be willing to see me?'

'What do you mean?'

'If I come over there, will you see me? So we can talk?'

'Of course.' I wanted to say, 'I haven't left you,' but I didn't know if I had or not. Instead, I said, 'I love you,' because I knew for sure that was true.

Twenty minutes later, I turned into Eleanor's street, and there was someone standing outside their house, leaning against the gate. A familiar person, who still made my heart beat a little faster, as it had the first day I met him. Standing together in the community college kitchen, laughing at the colour of the coffee, his kind eyes looking down at me, seeing me, Pearl, for who I was.

'Hello,' Denny said, smiling uncertainly.

'Have you built yourself a teleporting machine from the finest oak?'

'I checked in earlier to the Premier Inn round the corner.'

'That makes more sense.'

'I've really messed up,' he said.

'We both have.'

'I've been overbearing.'

'I've loved you looking after me.'

'You're using the past tense.'

'We thought I was a fragile little flower,' I said, 'but I'm not.' I put my hand out, and he took it. 'I don't think I need so much looking after any more. I think perhaps you're the one who needs looking after.'

'I've been thinking about that, too. I think you're right, I need to see someone. Like you did.'

'A therapist?' I said.

'Counsellor, maybe.'

'That's a really good idea,' I said, managing not to smile at his preference for the less therapy-sounding word.

'Eleanor is peeping at us out of the front window,' he said.

'She's a fan of yours.'

'She always had good taste.' He blew out his cheeks. In a rush, he said, 'Since your dad died, I haven't understood what's going on with you, what you're thinking. I liked the way things were. I thought you did too.'

'I did.'

'I really, really don't want to lose you. Is it too late?'

'I want to say that everything will be fine, but I don't know if it will be. I do know that I can't live the way we've been living any more. It worked for a while, cutting ourselves off from everyone, but I'm ready for more than that, now.'

'I'm ready to try, then. I don't want anything that makes you unhappy, Pearl.'

'Well, that's not realistic, is it? There will be times when I'm unhappy. That's life.'

'You know what I mean. Whatever the best version of life looks like to you, I'll try to make it happen.'

'You will? If I say I want to move back here? Go to art school? Or return to Sévérac and open up the wood to the public? If I want to see Carrie every week?'

'I'm here for it. All of it. Any of it.'

'You weren't there when I told you about Carrie and Emmie. I wanted to share it with you, but—'

'I know. I was blindsided. Really blindsided that you never told me you'd had a baby before...' He paused, and at long last, said her name to me. 'Tilly.'

As he said it, I pictured her, standing next to Gracie. For the first time, imaginary Tilly was no longer a baby, but a school-child, out in the world. She looked a little like an older version of Emmie. She looked confident and happy.

Denny went on, 'But I understand why you didn't tell me, I really do. I've had a lot of time to think, while you've been here.'

'I've told you some of what I might want,' I said. 'But what do *you* want? It sometimes seems as if we've spent the last six years thinking only about me. What about you?'

'You already know what I want, Pearl. I want you to be happy. Whatever that looks like.'

'There must be something you'd like to be different.'

'Well...' He smiled shyly. 'I'd like it if you'd come to see the work I've been doing in the chapel in Rodez. I'm really proud of it.'

'I'd love to see it.' I thought of what Ellie had said, about who the important people in Denny's life were. It was quite an honour, to be one of those people. But I hoped he would be willing to let a few others into his life too. 'Have you liked hiding away, just us two, these last years?'

'I can't lie,' he said, 'I have. But I do know that we are differ-ent, that you like being around other people, and I want you to be able to have that again.'

'That's a lot of compromising on your part, Denny.'

'For nearly six years you've been living in the house I built, in the country I chose, with no-one for company but me. That's quite a lengthy custodial sentence. I think it's fair if I do some compromising now.' He raised my hand to his lips and kissed it. Then he said, 'I haven't been idle while you've been here. Look.'

He gave me his phone, and I scrolled through several pictures of a wooden high chair, designed for a toddler. It had smooth rounded bars to prevent them falling out, and a carved heart on the upright back of the seat. It was exquisite, like all his carpentry. I was married to an artist.

'It's for Emmie,' he said. 'For when she comes to stay.'

'Thank you, it's beautiful.'

'Is it enough?' His face was a picture of misery. 'Will you come back?'

I'd have loved to be able to say yes, it was enough, and yes, I would come back. I honestly didn't know, though. Words were easy. Actions were hard. I loved him, but we got together in a crisis, two passengers clinging to what was left of our parents' shipwrecks, and then we lurched into a new crisis when we lost Tilly. I didn't know what we were like, just Denny and Pearl, looking towards the future rather than being defined by the past.

'Why don't we see how it goes, for a while?' I said, and I kissed him. 'Let's stay here a few days, hang out with Ellie and Greg, and then we can go to Bristol, and you can meet Carrie and Emmie.'

He nodded. 'I'd like that.'

My mother always used to say that Greg was the optimist, Benjy was the realist, and I was the pessimist. My father saw me as Peppermint Patty, and to Jeanie, I was Little Miss Mouse. But if the last two months had taught me anything, it was that you didn't always have to go along with the ideas other people had about you. You could create your own version of who you were, and how you wanted things to be. I led Denny into the house, where we could sit with Eleanor and Greg, and talk about Tilly, and Dad, and Carrie, and see if, between us, we could start to paint a different picture of our lives.

A LETTER FROM BETH

Dear reader,

Thank you so much for choosing to read *The Woman Who Came Back to Life*. If you enjoyed it, and want to keep up to date with all my latest releases, just sign up at the following link. Your email address will never be shared and you can unsubscribe at any time.

www.bookouture.com/beth-miller

I do hope you loved *The Woman Who Came Back to Life* and if you did I would be very grateful if you could write a review. It makes such a difference helping new readers to discover one of my books for the first time. I read all the reviews, so don't hold back!

The events of this book are mostly made up, smooshed together with some real-life events inspired by people I know. I therefore ought to clarify that the heroine, Pearl, while named for my mother, is absolutely not based on her, other than in two particulars. My mum, Pearl Cohen, died in 2017, and like my made-up Pearl, she was rather artistic. She was also the middle girl of two brothers. But there the similarities end. She was born before the Second World War, not in the sixties, and her gentle, loving parents barely spent a day apart from each other. As far as I know, my mum did not have any secret or lost children, and she was not particularly fond of France, or any kind of 'abroad'

– born in Stoke Newington, she lived in London her whole life. As this book contains so many parents and children, I wanted to remember one parent in particular, and hope she wouldn't mind that I've used her name to do so.

Thanks,

Beth

www.bethmiller.co.uk

 facebook.com/bethmillerauthor
twitter.com/drbethmiller

ACKNOWLEDGEMENTS

Written mostly during lockdown, this book allowed me to go to France without having to leave my room. I asked Remy Wheeler and Sevi Lawson many questions about French language, food and wildlife, and their generous and vivid emails made me feel like I was there. I haven't actually been to Sévérac-le-Château in more than thirty years, when I fell off a motorbike and the locals were terribly kind. But I hope to go back there one day.

Words are insufficient to describe what I owe to my long-term writing partners Jacq Molloy and Liz Bahs. Their unstinting support, fiendishly smart critiquing, wisdom and humour are qualities I never take for granted. These qualities were scarcely diminished even by Zoom, though I can't flipping wait till we're meeting in real life again.

Thanks to Saskia Gent, my essential first reader, who knows exactly what matters, and whose response to this book took me by surprise.

Thanks also to Amy Lavelle (author of the delightful debut, *Definitely Fine*), for sharing her unexpected knowledge of Teeline shorthand.

Thanks to the people who know all about the writing life and who were a much-needed source of socially distanced support: Melissa Bailey, Jo Bloom, Sharon Duggal, Juliette Mitchell, Laura Wilkinson, and the Prime Writers.

The book was steered safely into harbour by two hard-working editors at Bookouture: Maisie Lawrence and Sonny Marr.

To the people I live with – John and my amazing teenagers – thanks for being there. Though where else was there for us to go, this year? While there was, occasionally, somewhere else I'd rather have been, there was no-one else I'd rather have been with.

Made in United States
Orlando, FL
20 April 2022

17055540R00200